Book Three

The Adventures of Jonathan Moore

Paladin's War

by
Peter Greene

The Adventures of Jonathan Moore Series

Book 1: *Warship Poseidon*

Adventure Writers
Grandmaster Award
Winner

Indenpendent
Author Network
Finalist

Indenpendent
Author Network
Book of the Year

"A robust story of a young lad in the British navy during the Nelson years. A thorough insight and beautiful portrait of those days under windblown sails and the creak of wooden hulls. Peter Greene has created a story that shines from every page. An excellent book. He truly nails an insight of nineteenth-century sailing ships and their crews."
— Clive Cussler, best-selling author of *Poseidon's Arrow* and *Raise the Titanic*

"A heartwarming tale of a boy essentially orphaned in search of his father, *Warship Poseidon* never ceases to entertain. Greene's swashbuckling tale of high-seas adventure is pure, uncomplicated fun!"
— *Kirkus Reviews*

"Equal parts saltwater and page-turning fun, WARSHIP POSEIDON is heir to traditions of Rudyard Kipling and Robert Louis Stephenson. Young adult adventure has a new master, and his name is Peter Greene."

— Jeff Edwards, THE SEVENTH ANGEL and SWORD OF SHIVA

Book 2: *Castle of Fire*

Independent Author Network Finalist Action/Adventure

"Chock-full of adventurous fun...Greene seamlessly weaves together several dynamic storylines, creating a rich, complex world for readers to enjoy. It's driven by an eclectic, well-drawn cast of characters Jonathan, Delain, and quirky best friend Sean Flagon, form a wonderful trio whose escapades will leave readers hooked. A spirited tale of high-seas adventure that will leave readers both young and old anxiously waiting for more!

— *Kirkus Reviews*

Book 3: **Paladin's War**

Chanticleer Historical Fiction Grand Prize

"Greene has produced another page-turner here, filling the seas with gunfire and knife fights, and London's streets with a network of spies and traitors hidden in tea parties and foxhunts. An exciting, satisfying historical novel with a touch of poignancy."

— *Kirkus Reviews*

Author's note: This book has been written so that it can be easily read aloud, with dialogue direction pertaining to who is speaking. This will make reading aloud more enjoyable for all parties. Also, chapters have suggested breaks approximately halfway through marked by a series of asterisks:
* * * * *
This makes it easy to stop at a sensible point and then continue the story the next day.

To purchase and learn more about Jonathan Moore adventure books, and to join the crew, please visit:

www.ajmbooks.com or www.paladinswar.com

Chapters

To my teachers:

Jane Beem
Dorn Kennison
Jo Ann Fox
Mike Aguilar
Steve Brown

I would literally and creatively be nowhere without your influence.

Book Three

The Adventures of Jonathan Moore

Paladin's War

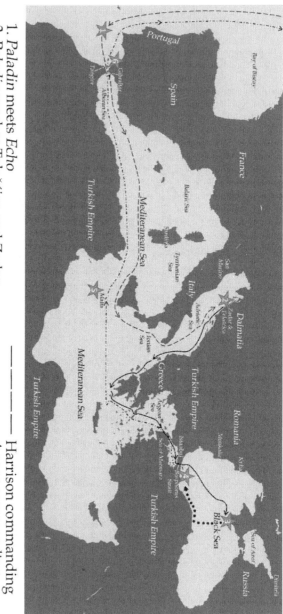

1. *Paladin* meets *Echo*
2. *Paladin* reaches Telašćica and Zadar
3. *Paladin* and *Echo* Mutiny
4. *Echo* and *Kérata Vátrachos* vs. Navarkhia
5. Harrison resupplies at Malta
6. Harrison repairs at Gibraltar, heads home

———————— Harrison commanding
———————— Aggar commanding
•••••••• Moore commanding
------------ Harrison re-commanding

1
The Lost Echo

Only stars and the faint glow of a cloud-veiled moon lit the way of the eighteen-gun, one-hundred-foot brig-rigged sloop HMS *Echo*. She seemed to float on the milky mist that rolled along the western edge of the island called Dugi Otok. Sailing under only topsails, not even the fluttering of canvas could be heard as the ship slipped through the calm water. Craggy and ashen cliff walls lined the coast and stretched over one hundred feet into the night sky as gentle waves lapped at their sides. Along the silent coast, no other ship was in sight, no people walking in this late hour, no fishermen readying nets — not even a single gull crying in the dark. There was only the sound of soft surf and at times a lonesome sigh from a slight breeze slipping through the rocks and scrub bushes of this desolate corner of the world.

To some persons in another place, the night may have seemed peaceful and calming; however, it was anything but that to the newly appointed British captain, Commander Joshua Gray. Standing at the wheel alongside his sailing master, he looked in all directions — for what, he did not know.

Formerly second-in-command of the fighting seventy-four-gun HMS *Trident*, Gray had only been commander of the *Echo* for the few weeks it took to execute his current mission, one that had him uneasy from its beginnings.

"Deep water," said Lieutenant Hayes calmly from the bow. There was no need to call out loud as was usually the proper procedure. Commander Gray had ordered all to be as silent as mice once the ship had reached just three hundred yards offshore. One could have heard a pin drop.

"Any sign of the inlet, Mister Hayes?" asked the commander, knowing full well the answer. Little could be seen through the darkness and fog, unless a breeze swept in and parted the veil of clouds for a brief moment, allowing a shaft of moonlight to reveal the rugged shoreline.

"Nothing, sir," answered Hayes softly.

The *Echo* continued on in silence, the crew searching the swirling mist for a sign or watching the black ocean for submerged reefs or sandbars. The stars were obscured most of the time; the moon continued to offer only the least assistance.

The odd nature of the mission had Gray on edge. On the second of March, he sailed from Chatham, and, much to his liking, the core of officers was solid and reliable, with a dependable senior crew. However, as was usually the case with His Majesty's Navy, he employed a less-than-adequate compliment of experienced seamen. Some new hands had professed that they had sailed for years on merchant vessels, but these were few. That left the fulfillment of the crew to the dreaded *press gangs*—thugs, basically—hired by the Impress Service of the Admiralty to comb the streets and alleys of port towns, the corner pubs, and, as rumor would have it, even jails, to acquire the needed sailors. Their methods were more often than not brutal and entirely unfair. Old men, men with families, boys, and anyone in between, if in an unfortunate place at an inopportune time, could be targeted and taken against their will, then forced to work aboard any of over a thousand British warships. This was a sanctioned procedure protected by law, and because of this practice, many of the newly assigned sailors were not exactly *pleased* about their sudden career change.

Gray watched several of these pressed men at the bow. They were ordered to observe the shoreline; however, some were not. Instead they were standing close together, talking among themselves.

"Styles! Ryder! Evans!" called Gray with some irritation. "Eyes on the shore!"

The men grimaced and slowly turned to their duty.

I will have to deal with them after this exchange is over, thought Gray. A commander needs to retain a firm hand to sustain order. Some form of punishment will have to be administered.

His original mission was to deliver mail to the naval station at Gibraltar, the British-controlled port that regulated access to all ships from the Atlantic as they traveled into the Mediterranean and the many waters to the east. This was a simple mission and very common for a "packet," such as the *Echo*—a fast ship second only to one other. She was not used as a fighting platform primarily but as a communications vessel that delivered mail and official orders for ships at sea.

The *Echo* had seen action, it was true, and Gray had seen her running fast with the wind to attack a French seventy-four in a multiship action on the seas south of the tip of Africa. The *Echo* performed with distinction, as did the other ships of His Majesty's Navy, in what was now known as *The Battle of Fire*, as it was fought in the channel just south of the Castelo de Fogo. At that time, Gray was aboard the *Trident* as first lieutenant under the capable command of Captain Jeremy Langley. There, aboard that ship, all was by the book, and nothing was ever out of the ordinary.

What was uncommon and suspicious about his new command was the literally last-minute change in his orders that had brought him past Gibraltar and deep into the Adriatic Sea east of Italy, to the maze of stone islands off the coast of Austrian-ruled Dalmatia. He was allowed to ask no questions, and no clarification was given—just the directive to proceed to the western coast of the island named Dugi Otok, just north of the small fishing village of Telašćica. There, he was to search northward and find an inlet described in his written orders as "a cove guarded by two gnarled pines, one with a dangling rope." Once located, he was to meet a party identifying himself by using the coded phrase "I am Volpone," and he was to reply, "And I am not."

The orders further dictated that he perform a prisoner exchange. The man he had transported, one Nikomed Aggar, was to be exchanged for an unnamed British subject of great importance to the Crown.

En route to their destination, the *Echo* had favorable winds, at times making fifteen knots as she traveled south past France and Portugal, then east past Gibraltar Station and continuing into the Mediterranean. The voyage to the eastern portion of the Adriatic Sea was completed in just twelve days. Speed was the weapon of the *Echo*, and accordingly, she was able to avoid any entanglements with French and Spanish warships with ease. There was rumor of a peace, a treaty being discussed in Amiens, France, and though not officially in effect, tensions had been somewhat eased.

The *Echo* continued along the coast of Dugi Otok slowly and steadily. All hands on deck and all officers searched the bank of dark haze, straining to see anything that resembled an inlet to a small bay flanked by two trees. At times Gray would look away to the open sea behind, suspecting something amiss, some threat.

"This is surely disquieting," he whispered to his sailing master.

"Yes sir, 'tis that," came the reply from Geoffrey Spencer. He was an experienced master, having sailed around the world at least twice. Spencer had been assigned to the famous HMS *Victory* as an assistant sailing master at one time, and he was a welcome addition to the crew of the small packet.

Gray strained to see through the night. Blast this fog! he thought. I've a mind to call off this entire operation and return to London. I just don't—

"A tree, sir!" came a slightly elevated cry. It was young Ike Williams, just eleven years old but an experienced mate. He had previously sailed aboard the *Echo* as loblolly boy, an assistant to the ship's surgeon, however, the blood and gore became too much for him. Now a deckhand—and one with superb eyesight—he was positioned in the crow's nest, and had spotted the first landmark. "And another tree…with a rope!" he added.

"Drop the bow anchor," called Gray calmly, though he was anything but calm inside. "Adams! Cardew! Reef the topsails."

As the men in the tops took in canvas to slow the ship, the crew on deck seemed to lean to the starboard side and strain their eyes to peer into, and hopefully through, the drifting fog.

"Back to your duty, men," Gray said calmly, more a reminder than an admonishment. He patted Spencer on the shoulder, then strode to the bow as the anchor silently dropped into the shallows. Within seconds, the slow-moving ship ceased its forward motion, though with a turn of the wheel from Spencer, the stern began swinging away from the coast. Another anchor was poised to deploy from the stern hawser, crew at the ready, looking toward Gray for the order. Within a moment, when the *Echo* was almost perpendicular to the coastline, Gray commanded the crew to drop the stern anchor.

"Slowly, men," Gray whispered.

The anchor dropped silently into the sea and within a few seconds had hit bottom. The hawser was immediately lashed tight, holding the ship in place. The *Echo* now pointed bow first, directly toward the inlet.

Still uneasy, Gray surveyed the surroundings. It was impossible to see anything moving on earth or sea; however, he searched still, looking for a lantern, a signal fire, a soul waving arms, or just to hear the call of the code phrase. There was no sound and only the bleak fog occasionally rolling just enough to give a glimpse of the shore. Again he caught sight of the tall, barren rock walls and now saw the opening that formed the entrance to the inlet.

His orders had stated that once the inlet was discovered, he was to proceed directly in, not with any of his smaller boats that were secured to the deck of the ship, but with the *Echo* itself.

"Mister Hayes, bring the prisoner to the deck, and

have Wilson and Sherland lower the boat over the starboard side," Gray said softly but firmly. "Spencer, captain the jolly boat."

"Beg your pardon, Commander," whispered Hayes cautiously as Spencer left his post and proceeded to the rail. "I understood there was to be no boat until we were inside the bay. Sir."

"Yes, that is what the orders state. Nevertheless, call me an old lady or a prissy young girl, but I am still suspicious of this entire affair." He paused for a moment, wondering if he was making the correct decision. This was, for all practical reasons, a simple exchange, and they would be on their way. However, why would a ship as famous and decorated as the *Echo* be used for such a mundane task? It was this portion of the operation that was perplexing.

"Discretion is the better part of valor, Mister Hayes," Gray said. "After we determine that the bay is safe, we will proceed inward with the *Echo*. Let us allow Spencer to explore a bit."

"Aye, sir," Hayes said as he went belowdecks to retrieve the prisoner, Aggar.

The largest of the boats the *Echo* carried, the jolly boat, was freed from the deck and raised over the side. Once lowered into the water, it was filled with Mister Spencer and fifteen men who all entered quietly and began rowing toward the shore.

"Spencer?" called Gray as the small boat slowly moved alongside.

"Aye, Cap'n?"

"Silently. Take a good look and see what you can see. I don't like this at all. Eyes and ears."

"Yes, sir," Spencer replied.

Within minutes, with only the sound of the oars dipping into and out of the water to mark their passage, the boat and its crew disappeared into the mist.

Gray remained on edge, his stomach in a sour knot as he waited. He eyed the point where the jolly boat had disappeared into the fog and turned about often, watching astern. He scanned the deck, noticing the few marines, guns at the ready.

"Here he is, Cap'n. As ordered," announced Hayes upon his return.

Gray turned to consider the prisoner.

Aggar was a dark-haired man, maybe in his later thirties, but he looked as if life had tested him physically. He seemed slightly ragged, more so than just any common criminal who spent time in captivity. Gray could see that in his eyes were many sleepless nights, and he was thin from lack of a proper diet. The commander had little to do with Aggar since he came aboard, just asking the crew if the man was fed, if he was behaving himself, and if he was seemingly in good health.

"Did you remove his manacles, Mister Hayes?" asked the commander, noticing the restraints were absent.

"They were already off when I retrieved him from below, sir."

"Come again?" asked Gray, slightly agitated that a prisoner had been left unrestrained aboard his ship.

"A *ca-rew-mon* did this," said Aggar in his heavy, Slavic accent.

"A crewman? Which one?" asked Gray, but Aggar only shrugged.

"The boat, Cap'n!" called Williams softly from the top. "She's returning!"

Gray shook his head as he moved toward the port rail. "Keep an eye on our friend, Mister Hayes."

"Yes, sir," said Hayes, embarrassed that somehow, some crewman had removed the restraints from the prisoner, and surely the commander thought Hayes might be that person. It was hard to please any captain, and the fact that Gray was one of the more amiable ones with somewhat more humane standards for managing a crew meant that no officer or hand wanted to fall from his good graces.

Gray looked overboard and addressed Spencer directly.

"Report?"

"Nothing, sir," replied Spencer. "There is nothing in there. The bay is not large — maybe three hundred feet to the far shore and no more than a hundred side to side. 'Seems at least ten fathoms deep. There's enough space for us to slide inside, but it will be tight."

Gray was still not certain at all if this looked proper. And what should proper look like? he thought. I have never exchanged a prisoner, and I don't think anyone in the entire service of His Majesty has done so under such secrecy and mystery.

"Did you see anyone in there? Another boat? Anyone on shore?" asked Gray.

"No, sir. The cliff walls climb as far as these here," Spencer said, motioning to where the tall bluffs were hiding behind the mist. "They surround the cove completely. If anyone is in there, they're made of rocks and fog, sir."

Or our contacts will come from the open sea as we did, blocking our exit, thought Gray.

"Is there any breeze in there?" asked the commander.

"Yes, sir, a wee bit coming from inland over the top o' these cliffs, though not much," Spencer replied. "The whole inlet is like a bowl, sir. High sides all around and only this opening here. Not much space for breeze to get going, if you catch my drift."

"Thank you, Mister Spencer," Gray said. He turned and frowned as he addressed Hayes. "I'll not be trapped in there, having to maneuver to get out."

Gray considered preparing the eighteen-pound, long-gun bow chaser to cover the entrance to the inlet. Unknown to many, the *Echo* had specially mounted bow and stern chasers on swivel mounts, actually bringing the total gun count aboard to twenty. Typically, these chasers were not used to crack hulls or blast masts into splinters. That was left to the powerful, short, light-iron, thirty-two-pound carronades that were secured to carriages on the top deck. Chase guns were too light for that work. Their specialty: a well-aimed shot that could damage rigging rope and wooden yards — the horizontal pieces of the mast — thereby causing the target to lose performance. Aimed through cut-out ports on either side of the bowsprit or the stern rail, these guns were effective and necessary.

Gray thought, somewhat in jest, that without the extra weight, he could possibly reach the same speeds as his sister ship, HMS *Paladin*. However, it was his opinion that the *Echo* was fast enough, and having chasers fore and aft to slow down an enemy either ahead or behind would be worth the loss of speed.

"Lieutenant Johnson!" Gray called, making up his mind. "Prepare the bow chaser. Have it loaded and manned. Also, have the marines posted on stern and bow, guns at the ready."

"Aye, sir," came the reply.

"Spencer," the commander continued, calling over the rail. "Secure a line to the stern cleat, and pull us in stern first. We may catch some wind in the bay and exit quickly if need be."

The jolly boat and crew, somewhat distraught at the fact that towing the *Echo* in stern first would take additional exertion, proceeded as ordered. Gray directed a half dozen men to work the stern anchor and raise it once Spencer had secured a line.

It was hard going. The supposedly experienced crew had some decent hands, but Styles, Ryder, and Evans, for example, left much to be desired. They fumbled a bit, almost as if they had trouble understanding orders. There were many, thought Gray, who were not educated or experienced in the English language let alone in the ways of the British Navy. As irritating as it was that he seemed to have more than his share of novices at the moment, he realized that he would need to give these men some further training. Hayes could do this, thought the commander. He has patience.

The going was slow; however, eventually the *Echo* moved toward the opening to the bay, with Gray himself at the wheel. The cliff walls loomed above them to each side, like great stone doors open only a crack, and to Gray, it seemed that once inside they would close shut, trapping him like an animal being caged.

Gray thought of the *Echo* as a beautiful bird, and many in His Majesty's Navy felt it was one of the most handsome ships afloat, second only to HMS *Paladin*. And like that ship, the *Echo* had strikingly sleek lines, slightly raked masts, and somewhat larger sails than most ships her size. She did not have the famous teak deck found on the *Paladin*. However, she was not without her charms—namely, a rich blue stripe down each side that was trimmed in gold and, most notably, a carved figurehead of a beguiling young woman with long blond hair, calling out with one delicate hand to her lips, the other to her ear. Like the Greek mythological figure after which she was named, the *Echo* was beautiful to many—not only to the gods. She was as fast as a wind and a smooth sailor in every measure. To trap such an elegant lady in a cage would be an injustice.

Gray took another look around the deck as the ship slowly moved onward. All men were in proper position, and the prisoner, Aggar, seemed alert, almost on edge, eyes darting about from time to time as he appeared to be searching the fog. Any slight noise, like the creaking of the ship or the *shhhhh* of some rope being dragged across the deck would cause him to start in surprise. He would then calm down again and resume his gaze, mostly looking outward and upward.

"I assume you know what this is about, Aggar?" asked Gray.

Aggar halted his search and addressed the commander. "I know nothing. I understand I am to go home. That is all I know," he replied.

"Well," continued Commander Gray, "I am not sure where you are going or who you are going with, but if all unfolds well, you will be off this ship and I assume on another."

Aggar grunted and returned to his search.

Whatever is he looking for? wondered Gray. Maybe he is as nervous as I, not knowing how this will turn out.

* * * * *

Tense moments passed, the *Echo* now moving beyond the two pine trees guarding the opening to the inner water. The mist lessened once the ship entered the cove, and all aboard could see the surroundings more clearly. Indeed, as Spencer had stated, the bay was much like a large bowl with high stone cliffs all around and not much room for anything except their vessel. The stone walls held a few scraggly bushes and saplings, impossibly hanging on to the steep face with great effort, scratching out a foothold by some means in the barren rock. The water reflected a few stars above. The slight wind was intermittent.

Once in the center, Gray called for anchors to be dropped at both bow and stern and for men to assume positions around the rail to keep an eye out for the presumed boat that would be meeting them. Others, he sent to the tops and had them prepare to let out all canvas at a moment's notice. The bow chaser was also positioned on deck, pointing straight ahead at the entrance to the bay, manned and armed.

After a few minutes, all was secured. The men were in place.

Commander Gray and Hayes escorted Aggar to the stern, where they each stared directly into the bay.

"Sir, I believe," Hayes said, "that anyone wanting to meet us will approach from the sea. I don't believe anyone could approach through the land side."

"It only makes sense, Mister Hayes, but let's keep an eye around us as well," the commander said. "It could be that someone is hiding in the few bits of scrub along the shoreline or in a hidden cave or crook that is invisible to us in the dark."

And they waited. No sound was heard except for the slight creaking of the ship, the occasional footfall of someone in the tops, and waves gently lapping on the hull. Shortly, a mild breeze parted the clouds and fog, and the moon shone brightly, lighting the scene. The men aboard the *Echo* could now clearly see their surroundings as the white, limestone cliff walls seemed to glow, exposing details that were previously hidden.

Then, quite surprisingly, Aggar let out a long, low whistle. He turned to Gray and smiled.

A shot rang out. Then another.

"Who is firing?" demanded Gray as he turned to look about. Two marines fell dead at their positions.

"Return fire!" called Hayes loudly.

"At what?" came the call from the remaining marines.

"Where is the fire coming from?" asked Johnson, though he never heard the answer as several more shots rang out, one finding his heart. A ball struck a spar by Gray, sending wooden splinters flying about, the commander turning his head just in time. Another shot, and another man fell, wounded. Men continued to be hit. Lucky members of the crew dropped to the deck, taking cover behind anything that presented a form of shelter. Soon, all was a cacophony of confused instructions and random gunfire.

"Does anyone see a flash?" Gray called frantically.

There was no answer. The sounds of guns continued, and more men fell. "Drop all sail!" called the commander. "Hayes, to the wheel! I will tend the anchors! Get the men off that boat!"

Gray ventured that if they could catch a slight breeze, they would have a chance of escape. He could feel a waft as the ship strained at the anchor. He had enough wind to move the *Echo*. Now, if he could cut the anchor lines, there would be a chance.

As he ran to the bow, he was struck hard in the back, not from a ball, but from a large, blunt object, as if someone had struck him with their shoulder. He toppled over, head first. He spun around. There, standing above him, was Aggar.

"You'll not be commanding the ship any longer, Captain Gray," Aggar said calmly, his accent a little less pronounced than it had been earlier. He produced two pistols from under his coat and leveled one at Gray, the other at Hayes.

"Aggar! W-what is this?" demanded Gray, trying to stand. He was answered with a quick kick to the chest and sent back down to the deck.

"Stay down, if you want to live," ordered Aggar. "Though to me, it would be just as easy to kill you now."

Shots continued to ring out. Men cried in anguish. Gray looked about frantically. Despite the fact that men were falling from the yards above them, the mainsail was almost down completely, and the *Echo* strained at her ropes.

Gray was now able to ascertain that fire was coming from many directions, including above them. He saw flashes from the edges of the cliffs, and soon he could make out men there, firing downward at the ship. Even more disturbing was what he witnessed on deck: several of the crew, namely Styles, Ryder, and Evans, were firing pistols at other crewmen.

"Do you surrender your ship, Captain?" Aggar asked with a laugh. Then he called out loud, his voice echoing off the stone cliff walls, "*Astanevische Vasha Gon!*" Two more shots were heard.

"Pachenko! Nababkin! Oleski!" called Aggar, yelling to Styles, Ryder, and Evans. He held up his right hand, fingers extended and palm outward. "*Ostanovit!*"

The men, now revealed as agents of Aggar, halted their fire.

Hayes had moved toward his captain and whispered so softly it was all but impossible to hear, "Who are these men?"

Gray could only shrug.

"Well, they are not speaking French," added Hayes. "They sound Slavic to me."

There were many dead, and many more wounded lay on the deck. From below there was the sound of scuffling, a shot or two, and then shortly, men appeared on deck, hands above their heads, followed by two more of the

Echo's newer crew members, each holding muskets and now joining the corps of traitors.

The attackers on the cliff tops were now rappelling off the stone walls. Evans and Styles, pistols ready, commandeered the boat, shooting and killing Spencer as he fought back. This froze the others in fear, and they complied with orders to return to the deck of the *Echo*. Within moments, the small craft had been taken and was headed to the rocky shore, obviously to collect the boarding party. Soon the ship would be crawling with the enemy—whoever they were.

"I ask you one last time," said Aggar as he cocked his pistols. "Do you surrender your ship?"

Gray glared at him, then looked to Hayes. The man was injured, a small bit of blood trickling down his temple from what looked like a splinter that struck him as a nearby plank was shattered by a bullet. Hayes was still sitting up as he regarded his captain.

"W-we are beaten, Commander," Hayes responded, holding his wound. "No use."

Gray looked down and took a deep breath. Is this how his first command was to end? By the looks of things, this is how his *life* would end. These men are stealing the *Echo*, and they will not want witnesses, he was sure. Time! He need time to think!

"Captain, I will count to—"

"Strike colors!" Gray called out strongly. "Lower our flag! Surrender the ship!"

Gray looked up and almost immediately saw the British flag from the mainmast being lowered. He had lost the *Echo*.

"Ah! Good!" called Aggar. "Very good, Captain! Now, leave your men in the tops, and have the deckhands form a line along the starboard rail. Hurry now!"

Gray knew the odds of surviving this event were slim. Standing slowly, he quickly realized that he had two choices: to take back the ship, which was obviously impossible at the moment, or abandon her and try to save the lives of as many of the crew as he could. To do this, it was clear that he needed to get his men off the ship before many more were murdered. Gray knew this game. Aggar, or whoever would be the commander, only needed enough Englishmen to complement his crew, maybe fifty or sixty at the most. The *Echo* had over one hundred hands.

"Echoes! Deckhands along the starboard rail! The rest, stay in the tops," he called. "Not you, Williams! Get down from there!"

As Young Ike Williams came down from the crow's nest, Gray grabbed his arm, and in the confusion whispered a final command.

The deck crew slowly complied with the captain's directive and gingerly walked, limped, and crawled to the starboard rail. Now boarding the ship was yet another boatload of men from the shore. Within another half hour there would be almost forty of Aggar's men aboard, all armed with various muskets, knives, and swords. With the men in the tops, Aggar would have almost a complete crew.

"Aggar," pleaded Gray, "allow me to attend to the injured as best I can! One of your men shot our surgeon—so I am the only hope the wounded have!"

"Captain Gray," Aggar said as he pulled him aside, "the injured...will not make it out of this, eh? If you follow my instructions to the letter, you and a small number of your crew may have a...fighting chance at living at least a few more days. Now, get in line."

Gray stared at Aggar, held his gaze, then moved slowly to the starboard rail. As he passed Hayes, he quickly whispered a few words. Hayes nodded ever so slightly, and the captain slowly moved aft along the line of men to take his place at the farthest point.

"The sail, Kowalski!" called Aggar to the jolly boat as it appeared with a batch of men. "Come aboard quickly, and have these fine British sailors reduce sails to only the tops. She's straining at the lines. Ha! She is a fast one, like a pony at a gate, ready to run!"

"Yes, sir," said Kowalski as he began his ascent.

Williams, according to Gray's orders, was now at the captain's storage, as the men called it, a small area at the base of the rear ladder. The captain's cabin on the *Echo* was pretty by any standard of the British Navy, however, it was too small to hold all of the personal effects of its commander. To remedy this, the shipwrights built a space about the size of a breadbasket placed behind a small door in the floorboards. In this nook, there was a locked safe holding the captain's valuables. In the case of Commander Gray, among the valuables were two exquisite German dueling pistols given to him by his great uncle, and a small flint, powder, and ball supply. Williams loaded the weapons, hid them in his shirt, and took them to the deck.

The jolly boat now headed back to the shore. So far, it had completed three trips, each producing a dozen or more of Aggar's crew. Once aboard, they took positions about the ship, eyeing their captives, now and again calling to them forcibly in a language none of the Englishmen could understand. Likewise, the British men in the tops had difficulty understanding Kowalski, who had begun ordering the taking in of sails; however, it was a slow process, and many of the men were confused and frightened.

"Attention, all you fine British sailors!" came the raised voice of Nikomed Aggar as he strolled the deck, already proud of his new command. "We thank you for this wonderful vessel! She is a fine lady, and even now, with the slightest wind at her back, she is anxious to be underway! This will suit our purposes well!"

Hayes stared intently, not at Aggar but at Gray, awaiting a signal.

After another moment, Williams arrived from his secret task belowdecks and covertly handed Gray the two weapons, now loaded. He then stood next to his captain, shaking with fear.

"I ask that you all turn toward the rail and watch the approaching boat," boomed Aggar. "It contains the last of my crew who will need assistance securing the skiff along-side. Once aboard, we will allow you to depart for the shore. If you do not assist us, you will die."

A lie, thought Gray as he fumbled behind his back.

"Cherepanyanko! Kowalski! Take some of these English dogs and have them haul up the boat!" commanded Aggar as the jolly appeared with the last of his men. They climbed like rats onto the ship. Within moments, the boat was secured on deck.

"All of you Englishmen, against the rail!" boomed Aggar as he laughed. "Yes, yes, keep turning."

This entire mission was a farce from the beginning, thought Gray. A traitor succeeded in changing our orders, leading us to this point, and allowing Aggar to pop up and steal the ship easily. Yet he is no pirate. Pirates are thankfully few these days and would never attack a British Navy ship. And the men under Aggar's command are too well trained, and some—Styles, Evans, and Ryder, surely—were placed aboard my ship in Chatham! He will leave no witnesses, thought Gray. We are all dead, except maybe the men in the tops. He means to kill the rest of us as soon as our backs are turned. It is now or never.

Ever so slightly, he caught the eye of Hayes and nodded.

"Abandon ship!" bellowed Gray as loud as a hurricane. "Overboard! Now!"

Gray grabbed Williams and tossed the boy into the water. Cardew and Adams immediately went over the side.

Using the marlin spike that he had loosened from its position at the rail, Hayes immediately struck the enemy closest to him in the temple. He grabbed the man's sword and immediately cut the hawser, freeing the stern anchor line. At the exact same moment, Gray produced one of his fine pistols, took aim, and sent a ball directly into the line holding the bow anchor.

Free of constraint, the *Echo* lurched forward, sending many on both sides of the conflict to the deck.

"I said over the bloody rail, Echoes! Or damn you all!" boomed Gray, livid that so few had gone overboard as of yet.

Hayes, done with his duty at the rope, reached an arm out to each side, grabbed Sherland and Hill by the collars, and tossed them over board. Wilson grabbed Neil and pushed him over the rail. Others immediately followed.

Aggar, seeing that his plan was being challenged, bellowed the order, "We need the men in the tops! Address them!"

His men immediately aimed their weapons to the sails and rigging, preventing many from escaping.

"Aggar!" yelled Gray, who now stood on top of the rail.

Aggar turned and pointed a pistol at Gray. However, the Englishman had produced his second pistol and fired. Narrowly avoiding the blast, Aggar dropped to the deck.

Gray turned to jump, then looked up. A bit of luck, finally! he said to himself as the moon set behind the cliffs, plunging all into almost complete darkness. The view from the *Echo* of the swimming men was fast becoming shrouded in fog and darkness as the ship exited the bay. He smiled and leapt into the water.

Aboard, the men in the tops were taken under control and worked the sails as best they could. The *Echo* was now almost completely out of the inlet, steadily slipping away into the dark sea.

"The English commander and at least a dozen men must have made it ashore, Captain Aggar," said Cherepanyanko, the tall, blond lieutenant.

Aggar cupped his hands and called to the unseen shore, laughing. "Very well, Captain Gray! Bravo! Though, you leave me with no anchors, so I must leave *you* – leave you to die in this forsaken place! Nowhere to go and no way to get there! Thank you most kindly for this beautiful lady!"

Gray had indeed made it to the rocky shoreline, exhausted from his strenuous swim in the heavy uniform he wore. He quickly assisted several other men—some wounded, others just having trouble climbing the rocks that dotted the coast. He took a moment to glance out to sea.

Through the mist, he saw the stern of the *Echo* disappear into the night, hearing only the continuing laughter of her new commander.

2

Ice Cream

"It is gooey. It is cold. It is sweet," she said, her eyes blindfolded, but not too tightly, "and I believe it is...chocolate!"

The ice cream concoctions Jonathan Moore and Delain Dowdeswell had just begun to devour were the specialty of M. Graham's Tea and Sweets, the establishment being highly recommended by Mrs. Walker, Miss Barbara Thompson, and even Lady Bracknell. Jonathan quickly appropriated a scoop of the towering dessert that was in front of Delain, even though he had a tower of equal size in front of himself. He swallowed the stolen spoonful immediately.

"Correct! It is chocolate! Your sense of taste extends beyond your obviously fine choice of jewelry, Miss Dowdeswell," Jonathan Moore replied with a smile on his face.

Delain also smiled and removed the silk scarf she had permitted Jonathan to tie about her eyes, allowing her to guess the flavor of the first ice cream she had ever enjoyed. Had it been almost a year since Jonathan had asked her to join him for this experience? It seemed a world away — and it literally was.

"The jewelry, Mister Moore," she responded, "was chosen *for* me, actually, by a fine young man I met in the Bahamian Islands. Presents, as a matter of fact." She paused, a smile growing on her face. "Not much to look at, actually."

Jonathan furrowed his brow. Did she mean the *jewels* were nothing to look at, or was it the *young man* who was less than attractive? Either way, the playful insult was against him.

"Miss Dowdeswell, I can assure you that those jewels

you are wearing are not only handsome, but exotic. The silver dolphin with the blue jewel for an eye, which you have cleverly turned into a bracelet, comes from one of the finer shops in Piccadilly, just near here a block or two. And the turtle, the one you are wearing around your dainty neck, comes from Ribeira Grande in the Canary Island archipelago. Exotic indeed—and beautiful."

"Is it my neck that is beautiful or the necklace?" she asked, taking in another spoonful of the delicious frozen treat.

Jonathan smiled, knowing he had turned the tables.

"The necklace, of course. Truly a work of art."

"Mister Moore," said the young lady, still playfully, "if you weren't a gentleman and a young midshipman in His Majesty's Navy, one of high standing and recognition, I would believe that your last comment was somewhat...boorish."

"And if you were not the respected daughter of the Governor of the Bahamas, the Honorable Lord Dowdeswell, a hero of the Crown," Jonathan said, "I would think you were fishing for compliments. But that would be beneath you."

"Never think a compliment is beneath anyone, Mister Moore. You will know what I mean—if ever you should receive one."

This made Jonathan laugh aloud.

Though Delain Dowdeswell had only been a resident of London for a few months, being sent from Nassau by her father to become "refined" in polite society, Jonathan knew that any attempt to change her in any way would end in utter failure. He had always believed Delain was a lady, proper and polite, from the first time he saw her. It was when she was away from her retainers and was rappelling down the side of an ancient fort, saving sea turtles on the beaches of Conception Island, or firing a cannon from a revitalized fort near the south seas of Africa, that the *real* Delain Dowdeswell, adventurer, came into her own. These actions would be remarkable for any grown man but were truly astounding when applied to a young lady. And it was because of these feats and more that Jonathan discovered his true affection for the blond-haired, irrepressible four-teen-year-old with a penchant for adventure.

"Delain, I see the polite society of London that you have now been exposed to for the past six months has not affected your sense of humor."

"I won't let them—as I am sure you expected, Mister Moore."

"I have learned that when it comes to you, Miss Dow-deswell, one cannot *expect* anything. One must simply ac-cept the fact that one is going along for the ride."

This was the reason Delain enjoyed his company and attention. She knew that above all others, he accepted her for what she was, and that was a kindred spirit. Delain looked into Jonathan's eyes and smiled as she considered him.

To many in London and most of England, Jonathan Moore, also at the age of fourteen, had accomplished much more than men five times his age. Growing up separated from his parents on the streets of London, he was above all else a survivor. Being searched for and found by friends of his father, at the time an imprisoned British Navy captain being held in France, Jonathan was accepted into the family of HMS *Poseidon*. There, he became an integral part in the success of that crew's mission. That fateful ship was com-manded by Captain William Walker. He was made a lord by the king himself, in gratitude for his recovery of a huge sum of Spanish gold and the capture of the prize of the French fleet, the now renamed HMS *Danielle*, a seventy-four-gun battleship. All admitted that without Jonathan, the mission would have been less than successful. His in-dustry, fortitude, and aspiration to learn resulted in a pro-motion to midshipman's rank. His patience and desire to find his lost heritage rewarded him with a special gift: a reunion with his widowed father, now *Admiral* Nathaniel Moore. At the conclusion of that series of events, Jonathan and the crew arrived at the Bahamian Islands for the refitting of their ship. A ball was held at the governor's mansion in Nassau to celebrate their accomplishment, and it was there that Midshipman Jonathan Moore made the acquaintance of Delain Dowdeswell, the governor's daughter.

The following year, the crew of the *Danielle* returned to Delain's island home and, after a series of small ventures, accepted the assignment of bringing the Ladies Dowdeswell—Delain and her two sisters, Rebecca and Penelope—to London. Her father had said they had *outgrown* the small island and now required exposure to the refinements of the world's most important city to become true ladies. Though the adventure that awaited Delain in London held promise, the mission to which Jonathan and the crew of the *Danielle* were suddenly assigned seemed to hold potentially more excitement. Delain, predictably, became a stowaway, and one thing led to another.

She and Jonathan, along with their particular friend, Sean Flagon, had the opportunity to turn the tide of a key action in the war against Napoleon. Her role of actually firing more than one cannon in the battle had even been mentioned in the newspapers of the great cities of Europe, making her somewhat of a celebrity. To her parents, however, there was a mixture of pride and confusion—though mostly horror—at her very unladylike behavior. Jonathan, who was with her the entire time, was completely accepting of her part and treated her as an equal conspirator in the actions.

As Delain considered Jonathan in his smart, navy-blue-and-silver-trimmed midshipman's uniform, she saw herself had she been born a man: a brave young soul, inquisitive and smart, fearless and competitive, someone always looking forward to the next adventure. She certainly had these desires now; however, as a man, she would be able to pursue such a life without ridicule for being the improper gender.

"We have seen and done much, Miss Dowdeswell,"

Jonathan said, surprising Delain, as if he had been reading her thoughts.

"Indeed we have," she replied.

"Is the minor adventure of living in the great city of London yet to your liking?" Jonathan asked.

"It has its attractions—namely, ice cream," she responded, looking at the now-dwindling tower. "Though I have found that none of the ladies I meet here do more than sit and...look pretty." She took another spoonful.

"An easy accomplishment for you, Miss Delain," Jonathan said, somewhat under his breath.

"Pardon?" she said through the scoop.

"What have you seen that you *do* find interesting?" Jonathan continued, ignoring her question entirely.

She thought for a moment. There were so many things that she did not relish about the crowded city. Her new school was actually not as hands-on as she had experienced in the islands, having her own tutor and the entire coastline as her laboratory. Her time was now filled with supposedly stimulating events arranged by her aunt, Lady Bracknell. There were teas and luncheons and visits to the massive library on the edge of town.

What became a worse torture than anything imaginable was the Swedish finishing school she attended near the Bracknell Estate. The simple history, mathematics, and English studies were not the issue; it was the dancing, manners, and etiquette lessons, learning to walk in a certain way, to present oneself in a ladylike manner, and to say the proper things as required by mannerly people. These drove Delain to madness. It wasn't that she was against learning these things or that she found them difficult. Her mother had taught her well, and as all who met Delain could attest, she could turn on the charm at will and become a princess if need be. It was the fact that her teachers droned on about poise and posture and refinement so repeatedly that Delain felt her only purpose in life was to sit as rigid as a statue and smile.

"I have fired cannon at passing French warships, Mister Moore," she answered, "and I have recaptured a stolen British gunboat off the coast of—"

"Yes, I was there. Do you not remember?"

"Indeed. That was part of the fun! And because of those experiences, well, London will need to become much more stimulating to keep me interested. But I do find the people very fascinating. Take that man there, by the corner, with the gray coat and the small packet."

Jonathan looked out the window of the ice cream shop and observed the man. He was taller than average height and a little plump. He had a small, unkempt beard covering only his chin, and all his facial hair was gray. He checked the time with his watch. He looked as average as any Londoner.

"He is quite unremarkable, isn't he?" Jonathan asked.

"His coat is too long for this time of year, Jonathan, and his beard is not trimmed tightly. His shoes seem a tad muddy, yet he wears an expensive wool coat, and his pocket watch looks to be golden. How does one have all those refinements and yet—"

"Have an ill-kept beard? Yes, mildly amusing," Jonathan commented.

"And that other man there, looking at him from behind the boards in the alleyway? He looks like a thief or at least a scoundrel! See how he eyes the bearded man?"

"A scoundrel? My! That is a harsh word," said Jonathan, laughing.

"We might witness a crime, Jonathan!" said Delain, dropping her pretense of ladylike addresses and calling Jonathan by his first name, a practice both followed when any situation or adventure became heated.

They watched in silence; however, the bearded man simply walked onward. The man in the alley only watched until his subject turned a corner, and then he followed him from a distance.

Jonathan and Delain continued observing, pointing out others that happened by, laughing, and trying to create entire histories to go along with some of the more interesting-looking people.

What the Midshipman and the governor's daughter did not realize, is that they too were being observed by another couple from within the shop, and this couple never took their eyes off them. There were whispered guesses as to exactly what the youngsters were talking about, and if at any time they should be interrupted. But it was decided that their conversation was still in its early stages, and for now they should be left alone.

When the youths turned back to what remained of their desserts, Jonathan became slightly nervous, and his breath started and stopped with small hesitations. Finally, Delain looked at him and opened her eyes as if to say, "Yes, what is it?"

"Miss Dowdeswell," Jonathan said, after clearing his throat and taking a large breath, "As you know I am to be stationed aboard HMS *Paladin* shortly —"

"Yes," said Delain, somewhat sadly. "And our dear Mister Flagon is to go along with you I understand."

"Yes, he and a few others you will remember are joining us," Jonathan said. "As a small test of the newly formed crew, we are assigned a position in a yacht race of some dozen craft tomorrow. The race begins at Portsmouth Naval Yard and is to head along the coast until reaching Hastings and then proceed to a point east out to sea, where the *Paladin* will sit as a marker of sorts."

"You will not be racing?" asked Delain, somewhat disappointed.

"Unfortunately, no," answered Jonathan. "The yachts must pass to our stern before they make their way northward toward the finish line at Dover."

"Oh. The *Paladin* will act as a buoy?"

Jonathan winced. Then he tried to hide his reaction.

"Well, no, not exactly. I would never call the *Paladin* a buoy, however —"

"Oh!" Delain gasped. "I didn't mean any offense."

"Not an issue, Miss Dowdeswell. There will be reviewing platforms set up at the finish, and I was w-w-wondering, if you have the time, if you would like to attend the race with my father and Miss Thompson, and perhaps j-join a small group of us at Captain Walker's home for dinner afterward. W-we are celebrating Mister Harrison's promotion to commander. And I would enjo-enjoy your c-comp—"

"Are you inviting me on a date, Mister Moore?" Delain asked, surprised.

"Well, n-no, of course not! I mean yes, it is a...B-but that would mean if you see it in such a way as y-you might—"

"I would be delighted, Mister Moore," she replied, smiling.

At this tender moment, the watchers decided to interrupt the two youngsters. They stood and walked slowly and carefully toward them.

"Jonathan? Delain?" said Admiral Nathaniel Moore. He stood straight and tall, looking handsome in his uniform, though still he was eclipsed by the beauty of Miss Barbara Thompson, who had accompanied him to the ice cream shop. They had enjoyed a new concoction called a banana split, a most delectable affair that both devoured with little pretense of manners.

"Yes, Father," Jonathan responded.

"Yes, Admiral," said Delain.

"Did you enjoy your dessert?" asked Miss Thompson. "Was it all you expected?"

Seeing the question was for her, Delain responded quickly. "Yes, indeed! I would like to have one a day if at all possible!"

"My!" said Miss Thompson. "Wouldn't we all?"

"Now, my Londoners," said the Admiral, "we have a busy afternoon and evening ahead—a big day tomorrow as well. Jonathan, you have fencing practice with Mister

Harrison in an hour, and afterward you will need to make certain that you and Sean are well rested for your duties tomorrow."

"Where is Sean?" asked Delain.

"He is with Hudson and Hicks at the firing range," replied Admiral Moore. "It seems that in all your adventures he has never learned to handle a musket, and frankly, what good is a marine if he cannot fire a shot?"

"Some are able to make *bombs*, as I understand," said Miss Thompson, in a somewhat defensive tone. It was well known in their circle of friends that there was a particular motherly affection that she displayed for both boys. After Jonathan had been reunited with his father, and the subsequent "adoption" of Sean Flagon into the Moore family, Miss Thompson assumed a role of protector, teacher, and promoter. Though not their mother, not yet at least, she doted on them like one, and the boys blossomed under her tutelage. Many in society watched not only the boys but the couple of Admiral Moore and Barbara Thompson, expecting that any day they would announce their engagement.

"I assume," said Admiral Moore, "that you are referring to Sean's unofficial title as bomb maker —"

"A title given to him by His Majesty himself!" interrupted Miss Thompson, again firm in her reproach. "Hardly could it be called unofficial!"

"Yes, and he is certainly well prepared for that task," said Admiral Moore. "I meant no slight to him, Miss Thompson. He is improving on his skills is what I meant to say."

"Yes," she said, now smiling as if she had achieved a small victory in the defense of one of her boys.

With that, the two couples collected their few belongings—mostly gift items purchased at the surrounding shops—and exited the ice cream parlor.

The bearded man observed from inside the ice cream shop by Jonathan and Delain had not spoken to a soul since he left Piccadilly. He now walked briskly away from the avenue, down a neat alley near Coventry and Haymarket that led to an unmarked doorway of a pub named The Raven and Snake. It was dark, crowded, and not at all well kept; however, the man ignored the condition and ordered a tall porter. As he sipped, he secretly eyed every person in the room. Most were quiet and to themselves, and all were certainly of the lower class. "Slightly ragged to outright degenerate" described not only their clothing but their physical look as well. These were the unrefined commoners of the great city of London.

Once he had finished his drink and completed the review of the patrons, he stood, dropped two pennies on the bar, then exited quietly out the front door into the busy street.

Walking a full block eastward, the man hailed a hackney coach and had the driver take him to the Palace of Westminster. It was now approaching five in the evening, and he could see the streets were emptying as the night's cold descended on the city. Gas lights illuminated the few corners and at times spilled out from the open doorway of an establishment or the window of a town home.

Arriving at Westminster, he tipped the driver and then walked toward the Thames and across the bridge to Lambeth. After walking a few blocks south, he hailed another carriage and instructed the driver to take him back across the Westminster Bridge to Pall Mall, just past the Admiralty Building. Most would take this as a short walk, but the man feigned a limp, and because of this, the driver asked no questions.

Once the short ride was completed, the man exited into the near darkness. He found a secluded shadow beneath a large, old willow next to the gravel path and stood there for a full eleven minutes. No one had followed him.

Purposefully he walked west down the mall and took a path through Saint James Park to Queen Anne's Gate, where he stared at the statue of the queen for a few moments as only the lights of nearby lanterns dimly lit the scene. The darkness surrounded him as the wind blew in short, cold gusts.

After a few moments, another man approached. He was dressed in a more ragged coat compared to the bearded man; however, he cared not. He blended in with many who walked the streets of London, and that suited his purposes.

"'Oo is this statue of, gov'na?" he asked the bearded man.

"Queen Anne of the House of Stuart," answered the bearded man.

"Don't know 'er," said the ragged man.

"Why would you?" asked the bearded man, completing the coded signals.

"Why do we meet here?" whispered the second man, losing his street accent. "We are close to many who would do us harm. You most of all, Orvislat, would know that."

Orvislat frowned and gritted his teeth. "Lupien! You just used my name!" he whispered hoarsely.

Lupien became alarmed, looked about in the darkness to see if anyone was near. Then he realized his partner's mistake.

"And you just used my name, Mister O!" he said.

"Forgive us both then," said Orvislat. "Do you have any news for me, Mister L?"

"Do you have my payment?" asked Lupien.

Orvislat removed a package from inside his coat, opened it, and removed an envelope. He checked the name on the front. It simply read "bocc" in scripted letters.

"Ah. This is not yours. This one is for the boss," he said, returning it to the package.

"It looks a tad thicker than the one I am to receive," said Lupien.

"You are not the boss, so you do not get the thick one. This thinner one is yours," replied Orvislat.

Lupien accepted the thin envelope and stuffed it quickly into his coat pocket. "Thank ya, gov'na," he said.

"Now that you have been paid, will you inform me of your findings?" asked Orvislat.

"Yes, yes. It is reported that our agent was successful. The plan went off almost perfectly," Lupien answered.

"Good, good!" said Orvislat. "Then I assume Kharitonov has placed an order for another one."

"Ian Kharitonov! Even the mention of his name makes me shudder," said Lupien. "Yes, he has placed another order. Shall we fulfill it in the same manner as the first?"

"No, we will deliver the treaty," Orvislat said, saying the words slowly, as if to imply more meaning than just the face value of the statement.

"Ah, it is time for that already? Well, then things *are* going according to plan," said Lupien. "I assume you would like an inventory of available merchandise for delivery?"

"Yes," said Orvislat. "As soon as possible."

"That may be a problem. Things have been heating up, as they say, and there are eyes on the watch almost everywhere. I can't work in daylight, and it is difficult to see details in the dark."

"Will it calm down?" asked Orvislat.

"Eventually," said Lupien.

"Then our betters will have to sit tight for a while. They will not like it."

"Kharitonov will not like it," corrected Lupien.

"*He* doesn't like anything," said Orvislat. "We will meet again at our other location in three days. In the meantime I will have the treaty signed, sealed, and dispatched with the utmost secrecy. Then, as soon as we have a ship, it is off to Zadar for the exchange."

"Dugi Otok will be better," suggested Lupien. "It is easier for our man. He is familiar with it and should be there and waiting."

"Agreed. I look forward to our next meeting," said Orvislat.

"As do I, Mister O," added Lupien, with a tap to the envelope in his breast pocket.

With that, both men walked away in opposite directions as a drizzling rain began to fall. Once they were underway, a third man, wearing a dark hood, slid out from under a shadow cast by a dim gas lamp that was shining on the nearby corner building's edge. He followed the man called Lupien to the east.

3
Paladin's Race

The following morning, just an hour past sunup, there marched three red-coated marines of His Majesty's service, arms slung to shoulders, making their way past the barracks at Chatham, home of the First Division. Under an overcast sky, they passed the last of the wooden buildings, across the parade field, to a smaller clearing on the outskirts of the grounds. To see them walking in a straight line, one behind the other, silhouetted against the rising sun, would make one laugh aloud. The leader was of average height and portly, and he strode with confidence and purpose. The second was shorter by far — muscular yet still smaller — and he walked with trepidation. The last one was tallest, thinnest, and was obviously disinterested in the whole purpose, looking about at the surroundings and completely out of step with the others.

In this clearing of approximately three acres sat a short, squat, structure of wood — a large crate actually — at one end of the field closest to the parade grounds. The field had no trees except about the edges. However, spaced a dozen or so feet apart and anywhere from ten to forty feet away from the crate were several odd-looking posts sticking out of the earth. They were more or less a man's height, almost like young tree trunks but noticeably missing branches and leaves. Closer inspection would show they had many holes in them, and chunks of their trunks were missing.

The largest marine by far was Corporal Hudson, a man seasoned in battle and in having sailed around the world at least twice by this time in his life. A steadfast sailor and excellent shot, Hudson was up for promotion. By luck or by being able to take great advantage of his assignments, Hudson had sailed with Captain William Walker several times, and each mission was as successful as the last. Many wondered why he hadn't been promoted to sergeant as of yet. A few good words from his marine captain after his last voyage almost assured the new rank would be his. It was now just a waiting game, waiting for paperwork.

He led the procession to a point next to the wooden crate.

"All right then, Sean Flagon," he said in a loud, authoritative voice. "Let us get you set for practice. Remember what we said about safety?"

"Aye," said Sean, the smallest of the marines. He was certainly no more than fourteen years old, but his exact age was a mystery even to himself. "Never point the musket at anyone or anything I don't mean to put a hole in."

"Right. Now, let's check and load. Private Hicks?"

The third marine, the thinner and somewhat less interested party, looked to the corporal.

"Aye?"

"Set up some bottles for Sean to knock off, eh?"

With that, Hicks opened the lid of the crate and removed six empty wine bottles. He walked into the field and began placing a bottle on top of each pole.

"All loaded, Sean?" asked Hudson.

"Yes, sir," said the boy. "Are ya sure I'll be needing to fire this? I am much better at the sword, ya know."

Hudson frowned.

"Flagon. We have been through this many a time. Swords are fine, and you are almost considered a master at such a young age. But we are Royal Marines! It's our duty to keep His Majesty's enemies *off* our ships. That is best done with a musket or one of them new rifles the colonials have. Swords are a last resort."

"But it seems…unfair," offered Sean. "A sword fight is more…"

"Ge'lemanly?" suggested Hicks as he placed a bottle. "They won't seem like ge'lmen and it won't seem unfair when they's shootin' back at ya. Best to mind ol' Hudson, Seany."

"Ol' Hicks is right," said Hudson. "Did you desire to be a marine just because you liked the fancy red coat and sashes?"

Sean looked to the ground, not wanting to answer. Yes, he desired being part of the prestigious service, but he was young and therefore small to be a marine. However, all who knew his story knew that the king himself awarded Sean the honor of joining the corps as a private.

"Now, let's get you set up correctly," continued Hudson. "Rest your arm on this crate, as if it were a barrel on the deck that ya might be hiding behind, and hold the piece like I told ya. That's it. Close your left eye—yes, yes. Now line up the sight with that red bottle—"

"'Oly 'ell!" called Hicks from the last post. "Give a man a fair chance ta find a safe place ta stand before ya start firin'!"

"Hicks!" yelled Hudson. "You're way over to the left! We are shooting to the bottle farthest *right*!"

"No offense, Sean," said Hicks as he placed the last bottle on the farthest post to the left, "but the last time I saw ya shoot, ya missed the mark by a good ten feet. Beggin' yer pardon, but yer only a beginner."

"He's not goin' to miss by *that* much!" bellowed Hudson.

Sean didn't agree. He believed that any person or thing within a hundred feet in any direction, be it in front, left, right, or even behind, was in danger of being accidently shot. The last time Sean had practiced, Hudson instructed him to concentrate on simply staying on his feet after the blast. It was entirely possible that any gun was too heavy and powerful; however, Sean was now committed, and marines were trained in gun warfare. At least now he could fire the weapon without falling over. Today's lesson was on aiming.

"Just a moment," said Hicks as he ran to stand directly behind Sean. "All righty, Sean! Now, give 'er a whirl. Dead-eye blind, as they says!"

Hudson now turned his attention back to Sean, checking his stance, his holding of the weapon, and his general aim. He squared the boy's shoulders a bit, then gave him an assuring pat on the back.

"Get the sight directly on the center of the bottle, and keep that left eye closed. That's it! Take a breath and hold it, then squeeze the trigger slowly."

Sean did as instructed. The musket fired in a blinding flash. The blue bottle exploded in a thousand pieces, sending glass in every direction.

Unfortunately, the bottle at which Sean had been aiming was red and on the second post to the right of the blue bottle.

"Glory be!" Sean said. "It's no use!"

The marines looked at each other, somehow trying to think of a positive thing to say. Then finally:

"Yer still standin'!" said Hicks.

"True! True as rain! Very well done!" said Hudson.

For Sean, however, his spirits remained unlifted. He realized that he had a long struggle ahead of him to be considered even slightly proficient. And would he ever get to that point? As low as he felt, however, he knew that he was certainly better than the first few times he fired the weapon. Many of those attempts ended in his being knocked to the ground by the force of the blast. Another time, the gun actually flew out of his hands, the shot going high, knocking off an overhanging tree limb just above his head. At the very least, he realized that he had his friends to assist him, and they seemed dedicated to the task of his becoming a decent shot. He couldn't let them down now, could he?

"Well," he said finally, "as long as they are in a line abreast and standing still, I should be able to hit someone!"

The marines nodded. Hudson began loading the weapon again.

"That's right, Seany! We can build on that! Again, dear laddie!"

The sun was peeking through a clouded sky as a tolerable breeze was blowing and the crowd gathered at the Marine Parade at Dover, a picturesque seaside town with a wide lane running parallel to the sandy beach. Stately homes dotted the edge of the hillside, and the Dover Castle rose atop the east cliff. Visitors strolled the wide streets and explored the shops at seaside. The beach was occupied by dozens of children, mostly playing in the sand as the water was, as it always seemed to be, still frigid.

In the center of the strand, a viewing platform had been erected for dignitaries to observe the upcoming yacht race. The ladies present were in their best finery, looking like flowers about to bloom in the spring. The men, drab by comparison, were formally dressed in dark gray and black. Only the navy men sported any color to their hats and jackets, though only dark navy blue.

In these stands sat a happy group of those related to the *Paladin* in some way or another: Admiral Moore and Barbara Thompson, Lady Bracknell and all three of the Ladies Dowdeswell: Delain and her sisters, Rebecca and Penelope. They had traveled all the previous day, a tedious but uneventful journey in the large carriage owned by Lady Bracknell, and had then spent the night at Loddington House, enjoying a fine dinner.

"Delain, can you see the racers?" Barbara asked.

Delain took up the telescope glass lent to her by none other than Admiral Moore and pointed it southeast toward the sea. She had previously found the *Paladin* in its position marking the final turn. Though still quite a small image, Delain could at times make out movement aboard the decks. As for the yachts, there was no sign.

"No, not as of yet. I believe they are coming all the way from Portsmouth."

"I wonder who will win," said Rebecca. "I am sure none of them can best the *Paladin*."

"And why isn't the *Paladin* allowed to race?" asked Penelope.

"Because, my dear child, this is a race for private

yachts, not for warships," answered Lady Bracknell. "The *Paladin* is a ship in His Majesty's Navy."

"Then why is it here? Why does it just sit out there at anchor?" asked Penelope. "Mister Harrison explained to me that it is the fastest of all the ships in the British Fleet — and the most beautiful too."

A man's voice interrupted from behind them.

"And to which ship do you refer? The *Paladin*, you say?"

The ladies and Admiral Moore turned about to see who had addressed them. A stately gentleman, thin of face, yet with deep blue eyes and a proud chin, smiled broadly. His eyes were alive with cheer, and his nose, a bit longer than most, was slightly raised as he expected his answer. Next to him sat a ravishing beauty with auburn hair, the complexion of a porcelain doll, and deep brown eyes that, despite their darkness, had a twinkling of light and purity. She too held her head high and smiled politely.

"Lord Wilder," said Nathaniel Moore with a surprised look and a nod. "So good to see you."

"Admiral," said Lord James Wilder, "a pleasure." The men knew each other in a professional manner. Lord Wilder had recently been awarded a post on the Navy Board, though even prior to his association with the Royal Navy, he had watched Admiral Moore's rise to the top over his twenty years of service.

"You remember my wife, Admiral? Lady Alina Wilder?"

"Yes, we met at the celebration of your appointment to the Navy Board last June, if I remember correctly. Are you enjoying the day, Lady Wilder?"

"The day, yes. But all these ships and navy business — I actually detest it, to be quite honest," she said, almost apologetically. "Though to support dear James, I will endure it!" she finished with a laugh.

"What a pleasure to see you again, Lady Bracknell!" continued Lord Wilder. "Could all these lovely ladies be your charges? I had heard that you had agreed to sponsor

Lord Dowdeswell's children here in London."

"Not all are my relations," she answered. "I believe you know Miss Barbara Thompson?"

"Yes! Of course!" said Lady Wilder. "We attended the Swedish School together."

"A joy to see you again, Alina," said Barbara.

"Barbara is my dear friend and sister to Sylvia Walker," added Lady Bracknell. "You know of Captain William Walker, her husband, I am sure?"

"Yes, of course!" Lord Wilder said. "A hero of the Crown!"

"Let me introduce my brother's children," said Lady Bracknell. "Rebecca, Penelope, and Delain."

"So *you* are Delain Dowdeswell!" said Lady Wilder. "I have heard much of your adventures. Barbara, you must bring Delain to tea! I would love to hear all the details of her escapades. I have only read what I found in the papers."

"I would be delighted," answered Delain, trying to sound excited at the prospect, though inside she felt that another stiff and boring tea was the last thing she desired. As she thought of this possibility, her eyes wandered. She observed Lady Wilder's wonderful manners, and her perfect posture. She and Barbara Thompson appeared to be the embodiments of proper ladyhood in British society: their clean and proper looks, their almost statuelike demeanor at times. They were perfect. Except—there was something different about Lady Wilder. After a few more moments, Delain had ascertained the defect: it was her clothes. Stylish, yes, but of a style that even a newcomer to London could see was a tad bit *out* of style. And her necklace was simple and plain, not adorned with gems or even polished chain. Her clothing, at the edges, showed signs of wear, though just slightly. A loose thread here and a scuffed sleeve there. Maybe, thought Delain, she is not as well-to-do as most nobility. The poor dear.

"Which one is the *Paladin*?" asked Lord Wilder. "I

should know, of course. Yet I am still new to all things naval, and honestly, I know nothing of ships. My responsibilities at the Admiralty, luckily for all, involve things of a secretarial nature.

"That one!" exclaimed Rebecca. "The one with the tilted masts! It is captained by our special friend, Commander Thomas Harrison!"

"Oh! I see it!" said Lord Wilder excitedly. "It looks fast even when at anchor! I have heard of her, of course; however, this is my first actual sighting."

"Yes," said Rebecca, "it is the fastest ship in the fleet."

"I have seen her at sea a few times," continued Delain, "and I can say that she moves faster than the wind, using sails that are larger than most ships and made of a secret type of cotton. Only the *Echo* can come close to her, but not really. I have seen both ships in action on the Horn of Africa."

"Indeed?" said Lord Wilder, impressed.

"Yes," said Lady Bracknell, sourly. "A series of unfortunate events led her to that experience."

"I found them quite fortunate," said Delain.

"The *Paladin*. Fast," murmured Lord Wilder.

Aboard the *Paladin*, newly appointed Commander Thomas Harrison gazed into his telescope as he looked to the south and west. At his side stood Lieutenant Chad Alexander, his second-in-command, and Midshipman Jonathan Moore. Alexander was a new acquaintance, a year younger than Harrison at nineteen, and a few years older than Jonathan. Alexander had come recommended by several other captains, and he was known as a kind, gentle, and thoughtful young man. He took extra care in doing his duty correctly, and because of this, he had an exemplary record. Alexander was tall and lean and had deep-set dark eyes and a stern countenance, until he smiled. Then his entire face lit up, his eyes squinted, and his laugh was accompanied by a head nod and easy chuckle. Harrison felt fortunate to have him.

Of course, Jonathan and Harrison were not only accustomed to each other, but they had become as close as brothers, sharing missions at sea, and in London they were rarely apart. Along with Sean Flagon, the three were a common sight in and about town, studying maps and history at the many schools, fencing, and being together in general. It was odd that Sean was not with them now. He was in training, and both wondered if, possibly, some of the fantastic luck they had become accustomed to might be slightly diminished by Sean's absence.

"I see them now," Harrison said, looking through his glass. "Maybe four miles away."

"How many, sir?" asked Alexander.

"The whole lot, all bunched together like peas in a pod! With this wind being at least twenty knots, why, it is a near gale! The *Paladin* would attain close to fifteen knots, and we are three their size! They are barely eight knots if I know my sailing. Slow coaches to a one!"

"And we are to sit here and wait, sir?" asked Jonathan.

"Yes," said Commander Harrison with a sigh, "and each of these lead-bottomed, worm-rotted, brick-hulled scows must circle us, then head with the wind at their backs almost due north toward the beach, past the reviewing stands by the Parade. That's the finish, there — that raft. It's insulting."

Jonathan was puzzled. It seemed easy enough to sit and watch the race from this vantage point. What is the insult? he wondered.

"I see, sir," said Alexander. "When we have such a fine mare, it seems a waste to...keep her in the barn."

"My thoughts exactly," said Harrison. "Especially with all these people watching. There are many admirals and the like."

Jonathan thought about this for a moment. Yes, it was true that sitting here like a *buoy,* as Delain had described it, did nothing for the crew or the crowd. It was a shame not to race. And that gave him an idea.

"Captain Harrison," he started, "our duties end when

43

the last ship rounds our stern—is that correct?"

"Yes. Then we are to sail back to the Port of London at Wapping and enjoy our last evening in the great city before we sail tomorrow morning."

"As an exercise for the men, sir, we could just add all sail when the last yacht passes," said Jonathan, "and then take a closer look at the Parade. On our way to Wapping, of course."

At first Harrison and Alexander had confused looks on their faces, not yet understanding what Jonathan was suggesting; however, it didn't take long before smiles slowly appeared.

"I see why you have Mister Moore around, Captain," said Alexander.

"Ah! Ah! I am with you!" said Harrison excitedly, taking the telescope from his eyes and putting it in his pocket. "Mister Moore? Lieutenant Alexander? Have the men to the tops and ready all sail. Jenkins?"

"Aye, Cap'n?" said Jenkins. He had sailed with Harrison on both the *Poseidon* and the *Danielle* and knew most of the men now assigned to the *Paladin*. Almost an officerlike figure aboard the ship, he was seasoned, one would say. Not that he needed any more reason to be loyal to this captain, but Patrick Jenkins recognized he was getting older, and if there was any chance for promotion, it would be through Commander Thomas Harrison.

"Get a crew together," instructed Harrison. "More men than you need—and man the anchor. When that last *barge* passes our stern, haul the cable as if Satan himself were whipping you. I want that anchor up and secured in less than thirty seconds."

"Aye, Cap'n," Jenkins replied.

From the stands, many began to rise as they spied the yachts through their telescopes. Barbara Thompson lowered the glass she had borrowed from Nathaniel. Then she leaned to Delain and motioned toward the *Paladin*'s position.

"Dear, you know more about nautical procedures than I," she said. "What are they doing aboard the *Paladin*? There is much activity."

Using Admiral Moore's glass once again, Delain could just barely make out men running up the rigging and positioning themselves on the yards, the mast's cross beams, of the *Paladin*. They seemed to finally get into position and then stopped all movement. They looked like birds, resting on a tree.

"I believe, Miss Thompson, they are readying to bend the sails, as if they mean to be underway."

"Bend?" asked Lady Wilder.

"Yes," said Delain. "They are not always on the masts, you see. One must haul them up from the deck, in some cases, so they can be set to catch the wind."

"Why would they bend sails now?" asked Barbara.

Delain only smiled as the first of the racers neared the waypoint that was the *Paladin*.

"Look lively, men!" called Harrison. "Are all in position?"

"Yes, sir!" called Alexander.

"All in position, Captain!" added Jonathan.

The yachts now were mere yards from the *Paladin*, rounding her as best they could to achieve an arc that allowed them to turn in the tightest space yet retain needed speed to come about and catch the wind.

The *Paladin* was a hive of activity, with men in the tops securely holding to the yards, ready to unfurl sails, and setting the square lower sails, the courses, that needed to be hauled upward into position.

"Topmen! Unfurl all sail! Set courses! Sheet us home!" called Harrison. And like a canvas waterfall, the topgallants began to fall, unfurling into position, and the courses were hauled upwards. Ropes would soon be pulling sails tight—*sheeting* was the word—tight enough so the full wind would fill the sails. *Paladin* now began to strain against her anchor.

"Only four more yachts, Mister Harrison!" called Jonathan as he watched from the port rail.

"Jenkins, ready the anchor," Harrison called.

"Aye, sir! We 'ave her taut as can be, actually sliding a bit 'cross the bottom!"

"Good! Good!" called Harrison. "Stand ready."

As the last of the yachts came alongside the *Paladin,* Jonathan could see the name, the *Gray Gull,* across the stern. It was a pretty ship in all respects but not a racer, in Jonathan's humble opinion. The crew of the tiny craft handled the turn with only the barest of ability, and once past the *Paladin,* they had additional trouble finding the wind as the sails luffed, fluttered, and flapped.

"Blast them!" yelled Harrison, "I'd give them a hand if I could! Hurry up you — "

His expansive and lengthy tirade aimed at the delinquent yachtsmen had the *Paladins* laughing to themselves. Those who knew Harrison while he served under the Grand Dragon himself, Captain William Walker, had watched him achieve a level of excellence in his use of colorful metaphors, and to them it was an art form. Though no Rembrandt, Harrison was certainly bound to be a great master someday.

"By all the saints! Inconceivable!" Harrison shouted as the *Gray Gull* finally made the turn and passed the *Paladin's* starboard rail. "Heave the anchor!"

His orders were carried out exactly as desired. Within a few moments, the anchor was hauled, the sails had been let down, and the lines tightened. HMS *Paladin* began to speed forward, as if she were driven by machines of almost magical design. White foam started along the sides, and the hissing of salt spray could be heard all about the ship's deck. The sails were now full of wind, and Harrison, manning the wheel himself, turned her slightly to port, leaning her just so. The stays — ropes holding the masts in position — strained slightly, the raked masts groaned, and the *Paladin* was alive, like a graceful bird, running as if a storm drove her.

"The *Paladin!*" called someone in the crowd, and all joined Delain and Barbara in watching the sleek sloop with the graceful purple stripe running the length of her black sides quickly gain ground on the last of the yachts. Harrison had chosen a course that had him to the port side of the racers, thereby giving the spectators the best and uninterrupted view of the *Paladin*.

The crowd cheered.

Lord Wilder and his wife noticed the late entry as well and smiled broadly.

"It seems Mister Harrison has joined the race!" cried Lady Bracknell.

Rebecca gasped aloud.

Delain knew, as only a sister could, how fond Rebecca was of Harrison, and that he had called on her numerous times since they had all settled into London. Since their arrival in June, Harrison and Rebecca had spent considerable time together, enjoying London's many attractions.

"Rebecca," said Delain to her sister playfully, "what on earth is Thomas Harrison doing?"

"Doing what he does best!" Rebecca answered eagerly. "Creating excitement!"

This made all within earshot burst into laughter.

Within a minute, the *Paladin* had passed all but the leading yachts. Crowds were lined along the parade and beach as the race neared its conclusion. Many wondered what had happened, and why the *Paladin* was now allowed to enter the race. Certainly she could not best the racing craft of London's elite. But here she was, gaining on the leaders.

"The beach is approaching quickly. Will we have enough water, Captain?" called Alexander as they saw the black-and-white flags of two barges marking the quickly approaching finish line.

"Just enough!" called Harrison.

"We are a hundred yards from the leader," noted Jonathan, "and not much more from the finish line itself!"

"Tighten stays!" called Harrison, even though he knew they could not be tightened further. Men tried to carry out the order, more from a sense of duty than practicality.

Onshore, all stood to see the *Paladin* rush upon the leader, come abreast, and as Commander Harrison waved ever so slightly to the viewers ashore, pass into the lead and split the barges. A smooth turn to starboard had the *Paladin* gracefully round the bay and head out to sea, quickly disappearing south around the point.

"I knew he would win!" said Rebecca.

As the *Paladin* and crew sailed off to Wapping, their friends in the stands took the opportunity to walk the few yards and visit the charming seaside town. Here, they sampled some of the local sweets found in a nearby shop. Delain and her sisters chose ice cream, as could be expected, and strolled along the beach walk.

Lord and Lady Wilder had joined them, and soon they were deep into conversation.

"Tell me, Admiral Moore," Lady Wilder asked, "are you still very active in the Royal Navy?"

"Ah! If by 'active' you mean do I sail, no," said Nathaniel. "Those days are past for me. I hold a position in the Admiralty."

"He is personal adjunct to the king for naval affairs!" boasted Lady Bracknell.

"His son is also in the king's favor, I hear," added Delain knowingly.

"Impressive!" smiled Lord Wilder.

"The Moores are one of the great families of Britain," added Lady Bracknell. "A proud reminder to us all of industry and service to the country."

"Admiral Moore's son, Jonathan, is stationed aboard HMS *Paladin*, the ship that won the race!" added Rebecca, who had been listening. "It is captained by Commander Thomas Harrison."

"Admiral? What type of ship is the *Paladin*?" asked Lord Wilder. "It does fight, but it is not a...frigate. Is it a corvette? Possibly?"

"You are correct, my lord," said Nathaniel. "The French use the label 'corvette,' however, we call them 'sloops of war.' Naval nomenclature is actually more of an art than a science. In my definition, the *Paladin* is a two-masted, flush-deck, brig-rigged sloop. However, *corvette* fits as well as any other term."

"What is her complement of guns?" asked Lord Wilder.

"Eighteen of them, each firing a thirty-two-pound ball from a carronade. Quite a display of power from such a small craft—she is just over one-hundred feet. However, her best weapon is her speed."

"Though she is most assuredly a fighting ship!" added Rebecca. "With her sister ship, the *Echo*, they engaged a French seventy-four off the southern coast of Africa and single-handedly captured her!"

"Not exactly accurate, my dear," said the Admiral, laughing, "but I am sure that is what Commander Harrison has told many."

Ignoring this, Rebecca continued on explaining the seeming magical powers of the ship and the origin of her nickname, the *Periwinkle*. "She hadn't even received her painted stripes when her captain took her out for sea trials. It was during these trials that she engaged with and sank six French frigates—"

"Sank six frigates?" Admiral Moore chuckled.

"Let her finish, dear," said Barbara Thompson, enjoying the tale and the embellishments Rebecca added. She had originally heard the story from Harrison, who was famous for the superfluities he added to every tale he told.

"Before returning to England, the captain moored at a remote naval yard and had the hull stripes finally painted. The only available color was purple, so that is how she got her stripe!"

"But *Periwinkle?*" asked Lord Wilder.

"That is what we call the small mollusk of the Caribbean islands," added Nathaniel. "They have the same purple color on their shells."

Throughout this final exchange, Delain watched and listened. But not to the tale of the *Paladin*—she had heard that many times. She had a strange feeling about Lord and Lady Wilder, one she could not identify.

4

The Silver Star

In the stylish neighborhood of Golden Square, London, just off Silver Street, a carriage pulled by two bay horses appeared at the residence of Captain Sir William Walker and his charming wife, Sylvia. Also at the address dwelled Mrs. Walker's sister, Miss Barbara Thompson. In juxtaposition to these polite and genteel residents was a small crew of noisy servants whose manners were slightly less than desirable. As was customary for a captain of a naval vessel, while ashore and at home, he would retain several of his seagoing crew as house servants, gardeners, cooks, and handymen. This was done to not only assist them while they drew no naval pay, but to keep them—the better ones—for the captain's next voyage. Walker was no exception, and this made the house, at times, a little lively.

Exiting the carriage into the calm evening, Jonathan Moore held the door and extended a hand to Miss Delain Dowdeswell. As she accepted his help, Delain glanced at the front door of the large brick home and was overcome with a bout of anxiety. Jonathan noticed this.

"Delain? Are you all right?"

"Yes," she said unconvincingly. "It is just that...I haven't seen Captain Walker since the holidays. I wonder if he has..."

"Mellowed?" suggested Admiral Moore as he appeared from the opposite side of the carriage with Lady Bracknell. "You will find that the longer William Walker is on land, the more relaxed and softened he becomes. I am sure he will be a pleasant and graceful host throughout the evening."

Delain and Jonathan both remembered the few times

they'd had the unfortunate experience of being the focus of Captain Walker's wrath. Granted, he never became angry without good reason. It was just the length and ferocity of his anger that were infamous among his crew and other naval acquaintances. His word choices were as legendary as they were colorful and fiery, and because of this, he was called affectionately by the crew the Grand Dragon—of course, never to his face.

"So," Admiral Moore said with a sigh as they approached the steps that led to the door, "let us enjoy a wonderful and pleasant evening at the hands of our most generous and peaceful host."

At that moment, the front door to the Walker's home was flung open rudely from within, and there stood Walker. He immediately threw what appeared to be a full tray containing numerous cups of coffee over the heads of the approaching guests.

"By all the saints! Just a simple cup of drinkable coffee is all I ask! Any dim-witted son-of-a-wagger could arrange that! That is why I have employed Claise as the cook!"

He disappeared into the house again, leaving the front door open, and then reappeared with both Steward, his boson from HMS *Danielle,* and Claise, his cook aboard that same proud ship, clawing at what he carried, begging him to stop his rant.

"Now, Cap'n! Just a misunderstandin', that's all!" said Steward as he tried to wrestle something from Captain Walker's grasp.

"Confound it, Steward!" cried Walker.

"Please, sir!' begged Claise. "It's a beautiful coffee vase! Don't—"

But Walker was determined and considerably larger than the other two men, and he finally tore the coffee urn free from the numerous hands grasping it and launched it into the air. All watched as it sailed over the stoop, over the heads of the guests and the Admiral's carriage, and into the street, crashing into a hundred pieces.

The arriving guests turned back toward the house as

Steward and Claise started past them to clean up the mess.

"G'd evenin', Admiral Moore," said Steward as he rushed past, giving a hasty salute.

"Good to see you again, Mister Moore. Miss Dowdeswell. Lady Bracknell," said Claise as he tipped the hat he wasn't wearing.

All turned back to Walker for an explanation—and possibly, in the case of Lady Bracknell and Delain, an all-clear signal from the Admiral.

"Ah!" said Walker, as if nothing had happened at all, his mood changing to charming and joyous immediately. "Lady Bracknell! A pleasure as always! Come in! Come in! Nathaniel! So nice of you to come! Is that my favorite stowaway, Miss Delain Dowdeswell, on the arm of Midshipman Moore?"

"Yes, sir," said Jonathan, warily.

"Spa-*len*-did! Spa-*len*-did!" Walker continued, reflecting the articulation of each syllable of the word, just as the king had done during Walker's audience with His Majesty the previous year. The pronunciation had remained with and become part of the vocabulary of the several participants who attended that day, and the use of it had now spread to many of their acquaintances. Interestingly, many of those not appearing that day had heard the tale so often and repeated it to others with such frequency that they claimed falsely, yet proudly, they had been present in person.

Walker rushed down the few steps to the cobblestone drive to greet them formally.

"William! What on earth was that all about?" asked Lady Bracknell.

"What was what, my dear?"

"The launching of the coffee!" Admiral Moore laughed.

"Oh that. Nothing at all. It seems that Steward decided he would assist Claise, who you all know I have promoted from cook aboard the *Danielle* to cook aboard my kitchen here at home, in the making of some coffee for tonight's guests. When I discovered the gross disregard for my standing order that Steward was to give up all culinary duties on land and sea, I sampled the batch. I have tasted better in the black pitch we use to caulk seams! But never mind! Mrs. Walker and Miss Barbara Thompson await the ladies in the dining room! The men, to my study! We have business to discuss!"

At this point, a second carriage appeared in the drive, and from it emerged Commander Harrison in his uniform, escorting Rebecca Dowdeswell dressed in a beautiful silvery affair, complete with a stylish wool shawl and a dainty necklace about her neck fitted with a single diamond. Individually, anyone would use the term *handsome* to describe them, though as a couple, the word didn't seem adequate.

Harrison noticed Steward and Claise bending over the mess in the street and approached them on the way to the door, Rebecca on his arm. He had a look of puzzlement on his face.

"The street is full of something resembling tar," he said. "Steward, is this your attempt at pudding?"

"Good evenin' to ya, Commander," said Steward with an agitated tone.

Once inside the study, the men were seated and offered a few hors d'oeuvres. Jonathan, always with an appetite, settled on the bacon-wrapped dates, while the Admiral and Captain Walker had somehow enjoyed the miracle of out-of-season anchovies delivered by Claise, fried and lightly battered. Harrison joined them, dipping his fish into an apricot sauce set just to the side.

Walker sat in his large easy chair, sipping a brandy and munching his favorite fish when he turned to Admiral Moore who had taken up residence on the lounge nearby.

"Nathaniel, I am bored!" Walker announced.

"And why is that, William?"

"I am bored because of the war," Walker continued.

"What war? The treaty of Amiens was signed less than

a week ago," said Harrison.

"My point exactly! I am a bird without wings!" howled Walker. "The *Danielle* is in dock for repairs, and once seaworthy, I have no prospect of doing anything but escorting merchants to India and back. Not even a trip to the blasted colonies to harass them!"

"They are no longer colonies, William," Admiral Moore stated as he chose a second fish. "They are a sovereign nation—"

"For now, yes, but we shall see," interrupted Walker. "The point is, even though we have peace with France, Spain, and the whole lot, it will not last. We all know that. We must remain ready, not sit idly by while Napoleon strengthens his army."

A voice came from the doorway.

"I am not sitting idle," said Marine Captain Gorman as he entered the room. He wore his splendid open red jacket, with large white facings, a golden sash, and white breeches. In his hand was his black bicorn hat. He looked very much the part of a captain of His Majesty's Marines— even his face, weathered with a deep tan and with facial features as if chiseled out of stone. With him was Sean Flagon, resplendent in his red uniform—with short jacket, white crosshatched sash, and white breeches—though his face had the look of exhaustion, like a worn-out soldier twice his own age.

Both were greeted warmly by all. Sean and Gorman both lost no time taking up temporary flanking positions next to Jonathan and attacking the bacon-wrapped dates with enthusiasm. Sean seemed to liven up as he devoured the delicacies, causing Jonathan to quickly grab two of the prizes, knowing it would now be more than difficult fighting off the marines.

Once all the dates had been spoken for, Gorman stood and moved to the hearth, searching for something he knew to be there but most certainly hidden.

"Now, Midshipman Jonathan Moore," the marine said, "it seems we have not been on a mission together in a while. Hopefully we can descend into the waves yet again someday. In the meantime, I have a special espionage assignment for you."

"Of course!" said Jonathan happily, licking the sugary goo off his fingers from the last date he had consumed.

"Assist me," he said in a mock whisper, "in locating Captain Walker's hidden trove of chocolate-covered cherries. He keeps them in here, I know. I can smell them."

"Good luck," laughed Walker. "I have taken great care in hiding them from you."

"As I was saying," said Gorman as he continued looking under every lid on every knickknack, jar, and container on every shelf, "not everyone is idle in our effort to defeat the French."

"Are you commenting on your surveillance activities?" suggested Admiral Moore with a smile.

"Unofficially? Possibly. My point is that the active military may be at rest, but my men are always watching, always looking — as I am for those blasted cherries!"

Gorman was known as a master spy to a small community of English acquaintances, but somehow, as he aged, he was able to pass some of the more dangerous activities off to his less-known subordinates. He did occasionally handpick a mission for himself — usually when he could enlist the help of friends he trusted. He became fast friends with Captain Walker during a mission to Isla Pasaje in the Caribbean, and they had since been through much together, their successes known to all, even the king.

"What does your network think of the truce? Is it true there is to be no war?" asked Harrison.

"Oh, there will be war, I can assure you of that," answered Gorman. "This truce can't last more than a year or two at most. Many are still fighting: the Russians *unofficially* against the Turks, and the Americans are fighting with the Barbary States in Tripoli. No one is ever really satisfied. Never can be. But an interesting fact is that the influx of Frenchmen into our country makes life both difficult for me and, in a way, easier."

"How so?" asked Walker, silently laughing as Gorman continued to overturn everything except the furniture as he searched for his prize.

"There are French spies now in London, Chatham— everywhere. We know many of them, but they task us with new suspects. That is the hard part. However, the easy part is that I have *my* men in Paris and all points about the French countryside. The amount of information coming in is unmanageable. It is hard to discern what is worthy of attention and what is not."

Walker laughed. "I wish I were as busy as you, Captain."

"Blast it! I give up! Where are the cherries?" Gorman finally exploded, sending Jonathan, Harrison, and Sean into hysterical laughter.

"I will tell you," said Walker, "for a bottle of the wonderful port you brought me last February."

"W-what? Are you honestly suggesting I pay for the information?" asked Gorman, shocked.

"You pay for information often and handsomely, I am told, in your line of work!" defended Walker.

"Yes," added Admiral Moore. "That was excellent port. Please pay immediately."

"Thieves! Villains!" cried Gorman. "All right, all right! A bottle for the location of the cherries!"

Walker stood and walked over to the sofa where the boys had just finished the last of the dates. He lifted the plate, and under it, in a bowl, were revealed a dozen or so chocolate-covered cherries.

"Right under your nose, Gorman," announced the captain.

"Ah!" said Sean, reaching for a handful, "Under *my* nose, literally, as well!"

"Halt! Unhand those berries, Flagon! That is an order!" cried Gorman.

The rest of the evening was pleasant enough. Dinner was wonderful and the conversation was lively. Claise had prepared several hens, with a ginger glaze and sesame seeds sprinkled on the lightly browned skins. Peppered potatoes with burnt butter roux and a side dish of the famous anchovies, lightly fried and salted. A blond beer was also served, and though it looked tasty and cool, Jonathan, Sean, and Delain were not allowed to partake. Instead, they enjoyed a sweet tea made by Miss Thompson after an American recipe that mixed it with lemons and extra sugar. The youngsters were satisfied.

After many toasts to commemorate the promotion of Lieutenant Thomas James Harrison to commander, and even more salutes to his appointment as captain of the *Paladin*, he announced his orders.

"As commanding the most excellent ship HMS *Paladin* will be exciting enough, I can only guess that the Admiralty thought that a simple mission to deliver mail and packets to Gibraltar would be a sufficient task. Our orders are to act as a packet."

"No action for you either," mumbled Walker.

"Good luck, Thomas. And you as well, Jonathan," said Miss Thompson. She paused for a moment and then stood, quickly excusing herself from the room. Nathaniel, seeing that she was upset, followed.

"Barbara," Nathaniel said softly as he came to her, "what is the matter?"

She had walked almost all the way down the hallway to the front door, and stood looking out a thin window that ran alongside the entrance. She had her back turned to him, her arms wrapped about herself. Nathaniel could see that she was trying to regain her composure. He gave her a moment. As she faced him, there were tears in her eyes.

"My dear," he said, and he put his arms about her shoulders.

"Oh, I am being silly," Barbara said. "I should not act this way. But I will miss them so. I—I know I have no right to be so attached, but they are like my own, Jonathan and

Sean. I can't really bear the thought of them going hundreds of miles away—"

"Actually thousands," said Nathaniel.

"You are making it worse!" cried Barbara. "What if they find trouble and need us? What then?"

"Well," said Nathaniel thoughtfully, "that is why Harrison—*Commander* Harrison—will be there. And though they might appear young to you, think of what they have accomplished already."

"Thomas is still a boy," she said, sobbing slightly.

"One that has been literally battle-tested. He has seen half the known world and even commanded a prize ship from the Horn of Africa all the way to London. He is no novice."

"Don't you worry about them, Nathaniel?" she asked.

He thought for a moment.

"Always, my dear. I worried about Jonathan for the years I remained in prison in France. I worried as I fought my way to return to these shores. But I have faith in their abilities. I rely on that for strength. Thomas will look out for them, I can assure you. Patrick Jenkins is also going aboard the *Paladin*. He's been at sea since he was a lad."

"Jenkins? Yes, I remember him. Yarn in his beard."

"A tradition of some sailors," said Nathaniel. "He is a good man and more than capable of managing Jonathan and Sean."

Nathaniel and Barbara returned to the others, possibly a little more at ease, though both had moments of doubt and concern.

"Exquisite meal, Claise. You have outdone yourself again," said Walker as Claise and Steward began clearing plates from the table. "It will be some comfort to me knowing that you will remain under my command and are not going aboard the *Paladin* tomorrow."

"Oh!" cried Delain, now realizing that her time with Jonathan, Sean, and Harrison was at an end. She had dreaded the date, April the fourth, knowing that they would be setting out to sea once again. Her heart sank. London now held nothing but boring tea parties, social calls, and endless books.

Seeing her discomfort, Barbara Thompson patted her hand. "Delain, I will make sure you and I have some adventures of our own."

"That would be...nice," she answered, unable to hide her melancholy.

"Well, then. The hour is late!" announced Admiral Moore. "The Ladies Bracknell and Dowdeswell must be returned to their mansion, and the navy men need a good night's rest before they sail tomorrow. One more night of comfort."

All stood and said their good-byes, then walked the long hallway from the dining room to the front door. Admiral Moore seemed to delay his parting as he stood close to Barbara and slightly behind the others. All watched — while not watching — as they shared a short embrace and a light kiss on the cheek. This caused the children to giggle and Lady Bracknell to sigh with favor.

As the guests waved good-bye and began to enter their carriages, Harrison was awarded a dainty kiss from Rebecca, after which she joined the Moores, her aunt, and her sister in the admiral's carriage. The horses were driven slightly more than three miles to Van Patten Wood's western edge and the estate of the Bracknells, arriving within a half hour. Jonathan and his father escorted Delain, Rebecca, and Lady Bracknell to the door. Before following inside, Jonathan and Delain paused at the doorway for a moment.

"A wonderful evening," said Jonathan to Delain.

"And the entire day," Delain said, turning to face him. "I will...miss you, Jonathan. I-I have grown quite accustomed to y-your company. Please take care. Without me to assist you, your adventures could be dangerous."

Jonathan smiled and looked down to Delain's hands. They were petite and beautiful. She had somehow taken her dolphin necklace and wrapped it about her delicate wrist. He took her hands in his.

"I will be careful," Jonathan said. "And you as well. London can be harsh, Delain."

She knew he spoke from experience. When she thought of how miserable his young life had been, living on the streets for years, it weighed on her heart. She imagined how difficult it must have been — and how lonely. Her breath skipped, exposing her grief.

"A tear, Miss Dowdeswell?" Jonathan asked softly.

"Just when I think of your hardships…"

"Ah," Jonathan said with a smile. "I am all right now, Miss Dowdeswell. And remember: without my life as it was, I never would have met Sean, never would have been set aboard the *Poseidon*, and therefore…I never would have met you."

Delain turned up her face to him and smiled, her deep green eyes glowing above her silken cheeks.

"Well, that makes it all worthwhile then," she said, extending her fair hand to him. In it, she held a small gift box wrapped in white paper. "For you," she said.

Jonathan considered Delain and the box, a look of curious confusion painting his face. He opened the wrapping slowly, as if each sheet of paper were sacred and valuable. The box had a simple lid of paperboard, and as he opened it, he could see Delain's face blush a faint rose.

"It is for you, on your travels," she said, "and to remember *our* adventures."

Jonathan held up the gift: a silver crescent moon upon a silver star, with the compass points, north, east, west, and south, each engraved on the corners.

"Delain," Jonathan said. "It is stunning. I thank you. Coming from you, it will be a great comfort to me."

"Please return, Jonathan," she said.

"Of course," he replied.

He lifted her hands to his face slowly, and kissed them ever so lightly.

Delain smiled even brighter, let out a slight gasp, then turned and ran inside.

On the slow ride home in Admiral Moore's carriage, a light drizzle began to fall. Nathaniel watched his son in silence as the boy stared alternately between the silver star and the passing scene out the window, deep in his own thoughts. Jonathan's face was neither happy nor sad, but it showed some emotion. Was it concern—or possibly even loss in a way? It was true; he recognized that Jonathan would get to know, quite intimately, this feeling of being drawn between two loves. He would never be truly happy with just one, and never be able to satisfy them both.

5
The Treaty of Akbar

At the close of the evening, after the dinner at Captain Walker's home, Delain and her sisters prepared for bed. Upstairs at Bracknell Manor, there was a small parlor that was afforded to the girls, with a private room for each off its sides. Every evening they sat at three vanities, each set with a large mirror. The girls brushed their hair, discussing what they had seen in London that day, what had happened in school, and what activities were planned for tomorrow. Delain had, of course, mentioned Jonathan's kiss, or what her sisters called "the long-awaited kiss." Though none of them would consider it a *proper* kiss, as Rebecca called her final sample from Thomas Harrison, to Delain it was ever so special.

"I thought of just taking one from him," Delain had told her giggling sisters. "Jonathan has had so many chances. But I am glad I let him deliver it in his own time."

After her admission, she suddenly became silent, and her sisters became curious, noticing her scrunched brow and frown. She even started murmuring to herself, as if trying to recount some activity or conversation. Though they loved her dearly, she seemed to be a bit, well, *off*. Normally, Delain would complain about the appointments for tea, the ridiculous poise-and-manners lessons, and the fact that Jonathan, and all her friends who provided any modicum of excitement, would soon abandon her. Tonight, however, Delain seemed to be in her own world.

"Delain," Rebecca said, "whatever are you thinking?"

"Pardon," said Delain, affecting a proper and sophisticated air. "Whatever do you mean?"

"You are almost completely silent, something we are

not accustomed to," Rebecca said.

"I have been formulating an opinion," Delain said flatly.

"About whom?" asked Penelope, who had finished her own hair brushing and came to Delain's side to take over the task.

"About Lord and Lady Wilder," she answered.

"The lovely couple we met at the race?" asked Penelope.

"Yes," said Delain. "Something is not right with them. I can't quite put my finger on it."

"Why on earth do you have a concern with them?" asked Rebecca.

"I can't get the fact out of my mind that they are nobility in London, yet...Lady Wilder dressed slightly, well, shabbily."

Rebecca laughed. "Look who is now a fashion critic of the London elite! I never thought I would see the day that my tomboy sister would ever make such a comment. I mean, coming from you? You actually own *pants!*"

"I am not a tomboy!" said Delain forcibly.

"But you *do* own pants," stated Penelope. "I have seen you in them. Ghastly!"

Delain shook her head as best as she could; it was difficult with her sister stroking her hair. She settled on rolling her eyes and sighing loudly.

"It is not the lack of fashion that has me interested. It is the condition of Lady Wilder's clothes. They were tattered and frayed. Also, the Wilders departed after the race with Barbara Thompson in Captain Walker's carriage. Wouldn't you think they would have their own carriage?"

"They do," said Penelope. "I saw it before the race. A gray affair. Not very nice, I will admit."

"Why not take that carriage home?" asked Rebecca.

"Because, I think it is rented. By the hour!" claimed Delain.

"Good heavens!" scolded Rebecca. "How can you say such a thing?"

"All I am saying is that something is abnormal about the Wilders. They are not very…refined, to use a form of your word."

"Maybe they have money complications," offered Penelope.

"Possibly," said Delain. "However, I would like to get a little closer. Someone must assist me in—" She stopped short, and an uncomfortable silence remained.

"Spying?" asked Rebecca.

"I wouldn't put it that way," said Delain.

"I would," said Penelope.

"And why not then, if you must label it?" retorted Delain, slightly angry. "There were a few other items they mentioned that made little sense. And there were contradictions."

Rebecca stopped her grooming and turned to her sister.

"Lord Wilder claimed he knew little about sailing ships," said Delain. "However, he had no trouble telling a frigate from a corvette. And he asked a few questions about guns, and, may I point out, did not use the term *cannon*, as many uneducated persons would. There is a contradiction if I ever heard one."

"Contradiction?" exclaimed Rebecca. "Delain! Lord Wilder knew one small fact about sailing ships, hardly a reason for an inquisition. He obviously knows a thing or two being on the Navy Board. Might he have had a few conversations?"

"It was the *manner* in which he stated it," said Delain, "as if he were trying to appear innocent."

"*Appear* innocent?" asked Rebecca. "Why do you persist? This is all an attempt to promote your dissatisfaction with London. You, Penelope, and I—like Miss Barbara Thompson—are destined to be ladies of London!"

"Miss Barbara Thompson," Delain said softly.

"And if you marry well," continued her older sister, "you will be a polite and sophisticated woman, living in comfort and enjoying what polite society can offer. Can you not accept that?"

Delain stood, smiled, walked over to her older sister, and put her arms about her. They both saw their reflections in the mirror.

"My dear Rebecca," said Delain, smiling. "The answer to that question is an unequivocal and unsympathetically stated *no!* And thank you for the suggestion."

"What suggestion?" asked Rebecca.

On the eastern portion of Van Patten Wood, the night had settled in, and a cool wind blew a gray mist across the estate of Lord and Lady Wilder. It had been raining lightly and had just recently stopped. Stars peeked out from the space between the departing clouds, adding a glimmer of light to the wet cobblestone. At the end of the drive leading from the house to the street stood a figure. Cloaked in a heavy coat and hood with head cast down to hide his face, the man stood close to the trunk of a large pedunculate oak, hiding from the weak light in the tree's shadow. Not wanting to be seen, he stood as still as stone, staring not toward the sleeping mansion of the Wilders, but outward to the road.

At precisely three a.m., just as it had happened previously, there came the faint creaking of a carriage and the soft clip-clop of a lone horse's hooves. The cloaked figure strained to see through the darkness and remaining haze. After a moment, he saw the carriage materialize just a few yards to his left and then slow noticeably to continue beyond his position. As it rolled past, he could see the carriage's black form pulled by a blacker horse. There were no lamps lit, inside or out, and no human shape. Not even the form of the driver could be distinguished. The carriage stopped several yards to his right. A moment later, the side door was opened from within.

After a long moment, the cloaked man waiting by the tree looked briskly to the left and right, then behind, and stepped quickly toward the carriage. He rushed inside, then closed the door just as the cart began to move once again. A voice greeted him warmly.

"Lord Wilder. A pleasure to see you again."

Removing his hood, Lord James Wilder nodded.

The carriage moved south, away from the posh country estates of Van Patten Wood, heading south through the night toward Camden.

These trips were infrequent, though Wilder had come to realize that they all unfolded in the same manner. A note would almost magically appear at his dinner table — once in his salad, of all places — or in his study next to the brandy vase and snifter. There would be a clumsily written note in almost juvenile handwriting, with simply a date written on it. All he was required to do was to appear at the end of his drive at three in the morning, ensuring that his wife and servants would all be asleep, and await the carriage.

The driver outside had never spoken to Wilder in all the trips he had taken. The man inside never spoke, except the greeting, until the carriage was far from his home. The eventual conversations were always extremely interesting to Wilder, and the subject and plans made were befitting of a man in his position and with his talents. He was, after all, a lord of not only the Crown, but a lord of His Majesty's Navy, and he held an important position on the Admiralty Board, presiding over a variety of ship's assignments. It was, however, this added duty of working with one of His Majesty's secret agents that was the coup de grace.

Finally, the spy spoke.

"Some good news, Lord Wilder. His Majesty has been so taken by our last bit of success that he has decided to entrust us with another, more important mission."

"Indeed?" said Wilder. "It is my pleasure to serve him, and in the least, to do my small part."

"A true Tory, you are, Lord Wilder, and modest. It was no small part, nor will be this new endeavor. Shall I proceed with the details?" asked the spy.

"By all means," said Wilder, quite pleased at hearing that his last effort had been well received.

Reaching Camden, the carriage proceeded down a

dark and quiet street and came to a halt under a small foot-bridge that spanned a brook. The driver stayed in his seat and looked in all directions, as if expecting someone to happen by at this late hour, curiosity and possibly an opportunity to better their financial position driving them. Of course, none did this evening. If one had, a simple look from the driver and a flashing of his long, French pistol gleaming in the gaslight from across the street would be enough to send anyone quickly on his way.

Inside the carriage, the spy leaned close to Lord Wilder, dropped his voice to a low whisper, and presented the plan.

"The king desires a stronger relationship against Napoleon with his allies. Though at peace for the moment, all know it will not last. Hostilities are surely to break out within the year. Our list of allies is short, and the quality of our relationships is fragile."

"Indeed," said Wilder. It was true he had heard rumors, but these political events and machinations placed him out of his element. He had always believed that these things were best left up to those who had an interest in foreign affairs and had some means to affect them.

Means! Without the special compensation he expected to receive for his part in all of this, over a thousand pounds for his last effort, he would not have the means to keep his estate afloat, much less change the course of European history. But in his small way, he believed he could use his position to aid the British cause.

"What is the king's desire?" he asked.

"To deliver a treaty to the tsar of Russia, Ferdinand the second. The Treaty of Akbar."

"Akbar? Russia? Are they not already our allies?" asked Wilder.

"Yes, yes, but it is a tenuous relationship," interrupted the spy. "The king and his ministers feel a more specific treaty will ensure our alliance. It is our duty to secretly, and with the utmost dispatch, route this treaty to the tsar. Only the fastest ship will do."

"The *Paladin!*" said Lord Wilder. "Why, of course! The fastest ship in the fleet, even faster than the *Echo*, if that seems at all possible. And a beauty, I must say. Eighteen guns, though her best weapon is her speed. I have heard she can make almost seventeen knots."

"Seventeen? That will surely do. Yes. The *Paladin*," agreed the spy.

"She will take the treaty to the Island of Dugi Otok in the Adriatic Sea. A ship will be waiting to receive the treaty and take it to the tsar. I have the details on rice paper," he said, handing the sheet to Wilder. "Please destroy it once you have committed it to memory."

"I will," said Wilder dramatically.

"In this packet is the treaty," said the spy, who handed the package to his friend. Wilder took it and placed it in his breast pocket, giving it a firm pat.

"I will have Captain Spears change their orders immediately and inform the crew before they set sail tomorrow. They will be honored to carry such a valuable—"

"Begging your pardon, Lord Wilder," said the spy. "The crew must not know anything about the treaty or its purpose. They must be kept in the dark completely. Too risky to let any details escape."

Wilder thought about this. His few discussions with His Majesty's naval captains had taught him one thing: they were not accepting of duty without extreme amounts of detail, and they were a suspicious lot to a man. Not telling them of the purpose of the treaty could cause them to attempt all sorts of dangerous departures and take unnecessary chances in the execution of their duty. And then what would happen? The treaty could be captured by an enemy or lost during the taking of a ship, burned in a fire, blown overboard.

"I think it would be prudent to tell the officers of the *Paladin* at least something about their duty," said Wilder. "Just sending them to a delivery point with a diplomatic pouch will raise a great deal of suspicion. They will question the order more than usual."

"I am worried, Lord Wilder—"

"These are good men, my friend. I have spent a day with them. A topnotch crew they are, and trustworthy. The commander, Lieutenant Thomas Harrison, is beyond well respected! Recovered the *Drake*, I am told, and fought in the Battle of Fire gallantly! We can count on them, I am sure!"

"As you wish it, my lord," agreed the spy, "but let us tell them only that they carry an important treaty—not its name or purpose—and that information is for officers only. We cannot afford to have tongues of ordinary seamen wagging in every port."

"Completely understood, my friend," said Wilder.

"In addition," continued the spy, "I must say the schedule is extremely tight. The *Paladin* absolutely must not be late to Dugi Otok. The ship meeting them will only wait within a short window of time. I am afraid that if they are tempted to pursue prizes, as all captains are, they will likely miss the appointment. We must find a way to keep them on course and on schedule."

"I have it!" said Wilder after a moment of thought. "The midshipman aboard the *Paladin*, Jonathan Moore? Yes, Jonathan Moore is his name, the son of Admiral Nathaniel Moore! He has been given favor by the king himself, directly. If we could have His Majesty send a personal request for him to influence Commander Harrison, if needed, then he will advise as we desire. It would be like having one of our own spies on the ship."

Wilder chuckled at this comment, as he thought himself the spy—and obviously his companion was one as well.

The spy thought about this for a moment and realized that an extra amount of insurance would help keep the *Paladin* on course to meet her appointment. He had his own insurance, of course, though no one can have too much in this business.

"I will speak to His Majesty first thing in the morning, and I will send word to you of his response. When does the *Paladin* depart?"

"Just before noon. We must hurry," added Wilder as he glanced out the window of the carriage. They were now moving once again.

The carriage continued in silence, mostly, and after half an hour arrived quietly at the Wilder Estate. The spy leaned over to Lord Wilder and grasped his arm.

"I also have a personal request, Lord Wilder. My nephew, Lieutenant Phillip Quinn, is a member of the Royal Navy and is awaiting assignment. I was hoping he would join the crew of the *Paladin* on this historic mission. Would it be at all possible to have him—"

"Consider it done, my friend," Wilder said holding up his hand. "Phillip Quinn? He will be assigned and will deliver the orders personally to the *Paladin*. Have it at my office by eight a.m."

"That is most gracious of you, Lord Wilder," said the spy. "Here we are."

The carriage stopped a short distance from the drive leading to the Wilder Estate. The door opened. Both men looked about to see if anyone had noticed them. The fog was thinning, and a slight glow of the approaching day could be seen to the east, turning the edge of the night's blackness into a thin line of deep purple. It was silent—still only five in the morning at the most.

"His Majesty relies on us once again. I thank you for your service to him and to my network." The spy smiled and reached for the carriage door. "A pleasure doing business with you, Lord Wilder. Good evening."

"The pleasure is all mine, my dear Orvislat."

With that, Lord Wilder left the carriage and proceeded toward his home in the remaining darkness.

Orvislat smiled broadly as the carriage moved on through the night. He thought of the *Paladin*, and yes, it confirmed what Lupien had told him: it was a fast ship and should be suitable for their needs. He tried to contain a laugh as the carriage rolled on.

6

Simply Lieutenant Gray

"He's dead," said Hayes, covering the form of seaman Bedard with a coat. "Too much blood lost."

"How many are left?" asked Gray as he stared out into the cove. It had been two weeks of fog and chill, enough to sour any mood. Each day, including this one, was dreary and overcast, drizzling rain almost constantly. But the continued loss of men, mostly due to their injuries and lack of even the most rudimentary of medical supplies, almost drove Gray to complete depression. Losing the *Echo* was unimaginable, and losing his crew to slow death was unbearable.

"Seven, including us, sir."

Gray surveyed the small piece of beach and reviewed their resources. There were clothes, now trying to dry in the few minutes of sun that reached the cove. They came from the men who had perished, and as unholy as it was, they had been stripped and buried ashore in a single grave, covered with sand and as many loose rocks as could be found. Certainly this was unfitting; however, their clothes could be used, if they ever could get dry, to protect the survivors from the cold that was surely to come if they remained even a few days longer.

In their possession was also some ten-odd feet of fishing line they had gladly accepted from young Ike Williams, who had taken it in his personal effects before he left the *Echo*. A single fishing hook was crafted from the pin of Commander Gray's Order of the Bath medallion he had received for his participation in the Battle of Fire. A few pilchards and anchovies had been caught and eaten raw, while a few others were drying in the sun, watched over by

Marine Private Hill, whose sole job was to keep the small, stinging flies off the food.

Gray had his pistols but no ball or powder. Hayes had two small knives, and Sherland, the assistant armorer, had found a few planks and poles that must have fallen overboard when the men abandoned the *Echo* to Aggar.

The ropes that Aggar's crew had used to rappel down the face of the cliffs had been taken away as Aggar's men departed. Those, thought Gray, would have been more than handy.

As for natural supplies, they had no fresh water, no food besides the fish they caught, and no shelter due to the rocky terrain and lack of trees. They did obtain a few dried sticks taken from the bushes growing out of the steep, tall cliffs that kept them in their prison on three sides, the ocean acting as the remaining wall. The tinder sources were now few within reach, and at one point, the men stood on each other's shoulders to reach and gather firewood from higher-growing plants. At least for an hour or so each night, they could afford a small fire for cooking and warmth. Gray and the survivors knew that this fuel would run out shortly, the weather would cool, and most likely, they would starve or freeze to death.

He and Hayes had both tried swimming to the mouth of the inlet, and a bit further into the ocean itself, to see if there was any way around the shoreline. They had hoped to find a steep path up to the top of the cliffs or some other way to escape, but it was not to be. They reasoned that they would all drown if they attempted to swim to their freedom.

The only solace Gray could take was that, since their current situation was so dire, the fact that his ship had been taken was the least of his worries. He could put it out of his mind for now.

"Any idea of a plan, Commander Gray?" asked Hayes as he began to start a fire with his bare hands and two of the driest sticks.

"Plan? No, but a goal: to get back to England, of

course. We are on the island of Dugi Otok, and most settlements are on the eastern shore."

"And we are on the west," said Hayes.

"If we can somehow escape this bowl we are in, I would think we are only a few days' hike from Sali, and then we could take a boat to Zadar and civilization. We could then arrange for transport back to London or steal a ship if necessary. However, our current predicament remains the same, Mister Hayes. These walls are sheer enough to keep us here forever. The ropes used by Aggar's men are either taken, or they remain above the cliffs—no use to us. The sea, though shallow, is still fathoms over our heads and the distance to anywhere else is unknown. There is no way out, except as angels."

Hayes shook his head and managed a smile. "Well, if it comes to that, we can fly out."

Gray looked up at the darkening sky. It looked like some weather would roll in, and that would make for a wet evening. Thunder boomed somewhere off over the ocean. Ah, to be onboard a ship, Gray thought, with all the comforts and abundant supplies: food, blankets, lumber if you needed it, and miles of rope, glorious rope. We have none. Otherwise we could have somehow climbed out of this godforsaken place, he thought. Rope was handy for a number of things aboard a sailing ship: binding barrels together, lashing boats and supplies to the deck and inside holds, tightening masts, creating hammocks, and even managing the deployment of anchors.

"I would give my left arm for some lengths of rope," Gray muttered.

Hayes nodded again as his sticks began to smoke. It would be a few more seconds of rigorous work before the fire started; however, he stopped.

"What did you say, Mister Gray?"

"I said I would give my...Oh! Oh, Mister Hayes! We *do* have rope!" Gray said, as he quickly sat up on the sandy beach and began to take off his shoes.

"Are you game for another swim?" said Hayes as he

joined his captain in disrobing, having realized the same possibility.

"We shall soon see!" came Gray's reply. "Sherland! Hill! Neil! Wilson! Lend a hand! Williams! Get this fire roaring! Mister Hayes and I are going for a dip!"

"But, sir!" said Sherland as he stood, "we will run out o' firewood if we build a large fire. We can't reach the other bushes! They're too 'igh!"

"No, no, we won't!" said Gray, laughing. "We will climb up for more in a few moments, and then climb out of this hellish bowl!"

Neil leaned over to Hill and whispered, "'Ave they been drinkin' seawater? Is it madness?"

The men watched as the two officers dove into the murky water and swam out to the center of the bay. They seemed to be having a small discussion as they treaded water, then both took deep breaths and dove straight down, their feet breaking the surface momentarily. Then they were gone.

"What are they diving for, oysters?" asked Sherland.

"Don't like 'em much" said Neil.

"Looks like thar diving deep," said Hill. "All the way ta the bottom. Don't know what's down thar that would 'elp us climb out o' here."

"Oysters can't 'elp ya climb. Ya need rope fer that!" said Wilson with a laugh.

"No rope on the bottom of the ocean," added Sherland.

The men watched, imagining what in the name of the saints Gray and Hayes were doing. They were swimming deep, popping up for air as needed, then plunging down time and again.

"Ya know," said Neil as a ray of clarity struck him in the head. "The only thing that could be on the bottom besides muck and goo would be…the anchors of the *Echo*. Remember?"

"Sure," said Hill. "The hawsers were cut on bow and stern to push the *Echo* out of the bay. I saw Hayes axe the stern line myself — *sploosh*, right into the water."

"Yup, rope and all," added Sherland. "Cap'n Gray shot the bow line clean in 'alf with 'is last pistol round. I saw it myself. Prob'ly 'bout fifty feet o' rope on each anchor if an inch."

"But ya can't use an anchor ta climb a cliff, can ya?" asked Wilson.

They stared at the captain and Hayes as they excitedly dove once again, this time with knives in their teeth.

"Ya think…" said Neil.

"…that they are gettin' something else?" asked Hill.

"The anchor rope!" Williams said. "They'll go fer it!"

They all finally realized that the *ropes*, attached to the two anchors, were the prize.

Immediately the men began rounding up all the sticks, branches, and twigs available, and worked feverishly to build a roaring fire for both their cold and wet captain and his first lieutenant, Mister Hayes.

Within a few minutes, Gray and Hayes returned, dragging fifty feet of thick, strong rope each. The men cheered them, slapped their backs, and hugged them to keep their officers warm. All stood by the fire and laughed.

The next morning, the men had dry clothes that had been heated by the wonderfully strong fire made from the many bushes they had taken from the cliff walls. Then they set to tasks. It was easy enough to separate the thick hawser lines into thinner ropes, thereby making them easier to throw and gaining additional length. Tying an oblong stone to the end of a length, Hill was able to use it like a grapple and set it around an outcropping of boulders jetting out from the cliff wall. Sherland, the thinnest of them all and most agile — besides the youngster Williams — had no trouble shimmying up the rope and tearing out bush after bush. Hayes had easily made warm food for the first time in days. Yes, it rained that evening, and even that was welcome as the crew devised a hastily made catch out of a spare coat, and now drank wooly yet fresh water, with fresh-cooked fish made over a fire.

"Cap'n?" asked Sherland. "I believe I could easily climb out o' this place with the lengths o' rope Hill is making, but they'll be heavy! I don't think I can carry 'em up with me."

"A fine observation, Sherland," said Gray. "Let us think about this. Hill? How much rope do we now have from the hawsers?"

"Yes, sir," said Hill. "Each of the two hawsers was fifty-feet 'er so, and quadruple wound as I like ta say, so Wilson and I unwound 'em. We was able to get almost two 'undred feet from each. We 'ave almost four 'undred feet o' rope."

"Good! Very good," said Gray.

"Those cliffs are about a hundred feet or so," said Hayes. "We can have Hill toss the lines as high as he can and somehow attach it to those boulders there. They are about twenty-five feet up. Sherland can then shimmy on up and carry some rope with him!"

"Sure I can, sirs!" said Sherland, assessing the climb. "I could then toss a few fathom o' rope ta those bushes — and again to the others. Soon I'll be almost to the top. Then, I'll shimmy some more, and I could make my way up without any more rope from there. It looks pretty rocky all the way. I just know I can climb the rest, easy!"

"I see," said Wilson. "But 'ow do the rest o' us get up? Is Sherland goin' ta carry a rope with 'im to let down, like Rapunzel's hair? It will be mighty heavy."

"Beggin' yer pardon, sir," said Hill. "Sherland won't need to carry rope. I believe I can toss the line to the top from here."

"That's the spirit!" said Gray.

With that, the men began to gather their meager belongings, including a string of dried fish and their fishing line and hook. Hayes pinned the "hook" back on Gray's lapel in a small and short ceremony.

"I award you this medal of honor, Captain and Commander Gray of the HMS *Echo*," he said.

Gray bowed slightly, then a look of sadness came over his face as he stood erect.

"I am not captain, for I have no ship. Probably never will again. So I am simply Lieutenant Gray. We must make our way home to tell our tale and find those responsible. Additionally," he said, swallowing hard, "I will need to answer for the loss of one of His Majesty's vessels."

"Captain," said Hayes, "we will stand with you. Something was not right from the beginning of this mission, orders being changed and all. I can't help but think that someone high up in the Admiralty is, well..."

"A traitor?" asked Gray. "Yes. I agree. It is clear now that our orders were changed, and the entire prisoner exchange was a ruse to deliver the *Echo* into enemy hands."

"And they were most definitely speaking a Slavic language. They could be Germans or Poles, even Russians," added Hayes.

"But Russians? Aren't they our allies?" asked Hill.

"They were when we sailed from Chatham," said Gray. "However, Aggar could be acting on his own. There are many privateers — legal pirates, one could say — performing under the permission and direction of their government. They would certainly desire a ship like the *Echo*. You may be correct, Lieutenant Hayes. There is one thing we know: someone who changed our orders is dirty, and we can never know whom to trust."

"Therefore, we don't know who we can turn to if we get back to London," added Hayes.

Gray stood and took a deep breath.

"Let us concentrate on getting back, Mister Hayes. We will worry about the rest once we are home."

After Hill had tossed the rope to the boulder outcropping, Sherland had little trouble scaling the cliff to that point. Once he cleared the boulders, however, he had some difficulty swinging the rope to the next set of bushes some twelve feet above his head. After a few tries, he finally had what looked like a decent grip, as the stone on the end of the rope seemed to wrap two times around a scraggly tree trunk. He pulled himself upward. This process was repeated several times until he had almost reached the last set of bushes.

The men below had positioned themselves to break his fall if he should slip, and, he did slip once, dangling from the rope for a few seconds before finally finding his footing.

"Almost there," he called down to the men who stood under him.

Sherland now would attempt the most difficult portion: scrambling, free of the rope, the last several feet to the top. He loosened the line and let it fall to the ground.

All watched as Sherland scrambled up the remaining twelve or so feet. A small slip here and there, but actually, an easy climb at the end, and the men cheered and gave a joyous "Huzzah!" as Sherland smiled and bowed.

"Like a spider monkey he is!" said little Ike.

"Excellent job, Sherland!" called Gray. "And now the easy part!"

Hill took the end of the long rope with the stone attached and began swinging it around his head, over and over, glancing upward now and again, gauging the distance and his timing. The others had made sure the rope was untangled, and laying just right so as not to catch on anything. There was to be no impediment to its flight to the top.

"Let 'er go, Hill!" called Sherland from the top.

"Don't try to catch it," warned Gray. "Just let it sail past and then grasp it after it has come to rest!"

"Aye, sir," answered Sherland.

Hill made a few more swings about his head, and then, with great effort, he threw the line heavenward. It sailed clear for almost one hundred feet—far enough; however, the stone struck a few bushes and rocks, slid a few feet more, then came bouncing down.

"Hell and smoke!" called Hill. "Beggin' the captain's pardon."

"No pardon necessary, Hill. Again, if you please! I

have full faith in your abilities," Gray encouraged.

It took three more tries before Hill succeeded in tossing the line all the way to the top, where Sherland grabbed the rope and attached it to a nearby tree, sturdy and close to the edge. Neil, being the largest of all, stayed to steady the line as the others prepared to scale the cliff. They would all assist in pulling him up in the end.

"Onward and upward!" Gray called, and they began their way back to London.

7
A Change of Orders

In the very early morning of April the fourth, Nathaniel Moore stood in the cold but dry air outside of Captain Walker's home in Golden Square with none other than Patrick Jenkins, newly assigned hand of His Majesty's Ship *Paladin*. Earlier, at the admiral's home in Charing Cross, they had loaded the carriage with the seamen's lockers of both Jonathan Moore and Sean Flagon. Miss Barbara Thompson, who had been added to their small group only moments before, was now in the carriage, sleeping along with her two boys.

"Lookin' right as rain, Adm'ral," said Jenkins as he lashed the last of the luggage to the top. "Sun might be up soon. I'll be drivin' ya as well."

"Yes," said Nathaniel, "and I am quite thankful to you, Jenkins."

"No trouble at all, Adm'ral," he said, now done securing all items up top and hopping down to the street. "As I am on the *Paladin* now, I could use a ride to Wapping. I've a few tasks before we sail!"

"A word with you, Jenkins?" asked Nathaniel. Looking into the admiral's eyes, Jenkins could see he was concerned deeply about something. It was an odd expression, he thought.

"Of course, sir," said Jenkins.

"You know how precious my son is to me, Jenkins. If anything should happen to him, or to Sean...well, I could not go on. Do you understand me?"

"Yes, sir," said Jenkins softly. "I think we all would simply perish from grief. We 'ave grown to love the lads."

"Yes, and of that I am grateful," added Nathaniel. "I

feel most fortunate to have you along on this cruise, and I am certain you know that I personally assured your assignment aboard *Paladin*."

A look of mild puzzlement appeared on Jenkins's face. "I didn't realize, Admiral, but I thank you."

"And I thank you, Patrick. Please give an extra eye and ear to Jonathan and Sean. Watch over them, as if they were your own. Can you manage that?"

"Aye, sir," said Jenkins. "Of course I will, and I look forward to it. Rest assured: nothing will 'appen to them under my watch."

"Thank you," Nathaniel said, now relaxing visibly. He extended his hand to the old sailor, who took it, and they shook firmly.

"I will, sir, you can count on it. I would give my life for either of them, gladly," the man said.

"Again, I am deeply in your debt, Jenkins."

The short ride to the pier where the *Paladin* was moored was concluded by eight o'clock. Even at this early hour, the dockyard was full of activity: ships being loaded with supplies, men rushing from ship to shore, repairs being made, and newly pressed crewmen being unloaded from carts.

The inhabitants of the carriage slowly woke, and with the help of Jenkins, stepped into the light. Before them waited the *Paladin*, tied to the quay, the sun now lighting the sloop.

"Ah," said Admiral Moore. "She looks fast just sitting still. The *Paladin* is a fine ship, and she will keep you safe."

"As long as she brings you home to us again," added Barbara.

"We all trust in the lieutenant's abilities, my dear," said Nathaniel.

"Lieutenant? I thought Harrison was now a commander," said Barbara, somewhat surprised.

"Hoy! Here we go again!" said Sean, smiling.

"I'll be attendin' to my duties, Admiral," said Jenkins.

"No one better to explain the terminology than you, sir," he added as he tipped his hat and made his exit into the wharf.

"Dear me," said Jonathan, laughing, knowing what was about to be discussed. He and Sean had this same question, and only after months of discussion with Jenkins and others aboard the *Danielle* did they finally understand. The boys attended to their lockers as they contained their most precious possessions: maps, telescopes, cooking gear, spare uniform pieces, whitening chalk, Sean's flute, and Jonathan's silver star he had received from Delain. He opened the locker and placed the star, on its chain, about his neck.

"Harrison *was* a lieutenant," began Nathaniel. "However, for this mission he is now a commander. He will captain the *Paladin*."

"So, he is a captain, like William Walker?" asked Barbara, trying to connect the facts.

"No, no, he is captain only while on the ship. He is a commander in rank," said Nathaniel.

"Isn't 'captain' a rank?" asked Barbara, innocently.

"Ah! I see the issue," said Nathaniel as the boys began to collect their belongings from inside the carriage. "Yes, 'captain' is the *rank*, being a title, and also it is a *position* on the ship itself."

"Oh," said Barbara, smiling, thinking she had finally understood the strange lexicon of the Royal Navy. "'Captain' is a *position* —"

"Yes!" said Nathaniel, nodding.

"Like port and starboard!" exclaimed Barbara.

Nathaniel frowned.

"Ah, no, my dear. You see, Thomas Harrison was a lieutenant, and up until recently, lieutenants could captain small, unrated ships, such as the *Paladin*, and the *Echo*. However, that has all changed, and in order to command a vessel of that size, Thomas had to be promoted to the rank of commander, you see?"

Barbara nodded.

"So, he is now Commander Harrison, able to command the *Paladin* and act as its captain, and even, at times, he could also be the *master*, however, I believe Mister Fawcett is presently assigned as master of the *Paladin*, and Harrison will only command her. Now do you understand?" asked Nathaniel.

Barbara considered him, pausing for a second.

"Perfectly," she said.

"I knew you would get it, my dear," said Nathaniel as he stepped toward the pier to admire the ship.

Barbara stood still for a moment, then quickly turned to the boys and whispered, "I have no idea what he just said."

Just then, a call came from aboard the *Paladin*.

"Mister Moore! Private Flagon! Nice of you to join us!"

It was Harrison, and next to him, Lieutenant Alexander.

"Are we late?" asked Jonathan, truly concerned.

"No, no," answered Harrison. "Lieutenant Alexander and I spent the night aboard and have already started the final preparations. Hurry up now!"

"Yes, sir!" said the boys, as they started pulling their lockers toward the plank.

"Excuse me!" called Admiral Moore. "A proper goodbye?"

Jonathan and Sean looked at each other, then quickly set down their belongings and rushed back to the admiral and Miss Thompson.

"Listen boys," he said, bending down to see them eye to eye. "Be careful. Just because there is a peace, the sea is still a dangerous place. And I know you know that; however, you are still young and inexperienced. Write us when you get to Gibraltar. There are many ships sailing from there to here."

"According to our orders, we will probably be bringing the letter back ourselves!" laughed Jonathan.

"Aye, we probably will! Then we can just tell you what we wrote!" said Sean.

"That would be best," agreed Miss Thompson.

"However," cautioned Admiral Moore. "It is not unusual to have your orders changed at a moment's notice. We may not see you for months."

Jonathan and Sean again met each other's glance. It was true that they were excited to be at sea once again; however, all they had ever wanted was to be a family. Since returning from Africa and the Castle of Fire, they had remained in London for only ten months, in their apartment at Charing Cross, under the love and care of Admiral Moore—and more often than not, Miss Barbara Thompson, as she visited regularly. Just as they were settling into a routine that had them comfortable, they were off once again.

Jonathan hugged his father tightly, and Sean attached himself to Miss Thompson.

"We will miss you both," Jonathan said. "And we will take care!"

"I will watch out for Jonathan, don't you worry!" said Sean. "I always have!"

"And watch out for yourself, little bomb maker!" said Miss Thompson, fighting back tears. "We love you."

With that, the boys turned to their lockers and dragged them up the plank to the *Paladin*. Once aboard, Nathaniel and Barbara watched them salute their friend and new commander, Thomas Harrison. He returned the salute, and all waved a final good-bye to those ashore.

Harrison had been in love with the *Paladin* since he had first seen her. Not only was she beautiful, she was a fighter if needed, carrying sixteen thirty-two-pound carronades on the main deck, with eight to each side. These powerful, short-range guns made the ship a formidable adversary for any unprotected vessel and for any warship close to her size. The guns were exposed to the elements and needed constant attention and maintenance. The only other guns were the two stern chasers, both much smaller at only sixteen pounds. Though many ships of her size had bow chasers, the *Paladin* was rarely *chasing* for long, and her speed made stern-mounted guns more practical.

She was roughly one hundred feet long and measuring thirty and one-half feet at the beam. She was similar in many ways to most brig-rigged sloops, however, due to design changes in her mast-and-sail construction requested by Admiral Asher Wells in his almost-secret dealings with the shipwrights in Scotland, she outperformed all ships near her size. The *Echo*, again of Wells's secret works, also had experimental design elements, though, as fast as she was, she sailed a knot slower than the *Paladin* in almost every test.

Both were technically cruiser-class ships and handled surprisingly well. Many vessels of that design had a tendency to roll in the waves; however, even the most severe critics of Wells's design had admitted that the rolling tendency had been reduced greatly on the *Echo* and *Paladin*, certainly due to some secret keel design that few had ever seen.

A few nonfunctional attributes of the *Paladin* included a teakwood deck—rare but not completely uncommon, a small galley underneath in the hold that had a permanent iron stove, and many fine wood-worked scrolls and flourishes inside the captain's cabin and surrounding its four paned windows that looked astern.

Harrison had read and heard all he could about the ship, and he came to a single critical conclusion among the many praises and admirations: the captain's cabin, for reason of the sleek stern design, was smaller than a ship of this size should have. Measuring slightly over eighteen feet wide and only five feet deep, it was *tiny*. Of course, he would never mention to anyone that he had even the slightest disapproval of anything about the *Paladin*, and he kept this thought to himself.

The ship continued to make final preparation for departure. Jonathan was assigned with Lieutenant Alexander, checking on late-arriving stores and securing material in its proper place. It seemed that the new lieutenant had been hard at work, and somewhat to Jonathan's displeasure, had done many of the duties that would normally be assigned to the midshipman. Watching him address the men and instruct them, Jonathan could see that Alexander was confident yet approachable. He was a leader, yet he pitched in with his own hands and back when necessary. He was efficient, intelligent, and even likable. This made Jonathan feel torn. He liked the young man, though he set a hard example to follow.

I will try harder, thought Jonathan, and he turned back to his work.

On the main deck, Sean was assigned to watch the gangplank, along with Private Hicks, both charged with making sure no unauthorized persons came aboard.

"Not sure what would cons'tute someone bein' unauthorized," said Hicks, "But the mere sight o' two rough-'n-tumble marines the likes of us should scare most of 'em away!'

"As long as we don't have to shoot anyone," said Sean with a sigh. "I don't want to fire this blunderbuss, and if I had to, well, I think I'd miss anyway!"

"Well, then," said Hicks, "nothin' to worry 'bout then, eh?"

No one, of course, needed to be fired upon, and the two had been able to welcome many of the crew, some new to them such as Crump and Crystal, two silent men for the most part, coming from the southern part of the city. They seemed angry and kept to themselves, accepting their assignments to begin the never-ending cleaning of the deck.

Jonathan joined Sean and Hicks at the plank and reveled in the happy reunions. More old mates appeared for duty, including the brothers Stredney — Nicolas and Colin — former apprentice cooks. Berkeley and Boston, their old crewmates from the *Danielle*, appeared with little Paulie Garvey, who had sailed with them aboard the *Poseidon*, the *Danielle*, and now the *Paladin*. Garvey, however, was not *little* anymore. Over the last two years they had been together, Garvey had now grown to be nearly as tall as Commander Harrison.

In favor to all was Garvey's bringing of his young cousin, Carl Southcott—who had agreed to sail with them after a year on the merchant ship *Angel*—and his mate, Jim Graham.

"Jim here is a Graham from the old Wadsworth Farms, famous for horse manure and the like!" said Garvey.

"You can see why I chose a life at sea!" laughed Graham. This sent the others into hysterics.

"Karl here, he's my mum's mum's sister's boy!" continued Garvey. "Known him as a brother, I have. An able seaman just as Graham."

"Sir!" said the new crewmen as they beheld Midshipman Jonathan Moore, bowing low before the officer, then standing straight as arrows, smiling.

"Glad to have you aboard, Southcott, Graham," Jonathan said in an official tone. "You were both on the *Angel*? A fine ship."

"Well, I'll be!" said Sean as he considered the two young men. Others were staring at them as well. Though not in a navy uniform, Southcott wore a dark-blue coat over a white blouse and white britches. If he only had silver piping around the edges of the jacket, he could pass for a midshipman—in fact, a certain midshipman: Jonathan Moore.

"Ya look almost the same! Yer hair's even alike!" said Sean. "Except the face, of course, but from the back, or with a quick glance, you look like twins!"

"I feel sorry for you then," laughed Jonathan as he also noticed the resemblance.

"Glad to be aboard either way, sir!" said Southcott. "I heard the food is better than what we got in the merchant fleet."

"I doubt that," said Berkeley.

"We know too. My brother and I, we used to make it," said Nicolas.

"Now Berkeley does," said Colin. "And it didn't get

any better."

Smith and Jones, their old mates from the *Poseidon*, had now arrived, and they continued their cantankerous arguing of inane subjects, even as they walked up the plank together.

"Ahoy, Smith! Ahoy, Jones!" called Sean happily as the men made their way to the deck. "Good to see ya!"

"Sorry we are late," said Smith.

"We are not late," responded Jones. "The ship is still here and now so are we, so how can we be late?"

"Well, it's not as if she is our personal yacht," countered Smith, "and is waiting for us before she sails on a pleasure cruise! We work here! Our mates count on us!"

"They can count on us again, then, and we will help them finish their duty," Jones said.

"Yer an imbecile," said Smith.

"Yer a moron then," said Jones.

"Both types are welcome," said Hicks as he shooed them aboard.

"I'm sure a happy man that today is Sunday!" added Smith.

"As am I," said Jones.

"Why would you be any happier today, than, let's say, tomorrow?" asked Colin Stredney.

"I'd ask the same," said Sean.

"Tomorrow? Monday?" asked Jones with a worried look. "Oh no! Dear me! Never set sail on a Monday!"

"Don't 'cha know?" asked Smith.

"Know what?" asked Sean.

Smith and Jones took a deep look at each other, frowned, and shook their heads.

"Monday's *unlucky*! Cursed!" said Smith. He looked about the ship, up at the heavens, as if to expect some danger from above.

"Tis true!" added Jones. "And tomorrow is the first Monday in April! Even worser!"

"Worser?" asked Hicks, with a laugh.

"You know what I mean," continued Jones. "The second Monday in April is the day in the ol' Bible that Cain slew his brother, Abel!"

"And that makes it unlucky?" asked Jonathan.

"Aye, sir!" said Jones and Smith in unison.

"Then it sure is a happy day that we sail on a Sunday!" added Colin Stredney.

"Is Sunday good?" asked Nicolas, looking upward as if to be prepared for the onslaught of an angry God.

Smith and Jones smiled broadly.

"The luckiest!" they said.

"Then you all best get your work done, or we will be delayed!" added Jonathan. "And that may mean Commander Harrison decides to set sail tomorrow morning!"

The men now went into action with earnest.

Sean just smiled; then something caught his eye, something ashore. There, he saw a red-coated marine walking with purpose along the pier toward them. His head was held high, and he was slightly heavy, but the extra mass only made him look even more splendid in a brand-new red uniform of the marines, complete with wide white sash, a sheathed sword, and best of all, a sergeant's insignia on his lapel.

"Look, Hicks!" he said in wonder. "Is that Corporal Hudson?"

"No," said Hicks, amazed and pleased. "That thar is *Sergeant* Hudson! Newly minted, it seems!"

Sean could not contain his excitement, and he left his post to rush down the plank and greet his superior.

"Sergeant, sir! Marine Private Sean Flagon reporting for duty!" Sean stood as straight as a board, smart salute executed, then stared out to some point in space that was toward the sergeant, but not directly into his eyes.

Hudson turned and slowly looked the private up and down with a sour face, almost too sour. He inspected every detail of Sean's uniform, every button, every inch of the sleeves, his hat, his sword, grunting disapproval every second or two.

"Flagon!" said Hudson in a deep, bellowing voice, now standing back and taking in the entire display of what was Sean Flagon. "You call yourself a marine?" he yelled.

This took Sean completely aback.

"Y-yes, sir, I believe so! I spent all night on my uniform—"

"All night?" Hudson exploded. Then he bent down to Sean's level and stared at him eye to eye. Slowly his face changed from a most horrible scowl, to a scrunched-up prune, and finally it rested upon the jolly, warm, and smiling face of Sean's friend and coconspirator.

"Good to see ya, Seany!" he whispered.

Sean smiled back and winked. "Good to see you as well, Sergeant Hudson. Kind of difficult to get used to the title after all this time of simply saying *Hudson*."

"Aye, we will all get used to it. Had to put on a show for those about us. Can't be showing any favor, you understand."

"Yes, sir!" Sean said loudly so all could hear. "I'll try to do better in the future, sir!"

This startled Hudson some, until he realized that Sean was simply playing along.

"Well, you sure-as-the-wind-blows better do…*better*, Flagon!" bellowed Hudson. "Take that poor excuse for a marine Hicks and report to the magazine. I will take plank duty. And for the king's sake, work on that aiming, ya hear! On the double!"

* * * * *

After an hour, the spring day had continued warming, and the rays of the sun painted a yellowish glow to the teak deck of the *Paladin* and to the sails, still furled and awaiting the orders to be let down. The entire ship glowed, even more than usual. The experienced men, the "volunteers," as Jonathan and Sean called them, knowing how special and privileged they were to be aboard such a fine ship, appeared slightly more joyous in their work, knowing that soon they would depart. The *Paladin*, under sail on the open sea, would be a sight for those ashore, but an adventure for those aboard.

As the preparations were complete and midday meals scheduled to be served once underway, Captain Harrison ordered all on deck to be addressed before they left port. Jonathan and Alexander made sure all were at attention and then returned to the stern. Hudson lined up the assigned complement of marines, twelve in all, behind the captain on the stern, to show their support of the commander and his officers, and to let the crew see that they were watching *everyone*.

Unlike the larger, rated vessels in His Majesty's Navy, *Paladin* had no poop deck—no raised area above the captain's cabin that designated the commander's special area. Nevertheless, it was clear to all that the space at the rearmost portion of the upper deck, behind the aft mast, was for officers only. Unless you had been specifically ordered to perform duty there, it was off limits.

"Men," started Captain Harrison. "Welcome aboard His Majesty's Ship *Paladin*, the swiftest, most beautiful lady to sail the vastness of the briny blue! For those who have previously served here, welcome back. For those who are new to this ship, mind her well. She is the fastest and most graceful sloop ever to sail the seas, and we will carry on her tradition of service to the Crown as a symbol of British might. She has a fine reputation, and we will not tarnish it. Look about you to your brothers. Look!"

The crew turned and took in the almost one hundred men making up the crew of carpenters, deckhands, armorers, sail masters, able seamen, and others.

"These are your brothers. We are your officers, here to lead you on safe journeys to exotic locations—and maybe even a little fun mixed in if some French barge gets a little too close!"

This set the men to laughter. The seasoned hands all knew of Thomas Harrison, and that his tutelage under the famous Sir Captain William Walker meant he was experienced in taking enemy ships, at times for great profit, and that was shared, though somewhat disproportionately, down the line from commander to deckhand.

"Our orders are to sail to Gibraltar and deliver packets to the authorities, then await further instructions or return to England in one month's time. We sail short on crew, so we will need extra work to carry out our duty. Enjoy the cruise, gentlemen! Dismissed."

Harrison turned to his officers. "Lieutenant Alexander, set men to their stations. Mister Moore, as soon as Jenkins arrives, we cast off. Man the gangway and prepare to order in the lines. We will set tables for the noon meal as soon as we are underway."

"Yes, sir," they replied and began to organize the men in their duties. Harrison met with Mister Fawcett, the sailing master. He would man the helm, the great wheel that directed the ship, and together, they would plot a course to Gibraltar.

As Jonathan approached the gangway, a voice came from below. It was Jenkins.

"Hullo, Mister Moore! Permission to come aboard?"

"Granted," said Jonathan enthusiastically. He was pleased to see his old shipmate, as they had sailed to fame and some fortune on both the *Poseidon* and the *Danielle*. Jenkins had been Jonathan's first friend in His Majesty's Navy and had trained him on many of the finer points of seamanship. Jonathan felt joy at having him aboard.

"A special delivery I have for Marine Private Flagon."

Hearing this, Jonathan sent a crewman to retrieve Sean from the stern. Jenkins ascended the plank carrying a package a tad larger than a common hat box. It had several holes in it, and due to his manner of walking, Jonathan was sure Jenkins had no trouble with the load.

Sean arrived almost immediately and stood at attention.

"Flagon, at ease!" said Jonathan.

"I've a package for Marine Private Sean Flagon, of His

Majesty's ship *Paladin*," said Jenkins with all propriety and pomp, "sent from none other than Mister Jobias Watt, sailing master aboard the illustrious *Danielle*." Dropping the formality, Jenkins extended the package to Sean. "He thought ya might need this."

Sean, as curious as a kitten, took the box and slowly opened the lid to find exactly that—though it was technically not a *kitten*. He stared into the fuzzy face of his long-time friend Stewie. A meow came from the box.

"Stewie!" cried Sean. *"Mon doux petit chaton!"*

The great mouser, Stewie, from the *Danielle*, had made the acquaintance of Sean Flagon, then an aspiring seaman, under stressful circumstances. Though all turned out better than planned, they had been through a great adventure together, even as part of the small shore party set on Isla Sello just before the Battle of Fire.

"They say cats are lucky!" said Jenkins. "Magic in their tails."

"No more superstitions!" said Jonathan. "It's all hogwash!"

"It may be, Mister Moore, but to the crew," said Jenkins, waving his arm to include the men on the entire ship, "they believe it absolutely."

With the appearance of Jenkins and Stewie, the *Paladin* was now complete with supplies and crew and cat—and ready to sail.

At the stern, Harrison stood by Fawcett, who manned the wheel. Seeing all was in order, he smiled.

"I thought we would never be off!" said Harrison under his breath. "Mister Alexander, are we done with the exposition?"

"Yes, sir, Commander," answered the lieutenant, smiling.

"It is about time!" said Harrison, who then cupped his hands about his mouth and yelled "Cast—"

"Ahoy! Ahoy *Paladin*!" came an urgent call from the pier. "Pressing news for Commander Harrison and his officers! Ahoy!"

"Good heavens!" cried Harrison, now dropping his hands to his sides in defeat. "It is as if some malignant demon is working against me!"

Once at the rail, Harrison, flanked by Jonathan and Alexander, watched a uniformed lieutenant rushing toward the ship and requesting permission to come aboard.

"Lieutenant Phillip Quinn reporting for duty. Here are my orders, sir."

Harrison opened the plain gray envelope as Quinn stood at rigid attention, now under the inspecting eyes of the officers. To Jonathan, he appeared young for a lieutenant, yet certainly older than Jonathan himself—possibly seventeen. He was only an inch or so taller than Jonathan, yet still shorter than Harrison and considerably smaller than Alexander. His blond hair reminded Jonathan of Sean, but his full face and stocky form gave him a more grounded look, as if he belonged on a farm, not aboard a naval vessel. His uniform appeared brand-new, and his small bag, instead of a locker, seemed well made. He must have come from a wealthy family, Jonathan thought.

"From the *Spartan*. Always nice to have another officer aboard," said Harrison cautiously, as he lowered the orders. "Welcome. I see you have another packet?"

"Aye, sir. From the Admiralty. New orders."

Harrison frowned at Jonathan and Alexander with a concerned look on his face as he took the second, larger envelope from Quinn.

"Lieutenants? Let us open these in my cabin," said Harrison. "Jonathan, retain a crew to set tables, and have the men stand down. Berkeley, the new cook, may serve lunch. He's an improvement over Steward, and not quite up to the standards of Claise, but he does make a fine spotted dog, so I am sure a fast meal of tack and eggs will be within his talents. And take Hicks to the plank to keep an eye on things. This is all very...irregular. Alexander and Quinn, to my cabin immediately."

"Is your midshipman not to join us?" asked Quinn. "Though not an officer properly, I know we treat them as such, and I hear he is held in high esteem. I assume his input would be valuable?"

This gave Harrison reason to pause. It was considered very poor form and against regulation to, firstly, address the captain of a ship without using the term *sir*, and secondly, to even question a superior officer's order, no matter how simple. Quinn had done both in one comment. Jonathan blushed immediately, knowing that Commander Harrison had realized this breech of protocol. He and Alexander shielded their eyes as they observed the young captain drawing in breath, as a dragon would before the belching of immense heat and expulsion of unbearable flame that would literally toast his enemy. But before Harrison exploded, he caught himself, paused, and exhaled a slow, nonlethal breath.

"Lieutenant Quinn? We follow all the proprieties and protocols when we address a senior officer aboard this ship."

"Oh!" said Quinn in surprise. "Please forgive me, Commander! I-I never, sir, would mean to offend y-you, or any of the other officers. How rude and inconsiderate I have been. If I may apologize?"

Harrison seemed to cool slightly.

"Please, not an issue. However, let us make sure it never happens again," said Harrison.

"Yes, sir. Then allow me to formally express regret. It was the excitement I experienced upon the sudden realization that I was now aboard the *Paladin*, sir. The *Paladin!* She's a beautiful ship, the most beautiful ship in the world. It is as if I am in a dream, and what lieutenant in service of His Majesty has not dreamed of attending aboard this graceful lady? Is there anything that I can do to regain your good graces?"

Dear! thought Jonathan. That was the most perfect apology he had ever witnessed, and the effect on Commander Harrison was noticeable, as he had used the same words to describe his affection for the *Paladin* while he was still a lieutenant. Jonathan could see his face break into a wide smile, and he nodded his head in response to the new lieutenant.

"Let us all perform our duties well, then. Apology accepted, Lieutenant Quinn."

The lieutenants and Commander Harrison then moved below to the captain's cabin, leaving Jonathan to oversee the deck. However, as they departed, Quinn turned quickly and gave Jonathan an odd smile and a quick wink. This was noticed by Sean and Sergeant Hudson as they passed by.

"Jonny boy," Sean asked. "What was that about?"

"I have no idea," said Jonathan.

"Then I will see you sometime this afternoon — if not, after dinner? I have this watch and will stroll the deck, giving newcomers the evil eye, as Hicks calls it."

"Just so they learn to respect the marines!" added Hudson. "I'll wait with Mister Moore, Seany. Carry on."

Within minutes, a creaking noise alerted Jonathan to look toward the end of the pier. A carriage approached, much like his father's, but different. It was not quite as nice — and a gray color instead of black. It seemed in a hurry, as many things at the dockyards had a tendency to be, and surprisingly, it pulled to a stop in front of the *Paladin*. The door opened — and out stepped Captain Spears and another man.

Captain Spears's official position was one of the many staff assistants of the Admiralty Board, his responsibility being to not decide upon what ships would go where and on what errand, but to track and set up communications for the delivery of the assignments via official orders. Jonathan had a more complicated relationship with him, and more specifically, with his son, Wayne.

"Mister Moore," called Captain Spears from below. "Just the man we have come to see. Would you join us here on the pier?"

Jonathan's orders were to stay aboard and watch the gangway and supervise the men if needed; however, Captain Spears did technically outrank Commander Harrison, though not aboard the ship where he was standing.

We are not actually underway, thought Jonathan. I assume he still outranks Harrison. It is best to be sure.

"Sir. Good day, Captain Spears. I have been assigned deck watch by my commander. I am not to leave the ship. May I assist you from here?"

Spears looked slightly agitated.

"Mister Moore, I would discuss this in private. Come down to the bottom of the gangplank. You will technically be on the ship, not the pier."

Jonathan looked to Hudson, who had been listening to the entire exchange.

"I'll keep a watch, Mister Moore," he offered under his breath. "And that other figure is Lord James Wilder. An important man on the Navy Board, if you need to know."

"Thank you, Hudson," Jonathan said as he walked down the plank. He felt silly standing upon the wooden bridge addressing these important men; however, he reasoned, orders were orders.

"Captain Spears," Jonathan said cautiously. "If I may, any news of your son?"

Jonathan was referring to the unexpected disappearance of the captain's son, Midshipman Wayne Spears, who had sailed with Jonathan aboard his last mission on HMS *Danielle.* The boys did not get along, to say the least, and after several altercations, the matter of their differences was solved when Wayne technically deserted his post and left the ship during a key battle action.

"No," said Captain Spears. "And none of your concern, Moore. What is your concern is the change of orders. Have you seen them?"

"Begging your pardon, no, sir," Jonathan said. "I believe this is Lord Wilder of the Navy Board. We have not been introduced."

"I am Lord James Wilder," the man said. "And I have heard of you, Mister Moore. A pleasure to meet you. I know your father, and because of this, we have special orders for you, Mister Moore. Orders that cannot be written down."

This surprised Jonathan somewhat.

"I see. I believe I do…at least," said Jonathan.

"It is like this," said Spears in a hushed tone. "The orders that have been delivered to Captain Harrison are of a very sensitive nature. He may or may not share them with you."

"That is why we have come to address you directly," smiled Wilder. "It is my understanding that you are an outstanding officer-to-be. Your reputation precedes you, and after special consideration, I chose to ask you for your assistance."

Jonathan was wary. He knew Spears was no friend to his family, and he was most assuredly aware of the issues that had arisen between his son, Wayne, and Jonathan. Spears certainly could not be trusted. However, Lord Wilder was an unknown. He had no way to judge him for either good or ill.

"Sirs, exactly how may I assist you?" Jonathan asked.

"Mister Moore," began Wilder, "the orders are for the *Paladin* to deliver a very secret treaty to Dugi Otok, off the coast of Dalmatia. The Treaty of Akbar. It was written and prepared by the king himself. He asked that you be made aware of this. I believe you have met His Highness?"

This was common knowledge but still true.

"Yes, sir," said Jonathan, still suspicious.

"The treaty is between England and another nation, a powerful ally for us should war break out once again," continued Lord Wilder. "It must be delivered on exactly April the sixteenth. The king personally requests that you do whatever you can to keep the crew and the officers on course, to use a phrase with which we are all accustomed."

"I see, and I am honored His Majesty entrusts this duty to me," said Jonathan.

Spears and Wilder both smiled.

"However," said Jonathan, "why not inform Captain Harrison? He is a gentleman and a fine officer. I am sure he will see the importance of delivering this treaty and give you all assurance that he will perform his—"

"Because, Moore," said Spears angrily, "he is not to know the particulars of the treaty, and not to open the diplomatic pouch. It would invalidate the seal. That is the *secret* part of the secret treaty, dolt!"

"Please, Captain Spears. No need to be impatient or rude," said Lord Wilder as he turned his kind eyes to Jonathan. "Jonathan, the king wants this to remain as secret as can be, with as few people knowing the particulars of the treaty as possible. There are many who do not want this to be delivered, and they would do anything to stop its success. That is why His Majesty asked that you do whatever is necessary to keep the crew true to the mission. Do you understand?"

"Well," said Jonathan, confused, "not exactly."

"Oh!" blurted Spears. "Of all the—"

Lord Wilder held up a hand to silence Spears.

"I am sorry, Jonathan," continued Wilder. "What is it that you do not understand?"

"Sir, what type of situation might arise that would make it necessary to even address Captain Harrison about the execution of the mission? It seems abundantly clear to me that we are to sail to Dugi Otok and deliver the treaty to someone. That's not very complicated."

"Ah, yes, yes," said Wilder. "However, what if there were another ship, for example? One sailing under no colors—and it crossed your path? Wouldn't it be to Harrison's advantage to give chase? Possibly capture the ship? Or, what if it were a ploy of our enemies, and the treaty were taken during the battle? Or maybe another ship or two appeared at an inopportune time?"

Jonathan thought of this. Yes, that would make sense.

"Or possibly," continued Wilder, "Captain Harrison might desire to spend an extra day or two in a port along the way. Such a delay could prove disastrous for this mission."

"Sir, isn't this explained in the orders?" asked Jonathan.

"Yes," said Spears. "The orders are explicit. His Majesty requires some reassurance, and you are that reassurance. Also—and quite frankly, many believe, and I share this—that Thomas Harrison is cursed at best and not actually up to snuff."

Jonathan slowly frowned, and narrowed his eyes in anger.

"He has already been aboard two ships that have been lost," continued Spears, "and I wouldn't be surprised if he lost the *Paladin* as well."

"Commander Harrison is a well-seasoned—"

"The king gave him this assignment as a favor to Captain Walker. Everyone knows that," said Spears meanly.

"The king is relying on you, Jonathan," said Wilder.

Jonathan now understood the issue at hand, as ill-founded as it was. It was simply that these men did not know Commander Thomas Harrison, and they were taken with rumors and jealous innuendo. Jonathan knew that Thomas Harrison was worthy of this command, had fought hand-to-hand in many battles, and had trained some of the finest crews in His Majesty's Service. He would execute the orders faithfully, with or without any encouragement from Jonathan. In that case, he thought, no harm in agreeing to do what he could to keep everything by the book.

"Sirs," said Jonathan flatly, "you are incorrect about Thomas Harrison, I can assure you. However, I will do whatever I can to assure the success of the mission, and I will advise Commander Harrison, whenever necessary, to follow the orders with the utmost accuracy and dispatch."

This caused both men to smile once again.

"Good! Good!" said Wilder, who reached to shake Jonathan's hand. "Now, just one more thing. The orders contain precise instructions of how and where to anchor the *Paladin* in order for the designated recipient to obtain the treaty. These must be followed to the letter. The anchoring procedures are the signal for the contact to approach the *Paladin*."

"I am sure, again, that Harrison will follow these orders to the letter," said Jonathan.

"Should he deviate," warned Wilder, "the mission will fail. We need you to make sure it doesn't. Make sure he anchors exactly as prescribed, Jonathan."

Jonathan agreed.

Wilder and Spears left the pier unceremoniously, and Jonathan returned to the ship. It was all highly irregular, he thought, but that seemed to define life in London. At least at sea, there was a rhythm of predictability, and surprises were few. He couldn't wait to be underway.

Of course, the thought of London made him look back to the city, and up its northern stretch that he actually couldn't see; yet, he imagined the winding road that led to Van Patten Wood, and to the Bracknell Manor, and to Delain Dowdeswell. He would miss her, he thought, and he already did.

"I'd better check all the jolly boats, Sergeant Hudson," Jonathan said as he reached the deck.

"And why is that?" asked the marine.

"Just to make sure Miss Dowdeswell does not succeed in a repeat performance of her last adventure," Jonathan answered.

"Aye!" said Hudson as they laughed together.

In his cabin, Commander Harrison reread the orders uneasily. Even Alexander found them bizarre. Quinn agreed that the change was also an uncomfortable one to swallow. After a brief discussion, Harrison dismissed the lieutenants and sat to concentrate on and digest the papers by himself.

They instructed him to proceed to Telašćica, a fishing village on Dugi Otok, off the Dalmatian coast, then head north to find an inlet marked by two pine trees, one with a dangling rope. He was also to enter the inlet, bow first—insane, he thought—and wait for contact to deliver the packet containing the Treaty of Akbar.

"Acceptable code phrases will accompany any contact," Harrison said as he continued reading aloud. "*One has only one shoe for both feet. Preposterous! Who speaks in such a manner? Tis Señor Mosca? Ridiculous! Master Garvino and references to holiday in Madrid.*"

He put the orders down and rubbed his head.

"I thought command was going to be joyous," he said softly.

A gentle rap came to the door.

"Enter," said Harrison, now standing.

"We are ready to cast off, sir," said Alexander as he peeked into the room.

Within minutes, the *Paladin* was unmoored and towed out to the open channel by two jolly boats. Once away from the pier, sails were finally let down, and as the wind filled the vast expanse of canvas, the ship smoothly gained speed. Commander Harrison ordered all remaining sail let down, all lines tightened, and that the crew attend to his every command for more speed.

"I want to put as much distance between us and the shore in the shortest amount of time!" he called to all within earshot. "One more delay, Mister Alexander, and I would have simply exploded!"

8

Two Plots

O'Sullivan's Cock and Bull was a whiskey pub in London's East End, famous for two characteristics. One was the hard-edged crowd it catered to. There were very few actual gentlemen who paid visit to the establishment—and even fewer ladies. Many patrons were suspected criminals, and a vast majority of the others were *more* than suspect. There were often disagreements that ended with fists and sometimes knives. Even the entertainers—the piano players, fiddlers, and O'Sullivan himself—were of a more salty nature.

The other trait of the Cock and Bull was unknown to almost all who attended. The pub was the preferred meeting place for the English spy network of London, and the man who presided over this network was Marine Captain Thomas Gorman, always incognito. This cool and rainy night, he was in attendance, dressed as a typical common man, a few extra tears in his worn coat, a few extra surprises under his belt than most were wearing. He normally carried only a pistol, though when in this pub, he had a few tricks up his sleeves, literally.

Gorman sat at a small table in the darkest corner of the room. In front of him was a candle, lit, that would have cast some light upon his face but for his action of placing a tall bottle of vinegar just so as to block the flame's illumination. With the cast shadow hiding his features, he could see rather well, and he noticed two men sitting at the bar, whispering. They were often stealing glances at him, before turning about to delve deep into their own conversation. After twenty minutes, they both rose and walked with purpose to the dark alcove where Gorman sat.

"Particularly nasty weather, ain't it, gov'na?" said the

first man, addressing Gorman.

"I assume a man the likes o' you would know," commented the second man.

"I would know as I have been in the rain enough," answered Gorman.

This deceptively absurd conversation served two purposes. It was not necessarily code to identify any of the three spies; they all knew each other well and had decided and arranged to meet here at this exact time and place. The code was used to explain that, one, they had information of a sensitive nature to discuss. If there was no need to meet, they would have said "Do you have pence for a needy man?" and Gorman would have responded, "No. I am poor myself." All would have left the pub within a few moments, going in separate directions. However, there *was* important information to discuss.

The second purpose of the code was to determine if they should discuss the information now, here, or leave. The comment on rain, and being *in* the rain enough, meant for them to stay within the pub and conduct business. Had Gorman said he had been *out* in the rain, it was well they should leave to discuss their secret topics.

The men then sat down with Gorman, at first chatting about nothing in particular. Shortly thereafter, the barmaid appeared, a woman who looked as if she had seen a worker's life and had benefited little. She took their whiskey orders and returned to the bar.

Gorman leaned into the middle of the table and blew out the candle, casting them all mostly into darkness.

"Frey. Fairchild," he said. "Good to see you each in one piece."

"Aye, Cap'n Gorman. It'as been a month since we saw you," said Frey. "It was right after we nabbed that Russian operator, Aggar."

"Odd one 'e is," said Fairchild. "Not much for spying, but 'e sure associates with 'em."

"He was easy to catch," added Frey. "We watched 'em and eventually, we followed 'em to HMS *Syrinx*, that ol' eighteen-gun sloop."

"He was all alone," said Fairchild. "Simply looking at the ship, its rigging and such. 'E had nothing on him but the clothes on his back."

"After we arrested 'em," continued Frey, "I 'erd news that the Russian ambassador didn't even file a complaint! Ha! One of their citizens, jailed in a foreign country! A criminal, they called 'im, and good riddance, they said."

The barmaid returned and placed three whiskeys on the table. She noticed the unlit candle and reached for a match within her apron.

"We are fine," said Gorman, causing her to shrug and depart.

"Caught Aggar easy as pie," continued Fairchild.

"A little too easy," said Gorman. "However, he is off our hands now. In a prison hulk off of Portsmouth—the *Verde Bay*, I believe."

"And 'ere's to that," said Frey as he lifted his glass. The others copied his example and took a long swallow.

"What have you seen lately?" asked Gorman, setting down his half-empty glass.

"I was followin' my other assignment, that strange bloke with the funny accent," continued Fairchild. "'E turns out to be Lupien, remember 'im?"

"Lupien," said Gorman, thinking for a moment, trying to recollect the man.

"Thin, not too tall, dresses plain, like we do? Dark eyes?" offered Fairchild.

"Yes, yes. Sharp features," said Gorman. "Came into town aboard a clipper from America."

"That's the one," said Fairchild. "But don't let that 'merican part fool ya. He's no colonial. I been into 'is place he keeps on Ayliff Street. 'e lives with a few other degenerates and the like. Found some letters in a strange language, I did. Couldn't copy 'em, though. No time. Funny that one so common gets around as 'e does. And mostly at night."

"Where does he go?" asked Gorman.

"'E meets with the same bloke all the time," said

Fairchild, "and usually somewhere on Pall Mall or south of there. I followed 'em three times this month to the statue at Queen Anne's Gate. And I 'erd 'em talkin' 'bout a treaty — but they laughed about it, like it wasn't normal."

"Did you get a look at the other man?" asked Gorman.

"I did," said Frey. "Fairchild 'ere suggested I follow one night, just ta get a tail on the other bloke. Good thing I did. 'e's older, taller, stouter, has a beard, well dressed."

"'E's a spy, I'm sure of it," added Fairchild.

"Name?" asked Gorman.

"Lupien called him Mister O," said Fairchild.

"By the saints," said Gorman. "There are so many spies in town we ought to have them registered and licensed!"

Frey and Fairchild laughed.

"I followed this Mister O fer a good while," said Frey. 'E tried to give me the slip, but I stayed with 'im until 'e lost me at Borough Road."

"We need to find out who this 'O' is," said Gorman. "There is no treaty talk coming out of the Admiralty or Windsor Castle, I can assure you of that."

"'Ow can ya be sure?" asked Frey. "Not meaning any disrespect."

"I can never be one hundred percent sure, so I will check again," said Gorman, smiling, though it was dark, and Frey and Fairchild probably couldn't see his grin. He respected these two men. They had a particular talent and an extensive network of reliable informants. Some of Gorman's minions went overseas to spy in other countries. Frey and Fairchild specialized on the shores of England and in particular, London itself. They knew their way around and were both thorough in the plying of their trade. Though dressed in rags, each had accumulated a modest fortune, being employed and paid by Gorman for services rendered over the past few decades. He trusted their information and their advice.

"Continue tailing them," Gorman said. "One will lead to the other. We must find out who this Mister O is — and what the treaty is about."

The men finished their drinks, each giving them a little extra protection, or so they thought, from the mild spring chill outside. They got up, one at a time with five minutes between them, and went home, none of them directly. They assumed, as always, that they were being followed.

The following day, London warmed to the ways of early spring, and the morning grew bright and pleasant. A small group of ladies enjoyed the groomed horse paths within the area known as Van Patten Wood. The slow and peaceful ride was not without its concerns for one of them.

"How can anyone sit like this?" demanded Delain, as she uncomfortably adjusted herself upon *Lilliput*, her all-black filly.

"Aside? This is how a *lady* sits," answered Miss Barbara Thompson. "So the answer is: like a lady."

"It's impractical," said Delain.

"It's polite and dignified," retorted Barbara playfully.

"I will fall off," continued Delain. "I have ridden astride before in the Bahamas, sitting as a man would. The comfort and feeling of balance was superior. I think men make us sit like this because they know we can ride faster than they."

"A handicap?" asked Barbara, smiling.

"Indeed," agreed Delain. "But to please you, I will attempt it."

The ladies rode on in silence for a few minutes, just the clip-clop of their horse's hooves disturbing the sweet songs of the birds and the occasional fluttering of some passing insect. The panting of Daisy and Daffodil, the two hunting dogs that would not be denied the trip, also joined in the soft sounds of the day. The Airedales, cute and curly blonde-haired, were always playful unless engaged in hunting the many otters by the water's edge, where they became not only ruthless and efficient, but extremely dirty. Delain simply could not say no to them as she set out on horseback with Miss Thompson. Both dogs sat politely, coal-black eyes sadly watching, button noses in the air, sniffing as their tails wagged in anticipation of being invited, which, of course, they were.

The sunny day was muted by the beautiful shade cast from the many trees that thickly populated the forest. Van Patten Wood stretched for miles through the Hampstead area north of the city and was made of over forty private parcels of land, approximately ten acres apiece. Each property had a mansion sitting on its street edge, and behind each mansion was a substantial rear yard. Arranged as such, the center area, made up of all the rear yards of all the owners, created an expansive private preserve, where fox, grouse, deer, and the occasional otter lived in a tranquil setting — at least, until there was an organized hunt.

Within this preserve were groomed paths between all the various stables attached to almost every mansion. The Bracknells, as well as the other human inhabitants, used these to not only exercise their horses, but to visit each other on occasion. The dense woods and the several streams that crossed the trails made for a beautiful and relaxing ride.

Today, Miss Delain Dowdeswell and Miss Barbara Thompson had decided that a ride would be most welcome. It was Delain's idea. She had sent a note to Barbara via courier to ask for some time to discuss her perceptions and adjustments to a life in London.

"And so? How are your lessons?" asked Barbara. She was happy to have time with the young girl, as they had grown close since the Delain's arrival in London. Barbara admired Delain: so young and intelligent, poised and mannered when she wanted to impress. Yet, there was a somewhat *uncertain air* about her, as if at any instant, Delain might simply jump up and perform some exciting yet inappropriate stunt that would embarrass everyone nearby. At least in this area of the wood, there was no one to care besides the two of them. Barbara felt safe.

"All my classes and teachers are extremely dreary and tedious, I must say, Miss Thompson, with the exception of

Master Franklin. He teaches history. I think he used to be a thespian, as he seems to perform his lectures, more than recite them."

Barbara smiled. "I was a student of Master Franklin as well. He was a highlight in an otherwise dim year. However, we can't be entertained all the time."

"And that is what I take issue with, Miss Thompson," said Delain. "In an exciting city such as London, I would think there would be more entertainment available. Yes, that is what is missing."

The ladies easily guided their horses across a small brook that split the path and continued on to the south. The Airedales took this opportunity to explore the water's edge, sticking their noses into the stream and into every hole they could find. Within minutes they were mud-covered and happy.

The farther away from the Bracknell Estate they rode, the more privacy the ladies enjoyed. Barbara knew that Delain had something important to discuss, and it was a puzzle to determine exactly when she would reveal her true reason for the meeting.

"I do miss the boys," added Barbara, watching Delain's response to see if this was all about her affection for Jonathan; however, Delain simply smiled and nodded.

"Possibly we could attend the theatre? That might add some entertainment to your days?" asked Barbara.

"That would be lovely. I would enjoy that," said Delain.

No, thought Barbara. I have not uncovered her purposes yet. Maybe I will employ silence. She will crack soon.

They rode on, calling for Daisy and Daffy when they no longer saw them about. They knew the dogs were, by now, miles away, on their own adventure as they knew the woods well and would return home when tired and most assuredly filthy.

After a few silent minutes, Delain began to talk.

"I was wondering about going to a proper tea," she stated.

"A proper tea?" Barbara asked. "You and I have had several teas at both the Bracknells and at Captain Walker's home. I do not understand. They have all been proper."

"I mean at someone else's home. Like...the Wilders, for instance. They did invite us."

"The Wilders?" asked Barbara. "You know, Lady Alina and I attended the Swedish School together, though she is a year or two older than I. Just yesterday I received an invitation to tea for Wednesday at Wilder Manor. I could inform her of our intention to attend. Would that do?"

"Oh!" said Delain happily, "if it wouldn't be too much trouble!"

"Not at all. It has been over two years since she has held a tea party. I am sure Alina would enjoy showing you off to her friends," added Barbara.

Delain seemed slightly surprised at this comment. Why would Lady Wilder desire to "show off" a fourteen-year-old girl?

"You may not have noticed, but you are somewhat of a celebrity. Your exploits, my dear Delain, have even been written about in the papers. Many in polite society discuss your firing of cannons, engaging in sea battles, stowing away to Africa — well, these are not the exploits of ladies of London. You are, and please excuse me, somewhat of an *oddity*. A pleasurable one, however." Barbara added a smile to the end of her point.

"An oddity!" Delain said, laughing. "Only to those who, excuse *me* for saying, never get *out*!"

"Delain," said Barbara, now becoming the motherly type, "you will soon see that our role is to be ladies, not adventurers. A woman of today must be more than a pretty face, I remind you. We need to be literate, engaging in conversation, intelligent, yet — "

"Do nothing with our talents and education?" inserted Delain.

Barbara now had a turn at being slightly taken aback.

"What would you do with your education and up-bringing, then?" Barbara asked.

"Whatever I could. Go sailing to South America! Climb a mountain! I am used to only small hills and a few fortress walls for climbing, but a mountain? That would be stupendous!"

"Delain!" exclaimed Barbara. "Really!"

"And maybe solve a murder! Or at least uncover a mystery. It is certainly better than being a, a *doll*, sitting pretty and waiting for a man to take me somewhere. I have to believe there is more to this life than just being silent and polite, like a..." she reached for words that would not come.

"Bird in a cage?" Barbara said flatly, staring off into the vast woods.

Delain did not comment immediately. She looked to Barbara, trying to read her thoughts. Was she aware of the possibilities that could await her outside of the formalities of London? If she only could have had the opportunity to grow up as Delain had, in a more untamed and adventurous setting. Would she have developed a different view?

After a moment, Delain continued.

"You have thought of this, haven't you Miss Thompson?" asked Delain, with a note of encouragement. "That women are meant for taking our part in this world."

Barbara paused, then continued. "It is a dangerous world, Delain, and best meant for strong men with purpose."

"We are strong *women* with purpose," countered Delain, "a purpose that is just the same as a man's: to live a full and exciting life. To do as we like, not as we are told!"

Barbara laughed. "You sound like an American."

"I have met some," said Delain, defensively. "The women are proud and knowledgeable. They even engage in political debate, in public!"

"That is what I would expect from them," said Barbara with a disapproving tone. "They are uncouth and, and..."

"Free?" suggested Delain. "I would give up all this prissiness, all this ladylike pretending to be what I want to be—in charge of my own affairs. And I *will* be one day."

They rode on in silence for some time, each in her own thoughts. Delain believed that she might have been too forceful in expressing her views, and she possibly could have insulted Miss Thompson. Was it right for her to even mildly suggest that Barbara should change her plans and her course in life? She was soon to be engaged to Admiral Nathaniel Moore—even the papers had printed speculation, and certainly they were in love—and if that was what Barbara thought of as her destiny, well, it wasn't an unpleasant one.

Barbara thought, for her part, that possibly Delain did have a point, though an uncomfortable one.

Upon their turn toward home, Daffy and Daisy now rejoined them, happily wagging their cropped tails, muddy and wet, each proudly carrying in their mouths some dark and furry creature they had killed. This set both human ladies screaming in horror, then laughter, which caused the dogs to stop and wonder what all the fuss was about.

At least *they* can do what they want, thought Barbara as she contemplated the grizzly scene. She *was* prissy, she had to admit, and Delain certainly was not, though at times, the youngster was very much a lady. Was there a way to be both? What would it feel like to be even a little bit free and have a future that was completely in her own control?

"Shall we race back to the Bracknell Stables?" suggested Barbara.

"Really?" asked Delain, with a look of hopefulness.

With that, Barbara Thompson deftly swung a leg over her mount's head, and now, riding astride as a man would, bolted onward.

"Well, ladies," Delain said to the Airedales as she quickly swung her leg over her black filly's head and soon was sitting as Barbara had done. "What are we waiting for?"

Delain nudged the filly, and Daisy and Daffodil followed in earnest.

9

The Bow Chaser

With two days' sailing behind her, the *Paladin* had put the Bay of Biscay to her port side with the French coast more than two hundred and fifty miles beyond. Though England and France were at peace, the *Paladin* took no chances, keeping close to fifteen knots and almost a direct course south.

Leaving his cabin, Commander Harrison ascended the small ladder to the main deck. He observed his ship on this windy and cloudy day and considered his crew from a position a few yards behind Fawcett, who was at the wheel as sailing master. He was currently instructing a young midshipman on the finer points of piloting.

"Easy, Mister Moore. Not so jerky, eh?" he said.

"Yes, Fawcett," replied Jonathan. "But she is so big, and the wind is not consistent in direction."

"Big?" repeated Fawcett. "At eighteen guns and one hunnert feet, she's not *big* by any standard. The one-hunnert-gun *Victory*—now that's a large ship."

"But the wind," said Jonathan. "And the sea is a bit rough."

"Let the ship move before ya try to correct your course, Moore. Small movements, wait 'n see, then another adjustment."

"But what if I go off course?" said Jonathan.

"Don't worry. Ya won't be hittin' nothing out here!" laughed Fawcett. "That's enough fer today. See ya tomorrow, and we will go again."

"I thank you," said Jonathan as he turned over the helm to its master.

The seas came with a slight chop today, breezes

strong. At times, a wave would strike her just right, and the *Paladin* would rock on her beam, slightly, sending a few of the novice crew to the deck, and causing them to wonder just how safe this expedition of sailing the sea could actually be.

Gathered in a small group at the starboard rail stood Sean, along with Marshall, the gun captain, experienced and just recently assigned from HMS *Orion*. He had assembled a group of seasoned men to assist him in checking guns as the seas tossed, assuring they were secure. In these rough waters, a gun breaking loose could not only damage itself, but also the ship and, most dangerously, the crew.

As Jonathan joined the group, the *Paladin* was once again struck by a wave coming from the starboard side, and she rolled once again on her beam, side to side. This caused the bell, usually secured with a series of ropes tied in knots, to mysteriously ring. *Dong, dong, dong!*

"Is that bell ringin' by itself?" asked Marshall.

"It is," said Bowman, an experienced seaman of many years.

"A bad omen, that is," said Welty, also new to the *Paladin* from *Orion*.

"And why is that?" asked Jonathan.

"Yes," said Sean nervously, petting Stewie quickly, as if to use the good luck of the cat to ward off the bad luck that was surely caused by the lone bell.

"A dead man's hand rings it," said Marshall, ominously.

"Aye," said Welty, shaking his head in fear. "I 'ave 'eard it before. Never a good sign."

"It was the tossin' of the ship," said Jonathan, with a laugh. "Nothing more."

"Beggin' yer pardon, sir," said Marshall. "I was aboard the *Argo* years past. The bell, it rang just like this one did. Lonesome it sounded, like the dead calling us to join them."

"The dead?" said Sean, now furiously stroking the cat. Certainly, a bell ringing with no human hand to blame, at least not a *live* one, well, that was reason for concern.

"Aye, the dead!" said Marshall. "An' the *Argo*, she went down, didn't she, Bowman? You were there with us!"

"I don't want ta talk about it," said Bowman, returning to his work.

"I was on 'er as well," said Welty, staring off into the distance as he remembered the scene. "She went down in the North Sea, and many of us tossed overboard in the tempest. The bell rang, and within minutes, we 'ad hit something—a reef or a sand bar. It was so dark. Many didn't live."

"I said I don't want ta talk about it," said Bowman, aggravated.

"Yer not! I am," said Welty. "It was all we could do to get the boats loose before she was smashed by ol' Poseidon and his fury. Some said it was because we had that Irishman aboard, him bein' bad luck and all."

"Irishman?" said Sean nervously as he looked to Jonathan for some reassurance that his Irishness wouldn't jeopardize the ship. Stewie began to whine as he was now being almost roughed by Sean's attention.

"Sean, this is not true. It's all superstition," Jonathan said.

"Yer fine, Flagon," said Marshall. "Yer a *blond* Irishman—thank God yer not a redhead! Then we'd be in a fix!"

"Plus," added Welty, "You've been past the equator! An' that gold ring ya got fer doin' so? It will bring us luck!"

"Gold ring?" asked Sean, now frightened. "What gold ring?"

"The gold ring! In yer ear," said Welty. "The one ya got for crossing the 'quator!"

"I never got one!" exclaimed Sean, moving his hair to show his naked ear. He looked from man to man, hoping for some assurance that there was some way to right this oversight.

"Ya didn't?" asked the chorus of men.

"Oh, dearest Lord!" said Marshall. "We might be on a cursed ship."

"With a cursed captain!" added Welty.

Jonathan held up his hand and scowled at Welty and the others.

"What is this talk?" he said forcefully. The men froze. "Now hear this! Who here thinks we have a cursed captain?"

The men fell silent, embarrassed and unwilling to upset Jonathan by calling his friend *cursed*.

"Speak up now!" shouted Jonathan.

The men looked to each other, not wanting to speak. Finally, Welty looked up, face red and worried. He nervously held his hat in his hands, fidgeting with the brim.

"So sorry sir, it's just that—"

"Just what?" asked Jonathan, obviously upset.

"It's just that Captain Harrison..." continued Welty slowly. "Men have been talkin'. It's true 'e has lost every ship he's been on."

Jonathan laughed.

"You men and your superstitions! Based in ignorance and fear! And it is not true besides! Thomas Harrison was on the *Danielle*, and she still sails. He was also aboard the *Drake*, and captured her! He sailed the *Annie* from the Battle of Fire!"

"Well, sir," said Welty. "He's not *totally* cursed then."

Jonathan stood upright and tugged his jacket tight about him to show he was upset and would now exercise his rank.

"I will have no more talk of this idiotic superstition, especially about Captain Harrison. This is a direct order. Am I understood?"

"Yes, sir," came the meek reply.

As Jonathan turned about and walked to the stern, the men watched him go, embarrassed.

"Just the same," said Marshall, "we need ta get Flagon 'is gold earring."

"Tonight," added Bowman.

"I got an extra," said Welty. "Not real gold, but it will do the trick."

Sean nodded his acceptance, continuing to stroke Stewie, to the cat's growing discomfort.

Within the hour, the wind had died down, the surrounding seas became more composed, the tossing stopped, and the sun appeared warm and inviting. On the stern, unaware of the previous discussion about curses and luck, Harrison observed his realm and the approach of Patrick Jenkins.

"You called for me, sir?"

"Ah, Jenkins, yes!" said Harrison. "Thank the maker for an experienced hand. I have a letter for you here."

"Aye, sir, and thank you," Jenkins said. He took the letter — a large envelope actually — and stood at attention.

There was a brief moment of silent awkwardness.

"Don't you want to read it?" asked Harrison in an amused tone.

"Yes sir," said Jenkins, and he immediately began to open the packet.

"I believe it is from the Admiralty," added Harrison.

Jenkins considered the envelope quizzically, as if to say, "What would the Admiralty want with me?" The envelope was slightly larger than the typical correspondence one received on a ship, and that meant it was no mere letter. He opened the wrapping and held it out. A look of surprise came over his face.

"I must say, Jenkins, that I was made aware of this order last week," said Harrison. "Congratulations! You are to go before the Navy Board upon our return and be examined for warrant officer, to become boatswain, to use the correct title, of HMS *Paladin*."

Jenkins appeared shocked. He had figured that holding a warrant in His Majesty's Navy was not in his future. He had thought that, yes, maybe years ago it was possible, but a series of unfortunate events and captains had moved the promotion further and further away. A seaman first class was as far as he could have hoped for. Yet here, at the age of forty-five, he had finally been given a chance.

"T-thank you, sir," said Jenkins. "I-I don't know what to say."

"No need to thank me," said Harrison. "Just make sure you do us proud and pass the examination! As a warrant officer for this ship, you were the natural choice. In anticipation of your most assured promotion, I have a surprise for you, actually from Captain William Walker. Your pipe!"

Harrison produced a small box, wrapped in plain brown paper, tied with yarn. Jenkins reverently opening the package, saving the wrapping and string. Once opened, he held up a fine silver pipe, small enough to fit in one hand with a bell-like buoy on one end and a long pipe, or gun that one was to blow into. The shackle, or ring attached to the keel-like structure that ran along the bottom of the gun had a sturdy chain of links attached to it. Jenkins immediately looped it around his neck, then removed it quickly, as if it had stung him.

"Jenkins?" said Harrison, surprised.

"Bad luck, sir, to wear it before I-I am tested!"

Harrison furrowed his brow.

"Jenkins! Hogwash! Do you know who the examiner will be? Admiral Moore!"

"Oh," said Jenkins. "I believe he is favorable to me?"

"Indeed! To not test the pipe, well, *that* would be bad luck!"

"May I then, sir?" asked Jenkins, like a proud child who had just received exactly what he wanted for a present. His eyes glowed, and his teeth shown in a wide smile of anticipation.

"Do you know how to play it?" asked the commander.

"Yes, sir! Maybe...something simple? A 'still'?"

The 'still,' of course, was the call to attention. Anyone hearing it aboard the ship would stand at attention immediately until the 'carry-on' call was piped.

"By all means," granted Harrison, now adjusting his coat and standing perfectly erect. "Proceed!"

Jenkins held the pipe in his right hand and covered the

small hole in the buoy with his index finger. He blew firmly, creating a single note, held it for eight seconds, and then ended it abruptly. Harrison watched as all on deck, and he assumed all below who could hear, immediately snapped to attention, ramrod-straight, arms at their sides. He chuckled.

"Spa-*len*-did!" he said.

Jenkins then took another breath, blew a second-long high note, then released his finger from the hole, causing the note to drop in pitch. He cut it immediately. The crew resumed their duties.

"Sir," asked Jenkins, excitedly. "Would you like 'hands to dinner,' or possibly—"

"No, no, Jenkins," said Harrison, smiling. "That was a fine example of your abilities. No more piping, except as dictated. You will soon be an officer of this vessel, and I expect you to perform your duties to the letter and with all dispatch."

"Yes, sir," said Jenkins, snapping to attention and staring out to sea, somewhere to the left of the commander's head.

"Jenkins, you are my eyes and ears aboard this ship. I rely on you. Tell me everything you see. Everything."

"Aye, sir!" said Jenkins formally. "Just as Steward was to Captain Walker, so will I be to you!"

"Well, let us have a little less of Steward, for the glory of the king, and more of Jenkins, eh?" suggested Harrison.

"Yes, sir," said Jenkins.

"Now, on to less exciting business," said Harrison. "Complete a full evaluation of rigging and sails after sending my lieutenants, my midshipman, and Sergeant Hudson to my cabin."

Now would come the true test of the captain's quarters. As Harrison knew, the space was small for what he needed by himself, and it would certainly be too small for five people to attend. No matter how he moved items—his large table that was to seat six full-grown men, chairs, tall dresser, lamps, locker—the available space remained the same.

A knock came at the door.

"Enter," he said, and in came his two lieutenants, his marine sergeant, and his midshipman. "Gentlemen, please have a seat, if you can find one. I have arranged and rearranged this room numerous times, and still, it is too confining. Let us try to fit the best we can."

"I wonder, sir, if the carpenter could arrange something for you, short of an addition?" suggested Alexander.

"Possibly," said Harrison. "A capital idea. Ask Streen to see me when we are finished."

"Yes, sir," said Alexander.

"Is Fawcett aware of our position?"

"Yes, sir," answered Alexander as he found a spot to stand between the captain's chair and the lamp on the dresser.

Quinn moved to the windowsill—actually only a small piece of wood trim by the bottom of the center window that protruded less than three inches, just enough to take some of the weight off a man's feet in exchange for, literally, a pain in the rear. This left Jonathan with no option except to stand in the center of the room, with Hudson acting, more or less, as the door.

"Men," Harrison began, "three orders of business. First, upon our return, Jenkins will be tested for his warrant."

"Sir!' Jonathan exclaimed, his heart swelling with joy and surprise. Hudson had the same reaction.

"He is long overdue and certainly more than able," added Harrison. "A shame it has taken so long. Makes no sense at all; however, it will be righted soon."

"Indeed, sir!" said Jonathan, smiling. He had always been fond of Jenkins, and now he was more than happy for him. It was as if the universe were finally recognizing that a good man must be rewarded.

"Next topic," continued Harrison. "I received a large crate that I had placed amidships just fore of the mainmast. You may have seen it. A gift it is, from none other than

Captain Blake."

"Sir? *Our* Captain Blake?" Jonathan asked, smiling at Hudson, who returned the grin.

"Yes, indeed. The one who owes his command of the *Drake* to us!" Harrison said as he too smiled. They had captured the *Drake* less than a year prior. Then under the name *Fiero*, it was captained by rumrunners. Along with Miss Delain Dowdeswell, Sean, Hudson, and Hicks, they successfully took the ship off the shore of Conception Island.

"As a fine thank you, Captain Blake has sent us one of the deck guns. I believe, Jonathan, it is one of those that you actually fired at the approaching boats."

"It was Miss Dowdeswell, actually, who did the firing," added Jonathan. "I had my hands full at the time. Might I suggest we name it after her?"

"A capital idea!" said Harrison, laughing. "What did you have in mind?"

Thinking quickly, Jonathan said, "The *Stowaway*?"

"What a fine sentiment!" said Harrison. "I would have it installed as our bow chaser. We need a crew to mount it properly to the deck."

"Please, sir, allow me to oversee the installation," said Jonathan.

"Excellent!" replied Harrison. "Employ Jenkins as well. He has experience in this area, as he does with most things. Marshall is the gun captain. Have him assist."

"I will gladly employ them, sir," Jonathan said. "I will alert you as we are near completion."

"And I would like to fire it to signal eight bells of the afternoon watch," said Harrison with a smile.

"We will make it ready by then," replied Jonathan.

"Lastly, and most importantly, let us discuss our new orders," Harrison continued.

"Sir? I thought we have already done so," said Alexander.

"True. But as Lieutenant Quinn suggested earlier, we may want the input of Mister Moore. Possibly Sergeant Hudson as well. Therefore, Jonathan, Hudson, here is the mission."

Jonathan was suddenly awash with a sense of dread, as he, of course, had previously heard the information from Lord Wilder and Captain Spears. However, he realized that he needed to appear not to know anything, and to seem as if he were absorbing and reacting to this all for the first time. He stood at attention, as he had been more or less since entering Harrison's cabin, and listened, with eyes and expressions that were possibly a bit too interested.

"Somewhat of an honor has been bestowed on us," began Commander Harrison. "We have been asked to deliver a treaty in the name of His Majesty. We are to proceed to the island of Dugi Otok in the Adriatic Sea, and search north of the village of Telašćica for a specific inlet marked by a small entrance with two trees on either side, one with a rope dangling. I am unfamiliar with it."

"Sir, that area is quite desolate," said Alexander. "There are many small inlets and hundreds of islands on the Dalmatian coastline. They are all isolated and indistinguishable."

"Sir, I have some knowledge of the area," said Quinn. "Nothing out of the ordinary. Telašćica is more of a settlement than a town. There are sheer cliffs that make up the coastline near there. Picturesque and quiet."

"The orders dictate we are to enter bow first," continued Harrison.

"Bow first, sir? I find that...odd," said Alexander.

"A sign that we are the proper vessel," continued Harrison. "We are to deliver the treaty to our contact and depart. I can only assume he will have a boat of some kind. Any mishap will mean disaster, et cetera, et cetera, and if we need to communicate, there are a series of code words— for my eyes only—to use as a means of verification."

"It sounds simple enough," suggested Jonathan. This caused a pang of guilt within him.

"It does sound simple," said Harrison. "Though that doesn't mean it will be easy. A beesting is a simple thing, but it has its downside, yes?"

The officers laughed.

"What is the downside?" asked Jonathan. "It seems straightforward. We drop off the pouch and go on our way. Following the instructions to the letter."

"Sir, a simple plan for simple success," added Quinn with a bow to Harrison.

Harrison rose and, though wanting to pace about the cabin as he had seen his previous captains do when they had difficult decisions to make, he simply had no room. Instead, he exhaled and took one step toward the port window. Quinn, uncomfortable being so close to his captain, moved aside, and that caused Jonathan to have to move to the area Harrison had just vacated. This meant that Hudson had to actually step out into the passageway to let Jonathan by, then reenter the room.

"The downside," said Harrison, "is the manner in which the orders are to be carried out. I don't like the fact that I am to place the *Paladin* bow-first in a small bay. And I also don't like the idea that I must approach the bay at exactly eight in the evening."

Seeing that Harrison's suspicions were dangerously near to changing the plan, Jonathan felt the need to encourage him to stay the course.

"It must be due to the secret nature of the transfer. It is a secret, yes?" asked Jonathan.

"I agree, sir," said Quinn. "This treaty must be seriously important. No need to let the world see in broad daylight."

"Who would see in Telašćica?" Alexander asked with a laugh. "I can't imagine a more desolate place on the globe!"

"Exactly!" said Harrison. "No one will see us even if we appear nude at high noon with a trumpet section and stand in the center of the settlement yelling, "Here we are with the secret treaty!" Why use the ship as a signal? I've a good mind to change this whole plan. With our speed we could arrive earlier, by a day at least, scout out the cove, then return to Telašćica and send a small party on foot to the bay."

Jonathan saw that this was exactly what Lord Wilder had warned against. Any change in the plan might jeopardize the mission, the treaty never making its way to the tsar if the plan was altered. He felt compelled to do something. However, Quinn spoke first.

"Sir, with all respect, may I suggest?"

"Please," said Harrison, deep in thought as he sat back down in his chair, causing the room's occupants to shuffle about once again.

"I believe that following the precise instructions is integral to the mission's success," said Quinn. "Do you think that changing them in the least way could scare off our contact? There may be more at play here than we know. I would think the plan has been put into place as described, as odd as it is, meaning it is no *accident*, and it is so for a reason. I do not think we should change it."

"I agree," said Jonathan. "Begging your pardon, Captain."

Harrison turned to face them. He considered what they were saying, and it did made sense. He might be overthinking the entire exchange. Yes, there was something odd about this mission; however, it could all be nothing. The bay was remote enough, more remote than even Telašćica—indeed, he had never heard of it. How dangerous could it be?

"Though it seems remote enough," said Alexander, "I agree with Captain Harrison. Bow first? Leaves us no room to maneuver! I too do not like it. What if we remain on schedule, then see what the bay holds for us? If it looks acceptable enough, then we proceed as the orders dictate. If not, we sail on and send a shore party on foot."

"But we will miss the deadline!" said Jonathan, possibly a little too strongly.

"Deadlines at sea are an oxymoron," said Alexander, nodding to Jonathan. "There is no surety, only approximation."

Harrison mulled the ideas over in his head as he stared

out the window yet again. The ocean slipped by quickly behind the *Paladin*. He was caught with the beauty of it all—not just the sea but the glorious ship he was lucky enough to command. He couldn't let anything happen to her. And he had to admit that, with the exception of the *Danielle*, every ship he had been on for any decent length of time had been ill-fated. He had heard the talk by some: the *Poseidon*, destroyed at the Battle of Isla Pasaje, and before that, the *Helios*, captured during the engagement with the French Captain Champagne. Could the *Paladin* be lost? Not only would that destroy his career, but he would not be able to live with himself. The well-being of this vessel and its crew was most important. The mission was the mission, true; however, the *Paladin* was the *Paladin*.

"For now, we will do as Mister Moore and Lieutenant Quinn suggest," he announced. "By the book."

* * * * *

The *Paladin* sailed on into the afternoon. The day had turned warm and clear, sun now shining through thin clouds to the south. The men were busy as usual, cleaning or painting anything made of wood and polishing anything made of metal. Ropes were inspected, sails repaired as needed. About the bow, however, more than the chaser was being addressed. The figurehead was being maintained and had been assigned to none other than Sean Flagon.

Jonathan, Jenkins, and Marshall concentrated on the sixteen-pound gun, the gift from the *Drake*. It was to be attached slightly to the starboard side of the bowsprit. Of course, securing it directly in the center would have meant that each time the gun was fired, it would destroy all the intricate rigging and spars that made up the foresails and possibly even damage the figurehead. Streen, the carpenter, had secured the gun by spiking it directly to the deck and had constructed a brace to add stability. A small wooden box that was likewise secured to the deck was being filled with a dozen sixteen-pound balls.

"The *Stowaway* can do some real damage," Quinn announced as he appeared at the bow. "But it can also be a bit of fun when you're chasing a merchant brig or a small French corvette."

"Aye, sir. It makes 'em nervous," added Jenkins, "and these balls are new. Called shells they are, or sometimes bombs, and they explode when they hit the target or when the fuse expires. Lots o' flame and such."

"They came from the army," said Marshall. "They're made of cast iron."

"They seem lighter than shot," said Jonathan as he inspected one.

"Hollow," said Jenkins, "with oil and powder inside that sets fires. Pretty, and if you want to start some flames, they could be handy."

"So we are ready, Jenkins?" asked Quinn.

"Ready for inspection, Lieutenant," answered Jenkins.

"Then, Mister Moore, I will take the gun itself if you and Jenkins inspect the mounting?"

Ahead, Sean worked on the figurehead. He had been in charge of more than a few beautification crews aboard his past ships, and many of the crew not engaged with duty had appeared to watch him work. Strapped in with rope and harness, he hung over the bow and juggled his paint cans and brushes.

"Not a single can nor brush has fallen into the sea, mates!" he said proudly.

"Be careful, Sean," Garvey reminded him as he turned to inspect. "If you were to fall, we'd never find you. The ship would take you under in a second."

"Aye, and don't I know it! Jenkins has me trussed up like a goose for Christmas. I couldn't fall in if I had a mind to."

In the case of the *Paladin*, the figurehead was slightly out of the ordinary. It was not a woman, like those of so many other ships, nor a mythological creature like the sun god with his flowing rays of light for hair that was placed on the *Helios*. The figurehead of the *Paladin* was that of a horseman, riding high on the neck of a rushing stallion, the beast's nostrils flaring and golden mane flowing about its black hide. The rider, being only the head and shoulders of a young man, was calling out, one hand cupped by his mouth, the other hand lower by his side, gripping a long, slender lance with a furled banner at its tip, trailing above and beyond the two figures toward the stern.

At the moment, Sean was applying a bold blue paint carefully to the eyes of the rider.

"I was thinking," he said, "that I would change his hair. Blond would be nice. I'd match my own."

"Bad luck," said Hicks, who was observing the task and holding Sean's red jacket. "Changing the colors! Ya'd be cursing our good fortune. It's bad enough thar's a male as a figurehead. Don't start the crew on their mystical and superstitious ways!"

Sean laughed. "Have it your way, Hicks! But I was told there was good luck in this head here. Always has been a lucky ship!"

"The headpiece of the *Paladin* is nothing to be toyed with," came the voice of Fawcett as he watched. "I've been sailing this lady for years and years, been on since Cap'n Brendan Christopher, I 'ave. That is a lucky head, and if it is changed in any manner 'cept general maintenance, like a touch of paint from time to time, well…thar's a belief that most of us swear by. I know what I'm sayin'. If the horse and rider of the *Paladin* were to be changed, or damaged in battle, say, that would spell the end of all aboard."

There was a silence as all considered the words.

"I don't want to have anything like that," said Colin Stredney as he stared at Fawcett.

"'Course ya don't," said the sailing master.

"All nonsense," said Boston.

"Is not!" said Berkeley. "And saying so is to cause bad luck besides! Stop bewitchin' us!"

"Thar's no such thing as witches, either," added Boston.

"Ahhh! Denying it is to tempt fate!" cried Berkeley.

"Ridiculous," said Boston. "Ya think the commander believes in all that? O' course not."

Berkeley and Fawcett, along with a few others, glared at Boston, shook their heads, and moved away from him slightly.

"Oh, by gosh!" said Boston.

After Sean finished his last few strokes, he was eased off the bowsprit to the deck by Hudson and Hicks and un-harnessed. He rather enjoyed the task, though he was happy to be done, with feet on solid ground, as it were.

"How is the bow?" asked Alexander as he appeared. The crew members with no assignment stood about the deck, amidships, hoping to witness the first firing of the *Stowaway*. Many knew or had just been told of the significance of the title. They smiled, approving of Jonathan's naming of the weapon after his sweetheart. Many believe that even though having a woman on board was the most horrible cause of bad luck, having a gun named after a young lady was certainly good luck, and this put many at ease. No one would dare mention it to Mister Moore specifically or ask for details of his fondness. Besides, they had Flagon to probe about the romance, and he was a re-nowned storyteller—second only to Captain Harrison—and certainly more accurate.

"All complete, sir, as far as the figurehead is concerned," said Sean.

"And the gun?" asked Alexander, turning. "Captain Harrison is on the way as we speak. It is ready?"

"It is," said Jonathan.

"Ah, glorious industry!" said Harrison as he appeared. "The gun and the figurehead! Smart, smart, and smarter." He inspected Sean's handiwork. "Flagon? Top-notch! Looks better than it ever has. I see no variation in color or style was applied…and a good thing. We wouldn't want to tempt fate—bad luck and all."

Fawcett, Berkeley, and the others glared at Boston knowingly, pleased that the commander was one of them.

Harrison turned to the chaser. It gleamed with the last few rays from the sun, and as Harrison ran his hand down the barrel, he smiled.

"Jenkins, pipe to attention, please," he said.

Jenkins stood at attention and blew his pipe. The ship was silent, men listening as they stood erect and still.

"Gentlemen," Harrison began as he addressed all within earshot. "Attention please! An announcement! Let it be known that on this day, our very own Mister Patrick Jenkins has received a letter—a long overdue yet well-earned chance for promotion—and will soon hold a warrant, becoming our boatswain!"

The commander paused as the crowd murmured in disbelief, then whispered a few words signifying general acceptance, and finally cheered and applauded in sincere congratulation.

"Here we have the first firing of the bow chaser, it being named *Stowaway*, after our very own Miss Delain Dowdeswell," he continued. Then he turned aside and said quickly, "Who is not aboard on this journey, or at least we don't suppose so." This caused a wave of laughter. "In honor of his promotion, I would like to offer the *inaugural* firing of the *Stowaway* to our newly minted bosun. Mister Jenkins? Please."

"Me, sir?" asked Jenkins, verily surprised.

"Sir! It's bad luck, Captain!" said Hicks. "Yer gift, yer honor."

"Is truth, sir," replied Hudson.

"As much as I appreciate the honor, sir, I wouldn't want to tempt fate," said Jenkins.

Quinn and Alexander laughed aloud.

"Yes, I suppose so," said Harrison softly, with a glance to the crew. They were a superstitious lot, he knew, and more importantly, he didn't want them on edge, thinking about bad luck and poor prospects. "All right then," he said. "Sorry, Jenkins."

"No need to 'pologize, Cap'n," said the acting bosun.

Harrison smiled, then gave the order for the cartridge to be rammed and the ball to be set. Within a minute it was done, and he grabbed the chain.

Jonathan, who was standing behind, moved to the side and glanced aft. No one was behind the gun, just the foremast.

"Remembering an old lesson, Mister Moore?" asked Harrison, referring to an incident that both had been involved in and narrowly escaped serious injury.

"Yes, sir," said Jonathan, somewhat embarrassed.

Harrison gave the chain attached to the firing mechanism a firm pull.

All expected the gun to perform as it had been designed. However, it did not. Instead of launching the ball directly from the mouth, the rear of the gun exploded backward, spewing fire and sending the iron cap, now a red-hot projectile, screaming aft toward the foremast. It struck with a BANG, sending splinters and chunks of wood in all directions. Men screamed in shock. The cap rolled harmlessly in a small circle, and settled on the teak, like a penny would on a floor.

When the smoke cleared, Jonathan checked to make sure everyone was in one piece. Luckily, no one had been hurt. The foremast, though still standing, was missing a sizable piece and had a long crack, almost splitting the lower section of the mast in two lengthways.

"No, I did not inspect the gun, Lieutenant Alexander," said Jonathan. "I assumed that all pieces had been replaced correctly."

"Assumed?" asked Alexander.

In his cabin, surrounded by his lieutenants and his midshipman sat a frowning Commander Harrison. Holding his tongue, he allowed Alexander to continue the investigation.

"Sir," interjected Quinn, "I inspected the gun while Mister Moore inspected the mounting."

"It was not your duty, Lieutenant," said Alexander. "But thank you for the clarification."

"Yes, it was not your duty, Quinn," said Harrison as he stared at Jonathan.

The boy's heart sank.

"I have asked Jenkins to repair the foremast with the carpenter," said Alexander. "We have removed all sail at the bow; though, with some luck and industry, we should be able to add some canvas within a matter of hours, Captain.

Jonathan was dismissed. He dejectedly walked the deck in thought. He had a long watch ahead in which he could contemplate his error.

Sean was now dressed in his red uniform, musket slung, and he strolled the deck in the opposite direction. Each time he passed Jonathan, he smiled. But all he received in answer was a downward glance of embarrassment.

He's my friend, thought Sean. I hate to see him so. It was just a simple mistake.

After Jonathan's second round about the ship with nary a word to anyone, he returned to the spot where Jenkins was overseeing Streen, the carpenter; Everett, his assistant; and Boston as they cleaned the debris left over from the accident.

"It was not Mister Moore's fault," said Streen. "'T'was all that blasphemous talk about tempting fate and superstition."

"My point exactly!" said Boston. "All foolish nonsense."

"Yup, and the Lord, he doesn't like that superstitious talk," said Everett as he continued gathering debris.

"Eh?" asked Boston.

"The Lord!" said Everett. "He's the one who loosened that cap ta teach the others a lesson on holding blasphemous beliefs in witches and old bones and such."

"The Lord did that?" asked Boston. "But—"

"Gentlemen," said Jonathan as he stood before them.

Seeing the midshipman, they paused and tipped their hats as he approached.

"Mister Moore, sir," they said in unison, then returned to their work.

"We'll 'ave this cleaned up in a jiffy, don't ya worry," Jenkins said with a smile. "Streen, Everett, and Boston know the drill."

"Jenkins, a question?" asked Jonathan.

"Did Quinn check the cap? Is that the question?" asked Jenkins.

"Yes," said Jonathan dejectedly. "It is my responsibility and I will mention nothing to anyone. I just want to know. However," he sighed, "it makes no difference."

"I saw him at the cap, and he looked ta be doing somethin' with it."

"He defended me in the captain's cabin and said it was his fault," continued Jonathan.

"A right thing he did," said Jenkins, nodding. "Always best to tell the truth."

The words stung Jonathan as he realized that withholding the information about his discussions with Spears and Wilder meant that he too had been withholding information from his commander and his friend.

"I have no idea how it came off," continued Jenkins. "I was sure I completed all correctly. I am sorry if it is my fault. Sorry as well if it isn't, actually."

Jonathan's face became flushed, and he almost turned away from Jenkins for a moment to compose himself. Finally, he fought back the humiliation, removed his jacket, bent over, and grabbed a broom.

"Mister Moore?" Jenkins said quietly. "What are ya doin'?"

"Cleaning up my own mess, Jenkins."

Horrified, Jenkins stepped between Jonathan and the others. He gently placed a hand on the broom.

"They can do this for ya, Mister Moore," he said smiling.

"I can be responsible for my own repairs. It is no one's

duty but my own. Let me be," Jonathan said, slightly annoyed.

Jenkins held the broom tightly and looked Jonathan in the eye.

"A word with ya, Mister Moore? Please? One old *Poseidon* to another?"

It was true that they had served before on the *Poseidon*, had seen battle together, and had traveled half of the world side by side aboard that ship and the *Danielle*. There was an unwritten rule that those formerly of the *Poseidon* were a particular class of brothers. They called each other *Poseidons*, just as some called themselves *Danis*, after the ships that were their homes. Because of this relationship, there were certain liberties taken from time to time. Additionally, Jonathan owed Jenkins much. He had taught him his basic knots, his basic protocol aboard ship in relation to addressing officers, and had even looked after Jonathan on his first day aboard his first ship. Jenkins was more like an uncle than a shipmate, and Jonathan respected him a great deal.

"Just a word with ya, by the rigging. A question, actually," Jenkins added.

Jonathan relaxed his grip on the mop and allowed Jenkins to take it. He moved to the starboard rigging. After placing the mop against the foremast, Jenkins joined Jonathan at the rail.

"Mister Moore," Jenkins started, "may I speak freely?"

"Please," replied Jonathan.

Jenkins took a deep breath, hesitant to continue, and worried that his comments could be taken the wrong way. Jonathan noticed his concern.

"Speak freely, Jenkins," Jonathan said finally.

Jenkins seemed immediately relieved. He smiled ever so slightly.

"Good then, Mister Moore. I know ya are a bit upset with yerself over this here—*incident*. And that's right, ya should be. But ya know, this kind of thing happens. As experienced as ya are, ya are...allowed to make a mistake."

"I know that, Jenkins," Jonathan said.

"I know ya know, but even the best of us make mistakes. Let us do this cleanup. It's our job. We do it with pleasure."

"Jenkins," Jonathan said, somewhat annoyed, "I have always taken responsibility for my errors. And I have always cleaned them up as well. It will not hurt for me to help the men—"

"Ah, but it will, Mister Moore, excuse the interruption. The men look to you as an *officer*. Can't have you being a common hand, now, can we?"

"I just want to fix my own mistake," Jonathan said quietly but firmly.

"We can appreciate that, Mister Moore," said Jenkins. "But ya need to see yerself as a leader. And the *men* need to see ya as such. A leader has his place, and the hands have theirs. Eh?"

Jonathan smiled, then sighed in resignation.

"Carry on, Jenkins. I will report to the captain that all is being attended to. And as an acting warrant officer, I don't want to see you assisting."

"That's the ticket, Mister Moore!" said Jenkins.

10
Black Riders and Tea

"The sky looks awfully dark, Steward. Will it rain?"

"Eventually, Miss Thompson, eventually. But let's hurry on now 'fore it does, shall we?"

Steward escorted Barbara and Delain from the front door of the Bracknells' estate to the waiting horse carriage parked in the circular drive. He was wearing the same heavy wool coat he wore onboard ship, and though warm and dry on the inside, it would only be a matter of time, if caught in the rain, that it would become a heavy, wet burden.

"I wouldn't want to get wet!" added Miss Thompson as she ducked into the carriage, Delain immediately behind her.

Steward closed the carriage door and walked around to the front of the car and grabbed the reins.

It began to sprinkle.

"Nor would I," he said under his breath. "Yet fer some, it's our lot 'n life. Serving others. Gettin' wet. Bein' ignored."

From inside, came a muffled duet of "Thank you, Steward!"

Steward smiled as he climbed to the top of the carriage and shrugged his shoulders.

"Good ta be wrong from time to time. Yah!"

The horses pulled the carriage lazily around the drive and out into the street. It would be a good ride east to the Wilder's estate. Steward pulled his coat up about his neck and then reached into his pocket to find his *Poseidon* cap. Though he also had earned the newer *Danielle* variety for his service aboard that vessel, now under repair, he pre-ferred to wear the *Poseidon* version while on land—a trib-ute, he thought, to the friends he had lost at sea.

"Yah!" he shouted to the horses. "Let's pick up the pace! Don't want ta be totally drenched by the time we get thar!"

Now nearing Hampstead Heath and the estates on Van Patten, Delain held opera glasses to her eyes as she rode in the fine carriage. They were a gift from Miss Thompson for their plans to attend the theatre. Delain real-ized that the glasses, though not as powerful as the tele-scopes she had used while adventuring with Jonathan and Sean, were remarkably well made. They allowed her a view of objects that were surely two hundred yards away but seemed less than fifty. Alongside her, Barbara sat looking out the window, commenting on the mansions they passed and offering up tidbits of information on each of the inhab-itants.

"And this brick chateau-style home belongs to Lord and Lady Wendricks. Delightfully fun they are—however, at times a little too much fun. It is said that Lord Wendricks brews his own ale—in the *cellar!*"

"Scandalous," said Delain, feigning interest.

As Barbara continued her ruminations on the Van Pat-ten Wood elite, Delain turned her glasses to the trees and was startled at how quickly they seemed to flash by. It was disorienting at first, but soon, she was able to focus on ob-jects farther into the forest: a small pond, a deer, and after a while, a man on a horse. He was riding at full speed and often watching over his shoulder.

Delain thought this odd. She looked behind the rider and was soon able to see two other horsemen giving chase. She watched excitedly as the first one made an abrupt change in direction and disappeared into the thick brush. The two men following missed the ruse, stopped, and turned away in the direction they had come.

"This next estate belongs to the Hathaways. Rich mer-chants. She is a wonderful lady of impeccable taste. Mister

Hathaway is eccentric and entertaining, Delain. You would like him."

Delain was busily looking through her glass to get some glimpse of the rider; however, he had disappeared. That was certainly exciting and mysterious, she thought.

"We are almost to the Wilders'," announced Barbara. "We could have ridden the horse paths here in less than an hour, if we set a brisk gallop from time to time. When I was young, I used to ride the length of the entire forest."

"You still *are* young, Miss Thompson. You can't be a day over twenty—"

"Let's leave it at that, Delain," said Barbara hurriedly. "Thank you for the compliment."

The carriage left the avenue and entered the driveway of the Wilder Estate. Rain continued its sporadic pattern as it fell, and the sky darkened to a shade of charcoal-gray. Ahead of them, Delain noticed a dozen or so carriages in the drive, all slowing down and some even stopping to avoid running into each other. She raised her glasses to get a closer look at the ladies exiting their carriages and then allowed her gaze to wander about the estate. It seemed pleasant enough, though some noticeable areas of the buildings possibly needed some care, and certainly some paint. The grounds themselves were slightly overgrown, and there was a single gardener attending to the hedges and flowerbeds; however, he obviously couldn't keep up. There were even small saplings sprouting in the once-manicured lawn area, proof that the forest was encroaching on the grounds.

As she trained her gaze deeper into the woods, Delain noticed a shape: there appeared to be something large moving in the deep afternoon gloom behind the house, where the woods crept close. It wasn't another gardener; it was too large and had an awkward shape and gait. After a moment, as the branches of the woods parted and the sun glowed minutely brighter for a moment, the shape became clear. A horse and a rider.

Delain caught her breath and watched as the horseman dismounted and hurriedly tied his beast to a nearby tree. He then sprinted alongside a row of bushes, crouching so as not to be seen. Delain lost sight of him for a moment but correctly assumed that he was making his way to a far door off the rear corner of Wilder Manor. In a moment, she saw he had reappeared at the doorway. He took something out of his pocket that had to be a key, and after wrestling with the door for a moment, opened it slightly, just wide enough to enable him to slip inside.

The curious activity had Delain more than interested; she was literally beside herself with excitement. The difficulty was hiding her enthusiasm from Barbara, who would, of course, scold her for being unladylike and prying into matters not of her own business.

What was going on? wondered Delain. This doesn't look right. And how do I find out what is transpiring? I will follow him!

"Look," said Barbara, unaware of the intrigue unfolding nearby. "I believe that is the carriage of Lady Megan Wildrige. Of all the nerve! And after what she had said about the Hungarian Countess Ritana Eder—"

But Delain did not hear what horrifying faux pas had been committed by Lady Megan. While Miss Thompson was engaged in her explanation, Delain had taken the opportunity to leave the still-rolling carriage. Silently, she had opened the door, climbed to the side of the carriage along a railing, then shimmied to the rear fender and finally to the trunk attached to the back end. Hanging almost by her fingers, her feet moved in a running motion as she dangled for a moment above the driveway and then dropped to the ground. She stumbled for a step or two but regained her balance, quickly ran to the hedges along the drive, and began making her way to the back door.

"Oh!" said Barbara after a moment. "The line of carriages has stopped! We will need to sit and take our turn before we can enter." She turned to Delain, who, of course, was no longer present. All that remained were her opera glasses on the seat she had occupied.

"Miss Dowdeswell?"

Looking out the open door, she caught a glimpse of a young woman running into the hedges.

"Oh dear," she said aloud.

"I think yer chick has left the roost!" said Steward loudly.

"Steward! Pull aside, and let us wait as long as we can for her!"

"I could go fetch 'er," Steward offered.

"No! Dear me, no!" exclaimed Miss Thompson. "Let's not call attention to her!"

Steward pulled the carriage to the side of the lane, all the while shaking his head in dissatisfaction. "Miss Barbara, she doesn't need any help in that area."

The day was now a deeper gray, and the rain fell on and off in its irritatingly consistent inconsistency. It had become cooler, and Delain now wished she would have either stayed in the warm carriage with Miss Thompson or at least thought to bring a heavier shawl. Crouching by the last row of hedges before the rear door of the mansion, she reached to pull the thin wrap tighter about herself.

She could hear a horse stomping and snorting in the woods. Could it be the same one she saw being chased? Ah, she thought. There it is! The beast is literally steaming in the cold. It had to be the same rider. Why was he sneaking into the Wilders' home? A thief? But he had a key!

Slowly, with the greatest of care and silence, she approached the house and tried the door. It was locked.

Possibly looking through a window would reveal something. She noticed that all the windows of the home, at least in this area, were made of stained glass. On closer observation, she noticed they were mostly exquisite images of angels. Some were full-winged images, others just silhouettes, and some were detailed profiles. Peering through the glass, Delain noticed that the colorations and lead piping of the artwork distorted her view, though she could still see someone inside, stirring. She stood on her toes, moving her head as high as possible, and was able to look through a mostly clear part of the window.

There were no lights on inside. It was impossible to see clearly, but the glow from the overcast sky lent just enough light to allow her to make out some objects within. A desk was placed to the right, with two comfortable chairs facing it. Behind was a massive bookshelf, completely filled. The rearmost wall was also covered in shelves and books—and there, she saw the horseman, moving slowly and deliberately. His hand rose upward as he stepped on something, possibly a chair or small ladder, and reaching, moved a book on the secondmost shelf to the top, directly center.

Then, the unmistakable sound of a book dropping to the floor with a soft thud.

Delain strained to keep her balance as she stood on her toes. They ached from holding the uncomfortable position for so long; however, she could not afford to lose this angle nor take her eyes off the rider.

He placed something on the shelf in the space where the book had been, then crouched and retrieved the fallen volume. He placed it back where it had been, then turned for the door.

A sound came from behind her.

"Whar's that darned rake?" came a voice.

Delain froze. The gardener, she thought. Not turning her gaze, her eyes remained fixed on the man inside the room. He moved to the shadows, yet he turned his face to the window at the last moment. Was he looking directly at her?

The gardener came closer, mildly cursing as he looked about. From the corner of her eye, Delain could see him checking under bushes and on the nearby lawn. Her legs now seemed to be on fire from holding herself as still as stone. The worker was now coming closer and closer. It was only the fact that his focus was on the ground, where he believed he had placed the rake, that kept the girl out of his sight.

Delain was still staring inward through the window, now unable to move. The rider, if he noticed any movement at all, would see her.

Unknown to Delain, the horseman *was* looking directly at her. Maybe it was the darkness, maybe the fact that he too had heard the voice and was shaken, but the stained glass also distorted *his* view, and though he examined Delain's face, only a few feet away, he never saw her. She looked to be part of the images that made up the stained glass window, simply one of the replicated angels.

She realized this and was almost beside herself in fear as he inched closer and closer. Would he soon realize he was unable to see through this face?

"Argh! Here 'tis!" said the gardener as he reached under a hedge and retrieved his tool. In a moment, he was gone.

Legs burning, Delain remained unmoved. Not even a breath escaped her lips; not even an eyelash fluttered. The rider had now come even closer, but his height placed his gaze at least a foot above Delain's face. She was staring at the buttons on his coat.

They remained like this for what seemed to be one hundred heartbeats. Then, ever so slowly, the horseman turned his back to the window. Delain immediately dropped to the ground. Legs still aching, she ran around the corner of the mansion and back into the hedges. She froze once again, unbreathing. The sounds of the key and knob were followed by the creaking of the door opening. The rider emerged and looked about. Shadows covered him almost completely as he stood as still as stone. He then stepped quickly into the woods. A moment later, Delain could hear the horse's hooves pounding the soft earth as the Black Rider rode away into the trees' gloom.

Delain took a deep breath to calm her nerves. She rubbed her calves for a moment as she looked about. When she was sure she was alone and no workers, horses, or mysterious riders were visible, she approached the door. Hoping it was unlocked, she planned to see just what was placed behind the book in the case.

She gripped the knob. The door was locked; however, her curiosity had been opened.

Miss Thompson had waited with Steward on the side of the drive until the last carriage had deposited its travelers at the front steps of Wilder Manor. They had been looking about the hedges somewhat nonchalantly, hoping to catch a glimpse of their missing party. After several fruitless minutes, Barbara had made up her mind to cancel her attendance.

"Steward, I cannot wait any longer. I will go inside and inform the doorman that we are unable to—"

"Shall we go in?" asked Delain, appearing from behind the carriage, trying to fix her misplaced strands of hair and brush water drops and several leaves from her dress.

Miss Thompson's mouth was literally agape.

"Delain Dowdeswell! What a caution you are! Your hair! Your clothes! Quickly, into the carriage! Dear, dear, dear..."

After a full fifteen minutes of hairdressing, leaf-picking, waving of a handkerchief over damp areas of her dress, and avoidance of any details about her sudden disappearance, Delain was almost presentable once again. Steward stood watch outside, now and then stating to curious passersby that it was "just some female delay" or "typical London weather, eh, gov'na'?"

* * * * *

The tea was most splendid, even by Delain's standards. Initially, she expected Lady Wilder might be a dull host, but to the contrary, she was lively, polite, and engaging. Dressed in a less-than-attractive and slightly out-of-style ensemble, Alina seemed happy to have a celebrity such as Delain in her company. She escorted the youngster by the arm, parading her about the greeting room, introducing her to various ladies of the city, showing her off as if Delain were her distant cousin. Many asked for details of her exploits as a stowaway aboard HMS *Danielle* and about her activities at the Castle of Fire. Of course, they then became shocked by her audacity.

Delain couldn't help but think that all in attendance disapproved of her behavior. I don't care, she thought. If people such as these actually *did* approve of my behavior, I would question my own purposes!

"And here is Mrs. Brookside!" exclaimed Lady Wilder, leading Delain like an immensely curious pet on a chain. "May I introduce to you the famous Miss Delain Dowdeswell, daughter of His Lordship Admiral Dowdeswell, Governor of the Bahamas."

"Ah," said Mrs. Brookside as she looked Delain up and down as if evaluating her for purchase. The frown on her face and turning of her double chin into at least several new chins signaled her displeasure, yet her eyes held a glint of interest in the subject. "This is the young *lady* who lived on a boat with a few thousand men."

"Not a boat," giggled Lady Wilder. "A vessel of such size as the *Danielle* is a ship. A seventy-four-gun, third-rate ship of the line, to be exact."

Delain stared intently at Mrs. Brookside and considered using a few moves she had learned while dispatching pirates from the *Drake*. She believed a quick stomp on the foot, then a hefty blow to the throat would be in order. As if reading her thoughts, Miss Thompson appeared and diffused the situation with a jolly laugh.

"Oh, Mrs. Brookside! Always a wonderful sense of humor you display."

The only one truly interested in the details of Delain's tale was Lady Megan Wildrige. Stunningly beautiful in her auburn hair, and only a few years older than Delain at seventeen, she was especially intrigued by Delain's firing of cannon. Besides her supposed rude remarks about Lady Eder, Delain almost tolerated her, to the point of actually liking the young woman.

"Are the cannon loud?" asked the young noble-woman, smiling with excitement.

"Extremely," said Delain. "And the flames were hot. I could feel them even standing behind."

"I wouldn't want to find myself in front!" laughed Megan. "I have seen and heard cannon fired from ships in the Port of London, but never up close. Does the ground shake?"

"Indeed it does," said Delain. "But remember that a ship's cannon are called guns, and a gun on land is called a cannon."

Confused, Lady Megan just nodded her head.

"I fired seven of them," added Delain casually. "Struck a few French warships as well. Frigates, actually. Most exciting."

All were, of course, dressed splendidly, Delain thought, with the exception of Lady Wilder. Her dress was of the same frayed and tattered condition as the one she wore to the yacht race. Money problems, Penelope had thought.

Topics of discussion, however, mostly remained dull and uninteresting. Once seated on a paisley pouf next to Lady Wilder and Miss Thompson in the drawing room, Delain listened to long dialogues on such topics as the weather, the fashions from France that were now flowing into the city, and slight gossip about so-and-so who said this-and-that to Lady Whomever. The only thing that kept Delain awake was her desire to see just what had been placed in the library by the mysterious rider—and the never-ending trays of small chocolates and cucumber sandwiches that were offered by the servants of Lady Wilder. And that gave her an idea.

After her third cucumber sandwich, Delain became silent and slumped ever so slightly in her chair. She waited a moment, unmoving.

"And how is Admiral Moore?" asked Lady Wilder of Miss Thompson. "All going well?"

"Exceedingly well," said Barbara.

"And his son? Out to sea again?" asked Lady Wilder.

"Yes," added Barbara, "aboard the *Paladin*."

"The craft we saw at the race?" asked Alina.

Delain ignored this small talk. She sat quietly for five minutes. Then, very slowly, to not be noticed, took a deep breath and held it as long as she could, and then held it longer. This caused her to make an odd squawking noise as she released the air from her lungs. That, in turn, caused Lady Wilder and Miss Thompson to interrupt their conversation and become concerned.

"Miss Dowdeswell?" asked Lady Wilder, "are you well?"

"Your face seems...slightly flushed!" said Barbara.

"I think having cucumber sandwiches may not agree with me. I have never had them," said Delain.

Miss Thompson knew this was not true. She had served them to Delain herself on more than one occasion; however, maybe it was the mustard dressing added to today's variety that was upsetting.

"Dear me," said Lady Wilder. "What can I do for you? Water? Fresh air?"

"She has had plenty of fresh air," said Miss Thompson, somewhat suspiciously. Could this be one of Delain's famous subterfuges?

"Maybe if I could lie down for a while?" suggested Delain.

Within minutes a servant arrived and, led by Lady Wilder, supported Delain slowly to a bedroom in the rear of the house.

Now alone, head resting on a pillow in the oversized bed, Delain remained still for a moment, listening to the footsteps of Lady Wilder as she walked the long hallway back to her guests. Noisy shoes on that wooden floor, thought Delain. I had better take mine off, which she immediately did. After another moment, she sat up slowly and slid off the bed. At the door, she listened for a full minute, hearing only the dull drone of dull conversation coming from the tea room. It seemed safe to peek out.

Opening the door ever so slowly, Delain could see the empty hall leading all the way into the tea room. She carefully craned her neck the other way, opening the door wider, to see a dark passage to her right that immediately turned left, in the direction she assumed led to the library and its mysterious contents.

Holding her shoes, Delain breathlessly tiptoed down the hall.

In the tea room, no one was the wiser, until Miss Barbara Thompson happened to glance down the hallway leading to the bedroom where Delain had been deposited. She immediately noticed the form of a young lady in white running down the hallway, shoes in hand, disappearing into the dark.

Oh my! she thought. What could Delain be up to now? Yet another trick? And here? At Lady Wilder's home? It would not be inconceivable that the entire illness was feigned—and all in preparation for another *stunt*. Why can't she just be a lady? It is as if I am managing a rambunctious filly, with great promise and no demeanor!

Delain continued down the dark hallway to the left. She was now able to breathe easily, being out of sight of the tea room. She took the opportunity to get her bearings. Looking outside a crinoline-draped window, she could see her location in relation to the library. There, outside, was Steward, sitting atop the parked carriage. From the inside pocket of his woolen coat, he withdrew something. It looked positively disgusting: a fish sandwich he had most likely made himself. Delain was sure she could make out the head that was still on the fish as he began to eat, and as appalling as it was, it was no matter. Steward was slightly to her left, so that meant the library would have to be to her right.

Walking onward, Delain had a moment to think of an excuse, should she be found skulking about. A simple "I was looking for a powder room" would be easily believed if she were seen en route or returning from her task. However, what if she were discovered in the library—on a chair, reaching up into the bookcase? There would be no way to explain that if caught red-handed. Creeping down yet another turn in the hall past portraits of staring eyes and noble glances, she continued to think; however, not a single excuse came to mind. Best to not get caught then, she reasoned.

When she reached the end of the hallway, there were no other turns or doors, just a simple wooden entry on her left. It had to be the library. She listened for a moment, heard nothing, then, heart racing, she entered the room and quickly closed the door.

The room was dark, with only a dim light shining through the stained-glass windows directly before her. To the left was the large desk, flanked by two overstuffed chairs, and a floor-to-ceiling bookcase behind. The walls on either side of the door and to her right were also made of shelves filled with books. Delain turned around to face the door and looked upward to the secondmost top shelf. Yes, there it was: a volume just slightly protruding from the row of books by almost a half inch. It looked to be a large tome, certainly capable of making the loud thud she had heard earlier as she was peeking in the window. All she needed was to grab it and retrieve whatever was behind. Unfortunately, she needed a ladder.

All libraries have a ladder, she thought. But not this one. Of all the bad luck! No issue, I will use one of these chairs!

The nearest chair had to weigh over a hundred pounds, and though tough and resourceful, Delain was just slightly that weight herself. She gritted her teeth, angled herself just so, and then, with all her might, pushed the chair as hard as she could. It budged, making a squeaking sound as it rubbed the wooden floor.

Had anyone heard? She couldn't stop now!

She pushed and shoved, and eventually the chair was positioned, back to the wall, directly under the suspected book. She stood on the seat, in her stocking feet of course, and reached above. Feeling for the protruding volume, she looked upward. She was almost two feet below her target. Delain climbed up on the arm of the chair, and then, steadying herself by grabbing the edge of the bookshelf in front of her, leapt up to the high back. The chair shook. She wavered helplessly as her hand lost its grip on the shelf. A fall was imminent.

However, this was Delain Dowdeswell, adventurer, one who had climbed the walls of fortresses in Nassau, dragged cannon from recesses of a great castle, and scurried about the warship HMS *Danielle* unseen for several days. She was used to being in precarious positions and getting out of them.

Literally balancing on the fulcrum of disaster, Delain realized her silly *poise* exercises from the Swedish School had some practical use in her current predicament. She leaned to her left, then right, then found a middle ground of stability somewhere in between. Once assured of her position, she slowly moved her hand back to the shelf and grasped it.

She easily found the book hiding the treasure and removed it, dropping it on the chair silently. She reached into the space behind. Yes, there was something there, a fabric bag? It was heavy but not unmanageable. She took it.

Climbing down, she went to the desk, sat in the chair behind it, and looked in the bag.

"Money!" she gasped, then covered her mouth. Delain began extracting piles of English bank notes, counting as she went: five piles, each with ten one-hundred-pound notes each, totaling five thousand pounds. That was a small fortune by anyone's standards.

There was more: a slip of paper with the words "April Seventeen, Three A.M." scratched hastily in juvenile-looking script, and a letter in an envelope. The envelope was not sealed, only folded closed. Delain carefully opened it. Inside was a letter over a page long, neatly written yet completely unreadable. It was obviously in a foreign language.

To Delain, it was as if the letter were daring her, begging to be translated. To take it would not only be stealing, but it would tip off Lord Wilder that someone was onto him and his mysterious rider. The best thing to do was to reproduce the strange script. Rummaging through the desk drawer, she found a stack of writing paper and a fountain pen. She began copying.

In the tea room, some of the guests began asking Lady Wilder as to the whereabouts of Miss Dowdeswell, to which she replied, "The poor dear was feeling a little under the weather. I am having her lie down in a guest room for a while."

"So kind of you," added Barbara. "I am sure she is just fine."

"Odd," said Lady Wilder. "All that time at sea and crawling about dirty castles, and a little proper tea has her flustered. Maybe I should check on her."

Trying to hide her shock, Barbara held up a hand and shook her head vigorously

"I will check, Alina. Please enjoy your tea."

"I will be right back, really!" said Lady Wilder politely.

"Then allow me to go with you," suggested Barbara, almost in a panic. "We can share a few private moments to discuss my *situation* as we walk."

Lady Wilder paused, thinking, and then slowly smiled. "All right, dear. As long as we have our time together. Shall we?"

With that, they left the tea room.

As she copied the letter, Delain noticed the odd and strange markings above some of the characters and some symbols that just seemed backward. As confusing as it was, she persisted, making sure to precisely and thoroughly replicate each shape, until she finished the last few lines of the letter. Then, after carefully blowing across the wet ink, she folded her copy in half, and in half again, and placed the letter in the folds of her dress. Quickly, she replaced the writing pad and pen in the drawer where they had come from. Now, the money, the strange note, and the original letter had to go back in the bag exactly as they had been. But wait. Was the money atop the letter or the other way around?

Dear me, she thought. As hard as she tried, it produced no result. She simply couldn't remember the proper order. In the end, she put the money on the bottom, all else above, and scurried up the chair to return it to the previous spot in the bookcase. She positioned the book as it had been, sticking out a half inch, then stepped off the chair. Again, she began to push at the massive piece of furniture.

"You mentioned your *situation*, Barbara," said Lady Wilder as they walked the hallway to the guest room. "Do you have anything to share?"

Noticing a picture hanging on the wall to their left, and wanting to delay the unfortunate future about to unfold, Barbara motioned to the portrait, and recognizing an opportunity to delay, asked, "Ah! This portrait! How wonderful! Who may I ask, is the subject?"

Alina frowned at her friend with a questionable expression. "Queen Victoria. Is it that poor?"

"Oh," said Barbara with a forced laugh. "Of course, how silly of me."

"Indeed," said Alina.

Barbara repeatedly stole glances down the hall at the doorway ahead, expecting at any moment the appearance of Delain in some awkward position doing some deplorable act.

"Now, Barbara, please tell me!" said Lady Wilder, excitedly, "is there any announcement concerning you and the admiral?" Her appetite for gossip was well-known— and also the fact that she could not keep a secret. Barbara had to be careful. Whatever she said would surely be repeated.

"Yes, there is!"

"Has he…proposed?" asked Lady Wilder.

"Not exactly, but he has hinted and seemed very nervous the past few days." This was safe to say—nothing really new in the statement that hadn't been discussed by many in town already.

"Dear," said Lady Wilder. "We all know that! If he doesn't ask you soon, I feel others may wonder. I mean, none of us are getting any younger."

Barbara ignored this suggestion that she could become an old maid if her relationship with Nathaniel did not turn into marriage. In fact, she had a feeling that as soon as Jonathan and Sean returned, she would become engaged.

"Here we are!" Barbara announced loudly. She had a feeling that it would be best if she entered the room first to check on Delain, just in case. "Let me check on her, and I will be right back!"

"Allow me," said Alina. "She is my guest."

Lady Wilder reached around quickly and opened the door, stepping in. Barbara grabbed her arm, whispering loudly: "She is my charge, Alina. I need to—"

Just then, Barbara saw movement from the other, dark end of the hallway. She saw a small, stocking-clad foot almost step out into her view, then retreat quickly backward into the shadow.

"Barbara!" Alina said with a laugh, "How strange you are!"

Miss Thompson looked into the guest room, knowing that with Delain not there, Alina would notice, and, well, she would rather not even contemplate what horrible scandal this would cause and what blemish would be placed on the young girl. Glancing to the bed, she was surprised to see the shape of a person under the covers. Then who is in the hallway? she wondered.

She looked back to the shadow, and a delicate face peered out. Delain.

"What has come over you?" asked Lady Wilder.

"Ah…" said Barbara. She glared at Delain as if to say, "What are you doing?" Delain simply made a gesture of surprise and then mouthed what could only be the word *pillows.*

"You are right, Alina. Let us go in together!" said Barbara. She quickly glanced at Delain and positioning herself out of Alina's view, motioned for her to wait.

The ladies entered the bedroom. Looking at the bed, both women paused.

"Is she asleep?" whispered Lady Wilder.

Barbara quickly but silently rushed to the side of the bed and put her face close to the pillow that was pretending to be a head. Acting as if she were listening to the breathing of Delain, she nodded and smiled at Lady Wilder.

Returning to the door, Barbara whispered, "The little angel is asleep."

"Asleep?" asked Alina. "But she seemed so uncomfortable..."

Thinking of a quick lie to make the first lie seem more believable, Barbara continued, "I believe it is not cucumbers but a cold coming on. Yes, she was outside all this morning with the two dogs, and, frankly, she was *barefoot.*"

"Barefoot?" asked Lady Wilder, surprised and shocked. "Oh my dear!"

"Yes," said Barbara as she moved out to the hallway, pulling Lady Wilder by the hand and then closing the door quietly.

"That little imp!" said Barbara, shooting a glance in Delain's direction and speaking loud enough for the girl to hear. "She is always up to something, and exploring the mud with those hounds is her sort of fun."

"Mud? Are you serious? Dear me!" said Lady Wilder.

"Yes. She is quite a caution!" added Barbara.

The two ladies began their walk back to the tea room.

The carriage ride home began in silence, at least from Steward's point of view. The evening had fallen, the air now chilly, and gas lamps around Van Patten Wood were lit along front streets and drives. The horses clip-clopped onward, heads down, tired, yet happy to be moving home again. Standing was as uneventful and boring for them as it was for Steward. He heard nothing from inside the car until they were almost back to the Bracknell Estate, and then just incomprehensible voices to begin with. Eventually, the conversation became heated, the volume rising to a point where he could pick a few words and sometimes a phrase. He was sure the discussion had to do with Delain's foray into the woods and her behavior during tea. After a few moments more, the voices became loud enough that the topics were clear, and Steward almost felt guilty for listening.

"All I am saying, Miss Dowdeswell," said Barbara, "is that there is a time to act like a lady, and for you, a fourteen-year-old girl, that time is now!"

"Don't call me 'Miss Dowdeswell.' Am I now not your friend?" asked Delain.

"Delain, the point is — oh! Friends? Certainly we are!" Barbara said.

Then she paused, considering the young girl. Yes, we are dear friends, she thought. And though such trouble as Delain is, there is something captivating about her, wise beyond her years, intriguing, and yes, I must admit, exciting. However, a lady must first be a lady. And it is my duty, in the absence of Lady Dowdeswell, still in the Bahamas, to look after *this* one.

"And I will call you Barbara, if I may?" said Delain.

"Of course," answered Miss Thompson. "Now, where were we?"

"You were admonishing my behavior at tea," said Delain flatly.

"Ah yes, thank you," said Barbara. "Delain, you have so much promise, a bright spirit, and a charming demeanor. Why do you insist on outrageous conduct?"

"I don't think it was *that* outrageous," said Delain softly as she looked out the window.

"Jumping out of a moving carriage? Pretending to be ill? Snooping around a private residence?"

"All right. It was outrageous," offered Delain.

"It was almost criminal!" gushed Barbara. "Whatever made you decide to puff up the bed with pillows and go off exploring the dark regions of the Wilder Manor?"

Delain turned toward Barbara and smiled.

"I will tell you soon; however, for now, I will keep it to myself. Please, Barbara. Do not ask me again."

11

The Echo Returns

Just after midnight, April the seventh, the *Paladin* continued toward Gibraltar under less than full sail due to the damaged foremast. In the deep of the night, she glided along as the stars began their dance about the clear heavens, their reflections vividly sparkling in the dark sea.

Jonathan awoke from his slumber at the sound of a single bell to start his night watch. He dressed quickly and woke Sean with a mild poke. As the Irishman rolled over, Jonathan saw blood on his pillow.

"Sean," he whispered. "Are you all right?"

"Huh?" said Sean, yawning.

"There is blood on your pillow!" said Jonathan, careful to not wake others. "And your ear!"

"What? Oh! Just my earring," said Sean. "I got it for passing the equator. Welty and Bowman did it. Hurt like Hades, I can tell ya."

"Sean!" whispered Jonathan as harshly as he could, "You are going to be an officer someday! You can't have an earring like a common seaman!"

"I'm going to be an officer?" asked Sean, still groggy.

"A marine officer, I would hope! Now get up and take that fool thing out of your ear before you offend Commander Harrison!"

Sean grumbled and removed the gold loop, then began putting on his uniform. The possibility of becoming an officer had never occurred to him. And as pleasant as it sounded, the thought of being Marine Captain Flagon would bring some amount of responsibility that would certainly require substantial effort. Could he really perform to that expected level of duty? Would it be possible for him to actually progress that far?

Jonathan turned and ran up the ladder to the main deck, slipping on his coat and hat as he went. Sean, now almost dressed and in relative privacy, replaced the ring in his ear and positioned his hair so as to hide it. He fed Stewie a piece of dried, unsalted fish, gave him a generous pat, and then proceeded to the main deck for duty.

There were men awake and men asleep, the ones in slumber snoring and wheezing for the most part. The conscious crew was either preparing for a watch or just coming off. They gathered by the few open water barrels, and there was Berkeley, handing out hardtack and an almost completely dry rind of lime to all.

Once on deck, Sean reported to Sergeant Hudson for duty. It was usually the same: walking the deck, arms shouldered, usually with Hicks, and learning how to grimace at the common crewmen, mostly Sean's friends. The crew understood the need for the marines aboard to perform as maritime police. They were the eyes and ears and sometimes hands of the captain, and the crew pretended to be somewhat afraid and respectful of the marines' presence, at least while they were nearby. After Sean and Hicks had passed, the men lapsed back into their usual jolly manner. It was true that, at times, Sean missed the deep camaraderie he had enjoyed with the crew on previous voyages. While in uniform, the men respected him, and that meant sometimes they were distant. At least when belowdecks, he was again one of them.

Jonathan quickly found Lieutenant Quinn at the helm with Fawcett.

"Ah, Mister Moore. Are you ready?"

"Yes, sir," Jonathan answered.

"Then the watch is yours," said Quinn. "Nothing to report. Garvey is in the crow's nest. We are a day from Gibraltar. The Mediterranean lies beyond to the east."

"I have never been to the Mediterranean Sea," said Jonathan.

"It looks as all ocean does," said Quinn with a smile.

"We will stop in Gibraltar and see the port from the ship at least."

"We are stopping?" asked Jonathan.

"Commander Harrison inspected the repairs to the foremast," said Quinn, "and as it is not mended fully, he has decided to seek additional lumber and then continue on, even at this slower pace. He felt it better than delaying the mission by fully repairing."

Jonathan felt awful once again. The *Paladin*, beloved by his commander, was now an injured lady, and it was his fault. He knew it had been a poor decision to not check the entire gun himself—as was his deciding to remain silent about his meeting with Lord Wilder and Spears.

"Another word, if you have a moment?" asked Jonathan.

"Surely," replied Quinn.

They began to walk the deck as night was closing in deeply, the wind gusting at their backs as they looked toward the few lights they could discern ashore. Peaceful it was, and quiet.

"Lieutenant Quinn," Jonathan began. "Two items, if I may."

"The gun? Is that what this is about?" asked Quinn.

"Partly," said Jonathan, "however, it is not for blame or retribution's sake I bring up the subject. It was my responsibility to secure the gun, no one else's."

"You just want to know," said Quinn. "I understand, Jonathan. And the answer is yes, I did inspect the gun and the cap. All looked fine to me for the most part, until I checked the cap. It seemed loose. So I tightened it a bit, but after I began, it was clear that it was really fine before I even touched it. I now believe it was imperfectly made, or damaged in the transportation process."

"An accident in the true sense of the word?" added Jonathan.

"I believe so," said Quinn.

"I should tell Captain Harrison," said Jonathan.

"Why bother?" said Quinn. "He is over it. To bring it

up again would be as if you are opening a healed wound, yes?"

Jonathan thought about this as they walked the deck, and after a while, he decided to wait until the right moment to discuss the incident again with Harrison. Maybe after the mission was over, and they were back in London.

"Your second issue, Jonathan?" asked Quinn.

"Yes. When you came aboard with our new orders and were called to the captain's cabin, you winked at me as you passed. Was there any meaning to that action?"

Quinn thought for a moment, looked about the deck, and seeing that they were, for all practical purposes, alone, smiled.

"Yes. Because I had knowledge of you. From Captain Spears and Lord Wilder."

"You were contacted by Spears and Lord Wilder?" asked Jonathan, shocked.

The young men stopped walking, now back at the bow. The few hands that were present could see they were in deep discussion and moved away, out of earshot and courtesy.

"Indeed. They changed my orders," said Quinn. "I was assigned to the *Spartan* but was reassigned to the *Paladin* at the last minute and given the treaty."

"May I ask what they told you?" said Jonathan.

"I was told by Spears and Lord Wilder to keep an eye on Commander Harrison."

This made Jonathan gasp. Of course, he had been told the same thing and was given the same secret duty.

As if reading his mind, Quinn smiled and said, "I was also told what you were told, Jonathan. That Harrison, though a capable officer, was possibly a bit too confident, too reckless, and would deviate from the expressed mission orders. I was told that you would also be contacted, as one who knows Harrison well, and that you would also attempt to influence him and encourage him to perform accordingly."

"I am relieved to hear I am not alone," said Jonathan.

"However, I can tell you that Commander Harrison is extremely capable, and all this is unnecessary."

"Possibly," said Quinn. "However, he is considering changing course, changing plans, and that could mean disaster."

"He is my friend and a proven officer," said Jonathan, "capable of missions considerably more difficult than dropping off a few pieces of parchment."

"I am sure," said Quinn. "I am only repeating what I have been told. It is true that he has had only a few assignments as an officer, and has gotten his first command by jumping the ladder, as they say, even if by the king's command. There are those who believe he is a bit unlucky as well. He has lost two ships, and in the Admiralty, that is where they concentrate."

Jonathan was not satisfied. There was more to all this. He had been put into a difficult position by being asked to withhold information from his friend, and in that way, he felt dishonest. He told Quinn of his personal feelings about the matter.

"Then, Jonathan, all I can say is this: we must follow our orders from the king, and in the end, when we are successful, who will get the credit and the glory? Commander Thomas Harrison. That can't be all bad. So we are actually helping him, yes?"

With that, Quinn clapped Jonathan on the back and headed off to bed.

The eastern sky above the continent had now a pale gray glow as the creeping morning sun lit the few wispy clouds. To the west, it was black as pitch, and to the south, still too dark to make out anything but a few crests of the small waves that broke all but silently ahead of the ship. The view north was shrouded in shadow.

Jonathan's first and middle watch continued without incident, and as a single bell signaled the morning watch, Lieutenant Alexander took over the deck, sending Jonathan to bed. He tossed and turned, unable to sleep as the past few day's events played out, over and over, in his mind. Frustrated, Jonathan returned to the deck and stood by Mister Fawcett, staring off the stern, watching the crests of the waves. Deep in thought, Jonathan stared, now and again, refocusing his eyes through his telescope on a different section of the sea, a habit he had been taught by Harrison so many months ago. It was a way to systematically scan the ocean, moving one's gaze a point at a time, then progressing on to the next point. At first, he saw nothing, though as the sun climbed a little higher, the gray shades of the cresting waves lightened — and one crest was actually a pale white. Within a minute, Jonathan could see two masts, then, square mizzen, topsails, and topgallants, and finally the triangular mainsails. Not all were set out, but it was clear it was a sloop, much like the *Paladin*. He lowered his glass.

"Two masts! Three points off the port stern! Steady as she goes, Mister Fawcett," Jonathan said.

"Aye, Mister Moore. Steady as she goes."

Harrison and Alexander appeared immediately at the stern and raised their glasses.

"Very nice, Mister Moore. I see your eyes are in perfect working condition. She's almost directly behind now. Looks like…a brig-rigged sloop."

"Yes, sir," said Alexander. "If I didn't know better, I'd swear we were looking in a mirror."

"The *Echo!*" exclaimed Jonathan.

"It must be," agreed Harrison. "Lieutenant Gray is in command, if I remember correctly. There is a union jack above the spanker," said Harrison. "We must invite him to breakfast if his errand allows. Jonathan, have the crew reduce the tops, keep the mains."

As his orders were being carried out, Harrison again took up his glass and watched the approaching vessel. He could now see plainly as the sun ascended, making the ship's identity clear.

"It is definitely the *Echo*," he said. "I can almost make out the figurehead. No wonder it has caught us. Without our foremast, we couldn't have been doing more than seven knots."

Aboard the *Echo*, not Lieutenant Joshua Gray, but Nikomed Aggar, the Russian captain, watched intently through his telescope at the ship ahead. He had hoped that he would be able to steal a quick glance at the vessel, positively identify it as the *Paladin*, then come about with great speed and agility to slip out of visual range. He would then know that all was on schedule and could prepare his crew.

"Is it she" asked Kowalski, standing at the wheel.

Both were now wearing uniforms that they had taken from the English crew of the *Echo* and ones found in other places, including Gray's cabin.

"Yes," said Aggar. "I don't dare get any closer. If she sees us...have the men reduce sail and come about. We will hide to the north for a while."

The *Paladin*, now with canvas reduced to only square sails on the mainmast, had given up speed perceptibly. This was done to allow the *Echo* to easily approach. As Harrison watched, the *Echo* also reduced sail and kept her distance.

"Odd," said Harrison to Mister Fawcett. "What in heaven's name is Gray doing? Why is he slowing? Alexander! Quinn! Add sail, Moore! Get the men to the guns! Come about, Mister Fawcett! Jenkins! Pipe to stations!"

"Yes, sir," said the officers, who rushed to carry out the order. Following the call from Jenkins's pipe, the deck of the *Paladin* was now alive with men. The crew in the tops began letting down sail. Others ran to their guns, rolling them into position and prepping them for what may come. The marines mustered at the bow as Sergeant Hudson gave his orders. Within seconds, the red-coated musketeers were in position along the rails and in the masts. Sean took his place at the stern with Hicks to his right. His gun was loaded, his hands shaking visibly.

"What's a matter, Seany?" asked Hicks.

"I-I'm all right. Just don't want to fire on the *Echoes*, if you catch my meaning."

"Ah, just a precaution. Showin' off a bit," assured Hicks.

"They have seen us, Captain Aggar!" came the call from crow's nest of the *Echo*.

Aggar now realized that the most undesirable event had now occurred: they had been seen. If the English captain could identify his ship as the *Echo*, he may approach, want to converse, or may try to take the ship back if he were suspecting foul play. Possibly, he might even request to come aboard for breakfast. That would never do. Though Aggar was confident in his ability to speak in an almost perfect English accent, he could never pass as an officer of His Majesty's Navy, not up close. He had only one option. He must assume that the operative aboard the *Paladin* had somehow sabotaged her, making it nearly impossible to catch the *Echo*. Yes, he knew the *Paladin* was the fastest ship in these waters—probably in the world—but injured, he might just be able to slip away.

"Cherepanyanko!" yelled Aggar angrily. "Hurry! Add all sail! Kowalski! Bring us about! Starikov! Put on that uniform! And take the British men below! Guard them with your crew."

"We need them in the tops, Captain!" argued Cherepanyanko.

"They will give us away!" countered Aggar. "Move all available Russians to the tops! And stand tall and proud, like real British sailors!"

* * * * *

As the *Paladin* now approached the *Echo*, Jonathan returned to the stern and stood next to Harrison in silence. Alexander strode up quickly and raised his telescope.

"This is odd," said Harrison. "Gray must be daft or worse. He had, just a moment ago, reduced so much sail he was almost drifting backward! Now, as sloppily as an American whaler, he has added more sail and come about!"

"He is running?" asked Jonathan. "That is peculiar."

"I don't like it. Not at all," continued Harrison.

"Could the *Echo* have been captured, sir?" asked Alexander. "It would explain the erratic behavior."

"She is flying a Union Jack," said Harrison. "However, it would not be the first time an enemy had used that trick."

"Captain Harrison," said Jonathan. "I thought we were at peace?"

"England has many enemies, Jonathan. Some are nations; some are privateers. And if the peace has ended, how would we know? A letter? By the time we heard about it, war could have been declared weeks ago."

"More than likely," added Alexander, "we would find out when an enemy ship attacked us!"

"If that is happening, let us be ready," answered Harrison. "Jonathan? Are the men to battle stations?"

"Yes, sir," Jonathan replied.

"I want doors open and guns rolled out now. We will show them we are prepared to fight. Mister Fawcett, keep *Echo* directly ahead."

"Ahead she'll be, sir," said Fawcett.

Aboard the *Echo*, Aggar could see that now he was being pursued. His men had sloppily added sail, and the turn executed by Kowalski was too wide. He had missed the wind by overcoming it, and now they were struggling to gain it once again.

"Cherepanyanko! Add sail! Add sail!"

"She is gaining on us!" called Sublieutenant Starikov as he assisted in adding sail by hauling. He, along with Cherepanyanko and Kowalski, was a capable seaman and knew his way about a ship as much as Aggar. However, they were only three men surrounded by many who were not as seasoned. If only there were more old salts, as the British would say, they could have executed the maneuver easily and escaped.

"Find the dammed wind!" called Aggar.

Though the Russians had eventually captured some of the wind, the *Paladin* and her expert crew had performed their duties well, and she was now less than four hundred feet behind the *Echo*.

Harrison stood at the bow with Hudson at his side. They both peered ahead through their glasses.

"I see men on deck, sir," said the marine captain. "Some are running below. I see...I see someone by the sailing master. It must be Gray. But when did he grow a beard, as light as it is?"

"That explains it," Harrison said as he watched them. "That is not Gray."

"Pogany!" swore Aggar in aggravation.

"What are we to do?" asked Cherepanyanko. "They are almost alongside!"

"Keep our men in the sails, have them continue working until all is let out. And keep quiet! No one speaks but me!"

Within another minute, the *Paladin* had caught the *Echo* and had taken a position less than one hundred feet off her starboard side. Still sailing with limited foremast sails due to the gun accident, Captain Harrison knew that eventually, if her sister ship could succeed in setting all sail, the *Echo* would pull away. However, for now, the ships seemed to be at comparable speeds.

"Ahoy, *Echo*! What news?" Harrison called across the waves as he and his officers approached the port rail. This was somewhat a breach of protocol as he should have waited for Jenkins, or in the very least a lieutenant to call for him. Harrison hadn't the time for that sort of propriety.

Shortly, the officer on the *Echo* waved in return.

"Ahoy, *Paladin*! Commander Andrews, newly assigned!"

"You were running, Commander. Did you not see our colors?"

"Ah! That is funny," said Andrews. "No, we just did not realize you were an English ship! The light was not assisting us from our angle."

"We noticed that you were slowing," called Harrison, "then adding sail. It was hard to discern your intentions."

Sergeant Hudson remained nearby, a concerned look on his face as he realized there was something missing from the *Echo*.

"We wonder about Captain Gray," called Harrison. "Is he not commander of the *Echo*?"

Aggar paused for a moment. Damn these English dogs! he thought. Do they know their entire corps of officers by name and ship?

"Gray?" called Aggar. "He was replaced. I am now in command. Are you readying to fire, Commander?"

"We are ready but would rather not," explained Harrison. "Standard procedure, as you know."

"Is it?" asked Aggar. "I didn't think so. I have not prepared *my* crews, Commander."

Just then, Quinn appeared, tucking in his shirt as he approached.

"Sorry, sir," he said. "I was undressed."

"I don't remember ever seeing an Andrews on any list. Have you, Alexander?" asked Harrison softly.

"No, sir. I have no knowledge of him," replied Alexander.

"I do, sir," said Quinn. "Andrews and I served together in the East India Station aboard the *Xerxes*. He is quirky but a good egg. Inexperienced, yet well connected. May I, sir?"

"Please," said Harrison.

"Ahoy, Andrews! Quinn here! I haven't seen you since Ceylon!"

"Ah! Quinn. A pleasure once again!" came the greeting from the *Echo*.

Harrison stared across the water to his sister ship.

There were less than thirty men in the tops, now setting sail on the foremast; however, that was enough. Soon, the *Echo* would pull away.

"A new lieutenant, as inexperienced as this, assigned to the *Echo?*" asked Harrison quietly.

"He is friends with Captain Spears, sir," added Quinn. "That would explain some of this. His family has friends in high places."

Following a head motion from Harrison, Fawcett brought the *Paladin* a few yards closer to the *Echo*, causing Aggar to hide his face whenever he could, using the rigging, the wheel, and even his hand. If he could only get a bit more sail set, he could get away. Noticing the damaged foremast of the *Paladin*, he smiled within. His operative had succeeded. He needed only a few more moments.

Harrison caught a longer glimpse of Andrews. My, he thought, he looks considerably old for a lieutenant. He must be in his forties!

"We must take our leave of you, Commander Harrison," Aggar said as his ship finally set his last sail and began to move ahead. "Our mission is on a tight schedule!"

"If so," called Harrison, "why did you pursue us, now only to turn away?"

"Our orders have us searching for a specific ship," called Aggar. "Unfortunately, you are not the one. That is all I can say."

"Did those orders come from Admiral Monteith? If so, they may coincide with ours," asked Harrison. "Unless they came from Admiral Edwards, then I could understand fully."

"Edwards," called Aggar. "So sorry! I must be going! Good fortune to you, my friends!"

With that the *Echo* had caught the wind sufficiently, and was off and away.

"That was…strange," commented Hudson.

"I agree, Sergeant," said Harrison as they all watched the *Echo* disappear quickly ahead. "I believe he is lying."

"Lying, sir?" asked Jonathan.

"He said he couldn't tell if we were a friendly?" commented Alexander. "That is unbelievable."

"Beggin' your pardon, Captain," interrupted Sergeant Hudson.

"Hudson?"

"Yes, sir. I noticed that, well, he was a tad short on marines. He should have had a half dozen at least."

"How many did he have?" asked Alexander.

"None."

They all paused, deep in thought.

"It could be as I said, sir," said Quinn. "He is inexperienced. The light was slightly — "

"He is lying, and I know it," stated Alexander.

"And how do you know it?" asked Harrison as he smiled broadly.

Jonathan also wondered how Harrison and Alexander were so sure. Yes, Andrews seemed like a clumsy oaf, and his ship was handled so poorly, it was simply an embarrassment to the Royal Navy. But they had all seen well-commanded ships and also others that were not so tightly run.

"I saw that you laid a trap for him, Captain Harrison," said Alexander.

"Continue," said Harrison.

"You asked him who gave him his orders — gave him a choice actually. Both wrong, of course. Orders do not come from Admiral Monteith nor Admiral Edwards. All come from Captain Spears through Admiral Barnett."

All now knew that Andrews was lying. But why?

"Is he just a grobian?" asked Alexander. "A clumsy oaf with a pitiful crew?"

"A fool, but a harmless one, I believe," offered Quinn.

"Possibly," said Harrison. "Fawcett! Resume our course toward Gibraltar."

Later that evening, as Jonathan tossed in his sleep, he decided to give up the fruitless effort and wake. The mission was not going as smoothly as he or anyone desired.

They had left port late, had received strange orders, and after his mistake at the gun, had now lost precious time. And Spears and Wilder making their requests for him to ensure the mission's success at the bequest of the king—it was enough to send his mind spinning. No wonder he couldn't sleep.

Of course, sleeping like a log on the hammock next to him was Sean. He had a smile on his face, and now and again, Stewie, purring softly as he lay on the boy's chest, would stretch and yawn, look at Jonathan through half-slit eyes, then drift back to sleep. At least some are confident and able to rest, Jonathan thought.

He stared at the beam above his head for a few more moments and, resigned to the fact that he was unable to sleep, rose and lit a candle. Sitting next to his locker, he opened it and searched inside to locate paper and pen. There he saw the small box that had contained the silver compass star Delain had given him. Fingering the trinket now about his neck, he smiled and decided to write two letters—one to his father and Miss Thompson and the other to Miss Delain Dowdeswell. The *Paladin* would be in Gibraltar by morning, and the letters could be delivered home on the next ship bound for London.

HMS *Paladin* moored in the port of Gibraltar late in the morning of April the eighth. Immediately, Harrison had sent Streen, the carpenter, and Lieutenant Alexander to the port master to inquire about needed lumber for the fore-mast. Quinn was dispatched to deliver mail and report to Admiral Crampton, the ranking officer of Gibraltar Station. None of the crew, however, were allowed to go ashore, and to add insult to injury, they enjoyed only the hardtack that was served for breakfast.

Upon their arrival, a light rain began to fall, and after securing the crew and ship, Harrison called Jonathan, Jenkins, Hudson, and Sean into his cabin. Berkeley had prepared a light snack of soft-tack and cheese, strong coffee, which he seemed to regard as his specialty, and after a quick jaunt to a local market, some cheesed eggs and sliced ham.

"Not bad, Berkeley," said Harrison smiling. "You will soon be preparing spotted dick and pigs' pettitoes along with all the other favorites."

"Thank ya sir," said Berkeley. "I aim to please."

"Speaking of aiming," said Harrison as he turned to Sean, "How goes the musket practice? Are you showing any improvement?"

"Yes, sir," said Sean as he secured a forkful of eggs from his plate.

"He no longer falls over after each firing," said Hudson.

"And I have yet to kill anyone accidently," noted Sean with some sense of pride.

"Well," said Jonathan as he sipped his coffee, "let us hope you never have to fire that gun in battle!"

"Hear, hear!" came the chorus from all those present, including Sean. Though he was progressing marginally, Sergeant Hudson and Hicks were worried that, if needed, Sean might prove ineffective in using the gun, and this had them holding target practice daily for the youngster, dropping various pieces of used lumber and other debris over the stern and having Sean fire upon them as they bobbed up and down in the waves and as the ship pitched and rolled. It was difficult, to say the least, but they encouraged him nonetheless and even commented that in such conditions, even appearing to send a round close, within a few yards, was cause for celebration.

"We have plans to discuss, gentlemen," said Harrison, bringing the subject back in hand. "I fear that the foremast will need complete replacing."

Jonathan's heart sank again. He stopped eating and sat as still as stone.

"Streen believes we will need to replace the mast completely; however, due to our timetable, that will not be possible to effect here in Gibraltar. I have sent Streen and

Alexander to see what lumber they can find to assist in supporting the mast."

"If I may," asked Jenkins, "No matter what magic Streen conjures, we will not be able to set all sail on that mast. We will lose speed."

"Are we able to make eight knots?" asked Harrison, knowing the answer.

"Hard to say, sir," responded Jenkins. "We 'ave to wait until Streen is done."

"Our only other option is to turn back to London and then to Scotland for repair," said Harrison.

"The mission will be a failure, sir," said Jonathan.

"Let us see what Streen can do with whatever lumber he can afford," said Harrison. "My desire is to continue on without delay."

Within the hour, Streen and Alexander returned to the *Paladin*. Fortunately, they acquired a good bit of lumber, iron bands, and bolts to more or less repair the lower foremast, and though it was not anywhere near perfect or even acceptable, Jenkins and Fawcett believed they might make eight or nine knots—maybe ten, depending on winds. No matter what, the mast would require constant attention.

"Commander," said Alexander, joining the officers at the stern, "I received some interesting news pertaining to the *Echo*. The yard commander, Admiral Crampton, asked specifically if we had seen her."

"Oh?" asked Harrison.

"I told him we had, and that she was under a new commander. *He* told *me* that *Echo* was due in Gibraltar on the sixth of March. However, she never reported."

"She's a month late, and we've seen her lollygagging about," said Hudson.

"I mentioned that to Crampton. I suggested that their orders may have been changed," added Alexander.

"Not entirely uncommon, is it?" asked Quinn.

"No," said Commander Harrison, "though still suspicious that word has not reached Gibraltar Station and

Crampton, isn't it?"

Streen had worked through the night with his crew, and by the beginning of the first watch, they had patched the foremast with various wooden braces and brackets designed and created from their knowledge and years of experience. Certainly not *repaired* by any sense of the word, the mast looked almost as if it were surrounded by a cage, made with several large planks of heavy oak, straps of iron, and wooden braces that secured the mast to the deck and rails. Streen had finally declared that they were ready for sail.

Once underway, experimentation was necessary to test the strength of the repairs, and Harrison ordered more and less sail, adjusted rigging, and discussed outcomes with Fawcett and Alexander. They each looked intently at the mast, checking its bracing and listening for stress-cracking or other unexplainable noises.

Satisfied with adding all but the fore topgallant, the uppermost sail on the foremast, they were soon away from Gibraltar, heading straight east at nine knots to Telašćica. Due by the sixteenth of April, Harrison and Fawcett had calculated that, if sailing on calm seas with mostly favorable winds, they could still make the rendezvous by that time, if luck would serve.

Meanwhile, alone in his thoughts, Jonathan continued his lessons with Fawcett when he could, enjoying the fact that he was finally getting the feel of piloting the great ship. He also appreciated the opportunity to concentrate on something other than his problems.

12
The Bridge at Wapping

As early afternoon fell on the busy city of London, April the tenth, Marine Captain Gorman, not dressed as such, stood in front of The Monument near Pudding Lane. The Doric column had been erected as a tribute to the damage and loss due to the Great Fire of 1666. He observed the copper-sculpted urn of flames atop the two-hundred-foot memorial and then turned his attention to each of its sides, seemingly inspecting the structure for cracks and imperfections. He murmured to himself, circling the monument, back and forth, around and about. This odd dance of course was a signal to his most effective spy.

After physically receiving a bump on his side as he was leaving the Admiralty earlier that morning, Gorman looked in his pocket to find a coded message that had been placed there. It simply read "Bordeaux on the plaza." What this meant to Gorman was startling. Bordeaux, of course, was the code name for Marine Lieutenant Scotty Slater, Gorman's finest and most experienced operative, who was stationed in southern France, Spain, and points east. The phrase "on the plaza" meant that Slater had news for Gorman, and they were to meet at The Monument.

Slater emerged from behind King's Brick Bakery, on the corner of Thames and Fish Street, and watched the path and pattern Gorman was taking about the structure. He was moving counterclockwise, meaning that something was suspicious about their meeting, and Gorman could have been followed. He then noticed Gorman turn abruptly to his left and cross the street, disappearing into an alley beyond. This told Slater to meet on the opposite corner in one hour, inside whatever business was there — in this case, a cheese shop.

In precisely one hour, under the cloudy afternoon sky, Slater entered the Gollon Cheese Shop and Winery and nodded to the shopkeeper. Making his way to the rear, he paused by the wheels of Dovedale Blue.

"Too soft and mild of taste for me," said Slater softly.

Out of the shadows appeared Gorman.

"Try some Wensleydale," said the marine. "It is a bit crumbly and has a honey, acidic taste."

This, of course, meant that Slater was free to speak and that Gorman also felt they were secure and had complete privacy. Had Gorman recommended Pont-l'Évêque – well, they would have been running for their lives, naturally.

"What's new, old friend?" asked Gorman, taking a seat at a small tasting table. "You are out of uniform, Lieutenant."

"Good to see you, Captain," said Slater as he sat, his dark eyes and hair almost completely hiding his features in the shadows. "And I haven't been in uniform for almost two years. Ever since I began working for you."

The men shook hands heartily.

"Some interesting news from Gibraltar," said the lieutenant. "The *Echo* is missing."

"Missing? Could she be late?" asked Gorman. "Not uncommon for one of His Majesty's ships to be late."

"Even for *late*, she's late," said Slater with a chuckle. "It's been almost a month, and she hasn't reported."

"That's not good," said Gorman. "No one claims to have sunk her?"

"No," answered Slater, "and while I was discussing the ships coming and going with Admiral Crampton – he's at Gibraltar Station now – he mentioned her. No reports of skirmishes, no reports of bad weather, nothing. Pirates, I thought, but they are rare these days – and besides, the *Echo*? Not one except *Paladin* can catch her."

"No ships lost since the truce was signed," said Gorman.

"I watched the harbors, asked a few of His Majesty's

sailors and several captains of merchant vessels. No one has any news."

"Well, Frey and Fairchild have seen Lupien about town," added Gorman. "Mostly at the docks."

"That Russian bottlehead?" said Lieutenant Slater. "He's never up to any good. We ought to take him to potter's field and be done with him forever."

"I sent Frey and Fairchild to bring him in for a nice, quiet cup of tea and a pleasant conversation," said Gorman, smiling.

"He takes sugar in his tea, I'll wager. Give him a few lumps for me?"

"With pleasure," said Gorman. "He is working with another man, though we have yet to identify him. Goes by the name of 'O.' Frey and Fairchild followed him after one of his meetings with Lupien. They trailed him to a public stable in Van Patten Wood, where he mounted a horse. They followed after renting two beasts themselves."

"Did they catch him?" asked Slater.

"He gave them the slip," said Gorman, shaking his head. "Have you any news?"

"Of this Mister O? Never heard of him before," said Slater.

The men continued sharing news, suspicions, and the whereabouts of some of the more interesting characters they had been following in their network. After an hour, they both grew nervous. They had been in the shop for a long while, and that could appear suspicious to others. Simultaneously, they both stood.

"Getting late," said Slater. "Where am I going next?"

"Back to Gibraltar as soon as you can. Keep an eye out," said Gorman.

"I will, Boss," said Slater.

At this same time, moored to the quay at Wapping and sitting as pretty as a picture, was the small brig HMS *Cay-*

man, with twelve guns and two masts. Sadly, she was overlooked by the many lieutenants seeking their first command, due to her small size and relegated duty of transporting nothing of importance. She was always instructed to avoid all contact with the enemy, though possibly, on very rare occasion, she was allowed to fire a few rounds of colored smoke at some local celebration. But to the man leaning on the corner of the first pillar of the Wapping Bridge, the *Cayman* was of great interest.

Next to the *Cayman* was HMS *Danielle*, still under minor repair. As famous as it was, even with the many people of town who came to see her and discuss her adventures, the sleek seventy-four was of little concern to the man on the bridge.

A few berths down, past some very uninteresting first-rates, sat HMS *Drake*, a thirty-six-gun sloop with shapely lines and a dark mahogany stripe down her sides. She was nearly ready to sail, the man noticed, and was most likely fully outfitted with crew. He smiled and wrote down a few notes in the journal he was carrying.

Specific ships in the harbor were observed and noted: number of masts, sail configuration, hull type, number of guns, tonnage, length, and beam. Many of these attributes needed to be estimated, but the man on the bridge had been observing ships his entire life and had taken pride in the fact that he was an accurate estimator. Had he decided to lead a more customary life, he could have possibly used this talent in service of the navy, a ship builder, or even an insurance company. But those were not his ways. He observed these ships for his master, Commodore Ian Kharitonov.

Lupien completed writing the essentials of the smaller ships in the harbor in his book, pleased that he had found a few vessels with an appropriate number of guns to suit the purposes of his employer. In the Black Sea, the commodore had little use for larger ships such as the *Danielle*. The prey in that area could only be caught with fast, agile craft with adequate firepower. Large, lumbering ships of more than forty guns would be easily outrun by the smaller frigates and sloops used by the Ottoman Navy. Their small size made for easy maneuverability, and to catch one—or more—a sleek, fast, and lightly armed ship would stand the best chance. Ships such as HMS *Echo* and HMS *Paladin* were the perfect models.

The *Cayman* and the *Drake*, though not as perfect as the *Paladin* or *Echo*, would do nicely. Along with the other ships he had documented, Lupien felt he could fulfill Commodore Kharitonov's next order with ease. He closed his book and turned to walk across the bridge to the east and begin the long walk home.

At first, he noticed nothing out of the ordinary: the sun was steadily setting, the breeze had picked up slightly, and the surrounding area was now quiet as many had gone home for the day. Even work on the ships in the dockyard had ceased. It wasn't until he had reached the center of the bridge that he noticed the man on the other side. He stood with his hands on his hips, his head slightly down, hood close to his brow, and his eyes burning a hole through Lupien. Stopping, Lupien immediately looked over his shoulder, and saw behind him another figure, gray beard visible under his hood, heading toward him quickly.

Gorman's men! he thought. How could I have been so foolish as to not notice them? I knew it was too soon to explore the harbor! Damn that Kharitonov and his orders!

Frey, the man now facing him, was moving quickly and produced a long knife, allowing it to flash in the failing light, making sure Lupien had seen it.

"Now, now, now, Mister Lupien. Time for a little talk is all," said Frey. "Be a good fellow and come along nicely."

Lupien answered by rushing as fast as he could in the opposite direction. Unfortunately, Fairchild had moved closer and now stood in his way. He pointed a gun at Lupien's head.

"Look at what I've got 'ere!" said Fairchild. "One o' those new percussion-cap pistols. Extremely accurate. And the reload? Fast, like magic. Shame to 'ave to use it, such a pretty thing it is."

Lupien knew he had only one choice. He relaxed completely, as if to say, "All right, you have me now," and after a moment, he spun himself to face the rail of the bridge, ran as fast as he could, and leapt over the side.

Gorman's spies rushed to the edge and looked down just in time to see a splash. Fairchild fired a shot, reloaded in mere seconds, then fired a second round into the water. It missed its mark. Lupien surfaced a few yards down the Thames. As he took a huge breath, Fairchild fired again. A small splash erupted in the dark water a few feet to Lupien's right.

"Darn!" cursed Fairchild.

"Ya missed!" said Frey.

"I know that! Go in after 'im!" said Fairchild.

"Me?" asked Frey. "I-I can't swim!"

"You were in the navy!"

"Nelson can't swim either!" said Frey in his defense.

"Hogwash!" said Fairchild. "Oh! For 'eaven's sake! 'E's getting away! 'Ere!" He handed the pistol to Frey. "And don't shoot! It's gettin' dark, and ya might hit me!"

Frey took the gun.

Fairchild leapt into the water.

By now, the sun had all but set, and Fairchild had enough trouble getting his bearings in the water, much less being able to locate Lupien. He swam about in the cold river for twenty minutes, though to no effect. Giving up the search, he turned toward the shore. He could see Frey sitting on a tree limb close to the edge of the river, looking at something he had found. Fairchild laboriously made his way to the riverbank. Exhausted, he climbed out and sat down.

"Take my coat," said Frey.

"Obliged," said Fairchild, who did so and wrapped himself in the garment. "What have ya got there?"

Frey smiled. "It seems our lit'le fish found it hard ta swim with 'is notebook in 'is 'ands. Must 'ave dropped it when 'e 'it the water."

Fairchild scrutinized the book in the dim light. He could see handwriting, some smeared ink, and some dripping pages.

"What does it say?"

"HMS *Drayton*," said Frey, "sixteen guns, two masts, three hundred fifty tons, small crew. HMS *Annie*, converted merchant to sixty-four guns, three masts, five hundred fifty tons. HMS *Cayman*, twelve guns, two-masted sloop, two hundred tons."

"All ships in the harbor," said Fairchild.

"Let's memorize the list 'n toss it back," said Frey. "He will surely look for it 'n 'opefully believe it is still secret."

"Excellent idea," said Fairchild. "Then we report ta Cap'n Gorman. He'll know what this is about!"

The men read the ship names to each other several times, using the light of the gas lamps from the bridge above. Then, satisfied, they tossed the book onto the bank of the river.

Hours later, at a small pub on Ayliff Street near Whitechapel, two men sat at a corner table near a small fireplace, one in a fine coat of wool, the other wearing nothing but a large quilt. With only the two patrons, the house seemed quiet enough for conversations, especially of the private kind. The men whispered and sipped their dark drinks as they looked into the fire. Besides lending light to the scene, the flames dried the wet clothes that had been draped across an iron grate, at times needing to be adjusted by the smaller of the two men.

"Getting drier," said Lupien as he pulled his quilt tighter about his neck.

"This is bad news," said Orvislat as he stared into the flame.

"Maybe it is; maybe it isn't," said Lupien. "I don't think they knew why I was there. I recovered my book. Surely they would have taken it had they found it."

Orvislat winced, and shook his head.

"No, they might have not. They are experienced. They

may have memorized the list and set the book down to fool us."

Lupien shook his head.

"We don't know that. It is as good a chance as not that they didn't see the list."

Orvislat snorted his discontent.

"Stay away from the dockyard and piers. You may have to move to Portsmouth."

"Kharitonov will not be pleased," grumbled Lupien.

"He never is," said Orvislat. "I will have Wilder arrange for the *Drake*. Then I too will lay low."

They sat in silence for a while, listening to the crackling of the logs, becoming captivated by the glowing embers. A simple thing like the warmth of a fire could calm them. To these men of the world of espionage, enjoying the simple things in life, and relishing them for a few hours, seemed like heaven. Eventually, however, they must come down to earth.

"And we have more bad news," said Orvislat, finally. "The boss informed me that the bag had been tampered with before it was opened in the library."

"Did you open it?" asked Lupien as he rearranged his wet socks.

"Of course not!" said Orvislat in a hoarse whisper. "I never touched the thing except to position it in the hiding place! Did you open it before you gave it to me?"

"Me?" asked Lupien. "Never! I don't want to lose my life for curiosity's sake! I simply take the pouches from my drop point and deliver them to you without stopping anywhere for anything."

"Here we are, the story barely a third done, and things are becoming unraveled," said Orvislat. "Someone is on to us, and it has to be Gorman. You are sure the men on the bridge were his?"

"Positive. It was Frey and Fairchild," answered Lupien. "Could they have been in the library at Wilder Manor?"

"No, I am sure I lost them in the woods," said Orvislat.

"They have seen you about town, and knowing your occupation, they followed you."

"They might be on to you as well," suggested Lupien as he took a warm and mostly dry sock from the fire and stretched it over his foot.

"Eventually, they will be," said Orvislat, taking a long drink from his glass. "Let us hope we can complete one more mission and move on. England isn't the only country with available ships, yet it is so convenient."

"Ah," said Lupien, raising a finger to make a point. "But it is the only one where your father is the ambassador and we have created a relationship with an insider to do our bidding."

Orvislat smiled.

"My father, Ambassador Orvislat?" he laughed. "I have a father in every Russian Embassy in every capital in Europe! I will be reassigned if need be, to one of them. Maybe I will become Wodka in Poland, or Karhuski in Italy. I could become the son of Ambassador Najera in Spain. They have many ships that could suit our purposes. We will begin again if we must."

Lupien shook his head, wondering who Orvislat really was, and what name was truly his own.

13
The Cove at Telašćica

On the sixteenth of April, the *Paladin*, under reduced sail, approached the fishing village of Telašćica from the south. Surrounded by rocky and barren hills that lined the coast of Dugi Otok, the town was now cast in the golden glow of the setting sun. The crew and officers could see the town's few citizens going about their activities, and soon, all settled into a calm silence. The small bay that was the center of town was sparsely peppered with a few fishing boats and a single felucca, its raked masts and graceful lateen sails being taken in and secured for the night.

Paladin sailed onward to the northwest.

Harrison was at the bow, telescope in hand, surveying. After an hour under reduced sail, he still saw nothing out of the ordinary.

"Alexander!" he called. "Anything to report?"

"All clear astern, sir!" came the response.

"Time, Mister Moore?" Harrison asked.

"By the bell it will be six o'clock," Jonathan answered.

"We are early, in spite of all our efforts to be late," Harrison said. "You see, Jonathan, even when you make a mistake, you still bring us luck. Is Sean in the crow's nest?"

"No sir," answered Jonathan. "Lieutenant Quinn called him down when he replaced me. He is manning the point."

"I hope his eyes are as sharp, then. Quinn! Quinn! Anything at all?"

"Not a sail to be seen, sir!" came Quinn's voice from above.

Harrison literally had men stationed about the main deck every few yards, all watching for a sail or the entrance to the cove. Additionally, he had Jenkins pipe the men to battle stations and had Alexander managing the guns and their crews, in case someone unexpected decided to appear.

At the stern, Marine Sergeant Hudson was flanked by Privates Hicks and Flagon, all leaning on their muskets, peering behind. They saw nothing.

"Pretty clear evening, eh?" said Hicks.

"'Tis that," responded Hudson.

"Still enough light to see by," said Sean.

"Not sure I like this plan, if ya catch my meaning," continued Hicks after a moment or two. "Seems hare-brained."

"I agree," said Sean. "When in London, we had a rule, Jonathan and I: never get in an alley that has no back door. And this cove we are supposed to find is just the same."

"Sure as all the sea is salty, I never heard of anything like it," said Hudson. "But those are our orders."

They continued staring astern. It was then that Sean thought he saw something out in the offing. He stared for a bit, blinking and then rubbing his eyes. Could he be sure?

"Sergeant Hudson. Do you see anything directly astern?"

Commander Harrison, with his telescope pointed at the waterline to the east, scanned the shore for the tree and the rope. It seemed that the coastline was an unending series of small cliffs, a few scraggly trees, and certainly no relief from the rock outcroppings. Then, as the cliffs began to rise, he spied a tree and…was that a rope?

"Mister Fawcett! Come to starboard. The cove is four points off the bow. Take us in as close as you dare. Quinn! Alexander! Anything?"

"No, sir," came their responses.

"Captain…" began Jonathan.

"Yes, Mister Moore," the commander replied, still watching the shore.

"We are early. I would think we want to avoid coming into the cove before our time," said Jonathan. "The orders were explicit."

"Noted, Jonathan. I don't think going in for a closer look will hurt a thing. I want to make sure that this cove has some room to maneuver."

"What of the contact?" asked Jonathan. "If he sees us, might he be scared off?"

"I did think of that, Jonathan," Harrison said, "but consider this: if our contact is there, watching, he may see us sail slowly by. He could get prepared. We can then return at the exact time and finish this business quickly. That is if the cove is to my liking."

"What if it isn't to your liking?" asked Jonathan, worried.

"You will see soon enough. Get the men to reduce all sail save the main foremast. Keep them in the tops. I might want to leave in a hurry."

"Yes, sir," Jonathan replied, and he rushed to perform his duty.

At the stern, the marines looked hard out to sea. There was still a small glimmer of light on the horizon; however, the sun was setting fast. Indeed, they had all thought they had seen something — possibly a sail — but they couldn't be sure.

"Seany," said Hudson. "Hicks and I will keep an eye out. You call to the crow's nest and see if Quinn has a better angle, eh?"

"Should we alert Captain Harrison?"

"Let's be sure first. He's slightly jumpy as it is."

With that, Sean moved quickly to the mainmast and called up to Lieutenant Quinn.

"Lieutenant! Sir! Do you see anything directly astern?"

Sean could see Quinn leaning over the edge of the crow's nest, examining the shoreline though his glass. He immediately turned his gaze south. After a moment he stared down to Sean, shaking his head.

"Some whitecaps, no more," he said.

"We thought we saw a sail, but couldn't—"

"I said nothing to be seen, Flagon," snapped Quinn.

His tone was out of place, thought Sean. He eyed the lieutenant questioningly and then nodded his head.

"Aye, sir!" said Sean, and he returned to his post, though not before another quick glance upward. Quinn was once again looking at the shoreline.

Sean returned to the stern, visibly upset as he held his breath, then let it out noisily.

"What'd he say?" asked Hicks.

"It's what he didn't say. He was looking to the shore, not all about," said Sean. "Isn't he supposed to be watching all points?"

"He is," said Hudson. "All points being everywhere *not* to shore."

Hudson knew that Quinn was being negligent in his duty, and though quite a breach of protocol for a marine sergeant to question the actions of a full lieutenant, he felt a responsibility to take action.

"As you were, boys. I will report to Captain Harrison."

As he walked away, Sean and Hicks looked at each other, worried.

"Oh my," was all they could say, knowing that this would cause a firm disagreement between Hudson and Quinn. And more than likely it would be Hudson getting the short stick.

The *Paladin* was now approaching the cove. Harrison was almost leaning over the bow anchor, glass to his eyes, peering inward. What he saw was not to his liking. The cove was small, only three hundred feet long and maybe fifty wide; the cliff walls seemed over one hundred feet high.

Jonathan returned and stood at attention next to Harrison. He cleared his throat.

"Ahem," he began.

"Report," said Harrison.

"The sail is reduced. Men in the tops awaiting commands. Alexander has men at the guns."

"Good. Good," said Harrison.

"What do you think?" Jonathan asked.

"Well, I'll tell you one thing. I'd be a fool to go in there," said Harrison as he closed his glass and moved quickly aft. "Mister Fawcett!"

"Aye, sir?"

"Bring us about and head back to Telašćica. We'll anchor off the bay there! Jonathan, have the men add all sail on the mainmast. We are leaving!"

"Harrison?" asked Jonathan.

"*Commander* Harrison, Mister Moore! Now let's attend to our duty!" Harrison called.

"But Harrison! The mission says that we are to —"

"Midshipman Moore!"

"Commander, begging your pardon. But we have an appointment to keep!"

"Jonathan!" Harrison yelled. Then, composing himself, he leaned in close to his friend and with a firm voice said softly, "First, how dare you question my order? Friends or not, I am the captain of this ship and responsible for the crew and His Majesty's vessel."

"I understand that, Captain, however —"

"And secondly!" Harrison continued, loudly, "Orders or no, this mission and all its inanity has been a comedy of errors from the start! If our contact is worth his salt, he will return to Telašćica and contact us there. Now, carry out my order!"

"Captain Harrison!" It was Hudson.

"What is it!?" snapped Harrison, expecting another officer questioning his intentions.

"Sir, pardon the intrusion," said Hudson, taken aback at the sudden outburst. "I think we are being followed. Thought we saw a sail directly aft —"

"Quinn! For all the sakes of the sinners!" called Harrison, looking up at the crow's nest. "Do you see a ship directly aft?"

As they looked upward, Harrison saw Quinn spin around and point his glass due south. After a moment, Quinn lowered his piece and leaned over the side of the basket.

"Nothing there, sir!" he called.

Harrison looked to Hudson for an explanation.

"Sir, I saw it, Hicks saw it—"

"Hicks? He can barely tie a sailor's breastplate let alone—"

"—and Flagon saw it," continued Hudson. "Beggin' your pardon. Sir."

"Follow me, the both of you!" said Harrison angrily. He continued to mutter and swear, mostly to himself, as he stomped aft. Once at the stern, he raised his glass and peered to the horizon.

"Still directly aft, sir," said Sean. "Hull is down, but sails are clear. As we were going slower now, they are having a hard time staying back."

Harrison saw, without a doubt, two tall masts with sails being taken in, the ship's hull barely visible from this distance. She was as clear as a bell, being silhouetted by the setting sun.

"Son of a gun! Can I get a crew who will do their duty?" he shouted. "Thank you, Sergeant Hudson. Get Flagon up to the crow's nest and send down Quinn before I go up there and throw him down! Moore, I want that sail let out immediately! And do *not* question me again! Fawcett! We are heading straight for those sails!"

"Yes, sir!" came the collective call.

Harrison returned to the wheel, steaming. As the *Paladin* came about and headed swiftly south, it was clear that the sighted ship was, again, the *Echo*, and she had now completed a turn to port and was fleeing.

The chase lasted nearly two hours. The evening descended, casting a dark canvas about the coast. Rain began to fall lightly as the lantern glow of Telašćica became all but invisible. With no moon to guide their way, the crew of the

Paladin could only see the faintest details of the sea about them. The foremast still being unable to support additional sail made the chase fruitless. The *Echo* had escaped.

"Jenkins, reduce all sail on the foremast and give it a rest. Mister Fawcett? Take us back to Telašćica, just outside of the deep bay, and set our bow to the southwest. Alexander, prepare to drop both anchors. I want men sleeping on their guns. Moore, set a rotation on all points. Notify me immediately if there is anything that remotely resembles a sail."

"Yes, sir," came the replies as the officers ran to perform their duty.

"And my duty?" asked Quinn.

Though almost impossible to detect color with such little light, those standing about would swear that the captain's face turned a devilish red as he responded to the lieutenant with a colorful string of similes, metaphors, allegories, expletives, and vulgar representations that boomed as loud as a sixteen-pounder. Only at the end of the performance did Harrison clearly use English when he finished with:

"In my cabin! Immediately!"

The *Paladin* sailed southeast eight miles to Telašćica. As ordered, Fawcett positioned the ship between the few islands guarding the entrance to the large bay and pointed the bow southwest. Both anchors were deployed and secured, holding the ship in position.

Alexander and Jonathan inspected the guns and set teams of three, according to watches, to each until further notice. Jenkins had the men in the tops remain at station. Deckhands manned the lines and hauled the sail to the yards, where the topmen gathered sail and used their gaskets — short pieces of rope — to secure the fabric to the yard. Those not on watch slept nearby, as best they could, on the deck and wrapped in what blankets they had to keep out the drizzling rain. The officers reminded the men belowdecks that, as a precaution, they were to sleep near the hatchways, as the captain would call at any sign of trouble.

Jonathan could see that the men were both restless and unhappy with the situation on deck. After all, he thought, they had been working extra watches since the gun accident—again his fault, and again, his pang of guilt—and they were now sleeping on the hard deck instead of their hammocks. Maybe he would check on them.

"What is going on?" asked Colin Stredney as Jonathan came by. "Seems a lot of bother over seeing the *Echo*."

"Captain Harrison feels that something is out of sorts here," said Jonathan. "No reason for the *Echo* to run, is there?"

"No, sir," came a chorus of men who were listening nearby.

"The commander has the ship and your well-being in the front of his mind," added Jonathan, "and in that order!"

This caused the men to laugh.

"She is a beautiful lady," said Graham. "He will have a plan to keep us both!"

"We will know soon enough," added Jonathan. "Stay alert, men."

Jonathan continued his tour of the main deck, checking ropes, double-checking hatches, though mostly reassuring the crew that all was being addressed. At the stern he found Hudson, Hicks, and Sean. Each had stayed at their post, each scanning the sea ahead and to their sides.

"Jonny boy," said Sean, "a little mystery we have here, don't we?"

"A mystery that you three are still on deck. Isn't your watch over?"

"It is," said Hudson.

"But we got reason ta stay on," said Hicks. "Seein' as thar's something afoot, well, 'oo could sleep anyway?"

"And, seeing that Captain Harrison is breathing fire at Lieutenant Quinn, well, it's only a matter of time before we all get called in for our share," added Hudson.

"You saw something, obviously the *Echo*, and reported it," stated Jonathan matter-of-factly.

"Aye, we did," said Sean, still gazing outward into the night.

"Then you did your duty," said Jonathan.

"But Lieutenant Quinn didn't do his," said Hudson, "and I was the one who ratted on him, Mister Moore. I have made an enemy tonight."

They all thought about the ramifications of what had happened. Quinn was supposed to be looking all about. He had missed something that three other crew members saw clearly, and they had a less-than-advantageous viewpoint. Quinn, in the crow's nest, should have seen the *Echo* clearly, and long before.

"What was he doing up there?" asked Jonathan.

"He was looking at the shoreline," answered Hudson after a short pause.

"The 'ol' time," added Hicks quickly.

Jonathan wondered what it could be that made Quinn look to the shore instead of out to sea where a threat could be. Did it have something to do with their shared secret orders?

"Harrison had told him specifically to watch for approaching ships," said Jonathan softly.

"Well, Jonny boy. Not too many ships are settin' on land, waitin' to attack us. He was looking for somethin' else I'll wager," said Sean.

"But what?" asked Jonathan.

In Harrison's cabin, a nervous Lieutenant Quinn stood before the commander and Lieutenant Alexander. Jonathan was summoned at the halfway point to also attend, though he positioned himself near the door, as far from Harrison as he could physically stand yet still be considered in attendance. He knew that there would be a few words for him specifically, having doubted Harrison's orders and questioned his plan.

The tirade aimed at Quinn was all but over, and the lieutenant looked visibly shaken. Harrison now actually took a moment to catch his breath.

"It is simply this," said Harrison in conclusion. "I expect my orders to be followed to the letter. Is that understood?"

"Yes, sir," answered Quinn meekly.

"Now that we have that issue exhausted, let me move to one more. What in heaven's name were you looking at onshore?"

Quinn looked up from the floorboards he had been staring at and seemed at a loss for words.

"Quinn?" asked Harrison again.

"Sir, I—" stammered Quinn. "I simply found it irresistible to *not* look for the cove, sir. I-it was like a puzzle, and—again, so sorry."

Harrison contemplated this. Quinn was an odd one, which was surely the case. But Harrison had met many odd fellows in His Majesty's Navy. There were several on every ship, and some were downright lunatic. Steward, for example, aboard the *Poseidon* and the *Danielle*, was regarded by many to be a good egg and able crewman, but the word *odd* didn't even begin to describe him. Hicks was also unusual. Some would even consider him as strange and base as an *American*—it was only his cockney accent that saved him from being run out of the corps.

Harrison decided that Quinn, as strange as he was, just needed more seasoning. He would be assigned light duty. Jonathan would have to step into a larger role. But now, even that seemed too much to ask. As Harrison's gaze now turned to the midshipman, he saw a young man who, for some reason, was slightly off his game. Maybe it was the new crew or the smaller ship, but Jonathan had not performed as he was certainly capable. It was not just the incident at the bow chaser, it was his questioning of orders that was completely out of sorts, not something Jonathan Moore would do. Was he fading? Was he at the end of his potential? No, it could not be that. It had to be something more. This was the boy—*a boy!*—who had foiled a French captain and found a treasure; had succeeded in cutting out his first prize, the recaptured *Drake*; and had rekindled the

Castle of Fire, turning the tide of a major battle against a superior French force. Of course, not everyone can lay golden eggs every day, Harrison reasoned. He will find his footing again, he thought.

"On to the more important matters," Harrison continued. "Does anyone wish to tell me why the *Echo* is stalking us?"

"I have given that some thought, Captain," said Alexander. He sipped some coffee and nibbled on a piece of egg that Berkeley had put into a cheesed roll. "After seeing the previous behavior of Captain Andrews, it can only be utter incompetence."

"Pardon me, sir," said Quinn softly. "I agree."

"Jonathan?" asked Harrison.

"It could have something to do with the treaty," Jonathan said. "It is an important mission, and possibly, he was sent by the Admiralty to make sure we do our duty."

They all considered this.

"With the last-minute change of orders, that could make sense," added Quinn. "Maybe that explains his odd behavior. He was told to watch us, to make sure we succeeded, but not to tell us."

"Why that part?" asked Alexander. "Why not send us both together? And why lie to us when we asked about their orders?"

"Andrews could have been told to watch and report. Not to interfere," said Jonathan. "Not to insult us by saying he was sent to keep an eye out."

"That sounds as plausible as it does preposterous," laughed Harrison.

"It *is* the *Admiralty*, sir," suggested Alexander.

That sent all, even Quinn, into laughter.

A knock came at the door.

"Beggin' yer pardon, sir," said Jenkins as he saluted the men inside.

"Jenkins?" asked Harrison.

"Sir, you might hear some gunfire from the deck,"

"Oh? Why is that?" asked the commander.

"The marines, Flagon in particular, are drilling," said Jenkins.

"Then you best take cover in here," said Harrison, laughing. "Have a treat then, plenty here!"

All laughed as Jenkins gladly accepted one of the small cakes still remaining.

"Now, onward. Regardless of the buffoonery of the *Echo* and Commander Andrews, we must complete this mission," added Harrison.

"I am sure the treaty is dearly important; otherwise, why would the king himself be so interested in its success?" asked Jonathan as he took the last remaining cake.

The room fell into silence.

"What did you say?" asked Harrison. "How do you know the king is concerned?"

Jonathan's stomach sank. How could he be so foolish? He could not tell Harrison about his meeting with Lord Wilder and Captain Spears at the pier. He was sworn to secrecy. Another gaff! he thought, but I have no choice. I must come clean.

Just as he was about to answer, Quinn spoke up.

"I was told the package I carried came from the king. I must have mentioned it to Mister Moore."

Harrison thought about this and could only shake his head.

"Is there anything else anyone knows about this mission that I do not? Speak now. Jonathan?"

His heart was beating wildly, his face was red, and he feared that Harrison knew he was lying. In a quick glance, he could see that Jenkins was staring at him. He certainly knew that Jonathan was hiding something.

"N-nothing, sir," said Jonathan.

"Blazes!" said Harrison. "I have a mind to open this treaty and see for myself what this is all about!"

"Sir, that would break the seal and invalidate the dispatch," offered Quinn.

"I realize that!" snapped Harrison. "And now, we

have missed our meeting with our contact in that godforsaken cove!"

Harrison stood and began to pace. Then he was reminded of the fact that there was little room to do proper pacing in such a small area. He would have had Streen, the carpenter, already building him a private locker somewhere outside his cabin, but the foremast had taken all of the man's time. An area large enough to hold all he had in his locker and chest would clear several square feet, giving him room to think. After a minute, he turned to his officers.

"We will sail up the bay to the village and anchor. Quinn, you will then come with me into town in the morning. We will take a small complement of marines and some of the newer deckhands with us and see if we can scare up our contact. I assume the townspeople will see all the uniforms, and word will get out quickly that we are ashore."

"Yes, sir," said Quinn.

"Lieutenant Alexander," Harrison continued. "You and Mister Moore are to stay with the ship and the treaty. We are at peace—at least we were when we departed England."

"If we see the *Echo*, sir?" asked Alexander.

"If she reappears, signal with three guns. I will return immediately."

"Jenkins, first thing in the morning, send in Streen!" the commander said. "Dismissed!"

The crew spent an uncomfortable night on deck, but once the sun came up, all activity seemed to return to regularity. Crews were ordered to secure the guns and to string hammocks in place belowdecks, allowing those off duty to spend a few well-earned hours in sleep. Jenkins was ordered to take a small party into town to see about fresh water, food, and supplies. Upon his return, Berkeley, with the assistance of Boston, began preparing the over two hundred eggs that had been purchased. Supplemented with some thick slices of fresh bread, the men welcomed the only hot meal they had eaten since leaving London.

Fawcett piloted the *Paladin* five miles north into the bay toward Telašćica under only the main topgallants. Unlike the tall and foreboding cliffs they had seen as they searched for the cove, the mainland about the jade-colored bay was comprised of gently rising and falling hills, populated with lush scrub and dark-trunked trees in various shades of green. White rock outcroppings accented the area, matching the few small and rocky beaches. As beautiful as the men found this place, Fawcett knew that sailing these unknown waters could be dangerous; reefs and submerged boulders were visible just a fathom or so under the crystal-clear water. He concentrated mightily, and using lookouts on all points, attempted to avoid disaster. Several islands within the bay interrupted his direct course. They rose from the emerald-green water, appearing as gently sloping mounds of white rock and sparse scrub, some as tall as three hundred feet and spreading possibly twice that in diameter.

At the northernmost point of the bay lay the town of Telašćica. Several white, stone-walled houses lined the waterfront, and farther inland other simpler houses and huts dotted the hillsides. The inhabitants had seen the *Paladin* approaching and had prepared a mooring for her in the deep water alongside the outer edge of the long pier.

"No mooring there," instructed Harrison. "Fawcett, we will sit nicely in the center of the bay. Jenkins, attend to sails. Topgallants furled and anchor at the ready."

His orders carried out to the letter, Harrison returned to his cabin. Shortly, Streen appeared as requested, with hat in hand. A personal request from the captain was a chance to shine, to gain favor, and many of the crew would give a right arm to be awarded such a chance.

"Ah! Streen!" said Harrison still in a sour mood. "Just the man I want to see."

"Yes, sir," said Streen. "What kin I do for ya, sir?"

"Well, I need space," said Harrison, chewing on his eggs and biscuits.

"Space?" asked Streen. He usually *used* space, not created it. He was confused.

"I need a place to store some things that now take up space in my chest and locker, and I want them out of here, so I will have more *space*."

"Hmm," said Streen, looking at the cramped room. "A cap'n *does* need ta pace—we all know that."

"Exactly! You catch my meaning then," said Harrison.

"I could get a few o' the bigger 'ands, and we could move the chest 'n locker down ta the lower deck. That would do, wouldn't it, sir?"

Harrison frowned as he gulped down a little coffee and then shook his head.

"Almost, Streen. I want the items close by, where I can get to them quickly. I can't be stomping down to the lower deck every time I need something."

"Yes, sir," said Streen, now concerned that he was not pleasing the captain. He certainly was correct: a captain can't be stomping down ladders all day. Maybe...

"Sir? If I may?"

"Of course, Streen. An idea?" asked Harrison.

"Yes, sir. Thar's a space next to the ladder right outside yer door. I could *thin* the ladder out just a bit, maybe an inch or so, and then remove a plank in the side bulkhead. Then, I could add a thin door 'n a lock to it, seal it up on the inside. That would give ya 'bout the same room as yer chest there, but sideways. Maybe a little more?"

"A lock, you said?" asked Harrison.

Smiling, Streen just nodded.

"See to it then!" said Harrison, now almost happy. "And I thank you, Streen."

"My absolute pleasure, sir," said Streen. "Might be a bit o' noise fer a while, though."

"Not an issue, my good man," said Harrison. "Carry on!"

After finishing a lonely breakfast in his cabin, Harrison emerged, mustered his shore party at the gangway, and boarded the jolly. The short rowing exercise brought them to the town's pier, and from there, the party proceeded into town. In a most flamboyant manner, they immediately began attracting attention by laughing loudly, speaking to any who happened by, and generally being seen.

14

Two Letters

The excitement in the Bracknell home was at a level so high, it seemed that some extraordinary event of unexpected delight and good fortune had been bestowed upon all three Dowdeswell girls at the same time. They squealed in joy, especially Penelope and Rebecca, and ran through the mansion alerting Lady and Lord Bracknell, the servants, the cook, and the valets to the news that not one, not two, but *three* letters had arrived from the Admiralty. Each one had been addressed to one of the young ladies: Penelope had a letter from none other than Marine Private Sean Flagon, Rebecca one from Commander Thomas Harrison, and Delain received a special correspondence from Midshipman Jonathan Moore.

"Let us read them to each other!" shouted Rebecca as the girls retreated to their bedroom suite.

"Oh, Yes! What a wonderful idea!" said Penelope. "It will be triple the pleasure!"

"Delain?" asked Rebecca. "Surely you will read yours aloud!"

"You are quite *incorrect*, dear sisters," said Delain. "My correspondence is my own. Keep your torrid love letters to yourselves, and we will each keep our own secrets. It may make your lives more exciting that way."

Rebecca continued to plead, goad, coerce, and finally, threaten, but Delain held her ground. Finally, to get some small measure of peace, she retreated to the confines of the horse stables and sat on a bale of hay to read in private. The Airedales were present, rooting about in the dark shadows, chasing some small rodent, or worse, and eventually capturing it. Delain tried her best to ignore their gruesome activities.

At times, she could hear squeaks of delight coming from inside the home — and giddy laughter. She was happy for her sisters. Nothing could please her more than the thought of Thomas Harrison and Rebecca becoming betrothed. Additionally, the idea that Sean Flagon had taken an interest in her younger sister was at least entertaining — especially since Sean mostly concerned himself with Jonathan, his marine uniform, eating, and sleeping.

And though Delain's heart was beating considerably faster than normal, she tried to contain her excitement as she opened her letter. Looking at the envelope as she proceeded, Delain could see many postmarks on the outside: one from Gibraltar, another from the Canary Islands, one from Chatham, and the final from London, with the Admiralty stamp clear and bold, almost covering her name. Taking out the letter, she began to read.

April the eighth, 1802
Gibraltar Station
HMS Paladin

Bracknell Estate
Hampstead, England

To Miss Delain Dowdeswell, Adventurer

I hope this letter finds you well. I will tell you that you are missed, and I look forward to my return. Hopefully you will find some time in your busy schedule to enjoy ice cream and possibly a picnic in the park?
The Paladin *has acquired a small deck gun from the* Drake, *courtesy of Captain Blake, his gift to Harrison for capturing a ship for his use. I told Sean that for such a small, dainty gun, it has a sharp tongue and can certainly leave a mark if fired. I suggested that it reminded us of someone we all know, and also that*

we name it "The Stowaway" in your honor. Commander Harrison agreed.

Unfortunately, as I am embarrassed to say, the gun and I committed a grievous error, and due to a malfunction, the gun severely damaged our foremast, and she is hindering our progress. My fault for not inspecting it. Needless to say, I am straining my relationship with Thomas Harrison.

One bright spot, at least a cause for laughter, is Sean's and the crew's insistence on following and believing in the most ridiculous rituals and superstitions. It is quite maddening, actually, and the only person benefiting from all this is Stewie, the cat. One such belief is that cats are lucky, and to keep that luck, one must keep them well fed. He is now quite portly.

We encountered our sister ship Echo today as we approached Gibraltar. She is almost as beautiful as the Paladin, though second place is all I can convince myself of in this matter. It was a strange encounter as its new commander, Captain Andrews, was peculiar in that no one knew of him except for Quinn, our new lieutenant. The Echo crew seemed like novices, but then again, I am used to serving exclusively on only the finest ships in His Majesty's fleet, so any common ship is not up to my standards (humor). As with all things nautical, I am not sure when we will return, but hopefully, soon.

Thoughts of my family and of course, you, keep me in good spirits, and I anxiously await our reunion.

Your friend and coconspirator,
Midshipman Jonathan Moore, HMS Paladin.

The next morning, Delain had the unfortunate responsibility of attending school. Tedious, deskbound and repetitive, the classes were more than tiresome. All this she could learn from her own reading, she thought. Of course, the etiquette lessons were sheer torture, and only by exaggerating her movements, diction, and posture to try the patience of her teachers could she remain sane.

When the day's classes were complete, Delain purposefully walked to the office of Master Franklin, the history and language professor. He was the only tolerable instructor of Delain's, and he was quite fond of her, mostly because he fancied himself a writer, as well as other lofty titles. He had approached Delain to propose he act as a possible author of a book based on her experiences aboard the *Danielle* and subsequent role in the Battle of Fire. Delain humored him, and from time to time, spent a few moments telling her tale. Unlike Harrison, her embellishments were few. However, she was visiting him for some other reason. She needed his expertise in languages.

His office was large, containing an old wooden desk and chairs; racks of strange oddities from around the known world; and books, books, and more books, towering higher and higher on surrounding shelves and tables.

Franklin sat at his desk, his slight frame bent over some volume, his countenance frowning and firm, nose inches from the pages, murmuring to himself as he studied. Noticing Delain, he immediately lit up in a huge smile, exposing a full set of slightly yellowed teeth.

"Miss Dowdeswell! How wonderful to see you!"

"A pleasure as always, Master Franklin," she replied. "I hope I am not interrupting anything?"

"No, no, no," Franklin said, rising from his chair and setting another to the side of his desk for her.

"Please sit down. May I offer you some tea? My assistant has just brought me a fresh pot."

"That would be most welcome," Delain said.

"Sugar and cream?" asked Franklin, as he moved to a small side table to prepare her cup.

"Just cream," said Delain. "Lately I have been advised to grow up, become a lady, and the addition of sugar seems…childlike."

Franklin laughed. "And who told you that?"

"A friend," said Delain. She wondered at that moment if she and Barbara remained friends, especially after Delain had insulted her during the ride home from the Wilders. Though holding different views from her own about living as a woman in today's world, she missed her time with the extremely likable woman and knew that sooner or later, she must make amends.

"So shall we begin our book writing?" asked Master Franklin. "I was thinking of a title — it helps me set the right frame of mind, not only for me, the writer, but for the prospective reader. I was thinking of *The Adventures of Delain Dowdeswell*, and the volume would be called *Voyages at Sea*.

"It is too long a title, don't you think?" suggested Delain.

"Hmm," muttered Franklin. "Do you really think so?"

"Before we begin," said Delain, changing the subject, "I have a favor to ask."

"Of course, Miss Dowdeswell," said the teacher.

"I have in my possession something from one of my...adventures."

"Indeed?" asked Franklin, now visibly excited. "Is this a new adventure?"

Delain thought for a moment, then smiled.

"Master Franklin, there could be a second book in the making, and it all depends on your assistance in my...investigation!"

"Investigation? A second adventure? How may I be of assistance?"

He was now hooked, and Delain knew he would assist her willingly. Eventually, she would need to actually give him detailed information of her past adventures, and though that was the unwritten agreement between them, Delain had not concluded that being the subject of a book would be in her best interests. For now, she would play along.

She reached into her pocket and produced a folded piece of paper.

"I found a letter in a curious place, and it seems to have been written in a foreign language, or a code of some sort. Knowing that you speak several languages, I thought possibly you could translate it for me?"

He smiled as he set the cup of tea down before her.

Delain handed her copy of the letter to Franklin. Gazing at it, he muttered a few words as he returned to the desk.

"Yes...um-hum...yes...Yes, it is Russian," he said as he scanned his finger across the lines.

"Russian?" said Delain. That was a surprise. Though nothing really should have surprised her about the letter. "Can you read it to me?"

"Yes...and no," answered Franklin. "I only am partially familiar with Russian though...and some of the passages are a little strange."

"Can you try?"

Franklin smiled once again and then concentrated on the text.

"Dear L. W." He paused, reading ahead.

L. W.? thought Delain. Surely that was Lord Wilder.

Scratching his head, Franklin continued. "Um...It...has been...a long time since we have...corresponded. I...hope? Yes, I *hope*...all is well with you. I...understand you have...successfully finished the job of...no, *task* of delivering the artwork to...my gallery, and I am sure...you will be pleased...to know that...the order was received in perfect condition. I noticed...eighteen pieces, short of the twenty-four or thirty-six you had promised, however...the gallery manager is quite satisfied. Please...accept? No, please *see* the payment for...the delivery. In addition...I understand the second delivery will be late, and I cannot express my dissatisfaction. I will...of course...default to your better ...judgment."

Franklin paused. "I am not sure if my translation is perfect here, my dear, though it is clear this letter is referring to artwork and a gallery of some sort."

"Yes," said Delain, slightly disappointed. She was hoping the letter would reveal some highly sensitive international spy network, or a plot to assassinate a duke or the king of Prussia, or even a simple murder-for-hire scenario. It seemed that Lord Wilder was simply buying artwork and selling it.

But no, that couldn't be all, she thought. Why so secretive about that? Many art dealers worked in London, and none needed to have payment delivered by mysterious Black Riders that hide money and invoices in bookcases.

"Is that all?" asked Delain.

"Yes, just a salutation at the end," said Franklin, looking back to the letter. "Something like 'May God be with you,' and then a single Cyrillic letter *K*."

After meeting with her sisters in the school library, the Dowdeswell girls were escorted home by Steward, who entertained them with his somewhat off-color renditions of sea chanteys, though Delain could only wonder about the translation of her letter. Was the Black Rider "K"? Or did "K" write the letter, and the horseman was simply a delivery man? Somehow, this needed to be discerned, and then possibly she could understand what involvement Lord Wilder had in all this. It was a tough problem, and she certainly needed more information, more clues. Then the answer struck her like a bolt of lightning. Her old naturalist teacher, Mister Tupper, had always told her that to find the true answer to a problem, one must get as close to the evidence as possible—not to settle for hearsay or conjecture. One must add new evidence and facts until the only possible conclusion had to be the right one. Delain now realized that she had some clues but not enough. And there was only one way to acquire more information.

15
A Charming Scar

There were more than a few ways to steal a ship from an enemy. The most popular method was to meet the "chase" in battle, so named for the fact that it was the ship being chased. If attempting to take a merchant or other un-armed vessel, one could simply catch her, show weapons aimed at the prey or her crew, and reach a peaceful settle-ment. If the prize was a war vessel, unless grossly outnum-bered by the attacker's guns, there was a battle, continuing until one ship surrendered, signaled by the taking down, or "striking," the loser's colored flag.

Yet, another version was to sneak up on a ship in port or at anchor, and with a superior force, board her, take her from her mooring, and dispose of the original crew over-board. Sometimes, if a large crew was required, the new "owners" would attempt to convince some of the original crew to stay on as hands. It was surprising how many agreed to switch their allegiance to a new nation; the pay usually remained the same, and sometimes the treatment of the crew was improved.

This last method was called "cutting out," and Ni-komed Aggar had completed this successfully with the *Echo*. He had hoped to repeat the performance with the *Paladin*; however, Commander Harrison was not as willing to enter the cove as Lieutenant Gray had been. Aggar had re-mained on the *Echo*, ready to block the *Paladin*'s escape through the entrance. He had deposited a complement of his men in their positions on the rim of the cove's high cliff walls, where they stood and watched the graceful ship sail past. Additionally, Aggar had received the report from the shore party that the previous occupants of the cove — Gray and company—had been found in a shallow grave, but the question remained: Who had dug the grave? Some of the crew must have survived. More than likely, a fishing vessel rescued these few, or they had tried to swim to freedom, most likely drowning in the attempt, the high cliff walls unforgiving and impossible to climb for miles in either direction of the cove. If they had escaped and returned to England, then possibly they could report that their vessel had been taken; but for the English Navy to locate Aggar? A possibility, however, a remote one. The *Echo* would undergo modifications that would make here almost unidentifiable.

Either way, the *Paladin* and her commander had not taken the bait. Aggar wondered why they had given up on the mission so easily. He needed to quickly devise another plan, slightly bolder than the first.

He would simply cut out the *Paladin* when it moored in the small bay at Telašćica.

As he stood atop a small rise just out of the town, he and his party, forty-seven in all, remained in the shadows of a small group of pine trees that crested the hill. The day was bright, and through the leaves and thorny branches they could not be seen in the shadows, though in this position they commanded an excellent view of the town and small natural harbor below.

The inhabitants of the town could be seen moving about, conducting business in a slow and peaceful manner. Most of the village's commerce pertained to fishing, boating, or even larger trade with the mainland city of Zadar to the east, or with San Marino, just across the Adriatic to the west in Italy. It was rare that business would be conducted with any sailing ships of the various navies that found their way to Telašćica; however, it was certainly a welcome and profitable opportunity when it occurred. Sailors could easily purchase and load fresh water, simple meats like salted fish, maybe some eggs, and a chicken or two. Flour was also easy to find, and of course olives, limes, grapes, and even wine when available.

Today, there was only one ship in the bay: HMS *Paladin*. The crew was conducting business, sending men ashore to obtain supplies. And each group that came and went was being closely watched by Aggar. He was counting them, assigning a number to what he believed to be the complement of men aboard.

"I see three more leaving. That reduces their number to sixty-seven men aboard," Aggar said to Kowalski.

"Have any officers departed?"

"No," continued Aggar. "Though…I do see three or more at the plank. They might be preparing to leave. Yes, it is the young captain, and one of his lieutenants. Ah! Also two marines as well! Good! Good! I believe the odds are now in our favor. Prepare the men."

Aboard the *Paladin*, Commander Harrison and his small crew readied themselves to descend the plank and march into town.

"I have added Crump and Crystal to the group," reported Hudson.

"No duty for them aboard?" asked Harrison. "I thought they were assisting Streen."

"Nonessential at this point," continued Hudson. "Honestly, sir, they are mostly taking up space and food, in my opinion. Even Streen asked if we could keep them out of his way."

"Then we shall use them to fill out our party," said Harrison. "I am sure they can make noise and be noticed."

"One can only hope," answered the marine.

It could not go unnoticed by Quinn, who now joined the shore party as they descended the plank, that Crump and Crystal were now part of the detail. Wondering if he should question the commander, he settled on the safer route and asked Hudson.

"Lieutenant, it's customary," answered the sergeant. "All nonessential crew, meaning those who are basically new and untrained, are fit for this duty. No knots to tie or shrouds to climb, eh? Just walk the streets and be noticed."

Quinn nervously nodded his head and settled into the group. He gave a quick glance to Crump and Crystal that seemed to convey some meaning, though Hudson could not ascertain the purpose.

Still aboard the ship, on the lower deck, Jonathan Moore began dressing for duty. His uniform coat he brushed and plucked, trying to concentrate on picking assorted foreign particles from the dark fabric. Unable to actually wash the coat, it was his only choice.

"G-day to ya, Mister Moore," said Jenkins as he approached.

"Good day to you, Jenkins," said Jonathan.

"Hmm…" said Jenkins as he beheld the midshipman and then inspected the coat. He began assisting in the primping process.

"Pretty little town, Telašćica, isn't it? The color of the water is like a shiny gem. Jade possibly, from China."

"Quite picturesque," said Jonathan. Then he smiled.

"I was 'ere years ago," continued Jenkins. "Had a few days' leave. Not much ta do in such a small place. Well, if ya can't find trouble, sometimes trouble can find you, I always say."

Jonathan nodded.

"I was 'ere with the *Snake*, a pretty little brig, if I must say so. Just a deckhand at the time, but I showed promise, and the captain took a likin' to me."

"Is that how you got your start?" asked Jonathan.

Jenkins smiled. "No, I was long started by then. Joined the navy at age eleven. Thought I'd see the world. Telašćica was one part of it."

"Who was your captain?" asked Jonathan.

"Captain Jeffrey Edwards, though now he is Admiral Edwards. He was a popular captain at the time — well liked, yet very by the book. He gave me orders to go into town and get a few bottles of wine for the officers when we were 'ere. Simple enough."

"A pleasant memory then?" asked Jonathan as he began chalking the silver lining of his jacket to cover the darker stains and scrapes.

"No, no, not really," said Jenkins.

"What happened then?" asked Jonathan. "I assume you have a point to this story."

"Maybe. Maybe I don't," said Jenkins, continuing picking lint off the jacket. "The wine was easy to find. I purchased a dozen bottles and was returning to the ship when a young lieutenant met me about 'alfway back to the pier. He suggested that I give 'im a bottle and tell the captain that all the money could afford was 'leven bottles."

"That's stealing," said Jonathan.

"Punishable by death under some captains," added Jenkins. "But what could I do? If I disobeyed the lieutenant, well, there would be hell to pay for as long as we served together. If I gave 'im a bottle, and the captain found out, well... "

"What did you do?" asked Jonathan, now concerned.

"I gave the bottle to the lieutenant. Then I brooded over it. For a long time. And you know what 'appened, Mister Moore?"

Jonathan shook his head as he gave the coat a final inspection.

"I couldn't do my duty. So once we got back to England, I requested a transfer, and when Captain Edwards asked why, well..."

"Well what?" said Jonathan anxiously.

"That's not important. What is important is that I made a mistake, then more mistakes, but eventually, it all passed." Jenkins looked to the deck and squinted his eyes as if looking for something in particular. "Now, well, I think I did all right. Never became an officer, never even 'ad a chance until now. It looks bad if ya leave a ship under somewhat questionable circumstances. My career, as humble as it may 'ave turned out, could 'ave been lost. I should have told the captain everything. At least I could 'ave said I did the right thing."

Jonathan knew that Jenkins had figured out exactly what was going on. He had seen Jonathan's reaction to the lie he told in Harrison's cabin, and more than likely, he had previously seen Jonathan speaking to Spears and Lord Wilder before they left England. Nothing got past Jenkins.

He thought about the story and felt pity for Jenkins. He was well respected, a fine teacher, and hopefully, soon an acting warrant officer aboard a small ship. If his career had not been cut off by this unfortunate incident, what height could Jenkins have attained in His Majesty's Navy? Maybe a lieutenant? A captain?

But his story was not for the purpose of pity. It was for the benefit of Jonathan Moore.

"Thank you, Jenkins," Jonathan said. He hugged the man.

"Not at all," said Jenkins, shocked yet happy at the sign of affection.

"I will need to speak with Captain Harrison as soon as he returns. I will tell him—"

"Moore! Jenkins!" came the call from above. "There you are!" said Alexander as he popped his head down the hatch.

"Sir," they replied.

"Ah. Spa-*len*-did!" said Alexander. "Not sure why you *Danis* articulate the word in that manner; however, I have taken a liking to it and will employ the pronunciation when appropriate."

"That would be…spa-*len*-did, sir," said Jonathan.

"Ah! Good! Spa-*len*-did," Alexander said. Still mostly on deck, yet leaning down the ladder a bit to converse, he continued, "Now, Captain Harrison and Lieutenant Quinn have gone ashore on their scouting mission. Mister Moore, once dressed, would you tour the deck and make sure all men are keeping an eye out?"

"Yes, Lieutenant," Jonathan said.

"Spa-*len*-did!" said Alexander, smiling.

A commotion at the plank interrupted their conversation, and Alexander turned his head. A gunshot was heard.

Alarmed, Jonathan donned his coat and grabbed his sword. Jenkins rushed to the bottom of the ladder.

Alexander turned his head back to Jonathan, a queer look appearing on his face. He broke into a strange smile as blood began to trickle out from behind his teeth. He coughed, then fell, partially blocking the hatchway.

"Lieutenant!" cried Jenkins.

"Help me!" said Jonathan, and they climbed the ladder and pushed Alexander aside, allowing him to slide to the deck.

Once above, Jonathan and Jenkins took in the scene. At the plank, they could see Hicks wrestling with a hooded man. His adversary had his skin coaled black to hide his features. Immediately behind them came seven or more men dressed and disguised similarly. Some had pistols. They fired upon the crewmen nearby.

Jonathan and Jenkins rushed to the fray. As they reached the fight, an intruder emerged from the melee and fired a single shot. It struck the plank next to Jonathan's head. Splinters flew as he shut his eyes and winced. A splinter lodged in his forehead, and though not a large wound, blood began to flow.

Another invader turned and pointed his weapon at Jonathan. Before he could fire, a small hand ax sailed through the air with a *whoosh* and struck him in the chest. He fell.

Jonathan turned to see Jenkins, still in throwing position.

"Attend to your duty, Mister Moore!" With that, Jenkins ran to the bell, which he repeatedly rang.

"To arms! To arms!" Jonathan called. "We are being boarded! To the port side!"

The crew of the *Paladin* answered within seconds, the remaining marines quickly firing upon the intruders, yet more appeared on the plank, rushing aboard. *Paladins* streamed from belowdecks, sword against sword, hand, tooth, and nail; the fight was on. And rising above the battle, commanding the men to positions, alerting them to threats, was Jonathan Moore—not the recently timid boy, unsure of himself and embarrassed by his mistakes and white lies, but the one who had performed superbly time and time again. Without conscious calculation, he attacked with relentless fury. Next to him was Jenkins, the old salt, thrusting and parrying like a young champion. The two of them called to others to keep up the fight, man the rails to stop others from boarding, and help the wounded.

Aggar was there, face also coaled, pistol empty, but sword being unsheathed. Seeing Jonathan leading the English sailors caused Aggar to pause and watch in astonishment.

Leading at such a young age? he thought. Amazing!

The Russian knew that to succeed, he must cut off the head of the resistance—this young boy. He was leading his men, shouting encouragement, and most of all, dispatching Aggar's men over the side and forcing them to run off the planks to escape.

"*Svoloch!*" he yelled, and he rushed at the boy.

It was difficult to see this young man clearly, as the battle was upon them, and, confound him, he was moving fast, ducking, weaving, and even at one point in the rigging, beating down his enemies. Astonishingly, Aggar saw the youngster dispatch several men with just his swordplay. Some were run through, others beaten skillfully to the rail, where they simply jumped overboard to escape injury or death. Finally, Aggar reached him. The boy's face was almost completely covered in blood. Was it his own or from the many wounded about the deck? His hat was still on his head—it too covered in blood.

"You little *ublyudok!*" yelled Aggar. "This ship is mine! Strike your colors, or I will have you as well as your ship!"

Jonathan stared at the man. Trying to blink away the fluid that was seeping into his eyes, the boy faked a retreat by a small step to his rear, then an immediate double lunge of almost unbelievable distance. Becoming airborne for a moment, his blade was trained at the heart of his enemy. Aggar missed the parry slightly. Jonathan's point pierced deep into the man's shoulder. Aggar staggered backward, gasping in pain. The boy continued his attack. Aggar tried to parry, again and again, and was successful — until he had his back to the gangway, with only a full retreat as an option.

"Where did you learn to fight like this?" demanded Aggar.

"On the streets of London!" shouted Jonathan.

"Retreat!" yelled Aggar, and his men began to run off the ship, some diving into the water, others rushing off the gangway. He knew that the British had carried the day. In anger, he lunged at Jonathan. The tip of the Russian's blade seemed to cut the young midshipman in the shoulder — but only his coat was sliced. Jonathan parried another thrust, then, as quick as lightening, flicked the tip of his blade at Aggar's face. The point caught the man's right cheek, opening a slanted cut to his lower edge of his eye. Blood slowly seeped from the wound.

"You little brat!" yelled Aggar, grabbing at the wound. "You will pay for this!"

"Send me an invoice! Until then, get — off — my — ship!" Jonathan said forcefully and leaped to the yardarm above him, swinging his legs forward to kick the shocked Aggar forcefully in the chest, sending him toppling over backward down the gangway to land on the hard planks of the pier.

After a moment, Aggar stood, shook off his pain, bowed to Jonathan, and ran off into the town.

"They are gone, Mister Moore," said Jenkins. "Orders?"

Jonathan, panting with exhaustion, wiping the blood from his eyes ineffectively, watched the attackers flee, then turned slowly to Jenkins.

"Mister Moore?" repeated Jenkins as he inspected the wound above the boy's eyes.

Jonathan looked downward at the deck of the *Paladin*. Several men lay wounded, already being attended to by their crewmates. Blood pooled on the planks and literally ran through the scuppers. The ship, the beautiful *Paladin*, looked like a slaughterhouse. It must be cleaned before Harrison returns, he thought. She is in no condition to be called the pride of His Majesty's Navy.

Blood dripped from his midshipman's jacket, and he quickly took it off, in a panic, as he thought of the grizzly condition of the thing. It dropped to the deck.

Jenkins held a piece of cloth, probably from his own clothing, to the wound on Jonathan's forehead.

Jonathan's eyes then rested upon a form lying near his feet. It was Alexander. He could only think how unbelievable this all was. A moment before, Alexander was smiling and alive. Now, he was gone.

"Mister Moore," Jenkins said softly. "Jonathan? Now is the time to take command."

"T-take command?" Jonathan said, still looking at the body.

"Yes. You are the ranking officer," Jenkins said as he placed a firm hand on the boy's shoulder.

"You, Jenkins—you should command."

"No, Mister Moore. I have no warrant, not yet," said Jenkins.

"B-but I am only a midshipman," Jonathan replied, still bewildered.

"But you are *our* midshipman," said Jenkins softly. "Orders, sir?"

Jonathan's mind raced. Again, he felt almost dizzy. He was now, even if only temporarily, the commander of the *Paladin*. Where was Harrison? Didn't he know what was happening? Could he have seen the battle? Then he realized.

"The guns! Jenkins, the guns!"

"Aye?" said Jenkins, nodding. "The guns."

"Fire three shots in succession. Alert Captain Harrison!"

"Aye, sir!" said Jenkins, managing a smile as he ran below to prepare the signal.

"Garvey, Southcott! Jones! Hoist the anchors!" Jonathan called. "Mister Fawcett!"

"Aye, sir?"

"Are you well?" asked Jonathan.

"A slight scrape on the arm, but nothing that will stop the likes of me. Maybe a glass of ale would help—a porter possibly, or—"

"Later, Fawcett! Position the ship at the mouth of the bay, bow to the east. I don't want any more action so close in."

"Aye, sir," said Fawcett.

"Bowman! Get the men in the tops! I need topgallants set immediately, and prepare to set all sail at my command."

"But, sir!" said Bowman, "what of Captain Harrison? Shouldn't we wait for him?"

"Confound it, man!" exploded Jonathan. "If I wanted your opinion I'd give it to you! Now carry out my orders, you—"

A light string of colorful metaphors and descriptive adjectives describing and comparing Bowman to various beasts of burden escaped Jonathan's mouth as the men ran to their duties.

Though busy, all within earshot turned to see this new little dragon trying out his flames for the first time. Some smiled.

"Sorry, sir!" was all that Bowman could manage as he scurried away to perform his duty.

"Golly!" said Welty. "I guess Mister Moore is ready for command. Not exactly the fire 'n brimstone we get from the likes of Cap'n Harrison, but a sparky lit'le flame all the same!"

"And I am still singed!" replied Bowman, smiling slightly.

Jonathan ran to Hicks, who still lay on the deck. Hands were attending to him, but he was shaking his head, trying to push them away.

"I'm all right!" he slurred. "Just a bit taken aback."

Three guns exploded in succession off the starboard stern. It was Jenkins, sending the signal to Captain Harrison.

"Hicks, can you get a boat into the water?" Jonathan asked. "Station it just to the side of the stern, and await the shore parties."

"Aye, Mister Moore. But, beggin' yer pardon, why not hold the *Paladin* close in and wait for Cap'n Harrison?"

"I want the ship out of danger and ready to move if another attempt is made! We can do nothing if we sit here all tied up! Now, move!"

"Yes, sir!" said Hicks, as he was helped to his feet. Quickly, he gathered available crew and soon had the jolly boat in the water.

Jonathan ran to the rail and, with his sword, cut the lines that moored the ship to the pier. Immediately, the *Paladin* began to move. He ran amidships and saw the plank fall into the water. Jenkins was waiting for him at the rail.

"To the helm, Mister Moore? A captain's place is there, so he can see all about him, see all the men at their duty."

"I am well aware of that fact, Jenkins."

"Then why do your feet move as if in tar?" Jenkins asked.

Jonathan knew the answer. It was unthinkable that at the age of only fourteen, after only two years of service, he was acting commander of a Royal Navy vessel, and the *Paladin* at that. He felt unready, uncomfortable, and mostly, unworthy.

"I am making it there, Jenkins, at my own speed," he managed.

"Aye, *Captain*," Jenkins said.

"That is not helping," retorted Jonathan. "I don't feel like a captain."

"Nonetheless, ya are," said Jenkins, "at least for a few more moments. Sir."

"I know," said Jonathan, now taking a deep, well-earned breath.

"I am sure you also know that one is to retrieve the

plank *before* cutting the lines?" the man said, pointing to the floating plank as the ship pulled away.

Jonathan laughed. "Touché, Jenkins. I guess that was not an 'A' grade for my first duty as commander."

"Hmm. I see," said Jenkins, contemplating the events that had just transpired. "If someone was asking me to evaluate the performance, I'd say it was a high 'B,' Mister Moore. A very high 'B.' Your fighting, well, that was certainly an 'A.' Well done."

Jonathan managed a thin smile. "Then let us man the guns with whatever crew we have available," he added. "Just to be sure."

"Aye, sir," said Jenkins, smiling. "Just to be sure."

16
Abduction

"My dear, an exquisite dinner. Bravo," commented Lord Wilder as he placed his fork neatly down on the edge of his plate. He and Alina had enjoyed a fine meal of roasted pork crusted with pepper and sea salt and glazed with honey. Accompanied by a tart lemon and white wine dressing for his mixed green salad, the Wilders also finished two small loaves of crusty baked bread with rosemary and creamy butter. Served on their fine china and within the formal dining room, they seemed to be, finally, dining like royalty.

"I am pleased you enjoyed it, dear," said Lady Wilder, "though it is not as if I had much to do with it. I hired a new cook today."

"A new cook?" asked Lord Wilder. "I thought we had discussed this, my dear. Our finances are improving, however, we must be careful—"

"I know dear; however, she was a *present*, actually. My uncle wanted to do something nice for my birthday, and he has paid for her through the end of the year. Isn't that wonderful?"

"Yes," commented Lord Wilder. He was somewhat taken aback, as he did not feel like accepting charity at this time.

The cook, a Mrs. Morgan, entered the room and took their plates away. "Mum," she said, addressing Lady Wilder. "The dessert is ready. You asked to bring it in yourself."

."Ah! Yes! Thank you, Mrs. Morgan."

"Dessert?" said Lord Wilder to the empty chair his wife recently occupied.

This was unexpected. He couldn't remember when last they had such luxuries. His current state of affairs had improved yet was not quite back to full health. Previously, he had feared that Alina was dissatisfied with him as a provider. After all, she was a lady, and he, a lord.

The estate where they now resided was part of his inheritance, passed to him, the only child. And the fortune that came with it was not paltry, if a fortune could ever be considered so; however, it was also not vast.

Years ago, as a bachelor, all was well, and his investments made modest profits. His accountant and bankers did quite well, maybe a little better for themselves than for their employer.

Things changed for both the better and the worse on his fortieth birthday: he met the vibrant and charming woman who became his wife. Alina was almost twelve years younger than he, though that didn't appear to matter; they fell in love. This was as unexpected and almost as unexplainable to Lord James Wilder, for he believed she was too beautiful, too proper, and slightly more refined than he deserved.

The downside came financially. Almost immediately after his marriage, every business venture had more of a downside than ever before, and each circumstance ended with a loss of his investment. Now, he had amassed considerable debt, and there seemed to be no way to solvency, save selling the estate.

Enter Seeja Orvislat, the son of the Russian Ambassador. He offered to assist Lord Wilder financially if the nobleman would support the most important British and Russian cause: stopping Napoleon. More than excited to assist his king, Wilder agreed, and though he asked for no compensation, Orvislat insisted, and Wilder, after some minor resistance, capitulated. The first payment had just come; he saw the receipt from Baxter's, announcing the deposit of one thousand pounds in his account.

Lady Wilder soon returned with two small dishes, each containing a cherry tart. She placed one in front of her husband, and took one to her seat for herself.

"Cherry tart!" she said. "Delicious, I am sure. Mrs. Morgan got them from the baker, but she added a few ingredients—secrets, she swears. Then she baked them again, with a drop of sherry for moisture."

"Secrets?" said Lord Wilder, laughing slightly.

"Yes!" answered Lady Wilder. She took a bite, slowly savoring it. "Ah...wonderful."

Lord Wilder watched this, and seeing the happiness on his wife's face, smiled in return and decided that scolding her for accepting a gift from her uncle would only spoil the mood.

"Please tell your uncle I am most grateful for his generosity," he said as he put his spoon into the tart.

Immediately he knew something was wrong. His plate didn't clink as his wife's did. It had a softer sound—a dull knock, almost. There was something on the bottom of the dish!

"What in the name of—" but he caught himself. It could only be a note from Orvislat. How did it get in here? he wondered. Ah! Mrs. Morgan! The new cook! She is a plant; I am sure of it! Secret ingredient indeed!

He carefully moved the tart to the side, ate a little bit here and there, and then realized he couldn't simply reach in and pull out the note, right in front of his wife. He needed a diversion. Yes, a spy, as he fancied himself, must have an entire inventory of diversions and plots to handily manipulate others.

"My dear," he said, addressing his wife. "Would you be so kind as to ask Mrs. Morgan for a little more cream for my tea? It would go so well with this amazing tart."

"Of course, dear," she said, and quickly moved to comply.

The moment she had left the dining room, Lord Wilder reached into the tart, extracted the paper, and unfolded it. He immediately made out the words "April Twentieth, Three a.m."

"Tonight!" he muttered. Why so soon? he wondered.

It had only been three days since the last meeting. Something must be wrong. Worried, he took the paper and ate it.

At eight in the evening, the Bracknell home was silent. The girls had gone to bed, Lady Bracknell had retired to her bedroom, and the lights were extinguished by the servants before they too returned to their quarters for the evening. Darkness was complete; not even a moon was out. A few stars twinkled through the cloud-veiled sky, and a slight breeze rolled quietly across the lawns.

Through this silent scene, a black-clad figure slowly walked, crouched, past the edge of the Bracknell home and made its way to the stables behind the main house. The hood of the cloak covered the figure's face almost completely, and black gloves covered its hands. Nothing was discernible, just the dark silhouette of a being moving noiselessly between darker shadows of trees and bushes.

Eventually, the figure reached the stable, opened the door with barely a creak, and then closed it behind. Only the soft sound of hay being stepped upon signaled that the figure was moving into the center of the barn. The door to *Lilliput*, the young, all-black filly, was opened, and the figure, with some effort, placed a saddle upon the beast, put the bit in the horse's mouth, and led her to the back door.

Immediately, the Airedales began to bark and whine, not in alarm, but in excitement, as if to say, "We will be going with you, yes?" Unfortunately, if they continued their mule-like baying, the plot would be foiled. The stable master would soon be investigating.

"Hush!" said Delain. "Daisy, shhhh! Daffodil, be quiet!"

The dogs paused for a moment, looked at each other, then returned to their miserable whining.

A muffled voice came from the stable master's quarters, just off the barn: "You two mutts! Keep it down in there!"

The Airedales continued.

"All right! All right, you can come!" whispered Delain as she slapped her thigh, finally exasperated. "Come on now!"

Happily, the dogs stopped their idiotic rambling and, with a few licks and nibbles at Delain's hands, they squeezed through the door as it opened and headed into the woods.

"Hopefully they disappear into the mud and gloom, chase some disgusting, furry thing, and leave me alone!" she said under her breath. Mounting the filly, she took a last look at the stable master's house to make sure she hadn't been seen, and satisfied, headed into Van Patten Wood and to the Wilders' estate.

After dinner, Lord Wilder sat by the fireside in his den, pretending to read a book that sat upon his lap. He watched the small pendulum clock sitting on the mantle. Next to him, Lady Wilder dozed restlessly.

At two in the morning, Lord Wilder patted his wife's hand and suggested she retire to their bedroom.

"What time is it?" she asked groggily.

"Almost two," he replied softly.

"You are coming to bed then?" she asked.

"I have just reached the interesting part. I will be in shortly," he said. "Good night, my dearest."

Placing a dainty peck on his cheek, Lady Wilder left her husband and went straight to bed.

After a few more minutes, Lord Wilder rose and walked silently to the bedroom to make sure his wife was fast asleep. Seeing that she was indeed, he went to his library, lit a small candle, opened the small bottom drawer in his desk, and retrieved a long black cloak. He considered it his spy attire and used it whenever he had a meeting with his contact, Orvislat. Donning the cloak, he extinguished the candle, slipped out of the library via the back door, made his way across the hedges, past the bushes about the rear of the house, and up to the small crowd of trees in front, near the lane. There, he hid in the shadows as he always did and waited.

He was not alone this evening, though he was unaware of that fact. In a clump of bushes less than twenty feet away was another cloaked figure, slightly smaller, much younger but certainly an expert at hiding her presence from many people, even a few hundred sailors that were within close quarters. Delain Dowdeswell was a master at lurking and remaining undiscovered. Here, she watched him, having tied her horse to a tree, oat bag in place, thirty or more yards away and deep in the woods. Even a snort from the beast would probably be of no concern. Not only the Wilders but also the neighbors all kept horses, and the way sound carried, a few animal utterances were not out of the ordinary.

Delain knew it was now April the twentieth, the date written on the small note she had found in Lord Wilder's library. It would soon be three a.m., the time also mentioned in the note. She had arrived early, and after waiting an hour, saw candles being extinguished throughout in the house. Soon, there was a dim light from a candle flickering in the library. The appearance of the person she assumed to be Lord Wilder afforded her the satisfaction that she had planned this event perfectly — and that something sinister was afoot.

A sound was heard from the street, and within a minute or two, a black carriage could be seen approaching. It was only because Delain had been in the dark for some time that her pupils had opened impossibly large, enough to gather in the slimmest amount of light and recognize the shape of the carriage.

Wilder emerged from his hiding place and walked to the cart. The door opened, and he entered quickly. Immediately, the car moved ahead.

"That does it!" said Delain under her breath. "I knew he was up to no good."

She turned back to the deep woods and retrieved her horse.

I can't just trot down the street at this ungodly hour, she thought. I will use the horse paths as best I can!

Mounting the filly, she took to the soft lawns and dirt paths that ran alongside the road near Van Patten. The damp ground hid the sounds of the horse's hooves almost completely. Up ahead, she could see the carriage moving between the bushes and trees that lined the way. In this manner, Delain followed Wilder for miles, heading toward the city.

Inside the carriage, the conversation became heated, and though both parties were whispering, the argument was in full swing. It sounded to the driver as if there were two snakes hissing and snapping at each other. Funny, he thought, why not just speak in a normal voice? The passengers were so loud, whispering had no effect on dampening the sound.

"Yet another request for another treaty? And so soon? I wonder if this is serious business or just some useless political wrangling that will have no effect on the relationships between England and Russia!" said Wilder.

"I understand your concern," said Orvislat. "However, these treaties are living documents, each side changing and rearranging wording and conditions. It is not uncommon to have several iterations!"

"That I understand, my friend; however, these last-minute changes in ship assignments and missions are going to attract attention, and eventually, someone will begin to question these actions. The *Echo* and the *Paladin* are packets, and changing their orders is quite common, but this last request will raise eyebrows, I assure you. There must be another way. Can't we send the treaty by land?"

Orvislat shook his head. "No, a land route is too treacherous. Spies are everywhere, and if the treaty were to fall into the wrong hands—"

"There are spies at sea as well!" shouted Wilder in a hoarse whisper that was now, basically, a normal voice. "And there is also a chance of capture!"

"Yes," said Orvislat. "However, my friend, I have studied the facts and figures. A land route is over five times more dangerous! We have tried it on several occasions with minor missions, and almost half ended in failure. A sea route with a new ship is the safest and surest method. You must trust me."

Wilder looked out the window in disgust. The night rolled by, dark, foggy, and cold, much like the business at hand. What Orvislat said made sense, though it did not change the fact that they had gone to this well too many times before. Spears, the actual officer who wrote up the orders, already seemed suspicious. He even questioned the secretive manner in which the treaty was discussed and complained that not telling the officers aboard the *Echo* and *Paladin* was unusual and considered an insult. Spears was a malcontent, it was sure; however, he was a proper navy man and cared a great deal about his fellow officer. Asking him to transport this new treaty would be difficult.

"I am telling you," continued Wilder, "Spears is already suspicious of all this. He informed me just today that the *Echo* is late to report. Soon, people will want to review the orders."

Orvislat took a mental note. If Spears became a problem, he would have Lupien take care of him permanently. It wouldn't be the first time they'd had to murder for a greater cause. Who would really miss him or even investigate his disappearance?

"Let me know if Spears becomes an issue," said Orvislat.

Something about the tone in the spy's voice chilled Wilder to the bone. He made a mental note to never mention Spears again.

"I am sorry this is hard for you," continued Orvislat in a much softer tone. He was no longer snapping or whispering hoarsely and was suddenly calm and kind once again. "Your country and king appreciate your efforts and your candor."

Wilder sat silently. He made no response.

"One other particular," added Orvislat. "The ship to be used for this mission may encounter some hostile forces. Activity in the Adriatic Sea has increased. The Turks and other factions of Napoleon have been active. A packet of eighteen guns will not be enough. We need a twenty-four or a thirty-six for this mission."

"Dear God," said Wilder. "Packets have a more fluid schedule. They deliver mail, orders, and critical supplies. It is not uncommon to see them on their own, cruising back and forth between stations. But larger ships are another story! They have missions and are usually part of larger operations — "

"There are those that cruise alone, for prizes — "

"Yes," said Wilder, "some. However, those captains have a certain way about them. Rebellious they are, and risk takers. Not the type you would like for this mission. Delivering a diplomatic pouch would be beneath them. I wouldn't be surprised if they accepted it and then immediately tossed it overboard! They are used to having their own way!"

"Then let us get a new captain, one who is grateful for his recent success and would relish such an honorable role in history. I do believe this will be the last delivery for a while."

"Impossible," said Wilder. "We cannot send more than a packet. It is too risky."

"I said a thirty-six!" snapped Orvislat.

"I beg your pardon?" said Wilder, now angry once again. "I am handling the ship assignments — not you, *friend* — and I believe I know what is best — "

"Begging *your* pardon, Lord Wilder, I am in charge of this mission," said Orvislat sternly. "And if I discover that you have violated my instructions or told anyone about our plans, your services will no longer be needed — and the payments, and many other *things*, will end."

Wilder took the meaning to be a threat. The look in Orvislat's eyes conveyed his sinister meaning: if you do not do as I say, I will kill you.

Orvislat could see that he had truly upset the noble-man, and now, after making his point, he needed to reas-sure Wilder that all was well. He wanted to ease his mind, not for any concern or affection he held for his lordship, but for the sake of the mission. He didn't need Wilder running scared, blabbering to people in the Admiralty about the treaty that obviously didn't exist. That would surely de-stroy any chances of providing Kharitonov his needed ships for his special purposes. After the pulling of a few strings, he would find himself before the commodore and be made to answer directly to him — and then to his sup-porters.

Officially, due to the Treaty of Amiens, there was no war between Russia and the Turks of the Ottoman Empire; however, they had been fighting for control of the Black Sea for a thousand years. Peace could tip the balance of power in the struggle, so what was in the best interests of Russia? To continue to press their advantage against the crumbling Turkish forces.

Orvislat and the boss knew that Kharitonov was act-ing outside of the official blessing of the tsar. He held an unofficial letter of marque, granted by certain members of the Russian Parliament and backed financially by several patriotic noblemen. The goal was to continue a secret war against the Ottoman Empire, harassing shipping, taking smaller naval vessels, and sinking them if needed. As Khar-itonov's activities were officially *unofficial*, he needed to gain his fleet quickly and quietly. His acquaintance, Orvislat, was posing as the son of the Russian ambassador to England, and England had the world's largest fleet, with over one thousand ships to choose from. It was obvious and simple to set up a small network in London that would choose, position, and then obtain vessels that fit their pur-poses from their ally, the British Empire. Hence, Orvislat needed Wilder in his position in the British Admiralty, calm and superficially in control, yet unaware.

"I am sorry, my friend," said Orvislat. "That was un-necessary and boorish. Please forgive me. But understand, these orders come from those high in our governments, and to change even a simple thing like the number of *guns* requested on the delivery vessel could fall back on us — hurt us — if the mission fails. Do you see my predicament?"

Wilder thought that it certainly would not help to question or go against the orders of his king and his advisors. God only knew what Russian officials were capable of doing to their own subjects.

"I saw a ship in the harbor by chance," said Orvislat hopefully. "The *Draker*, I believe?"

"The *Drake*," corrected Wilder. "Yes, she's a small frigate, though she mounts thirty-six guns. A newly promoted captain, Blake, of only a dozen months with a decent crew."

"That would do?" asked Orvislat in a conciliatory tone.

"Yes," said Wilder. "I will see to it."

Delain watched as the carriage came to a halt just to the edge of a row of small warehouses. She dismounted her horse and tied it to a nearby tree once again. Creeping slowly toward the lane, she watched for any movement. It was cold now, and she suddenly realized that as exciting as this evening was, it would not get her any additional information besides the fact that Lord Wilder, the recipient of the secret note, had only gotten into a carriage. She needed to hear or see something more.

A shadow of a nearby wall stretched all the way to the carriage. Possibly, she could sneak closer if she was careful, remain unseen by the driver, and maybe pick out a word or two — or see the face of the other occupant.

"Then I will take my leave of you, Lord Wilder," said Orvislat from inside the carriage. "I am indebted to you, as is all of England and Russia. My driver will see you back to your estate. I will convey your most excellent plan to my superiors."

With that, Orvislat exited the car and addressed the driver.

"Take him back quickly. The hour is late."

The driver whipped the horses, and they ran off at an alarming pace.

The spy hastily entered into the shadows of a nearby alley, behind the warehouses. In his haste, he was not as diligent in checking his surroundings as he was usually. Maybe it was because he had nothing of importance on his person, no official papers or incriminating evidence. He was rushing to an important rendezvous at the Log and Loaf Pub with Lupien. The establishment was surely closed, but all the better. It was a location with which both men were thoroughly familiar, and the lack of patrons at this hour would make them both comfortable in the fact that they were safe and their goings-on private. No matter what the reason, Orvislat missed the small, silent black figure in quick pursuit.

Orvislat paused at the entrance to yet another back alley that led directly to the rear door of the Log and Loaf, and just before proceeding, out of habit, he turned to check behind.

Delain dove across the entrance to the alley, landing on one knee behind a pile of refuse, banging her bone. Unable to cry out in pain, she lay still, hoping she had not been seen. She waited a moment, but then, to her horror, she heard the steps of someone coming back to the street from the alley.

Her mind raced. It had all been a game up to this point, but what would happen now if this man—surely the Black Rider—captured her? Dear Jonathan Moore, she found herself thinking, how I do wish you and Sean were here now with me. Then I wouldn't be such a scaredy-cat!

A cat? That gave her an idea.

Orvislat came closer, his hand in the pocket of his coat where he kept a small pistol. He removed it, looking warily at the entrance to the alley.

The sound had come from the left, less than ten feet away. He didn't want to reappear in the street. That would look suspicious; however, if he was being followed, he would shoot his way out if he had to and then disappear for a while. Lupien would surely meet him in their contingency location, checking for him every three days.

He raised the gun and aimed at the pile of garbage to the left of the entrance.

"Mee-ow? Rarraaar! Sssss!"

Orvislat lowered his weapon. A cat, he thought, and turned back to the pub.

In the pile, Delain had all she could handle simply suppressing a laugh. The great relief she felt when she heard the door to the building open and then close once again gave her a renewed energy. I must probably call it a night, she thought. As uneventful as all this was, I at least know that Lord Wilder is indeed involved with this character, and they are planning something. The black horseman frequents this place, and I will have to find a way to ask a few questions of the patrons. I will need the help of someone used to appearing in these lowbrow establishments, someone who knows his way around the bowels of London. She thought for a moment, then began to rise from the ground. Yes, she realized, Steward is just such a man.

As she wiped herself off, she couldn't wait to get home and bathe. It was cold and wet, and now she was full of filth. As she thought of a better way to end her evening, like the spy she followed, she wasn't as diligent as she should have been in considering her situational awareness.

Adjusting her hood, she tightened her cloak and took a few steps back toward her horse. In a flash, a figure darted out from a nearby doorway, rushed behind her, and stuffed a handful of cloth in her mouth. She then felt a sack of some sort being pulled over her head. Then the strong hands of a brute lifted her off her feet and slung her over his shoulder.

"Got the little sneak!" said a voice.

"Back to the boss, then!" said another.

17

Cursed Captains

It was much to Midshipman Jonathan Moore's relief that within a half an hour's time, the former captain of the *Paladin*, Commander Thomas Harrison, assumed control and responsibility of his ship. Harrison had heard the signal guns while in town, and with his shore party, he immediately rushed to the pier in the harbor at Telašćica. Somewhat shocked at the sight of *Paladin* moving out to sea, he was comforted once told by the jolly boat crew that Mister Moore was in command and had believed moving the ship from shore was a necessary precaution.

Appearing on deck, Harrison took in the scene. There were wounded men lying about, and blood seemed to be everywhere. His first thought was of Jonathan, though he could not locate him. As his fear rose, he saw Jenkins attending to a young crewman who was bare-chested and covered in blood. It was Jonathan.

"Jonathan! What happened? You are bleeding!" said Harrison with a mixture of worry and anger as he saw his friend's blood-soaked appearance. Sean ran to his friend and began inspecting him closely.

"Dear Lord!" exclaimed the young marine.

"It is not all my blood," Jonathan said as Jenkins applied a wet cloth to the boy's face, wiping away blood and dirt.

"Where are your clothes?" asked Sean.

"We sent them overboard," replied Jenkins. "The jacket was torn, all was blood-soaked."

"Where is Alexander?" the commander asked.

"Dead, sir," said Jenkins.

Shocked, Harrison looked about, then rested eyes on

Jonathan.

"Garvey!" called the commander, "retrieve a spare white blouse from my locker, and see if Alexander has an extra coat!

"Aye, sir!" said Garvey as he ran to the stern. He returned in a few moments with a spare shirt, a borrowed pair of breeches from his own supply, and a lieutenant's jacket from Alexander's locker. It was a bit large for Jonathan, though the fit was tolerable.

"Jonathan, can you explain what happened?" asked Harrison, now calming.

"We were boarded," Jonathan said, still obviously shaken. "Men in masks, faces coaled black. A fight ensued."

"How many men have we lost?" asked Harrison.

"Fourteen dead, and Alexander," answered Jonathan.

"Any survivors from the attacking force?" continued Harrison.

"None, sir," answered Jonathan. "One man was muttering something before he died. Fawcett heard him and thought it was a strange tongue, definitely not French or English — maybe Dutch."

"Are we at war with the Dutch?" asked Sean.

"Not at this moment," answered Harrison. "But who is to know? The Dutch seem to have their own agenda — and always have."

"But why not try to take us at sea? With their navy and large ships, we would have been outgunned surely," suggested Hudson.

"If they could catch us," said Harrison. "Even with a damaged foremast, is there any Dutch ship that can match the *Paladin*?"

All agreed there was no such ship, and that the Dutch certainly would have no need to steal a British sloop.

"How many men were there?" asked Harrison.

"Hard to tell," said Jenkins. "We figured about forty to fifty. Pistols and swords mostly."

"I can tell you that one spoke almost perfect English,"

said Jonathan. "He asked me to surrender the ship."

"What did ya say to him?" asked Sean.

"I told him to get off my ship, and I kicked him in the chest."

"That would do it," said Sean, laughing slightly.

"A job well done, Jonathan. You saved the ship. I am most grateful," said Harrison with a smile.

"I lost Mister Alexander, however," said Jonathan softly.

"He's gone, Jonny, that's true," said Sean. "But it wasn't you who lost him."

"That's right," added Harrison. "Alexander was in command. He lost his life defending his brothers and this ship. Any of us would have done the same."

Quinn stirred uncomfortably.

They stood quietly for a moment. Berkeley appeared with a hot pot of coffee, and Boston provided cups.

"Then who would attempt a cutting out like this? From land?" asked Jonathan.

"It could be the Austrians," suggested Harrison as he continued the conversation. "The war may be on again, and we are a fair target."

"Maybe it was privateers or slavers," offered Quinn. "A fast ship such as this would be most welcome. Maybe they were stranded here for some reason and thought we would be an easy mark."

"They were prepared and had a plan," said Jonathan. "They were very organized, waiting until many of the crew and officers were off the ship. It was no opportunistic lark. It must be the treaty. Someone wants it badly."

"Or doesn't want us to deliver it!" exclaimed Harrison. "By the powers of heaven, I am sick of this whole business!"

"Pardon," said Bowman as he approached the officers, tipping the hat he wasn't wearing in salute. "Marshall spotted a man ashore waving a white hankie. He is certainly trying to get our attention."

Harrison took up his telescope and observed the pier

for a moment. Yes, there was a man, dressed in finery —a neat coat and brushed hat, a pair of high boots, and a white wig. He was waving his handkerchief and calling out to them.

"Prepare the boat, Jenkins," Harrison said lowering his glass. "I will go to the pier and see what this man wants. He might be our contact. Hudson, I will need three tough marines, all with guns loaded and not afraid to shoot."

"Then I will accompany you," answered Hudson. "Hicks! Flagon! Get your weapons."

"Me?" asked Sean.

"No, your twin who's about to get a lickin'!" shouted Hudson sarcastically. "On the double!"

Sean immediately stood, gave Jonathan a quick, worried glance, and ran.

"I'll take a full complement of men to row as well," added Hudson, "and arm them with pistols."

"Good," replied Harrison. "Jonathan, set the stern deck guns at that pier; at the slightest hint of trouble, blast it to smithereens. Quinn, keep an eye out to sea, and I mean it! Leave the men in the tops to look as well."

"Aye, sir," came the replies as the orders were carried out.

"A word, with you Jonathan," whispered Harrison.

Once they were away from the others, Harrison spoke softly and firmly to his midshipman, looking him directly in the eye.

"Jonathan, I am ever so grateful. I am indebted to you. Losing the *Paladin*, well —" he paused, looking as if a tear were welling up in his eye.

"Harrison, it was a poor —"

"No. It was not poor anything," interrupted Harrison. "It was leadership. It was putting to action what you have learned. And I need *that* Jonathan Moore aboard, at all times. Do you hear me?"

"Yes, sir," said Jonathan.

"I know something seems to be, well, *off* in your self-confidence, and I am not sure what that may be. However, as *off* as you are, I trust you. And I do not trust Quinn. At best he is a fool, but he seems to know quite a bit about this Andrews character commanding the *Echo*. How is it that Quinn is so informed, yet none of us, with the connections we have in Whitehall, have ever heard of Andrews? I can't help but think Quinn is tied up in this mess. At least he knows something and is not sharing it. And, did you see him when I mentioned that any of us would die to protect the ship and crew?" continued Harrison. "He seemed uncomfortable with the notion."

"What can we do?" asked Jonathan.

"Be ready," said Harrison. "There is a pistol in the locker that Streen built. Here is a key. The treaty is contained therein as well."

He handed Jonathan the long, dark key and again looked him in the eye.

"Jonathan. Move any personal effects into the locker that you may need at a moment's notice. It is in a handy position while commanding from the stern."

Jonathan thought for a moment, and considered what items he would need quickly, should situations get out of hand. His blade, surely — and Sean's as well. He slipped the key into the pocket of his pants.

"I might be wrong about Quinn," said Harrison, "though I am nearly persuaded that he is mixed up in this mess. And Jenkins tells me he spends an inordinate amount of time with Crump and Crystal. Why would that be? In any case, retrieve my pistol and keep it on your person at all times."

"Aye, sir," Jonathan replied. "And when you return, there are a few things I believe we should discuss."

Harrison smiled, knowing that, finally, Jonathan's internal struggle, which was surely behind his less-than-by-the-book performance, would be brought to light.

"Yes, let us talk when I return," the commander said. "Remember — watch Quinn."

Joining the boat crew, Harrison and his party were lowered into the water.

Within minutes, the jolly arrived at the pier but did not tie up. Instead, men held on to the planks of the structure to steady the boat. The marines stood as one, leveled their guns at each villager nearby, and of course, at the man waving the handkerchief. The sight of three muzzles aimed his way caused the man to stop waving.

"Excuse me!" said the man. "I am Bogát Gogomán! Please! I mean you no harm!"

"I am Commander Harrison of His Majesty's ship *Paladin*. What is it you want? We are on urgent business!"

"Ah, this I know!" said Gogomán. "As am I." He looked about, leaned as close to the boat as he possibly could without falling into the water, and whispered, "I happen to have a message from a friend who, unfortunately, had missed a meeting he was to attend earlier."

"Go on," said Harrison, not yet trusting the man.

"His message is making little sense to me, but I am a poor messenger, a local magistrate who tries to help all who moor here or anchor nearby. You know our livelihood depends on the visitation of ships such as yours —"

"Yes, yes," interrupted Harrison. "Now, what is the message?"

Bogát Gogomán nodded. "Yes, the message. Again, I find it *nonsensical*, I think you say? Yes. It makes little sense to me. Though I am from a poor family with little education. What would I know of the world and its ways? Though in this town of simple fishermen and farmers, I am seen as a superior intellect!" Bogát Gogomán began laughing.

"Good heavens, man!" exploded Harrison. "Whatever is the message?"

"Ah, yes. Here it is. Are you ready?"

"Please, yes," said Harrison. "Deliver it with all due haste!"

"Because, if you are ready, I could possibly suggest that we sit over a glass of wine in one of the local establishments, yes? Then we can have a pleasant conversation —"

"I swear," said Harrison, now losing his temper. "If you do not tell me the message in your next breath, I will order my men to open fire!"

This shook Gogomán visibly. He took a breath and closed his eyes, as if trying to remember the exact words he was to say.

"A man approached me in my office just an hour or so ago. He said that if I saw the captain of the ship *Paladin*, that I was to say, ahem, 'One has only one shoe for both feet.'"

Harrison recognized this as the emergency phrase set into his orders.

"Do you understand the meaning?" asked Gogomán.

"Yes, I do. Is that all he said?" Harrison asked.

"He said if you understood that phrase, then you would accept this note."

Bogát Gogomán handed Harrison an envelope, almost falling in the water as he reached toward the boat.

Harrison read it quickly.

"Who were the men who attacked my ship?" asked Harrison.

"One cannot be sure," said Gogomán nervously. "But I would assume they were separatists. Many here feel little allegiance to the Austrian throne. Many Italians are assisting. There have been other incidents. Were these men, perhaps masked or with—how do you say—with darkened faces?"

"Indeed they were," said Harrison.

"*Esercito di Piccola Capre!*" Gogomán said, nodding. "Italian-backed Dalmatians that have been stealing small boats and barges to sell and purchase arms for their rebellion! Fools! Was anyone hurt?"

"We lost fourteen men, and some were injured."

"Be careful, Captain!" exclaimed the magistrate. "They have now an appetite for larger game!"

Upon Commander Harrison's return, HMS *Paladin*

made ready to sail and moved southward out of the Bay of Telašćica into more open water. Harrison thought this best. If trouble was approaching, he could maneuver in any direction or take advantage of any wind. Too close to the shore, or within the bay, and some of those advantages would be lost.

In his cabin, Harrison reread the note Gogomán had given him, and as far as he could tell, he believed it authentic. He had secretly summoned Jonathan to his cabin, purposely leaving Quinn on deck and out of the discussion. Jenkins was informed of the captain's concerns and remained within viewing distance of the new lieutenant at all times.

"Jonathan, what do you make of this?" Harrison asked, handing him the note.

My dear Captain Harrison,

Please forgive the hasty note. I can only assume that something prevented you from following the strict orders given to you for the prescribed delivery. I have now seen your party in town, plainly, and also assume that you are attempting to contact me. A new plan to complete the order requests that you proceed directly to Zadar and seek the Viscount Baron Ragusa. He lives in the mansion on the top of the hill to the east of town, a marvelous stone villa. You are to use the code word Garvino. *The Viscount will reply with the words* Madrid *and* Holiday.

He will accept the package. Arrive on the eighteenth of this month, no sooner or later. Good luck.

Señor Garvino

"Your thoughts, Mister Moore?" asked Harrison.

Jonathan wondered if this was a good opportunity to not only suggest they follow orders to the letter this time but also to detail his meeting with Spears and Lord Wilder.

Maybe one thing at a time, he thought.

"It seems authentic," Jonathan said after his reading. "Though I wouldn't know how to judge such things."

"The note mentions me by name. That means someone knew we were coming. Also, *Garvino* is one of the passwords mentioned in the mission orders. The magistrate, Gogomán, also knew one of the secret passwords as well. I feel confident that it is legitimate."

"Did he mention who attacked us?" asked Jonathan.

"He did. He believes it was a separatist group, the *Esercito di Piccola Capre*. They have been taking smaller craft but seem to have an appetite for something larger."

"Have you ever heard of the *Esercito di Piccola Capre?*" asked Jonathan.

"No, though I have to say that I don't understand the Italians nor the Dalmatians one iota. Maybe they want the treaty. Maybe they want our ship."

"What are we to do now?" asked Jonathan.

"We should proceed in the morning, surely," answered Harrison. "It is a treacherous path to Zadar — many islands and shallow waters — and I would not chance it at night."

"Yes, sir," said Jonathan.

"Jonathan, I can't help but believe that all these strange events are linked: this cutting-out attempt and that blasted Andrews aboard the *Echo*," said Harrison, exasperated. "He has something to do with this as well."

"It would be convenient to believe so," said Jonathan. "But we don't know. Not for sure."

"You are right, Jonathan," sighed Harrison as he began to pace the cabin slowly. "I just feel that I am not seeing the entire picture..." he said, his voice trailing off in frustration. He sighed heavily and closed his eyes as he leaned against an overhead beam.

It was to be now or never, Jonathan thought.

"Thomas," he began. "I am ashamed to say...that I have withheld information from you."

Harrison slowly turned to face Jonathan. He looked deep into his eyes.

"Continue," was all he could say.

"Thomas, I was sworn to secrecy by none other than the king."

"You spoke directly to the king about this mission?" asked Harrison, now turning his back to Jonathan. He moved to the stern window.

"No. I received his desires through Captain Spears."

"Spears? And you trusted him?" asked Harrison.

"He is one to be wary of, I agree," said Jonathan. "However, he appeared with Lord Wilder on the quay at Wapping immediately after Quinn arrived with new orders. I begged them, Thomas! I begged them to allow me to share the information with you. They refused!"

Harrison thought about this. Certainly, Wilder was well respected by many and his association with Spears, as odd as he was, was a matter of navy business, and many in the service believed that 'odd' didn't even begin to explain the purposes and pronouncements made by the Admiralty.

"And why tell me now?" asked Harrison, turning to face his friend.

"Because my duty to you…means more to me than my duty to the mission or the Crown. Treasonous words, I am sure. But I would rather do the right thing by you, and suffer the consequences, than lose your trust and friendship. I sincerely am ashamed."

This touched Harrison.

"It is understandable, Mister Moore," he said with a kind smile. "What can you tell me?"

"Spears and Wilder told me to encourage you to complete the mission precisely according to orders. They assumed you would vary, and honestly, you did."

"With good reason," replied Harrison, calmly. "So they sent you and Quinn to watch me, is that how it is?"

"Quinn admitted to receiving the same instructions that I received when his orders were changed," said Jonathan.

"Why not tell me to my face?" asked Harrison, notably upset.

"My question to them, exactly," said Jonathan. "They said they were not as—confident in you as others were."

"Really? And why was that?" asked Harrison, taken aback.

"I'd rather not say, Captain Harrison. It was a pithy remark that had no credence, no basis—"

"Jonathan?" said Harrison, somewhat firmly.

Jonathan paused, closed his eyes, and forced the words to be spoken.

"They said that...you were cursed. That you had already been aboard two ships that had been lost. And that they wouldn't be surprised if you lost the *Paladin* as well." Jonathan opened his eyes and looked upon his friend, his brother, with sympathy.

Harrison stood, eyes to the deck. His face turned red, not from anger, but from overwhelming embarrassment. After a moment came a slight smile, a masking one, surely. Yes, he had thought of the fact that he was party to some monumental defeats in his short career. But he never felt anyone else had taken notice.

"Well, Jonathan, they are correct," he said softly as he went to the window. "It is all true. The *Helios* and then the *Poseidon*, and now almost the *Paladin*. And the mission is not yet over."

They both remained in silence, listening only to the creaking of the ship and the light footsteps of the crew as they went about their duties. It was quiet down here in the small cabin. Peaceful. Away from the trouble that surrounded them.

Harrison sighed. Then he returned to his chair, slumped down, dropped his chin to his chest, and closed his eyes. He exhaled deeply.

"If it matters any at all," Jonathan offered.

Harrison opened one eye. "Yes?"

"Captain, you have also been part of *acquiring* two ships, the *Danielle* and the *Drake*. So gun for gun, I'd say you are even, and maybe just slightly ahead. Correct?"

Harrison let out a soft laugh.

"That is also true. I was even part of the taking of the *Annie* during the Battle of Fire, so I assume I am indeed ahead of the game."

A knock came at the door. It was Jenkins.

"Time, sirs," he said quietly.

As the sun began to sink lower on the horizon, casting a pink color to the sparse clouds painted above them, the crew of the *Paladin* held a somber ceremony on the deck. Harrison had ordered only the topsails set, and now the ship was gliding easily into the open sea, her passage marked by the sound of the water passing alongside, like the trickle of a soft brook in the country, bubbling away. At the starboard rail, the captain and his officers stood at perfect attention. Midshipman Moore stood next to Jenkins. In front of them was the last of fourteen long burlap bags, heavily weighted with chain and ball, sitting upon a long wooden plank, flanked by four men, two on a side.

"Ashes to ashes..." said Commander Harrison, "and dust to dust. We commit the soul of our friend and brother, Lieutenant Chad Alexander, to the deep. May his soul rest in peace."

Three bells were rung. Jenkins raised his pipe, and blew three long blasts, the final one trailing off slowly as the wind picked up, causing the sails to luff, flapping gently in the wind. The men lifted the end of the plank, and Alexander, dressed in burlap and chained with ball, slid over the side, silently into the deep.

* * * * *

Back on the hill outside of Telašćica, Nikomed Aggar prepared his men to move. It would be a lengthy hike to a remote inlet where the *Echo* waited for them. They had suffered a defeat at the hands of the British, and worse yet was the fact that the sailors aboard were under the command of a young boy. This fact ate at Aggar. Twelve men were dead! Six more would be left behind due to their wounds! That reduced his force to only forty-six remaining Russian men. Further angering him was the fact that, Tretiak, his man placed aboard the *Paladin* in London, was supposed to kill the officers once the cutting-out crew boarded the ship. However, he was not in the battle at all, nor were the other plants, Myshkin and Krutov.

"Incompetent fools," Aggar mumbled as he held a cloth to the gash under his eye. The bleeding had just now ceased, and his shoulder wound, though painful, would not kill him.

Because of this failure, Aggar would now have to meet Kharitonov at the rendezvous point near Zadar, where he was supposed to deliver the *Paladin*. The commodore would not be pleased. In fact, he might simply murder Aggar upon seeing him without the prize. To ensure his safety as best he could, Aggar had developed a plan to get the *Paladin* to Zadar and, with little chance of failure, take her. He knew the waters near Zadar and the surrounding coast well, and if that old hulk, the decaying barge he had seen anchored off the coast was still there, it would assist in his plan. The barge had been there for the past few months, unmoving and silent except for the waves that lapped against its side. And to assure that the British Commander followed the plan, he had sent Cherepanyanko to hire a messenger, the magistrate from Telašćica. Bogát Gogomán was his name, and he was paid in gold pieces to deliver a note and tell a story to Captain Harrison. Anything could be bought in all of the world, even here, thought Aggar. Lies and spies. Gold worked both miracles and madness.

As things were unfolding, Aggar had an aching desire to run. Run away. Why not just leave with the *Echo* now and avoid all this danger? Possibly pursue his true desire? He had waited long enough, had done enough for others. However, he knew the answer: Kharitonov. It was the fear of his commander that drove him. Kharitonov was known to have powerful friends and ruthless means, and he held

Aggar in his employ against the man's will. If the commodore didn't get what he wanted, many of Aggar's people would be punished, many innocents. Many friends and family.

Aggar had no choice but to continue. He would take the *Paladin* or die trying. And if he failed, he could not bear to think of what suffering would be forced upon his loved ones.

The gods had cursed him, he was sure.

He would navigate through the islands off the western coast, and arrive in darkness, secure his ship, and await Kharitonov — and his temper.

The night fell upon the Dalmatian coast, and a full moon was waxing as the *Echo* sailed past Zadar to the north. Nikomed Aggar instructed his men to reduce sail as they neared the city with its rising citadels and minarets, staying far enough offshore to avoid detection. They would anchor near Petrčane and await the commodore.

Kowalski sat next to his captain, addressing his wounds, trying not to do more damage than was already inflicted on Aggar. Kowalski was a sailing master; he had no training, formally, as a doctor and had no medical books to which he could refer. His skill, as it was, came from observation. Being in numerous battles, he had seen many injuries — some dire and some merely scrapes and bruises. He learned from trial and error and, unfortunately, more from the latter.

"Now," said Kowalski as he held a patch of cloth under Aggar's wounded cheek. "Hold this for a moment while I sew you up. The gash is quite deep. It will leave an…interesting scar."

"That little English brat!" Aggar said. "He thinks he can slice open my face and get away with that? I will be looking for him. And I will find him. And I will pay him back!"

"Nikomed," said Kowalski. "He was covered with blood. You will have a hard time recognizing him among the many boys on that ship."

"I will know him!" shouted Aggar.

"But, my friend, how?"

Aggar smiled, calming, thinking of the revenge he would exact. "It is simple. I did not see his face, but I did see his uniform. He was the only midshipman aboard."

"Captain Andrews, er, I mean Captain *Aggar!*" interrupted a crewman.

"What is it, Nababkin?" Aggar snapped. "Can you not see that I am engaged?"

"Yes, Captain. But…Commodore Kharitonov! He is here. The *Navarkhia* has been spotted ahead!"

Aggar's face went pale.

"Kharitonov is here?" asked Kowalski, obviously shaken by the thought. "Already?"

"Yes," said Nababkin. "We were supposed to deliver the *Paladin* to him! We have failed."

"We have not failed!" exclaimed Aggar. "We are *delayed*. I have already put the alternate plan into effect. That should please the commodore."

"Begging the captain's pardon," said Nababkin, gulping nervously. "Kharitonov is rarely pleased. Ever."

In the bay of Petrčane, just north of Zadar, two ships met. One was larger, designed with two decks and thirty-six guns—the other, a sleek eighteen-gun sloop with slightly raked masts and sails brig-rigged.

Commodore Ian Kharitonov commanded the thirty-six gun *Navarkhia*. He was angry and disappointed.

Captain Nikomed Aggar commanded the eighteen-gun *Echo*. He was afraid.

The ships anchored within fifty yards of one another, and even in the darkness, Aggar could see the small boat splash into the water off the side of the larger warship and immediately begin a rapid approach. He recognized the form of Kharitonov, over six and a half feet tall, standing at the bow of the craft, arms folded. His scowl was visible in the moonlight.

The small boat reached the *Echo*, and a Jacob's ladder made of rope wound as steps descended from the deck.

Though his large frame had to weigh at least three hundred pounds, Kharitonov scaled the rope ladder to the main deck with ease. Only a few lanterns lit the scene, casting an ochre glow to the beams and rigging. Kharitonov surveyed the deck quickly, and there he saw Aggar, standing at attention.

"Commodore—" was all that Aggar was able to say before Kharitonov lunged at him, slapped him across the face, then landed a blow to the head with a massive fist.

"You!" yelled Kharitonov. "You have failed us! You could not obtain this ship the simple way at Telašćica. No, you needed two attempts! Now, I must take over!"

Aggar sat up, holding his jaw, and spitting blood. Blood from the reopened sword gash on his cheek began to flow.

"Without me, you are *nothing*!" yelled the commodore.

Aggar looked to Kharitonov and then to the deck. His instincts told him to avoid eye contact and show complete submission to this monster. However, a small part of him encouraged retaliation, a wave of embarrassment and hatred washed over him, until he took another breath. He calmed himself, his mind regaining control. Noticing his own crew, he could see that they too had been berated, subjugated under the wrath of Kharitonov. They hid their eyes, as if to ensure that they would not become involved or be in a position such that the commodore saw them, even for the briefest of moments, and his anger scorch them.

"I know I have disappointed you, Commodore," Aggar finally said, "however, the English captain! He did not follow his orders. He would not come into the cove!"

"So was it then that you gave up?" asked Kharitonov, getting angrier.

"No, Commodore. I developed a plan, executed the first part, and now, together, we can capture the *Paladin*, the gem of the British Navy."

Aggar stood slowly.

Kharitonov considered him as he stood within striking distance. Well over a hundred pounds heavier and two hands taller, the commodore towered above Aggar. His face was in a permanent frown, his tight white beard outlining a square jaw, his reddish skin made of rock. His light blue eyes flickered in the lantern's light, and they bore a hole into Aggar's soul.

"Aggar," said the commodore softly. "Do you think I need you? Do you think that you are special in some way?"

"No, Commodore," Aggar replied.

"I can find a hundred men like you and have all of them willing to do my bidding. I don't need you or your ideas, your plans, or your dreams."

Aggar thought this ironic. He had no dreams—none anymore. His only thought was for his family, wherever they were.

"I would be most honored if you would listen to my plan, Commodore. I think you will approve."

Kharitonov folded his arms across his massive chest and smiled.

"I had *better* approve," snarled the commodore, "or else I will take what is left of your life."

18

The Viscount of Zadar

At the break of day, HMS *Paladin* continued southeast from Telašćica on fair winds and calm sky, approaching the large island named Kornati. From there, the ship navigated through the many islands that dotted the Dalmatian coast, approaching Zadar. It now seemed familiar to the crew, the mixture of tall, chalky cliffs and the lush green hills giving way to beautiful white-sand beaches and turquoise bays. In any other circumstance, Harrison would have anchored off a small bay and let the men enjoy the warm sun and a bath in the clear waters.

It was hard sailing, and as the crow would fly at ten knots, if one was able, the trip from Telašćica would have taken less than two or three hours. However, with the many turns and mostly unknown waters, the trip to Zadar would take almost half the day.

Now approaching their destination, Captain Harrison had ordered the crew to reduce sail to all but the topgallants, bringing the *Paladin* to almost a complete stop. He instructed Mister Fawcett to remain as long as was possible at the mouth of the bay.

The entrance was marked by two small towers, one on the north side of the wide inlet and another to the south. The bay then turned with a protected waterway to the south that was narrow, with a series of piers and a long quay along each side. Along the shoreline looked to be dense woodland and a few rolling hills beyond. One hill rose above the rest, possibly two hundred feet above sea level. Atop, stood a magnificent stone villa as described in the letter Harrison received from Bogát Gogomán at Telašćica.

Normally, there would be only the usual fishing skiffs and caïques plying the waters off Zadar. There were at rare times larger ships belonging to the Austrians who controlled the area, as well as the Venetians: Italians who had recently lost the area due to the war with Napoleon. All three parties continued to trade among one another, carrying goods of various types, and were sometimes in the company of protection—small- to medium-sized warships of similar proportion to the *Paladin*.

Today, only a small Austrian vessel of possibly twelve guns and an Italian merchant ship sat in the main part of the bay, anchored. Looking through their telescopes, the officers could see a dozen smaller fishing vessels and a yacht tied to the pier at the deepest end of the southern channel by the quaint village center.

British ships of His Majesty's Navy took proper precautions when approaching other vessels anywhere other than their home port. Harrison knew this well. He instructed his two officers to place men in the tops to man sails; send Garvey, who had the best eyes of all the crew save Jonathan, to the crow's nest; and send men to the guns on both sides and marines to various positions, muskets loaded and standing at attention. This accomplished two goals: one was to show the other ships that the British Navy was indeed the dominant force in all waters of the world and its crews professional, experienced, and most of all, dangerous to any who thought otherwise; and two, to be ready for battle at any time.

The *Paladin* had been at sea for just over two weeks, and news of political changes, in other words, the war, traveled slowly. Who was to know if at this given instant, as the *Paladin* sailed into Zadar, that hostilities might have once again broken out between Britain and any other country? Alliances were being forged between likely and unlikely bedfellows constantly, the pieces of the grand game of world trade being positioned through secret doings, public announcements, and not-so-public treaties.

Standing next to Captain Harrison on the bow were

Midshipman Moore and Lieutenant Quinn. They continued to scan all parts of the Zadar coast, observing every ship in the main harbor or moored at the long quay and each building at the shoreline.

"I believe," said Harrison, "that the inactivity aboard the ships in the harbor means the peace still holds in this pocket of the world. Otherwise, the crews would be ordered at least to stations. Still, our best position would be to anchor just at the mouth of the main bay, guns manned."

"Why that position, sir?" asked Quinn. "I would assume any of these moorings at the pier would suffice, possibly one closer to the center of town. It would make loading supplies easier."

Harrison lowered his telescope and stared at Quinn. Before he could speak, Jonathan stepped in.

"A pier would be easiest and most convenient," said Jonathan, "however, it would also make a repeat performance of the Telašćica attack easier as well."

"But the bay is large," argued Quinn. "At least a mile wide. I believe we could almost fight a battle in here with plenty of room to maneuver."

"If we had forty-four guns, yes!" answered Harrison. "But our weapon is our speed. I will not lose that advantage. The wind is blowing off the shore, and we will keep it at our backs. Mister Fawcett?"

"Aye, sir?"

"Bring us to just the mouth of the main bay, then point our bow to the west. Moore, man the anchors and place axes by all the lines in case we need to leave in a hurry. Get the men to the guns."

"Yes, sir," Jonathan said and ran to execute the order.

"Quinn," said Harrison softly. "I am not sure if you are simply an imbecile or have dropped below the line of common sense and descended into moronic stupidity."

"Sir?" said Quinn, shocked. He lowered his telescope.

"Did you just suggest that we dock in a strange port, and then when I informed you of the ridiculousness of that idea, suggest that the bay is large enough for an engagement?"

Quinn swallowed hard.

Harrison looked him in the eye. He spoke quietly yet firmly.

"I am not sure if you are up to anything unsavory, but let me remind you, that I am watching. As are others on this ship."

"But, sir!"

"Do not contradict me, Quinn! Carry out your orders to the letter for the remainder of this cruise, or, so help me, I will have you in front of the board upon our return, if I don't dispose of you as is my right as captain of this ship! Is that understood?"

Quinn recoiled during this verbal attack and then recovered. He stood tall and stern facing Harrison, squared his shoulders, and pulled his coat downward with a firm tug to straighten out any creases or wrinkles — all in an effort to look serious, subservient, and in complete agreement.

"My apologies, Captain. I will endeavor to impress you and make amends for my incorrect assumptions."

Harrison sighed. "That's better. Please have the men in the tops ready to reduce all canvas on my command."

"Yes, sir," said Quinn. He marched off briskly.

Within a fraction of an hour, HMS *Paladin* had maneuvered into position and set anchor at the mouth of the wide bay, bow to the west, and all guns manned, yet doors closed. There was no need to ask for trouble; however, Harrison was sure to be ready if anyone approached the ship unannounced.

It was now time for a late breakfast. All crew not in the tops or manning guns were seated at prepared tables, eating a simple meal of hardtack, coffee, and some honey that had been saved for the halfway point of the journey. All had expected to be on their way home by this date; however, with the delay at Telašćica, only now did they feel it was time for the honey.

Normally, a breakfast for the officers would be served in the captain's cabin, and Berkeley had prepared one of Harrison's favorites: lightly fried and breaded flying fish fillets, with coffee and small corncakes. Berkeley had obtained the recipe from Jenkins, who had discovered it on a previous trip to the Lesser Antilles. Together, they had perfected the preparation with a few secret attempts over the last two weeks. Today, this feast was served on a small table placed on the stern deck, where Harrison and his officers could keep their eyes on the shore, the bay at Zadar, and the sea beyond.

Sean Flagon was also in attendance, and he took the opportunity to enjoy the fish and the slightly better bread. The coffee, growing on him each day, was strong and hot, and though in an almost tropical environment, it was still welcome. Sean had been up all night, walking the deck with Hicks and worrying. He knew he was to be part of this morning's shore detail that would be led by Captain Harrison. He knew his musket would also be attending.

About them, marines marched around the deck, and Jenkins had a small detail of men scrubbing the teak, removing any signs of the bloody battle from the day before. There was much to do, as usual.

"Gentlemen," began Harrison after finishing his third fillet, "let us review this morning's mission. Most of all, I want to make sure that all know my most dire concerns."

All stopped eating or drinking, wiped mouths and hands, and turned to the captain, giving him their full attention.

"I do not trust the information we have received," said Harrison, "nor the information I have come to discover regarding this mission."

Jonathan squirmed uncontrollably. Harrison was referring to his retaining of information. At least his friend had the manners not to call his name out loud.

"I am not going to simply hand over the treaty to this new player, Viscount Ragusa. He will need to know all the correct codes and passwords — and have at least an excellent bottle of Madeira before I am satisfied!"

"What do you propose?" asked Jonathan.

"I will leave the treaty aboard the *Paladin* and lead a small shore party to the viscount's villa. Once there, I will test him. If he seems to fit all the criteria and know all the code words, then I will return to the *Paladin*, retrieve the treaty, and only then will I deliver it."

Harrison looked at Quinn. He half expected him to begin a counterargument, considering he was once again greatly altering the particulars of the plan. Instead, Quinn nodded.

"A fine plan, Commander," said Quinn. "Sensible and proper considering all the mishaps and unexplained events."

"Thank you, Lieutenant Quinn," Harrison said, staring. "I will have you remain on board with Mister Moore."

"Aye, sir," said Quinn, apparently satisfied.

"Jonathan," continued Harrison, "You are in command of the *Paladin* in my absence. Have Jenkins assist you if needed."

Quinn was shocked.

"Sir!" he blurted out. "I'm a lieutenant! And though I respect and value Mister Moore, he is only a midshipman. I am surely the ranking officer!"

"I am well aware of that, Lieutenant Quinn. You will follow Mister Moore's every command — and pay particular attention to the gun deck. Am I clear?"

There was a silence as all within earshot had heard the command for Jonathan to assume the role of captain. Jenkins and Welty had maneuvered their cleaning of the deck close to the officer's table and had been listening since before the coffee was served. They smiled.

"I asked if I made myself *clear!*" exploded Harrison.

"Yes, sir!" they all said, even Jenkins and Welty.

"Quinn, I want every gun checked, loaded, and ready to fire. Do you understand?"

"Yes, sir, said Quinn, standing at attention. "I will attend to it personally."

"Await our return, Mister Moore," Harrison said, calming. "At any sign of trouble, use your speed. Warn us with three guns, then set sail. Keep the ship out of danger. Come back in three days' time if you can—and every three days after, if necessary. Am I understood?"

"Yes, sir," answered Jonathan.

"Hudson, I will need you, Hicks, and Flagon, along with twelve more able men. Assign Welty, Marshall, and Bowman as well. They are experienced fighters. Get your party organized and meet me at the jolly."

Once the second shore party departed, Jonathan assigned eyes to all points about the ship, men to the tops, and Quinn, with his small crew of Crump and Crystal, inspected each gun, clearing touchholes and generally inspecting each piece.

Atop the hill overlooking the bay, the viscount of Zadar stood on the balcony of his home. Less than a mile from the shore in a wooded park, the superbly crafted stone villa had a commanding view of the area. Certainly, all in Zadar knew that this estate was home to the most important man in town. His wealth had been generated by much industry, some being legitimate business, though the vast majority was obtained by performing duties for some of his wealthy and powerful friends who had less-than-honest proposals. Sometimes, his services included murder, theft, kidnapping, or even more intricate performances that might require multiple crimes. Hidden behind his title of viscount, Baron Ragusa, an Austrian by birth, could claim his riches were part of his family's wealth. They allowed him to employ a small band of men to do his work in this busy trade region—and also to afford the beautiful home overlooking Zadar.

Ragusa had been observing the English ship since he'd spotted her at the entrance to the main harbor earlier that morning. The fine telescope of superb workmanship he used was positioned on a pedestal in his loggia. Much stronger than the ones used by most seamen, he was always the first person to see any vessel approaching and even discover details others would not see until the ships had literally entered the bay.

The viscount had been paid—most handsomely, in fact—to alert Commodore Kharitonov of the arrival of a particular ship. He also was paid to perform a certain part, like an actor in a play, and convince his audience that what they were seeing was real. Challenging, yes, but he had a plan.

He could see the ship clearly now as a small boat left its side and headed for the shore. Its bow almost facing directly away from him, he could make out the letters across the ship's stern. It read *"Paladin."*

Now certain it was the ship he was looking for, he called his page.

"Chase!"

In a moment, his servant arrived.

"Send word to our friend that his ship has arrived. Take my quickest horse, and do not dally for any reason, understood?"

"Yes, Viscount!" said Chase. In less than a minute, the page was mounted on a white Arabian and speeding the well-known five miles over the hills to the north and to the small bay at Petrčane. There, the two Russian ships of Commodore Kharitonov sat anchored.

The jolly boat of HMS *Paladin* arrived at the southeast pier, deposited Harrison and his shore party, and quickly rowed away, returning to the ship. But as they departed, a scurrying was heard, and, leaping the yard or so from the jolly to the pier, was none other than Stewie, the cat.

"Dear Lord!" exclaimed Harrison. "What in the name of the saints is that cat doing here?"

"Stewie!" called Sean, who immediately broke ranks and ran to the animal.

"Get back in line, Flagon!" called Hudson angrily.

"But it's Stewie!" he exclaimed, reaching for the cat.

"Now, Flagon!" called Hudson, turning red.

This outburst frightened the mouser, who immediately ran away, hiding under a nearby fruit cart. Sean could only look and slowly return to his position.

As they marched away, he glanced over his shoulder, hoping his furry friend would follow; however, he saw nothing more of the cat.

"Don't worry, Seany," said Hicks softly. "I bet 'ell wait fer us right thar!"

* * * * *

Harrison led the small party deeper into town. Before long, they began to climb the hill to the viscount's villa. Sean, nervous and alert, seemed to believe that everyone in town was staring at him and his armed friends. Of course, they *were*, as all the *Paladins* were in full uniform: Harrison in his best-kept deep-navy-blue jacket, hat trimmed in gold, and sword in a silver sheath at his hip. The three marines — Hudson, Hicks, and Flagon — in their scarlet coats and the several deckhands in their embroidered and tasseled hats were a sight to see for the townspeople.

"Stay alert, men," reminded Harrison.

A well vocalized chorus of "Yes, sir!" echoed through the streets off the stone-walled buildings. This, of course, set the townspeople into wide smiles, as if the parade were staged for their enjoyment; several began to clap, almost encouraging the Englishmen to perform again.

"This day will not end soon enough for me," said the commander under his breath.

Aboard the *Paladin*, Jonathan paced the deck after putting men at the corners of the ship to keep watch on the surroundings. He spent most of his attention overlooking the starboard rail, with Jenkins at his side. Both had agreed that the most dangerous adversary, if there was to be one, would come not from shore, but from the sea.

There was more on Jonathan's mind than enemy ships or cutting crews.

"It is peculiar, Jenkins, that I am now in command instead of Quinn, is it not?"

"Aye, sir, it is," said Jenkins. "But not totally unexpected," he added with a slight smile as he gazed outward to the sea.

"And why do you say that?" asked Jonathan.

"It is obvious that Captain Harrison has no confidence in Lieutenant Quinn. He has considerable respect for you and your judgment, on the other hand."

"But I have not been exemplary on this cruise, with the withholding of information and, well, basically destroying the foremast with sheer stupidity. I don't even have a proper uniform to wear," commented Jonathan.

Jenkins smiled. "It's not the uniform, my dear departedpappy used to say, but the man inside it!"

"Well," said Jonathan, "I hope the angels are looking over us, because we will need all the help we can get!"

Jonathan looked to Quinn, who was at the bow speaking with two of the new men, Crump and Crystal. Jonathan felt uncomfortable with the command arrangement, but Quinn had done this to himself. He had second-guessed Harrison more than once—and in an unprofessional manner.

After a few words with Quinn, the two new men descended belowdecks, and Quinn approached the starboard rail.

"Mister Moore, I have sent all the men to their guns, and Crump and Crystal are teamed with the more experienced men I sent below to inventory and secure. I thought it would be good to have them gain some experience."

"A grand idea, Lieutenant Quinn," Jonathan responded. "Would you join us in our observation of the surrounding bay, then?"

"With pleasure," said Quinn, and took up his scope and began searching the mouth to the bay.

He seems content and comfortable, thought Jonathan.

This might be easier than I thought!

Harrison stood back and allowed Sean to raise the giant door knocker that was affixed to the entry of the villa. He rapped three times, loudly.

"Almost as stunning as Captain Walker's back home!" Sean said. Then he took his place next to Hudson and Hicks.

Within a moment, the grand door opened and the viscount of Zadar stood smiling.

"Captain Harrison, I presume?"

"Indeed. And you must be Baron Ragusa, Viscount of Zadar. Mister Garvino sends his regards."

"Ah! Garvino, that old wagger!" the viscount said, laughing. "I have not seen him since we spent a holiday in Madrid! He told you of that, I am sure?"

Harrison felt slightly more at ease. The acceptance of the name Garvino and the mention of *Madrid* and *holiday* would not be coincidence. The viscount was certainly privy to the plan, or the charade, thought Harrison.

"He did mention that event," answered Harrison.

"Please! Please! Welcome to my home! Enter! Would you and your men join me on the loggia? The climb up the hill will take the breath away from even one of His Majesty's Marines, and build quite a thirst, yes?"

The viscount's smile and polite manners were disarming. Harrison agreed, and the party stepped indoors.

"Ship! A ship!" called Garvey from the crow's nest of the *Paladin*. "Three points off our port bow!"

All raised their glasses and trained them to the sea. Jonathan clearly could see a two-masted ship flying the English Union Jack. Its sails were only partly functioning, there was smoke about the deck, and men ran to and fro.

"The *Echo*!" Garvey exclaimed. "She is under attack!"

"But from whom?" asked Quinn.

"Ah! A ship to her stern!" called Jenkins.

Jonathan pointed his glass astern of the *Echo*. Yes, he

saw it: a three-masted brig, possibly thirty-six guns. They fired. Looking back instinctively to the *Echo*, he saw men fall on deck—but no damage to the ship.

"Grapeshot!" said Quinn. "They are trying to take the ship, not sink it. The attackers have…the Turkish flag! I see the white crescent and star on a field of red!"

"We must give aid to the *Echo*!" cried Jonathan. "Jenkins, fire three successive rounds from the stern deck guns!"

"I will do it!" said Quinn and ran immediately to his duty.

"Jenkins, with this pitiful breeze, we will be lucky to crawl out to sea, but have the men add all sail. I will see to the anchors!"

"Yes, sir!" said Jenkins.

At the Villa Ragusa, Harrison sat across from the nobleman, sipping cool tea. The remaining Englishmen stood about, also enjoying a beverage. Sean and Hudson sipped nervously as they watched both men closely.

"Splendid tea, Viscount. I thank you most happily."

"You are welcome, Captain Harrison."

"Though, this is not why we are here, is it? To sip tea? I believe I have something for you?"

"Why rush to business?" said Ragusa. "It is a lovely day, we are both gentlemen servicing the side of peace for our nations, and our duty is mostly done. Let us relax and celebrate our success."

"I would assume you would desire to get the treaty to the tsar with all haste. Being in Austrian-controlled Dalmatia, it might be difficult," added Harrison.

"Not at all. The current peace makes communication to all parts of the world much easier. I have a fast yacht, the *Kérata Vátrachos*. She will sail tomorrow. What could possibly happen that would stop our efficacious conclusion of this mission?"

Almost on cue, all in the loggia heard three booms fired in succession, coming from the bay. The Englishmen immediately ran to the edge of the balcony.

"The *Paladin*!" exclaimed Sean.

"Is there trouble?" asked the viscount.

"That is our signal!" said Harrison. He pointed to the nearby telescope. "Viscount, may I?"

"Of course, Captain!"

It took no time at all for Harrison to locate the *Paladin*, now under sail and heading out to sea. He could also see the *Echo* under attack from a larger, unmarked ship astern and slightly to port.

"*Paladin* is moving to assist *Echo*!" he said. "There is a thirty-six attacking! That fool Andrews! His sails are luffing, and he is scrambling about like an ape! He is not returning fire!"

"Who is attacking?" asked the viscount.

"The flag is…red, with white crescent and star," said Harrison.

"Rogue Turks!" said the viscount. "They appear from time to time off these shores. In these days of peace, many have turned to piracy. They are trying to gain ships for their future wars against the Russians that surely will resume!"

"What will Jonathan do?" asked Sean. "Shouldn't we return at once?"

"There would be no use," said Harrison, still with an eye glued to the glass. "He is underway. Dear Lord! How could I have put Jonathan in such a predicament? He's just a boy!"

"Commander Harrison, beggin' your pardon," said Hudson. "He's no ordinary boy."

"Jenkins!" Jonathan called. "What are we to do?"

"You are in command, Mister Moore."

"Damn it, Jenkins, I know that! But I have never maneuvered a ship in battle! Stop giving me lessons like a schoolmaster and suggest something!"

"Well, sir, you want to assist the *Echo* with your guns. Put as much firepower on the enemy as possible, then get away quickly to remount a second attack. She's a bigger ship, and one broadside won't do the whole job. Sir."

Without hesitation, Jonathan called to Fawcett.

"Fawcett, dead ahead west. Approach the thirty-six and a hard starboard turn with the wind assisting will put our portside guns to her side. If Andrews can come to his port and fire his guns, we will have the thirty-six between us."

"A sound improvement, Mister Moore!" said Jenkins.

Aboard the fast cruiser *Navarkhia*, Commodore Kharitonov smiled as he himself piloted the ship in battle. He had seen the *Paladin* approaching to assist her sister ship, thereby taking the bait. Also, and surprisingly to him, he saw that Aggar had successfully moved the old hulk — the rotting ship — from its position behind the small islands to the north, closer to the mouth of the Bay of Zadar, yet still out of the view of anyone in town or at the stone villa on the hill.

"Morozov!" he bellowed. "Take the wheel, and hold a steady course!"

"Aye, sir!" said Morozov as he took control of the helm.

"Skryrabin! Fire another smoke round above the deck of the *Echo*!" Kharitonov called to his lieutenant as he approached the rail. "It will look as if we are thoroughly engaged! Then load grape shot!"

The *Paladin* now had a fair amount of crosswind filling the sails as she entered the open sea past the entrance to the bay. Jonathan saw that the large thirty-six was now almost directly ahead, possibly two hundred yards. There were no men aboard observing his approach, and the deck guns were not firing upon him. Am I lucky, he thought, or are they too bent on the *Echo*?

"Come to starboard, Mister Fawcett. Now!"

"Aye, sir!" said Fawcett.

Paladin performed the maneuver, and catching the

wind, came fast alongside the cruiser, only fifty feet away. Jonathan now noticed a change in his enemy's tactic: the gun crews were now directing their weapons low to the deck of the *Paladin*.

"*Paladins*! Fire!" he called.

Nothing happened.

"Fire!" he called again, turning to the main deck.

The gun crews stood beside each piece, torches lit, and tapping the holes atop the guns. But no piece would ignite.

Aboard the *Navarkhia*, Kharitonov quickly called out his command.

"Strelyat!"

His starboard guns, all eighteen, let loose round after round of hot shot, all into the deck of the *Paladin*. Jonathan and others reacted fast enough and fell quickly to the deck, avoiding the deadly raking. Others were struck and killed.

There had been enough momentum building that the *Paladin* kept her speed and sailed on past the *Navarkhia* to the north.

As the enemy fell behind, Jenkins appeared at Jonathan's side.

"The guns?" said the man.

"What happened?" Jonathan yelled to the deck.

Marshall was inspecting the touchhole on his gun, and even from Jonathan's distance, he could see the man's face turn pale.

"Somethin's jammed in the touchhole, sir!"

"Mine as well!" called Jones.

"Here too!" said Smith.

Quinn! thought Jonathan. He was to inspect the guns! Harrison was right! Quinn was more than inept; he was a saboteur! He must have spiked the touchholes with something—wood, or worse. It was probably also Quinn who caused the chaser to backfire into the foremast!

"Smith! Jones!" Jonathan yelled. "Find Quinn and bring him here immediately! And bind his hands tightly!"

"He went below!" called Southcott. "I saw him!"

"Yer with us, then!" called Smith as he and Jones ran to the ladder and disappeared below.

"The *Echo* is escaping to the north!" called Garvey from the crow's nest.

Indeed, Jonathan could see that the *Echo* was a hundred yards ahead of them, fleeing. They had added sail and moved while the *Navarkhia* was engaging the *Paladin*.

"Jenkins, get the men to add sail," ordered Jonathan. "We must run away to—"

But as Jonathan looked ahead, he froze in terror. Another ship lay in their path. It had no colors. Looking to the *Echo*, he witnessed another disturbing image: she was striking her colors.

Harrison could see the action unfolding before him, and he gave voice to what he saw so all on the loggia could hear.

"There is no return of fire from *Paladin*!" exclaimed Harrison.

"The *Paladin* did not fire?" asked Sean. "Why not?"

"I haven't a clue!" cried Harrison. "She is taking damage to the deck but still maneuvering. I cannot see the *Echo*—she has moved past the tower to the north. The Turk ship is pursuing! She is turning to starboard to give a side to the *Paladin* as she flees! Hurry, Jonathan! Hurry!"

Aboard the *Navarkhia*, Kharitonov was in full glory. He laughed and shouted commands to his crew. Aggar's plan was working perfectly. He knew his spy aboard the English ship, Tretiak, would not fail them. He surely knew enough to ensure that the *Paladin* never fired a shot. That is initiative, thought Kharitonov. He would reward him with his own command once they had secured this pesky little English brig. Possibly, he would have Tretiak command the *Paladin*, and Aggar would remain on the *Echo*. Yes, that would do nicely. Of course, the ship names would be changed and their appearance altered. No one could know that these were English ships at one time—especially the English. There was no need to worry, though. The Royal Navy rarely made appearances in the Black Sea. Kharitonov and his small flotilla could cruise the inland waters unmolested for years.

The perfectly executed turn to starboard had *Navarkhia* facing almost directly to shore, the tower on the northern point of the bay just ahead. Kharitonov looked over his right shoulder and spotted the viscount's villa immediately, high on the hill. Within another few seconds, it would move behind the rise of the tower and out of view. Anyone there, watching, would see no details of the final actions of the plan.

"I hope you are paying attention!" he called to the villa with a laugh, then yelled his command to the crew, as loud as thunder: "Strelyat!"

From the hill, Harrison saw the *Paladin* disappear from view.

"I can still see the Turk!" he said, referring incorrectly to the *Navarkhia*. "She has completed her turn!"

Sean stared out to sea, watching as best he could. The land to the north rose slightly, and his view was masked by woodland and stone structures. However, it was unmistakable that the *Navarkhia* had just fired a broadside.

"She has fired," said Harrison.

Immediately, the men heard two explosions: the first, a muted ripple of the guns from the *Navarkhia*. Then, immediately after, there was a thundering boom, much larger than any sound coming from guns. It was accompanied by a flash of light beyond the tower. Harrison could easily see planking and other debris flying through the air.

"W-what was that?" cried Sean.

"An explosion!" said Harrison. "A ship's magazine has been hit!"

"A magazine? The gunpowder?" asked the viscount.

"Harrison! Not the *Paladin*!" cried Sean.

Harrison watched as the *Navarkhia* turned slightly to

starboard, slipping behind the tower.

"Was it the *Paladin*?" asked Hudson anxiously.

"I cannot tell. They have all passed out of sight!" said Harrison.

"We must go! Now!" cried Sean, grabbing at Harrison's coat. "Jonathan may need us!"

"Just hold!" Harrison said, obviously upset. "Allow me to observe a moment longer!"

Harrison remained with his eye to the glass, staring at the edge of his view, the last place where the large Turk ship had disappeared. He was waiting for something, anything, that would help him decide on his next move. Eventually, if his notions were correct, the Turk would run back south from where it came, in an effort to turn east and use the Bosphorus Strait to return to the Back Sea. Surely, that is where she came from and would want to deliver her catch — either the *Echo* or the *Paladin* — to home waters. Only one ship would follow it, he was certain, the one ship that had been taken; the other was surely destroyed.

"Please," he said softly, "let the *Paladin* be afloat!"

After a moment, Harrison's hopes were dashed. Through the telescope, he could clearly see the *Echo*, flag struck, sailing back to the south. The *Navarkhia* was right behind. It was clear that the ship that had exploded could only have been HMS *Paladin*.

"Dear God," was all he could say.

"I will gladly loan you my yacht," offered the viscount. "You can use it to look for survivors."

Sean and Hudson dropped to their knees in shock and sadness.

"Oh," cried Sean. "J-jonny. M-my brother —" He then collapsed in utter despair, sobbing uncontrollably.

19

Interrogation

Delain could ascertain a few facts about her surroundings even though her mouth was gagged, her eyes blindfolded, and something was shoved in her ears, partially blocking out sound. She was in a basement. This she knew because she was jostled as her kidnapper stepped down a short flight of stairs. It was also warm, so they were probably in the basement of a building near a furnace warming the basement and rooms above.

She also knew that two men had abducted her. She had heard their voices, and during the process of tying her to the chair she sat upon, she counted at least four hands on her, securing ropes.

Never did they speak once inside, never did they remove the sack over her head that covered the upper half of her body. The gag in her mouth was not only slightly irritating, but it tasted like an old sock. She worked to spit it out of her mouth, but it was slow going.

She was petrified. Again, she thought of Jonathan, and wished that somehow he could rescue her. Yes, that was an odd thought for Delain Dowdeswell, so sure of herself and her abilities; yet even for her, there were times when receiving even a little help was acceptable, and this was certainly one of those times.

After what seemed to be an hour of sitting in this condition, the door opened. She could barely hear it, but the pressure changed in the room: it lightened. Then, the door closed again. She could hear muffled voices.

"I came as fast as I could," whispered a man with a deep voice. "Are you sure no one saw you?"

"Aye, sir, we was as quiet and as quick as a bunny,"

said another man with a softer voice.

"And you have asked no questions?" asked the deep voice.

"Not a one," answered the third man, with a more raspy tone and manner.

"Well, then," said the deep voice, loudly enough that Delain could hear clearly. He moved behind her and grasped the sack. "Let us have a look at the mysterious spy!"

The sack was instantly and violently pulled upward.

"Mister O!" said the deep voice triumphantly.

"O?" said Delain, spitting out the gag. "Who in the name of the king is Mister O?"

The men were shocked, though Delain could not read their expressions as the sudden light from the furnace blinded her momentarily.

"Who the 'ell are you?" said the closest man.

"A girl!" said the raspy-voiced one. "I knew the load was too light! I thought 'e was a midget!"

The deep-voiced man now walked from behind the bound subject to see for himself. Shock, surprise, bewilderment, and abject confusion all flooded his senses at the same time.

"Now, as I have said once before, I have seen everything in this life!"

Delain's eyes finally focused, though it was unnecessary for her to see who said these words. She had heard them before, and she instantly knew who had captured her.

"Captain Gorman!" she said, relieved.

"Delain Dowdeswell!" he said, still beside himself with confusion.

"You know her?" asked Frey.

"This isn't Mister O," said Fairchild.

"I know that!" exploded Gorman. "Why did you grab *her*?"

"We didn't know it was a *her*, Captain!" said Frey. "We thought *she* was a *he*, all cloaked up 'n skulking around."

"We were watchin' the alley be'ind the pub," said

Fairchild, "'cause the last time we followed Mister O, that's where he went with Lupien."

"Is Mister O the Black Rider?" asked Delain.

"Black Rider?" asked Gorman as he removed the wax plugs that had been placed in her ears. Delain looked at it, and gasped.

"Ee-yew! What is that?"

"We're doin' the askin' here, missy!" said Frey.

"And ya had best answer us truthfully, ya hear?" added Fairchild.

"I do not think so!" said Delain. "You have kidnapped a daughter of a member of the House of Lords, and you will—"

"Enough!" said Gorman. "Everyone be quiet! I will ask all the questions, and all of you will answer! Is that understood?"

"Why did you kidnap me?" asked Delain angrily.

Gorman was beside himself. "What did I just say? No one talks but me!"

"If we can't talk," said Delain, "how can we answer your—"

Gorman reached in his pocket and drew a long knife.

"I swear! The next one who speaks out of turn will regret it!"

They all became silent. Gorman approached Delain with the knife purely visible. She saw the blade and was suddenly confused and scared.

Gorman regarded her, anger plainly visible on his face. Then he used the long knife—to cut the bonds about Delain's wrists and feet.

"Bring Miss Dowdeswell a glass of water immediately," commanded Gorman.

Delain was relieved, as were Frey and Fairchild, who both complied and soon returned with the glass for the young girl.

"Delain," began Gorman, "does Lady Bracknell know you are not at home?"

"Of course not!" she snapped, insulted by the suggestion. "I was careful to sneak out unnoticed. Do you think I am some rank amateur?"

"Why are you here?" Gorman asked.

Delain took a drink of water from the glass. It felt good going down and had a calming effect. Now out of danger, she had a chance to think. Certainly, she and Gorman were investigating the same events, though from different sides. It was surely time to join forces and see what each network had uncovered.

"I was following the Black Rider," she said matter-of-factly.

"And who would that be?" said Gorman.

"I don't know his name; however," started Delain, "it all began last Wednesday, as I was on my way to tea at the home of Lord and Lady Wilder with Miss Thompson. Whilst still in the carriage, I saw a man in all black riding a black stallion through Van Patten Wood. He was being pursued by two men on horseback. It was exciting to watch, especially when he gave them the slip—easily enough, I might add."

Frey and Fairchild looked at each other, frowning.

"The pursuers," said Gorman with a sigh, "were none other than your kidnappers, Mister Frey and Mister Fairchild, my associates."

"At your service," both men said, bowing their heads in embarrassment.

"They were tailing this Black Rider of yours, known to us as *Mister O*," said Gorman. "Do you have any idea why he was in the woods?"

"His business was not in the woods," said Delain. "However, I saw him emerge from the thicket after I arrived at the Wilders' estate. He slipped into the house through a back door, so I left the carriage and went to investigate. Through the library window, I watched him place a package in the shelves of books. Later, I discovered it was a bag containing two handwritten notes and exactly five thousand pounds sterling."

Frey and Fairchild each let out a low whistle.

Gorman looked surprised. "I hate to ask this, Miss Dowdeswell, because I am sure I will not like the answer; however...how do you know what was in the bag?"

Delain smiled with satisfaction.

"I looked!" she said.

"Dear me," said Gorman.

"Let me start at the beginning of the tea party," Delain began.

"Always good to start at the beginnin'" said Frey.

"After an hour of the tea, I affected illness!" she continued, now directing the story to Frey and Fairchild, who listened, completely captivated. "And once I was led to a guest room to recover, I slipped out and made my way to the library. Behind a book that had been disturbed, in the otherwise neat and orderly row, I found a bag. I opened it. Inside, I saw and counted the money. There were also two notes. One note had today's date on it and the time of three a.m. That is how I knew to follow him! So earlier this evening, I left the Bracknell Manor, took a horse, and rode through Van Patten Wood. I stood in the shadows of the trees about the Wilder Mansion, and waited."

She paused for effect. Frey and Fairchild were standing, eyes open wide, anticipating the next part of the plot.

"G'won!" said Frey.

"What's next?" asked Fairchild.

"Dear, dear, dear..." said Gorman, shaking his head.

"Lord Wilder emerged from his house by the back door, wearing a dark cloak and hood," said Delain. "He hid in a tree shadow not twenty feet from me! Then I saw him enter a carriage that appeared right in front of his home. I followed on my filly."

Gorman held his head in his hands. "The other note, then. You said there were two."

"The other note was longer—a letter, really. At first I thought it was in a code of some sort," stated Delain. "So, not wanting to steal it and alert Lord Wilder that I was on to him, I copied it! I had it translated by my professor. It

271

was in Russian."

"Russian?" asked Frey.

"Lupien is Russian!" added Fairchild.

"Who is Lupien?" asked Delain.

"He is a Russian spy we have been watching. Let me see the letter, if you please," asked Gorman.

Delain frowned and thought that, surely, once Gorman had all the pieces to his puzzle, he would cut her out of the investigation—possibly even inform Lady Bracknell to keep Delain under house arrest or some such thing. That would be totally unfair. How can I keep myself in this plot? A deal? Yes!

"I will show you the note, if…you allow me to continue my investigation."

"No," said Gorman. "Out of the question."

"Yes."

"No."

"Yes," said Delain firmly.

"No!" said Gorman, more firmly.

"Then I won't tell you what the second letter said."

Gorman knew that the young girl had a point. He would have to figure out a way for Delain to be involved with the investigation but never be in danger. At least creating a plan with her would give him some control over what she would be doing. He could then possibly keep her safe.

"All right," he said reluctantly.

"And you are a man of your word?" she asked.

"As far as you are concerned, yes," said Gorman.

"Then here is the note," she said, retrieving it from the folds in her cloak.

Gorman studied the original note, then read the translation. Art? Odd. Here were numbers: eighteen, thirty-six. Gorman handed the letter to Fairchild. Then he stood and began pacing. He seemed to be trying to put two and two together, but there was something missing.

"Let us review what we know," he said. "First, there is a Russian spy, Lupien, whom we have seen about the docks. Second, Lupien had a book with ship names in it, listing their armaments, sizes, et cetera. Mildly interesting by itself; however, three, we have witnessed Lupien associating with this horseman of yours."

"Mister O," said Frey, attempting to keep things clear in his own head.

"Four, Wilder is dealing in art, it appears, and five, Mister O is associating with Lord Wilder on the matter, in the middle of the night, and is paying him great sums of money. And since Lupien is a spy, and Mister O seems to be a spy—"

"Then Wilder is up to no good!" said Delain triumphantly. "I knew it!"

"But what 'no good' is 'e up to?" asked Fairchild.

"That is where, I believe, we are missing some information. Art dealing is not a crime, though it is suspicious that he would be discussing it at three in the morning in a private carriage."

"With a spy," added Delain.

The room fell silent. Only the crackling of the wood in the furnace interrupted their thoughts. Delain stood, rubbing her wrists where they had been bound. Frey and Fairchild stood looking at the ceiling and then the floor, deep in thought.

Gorman ran over the facts in his head, over and over, and eventually began murmuring them out loud.

"Lupien. Wilder. Mister O. A book of ship names. Money. Russian notes about art."

"Art," said Delain. "That tidbit is the odd one."

Gorman took the letter from Frey, who had now finished reading and inspected it once again.

"Eighteen pieces...thirty-six pieces..." he said.

Then it hit him, like a ball from a gun—a gun aboard one of His Majesty's...

"Ships!" he exclaimed.

"Ships?" asked Fairchild.

"The letter!" said Gorman excitedly. "It is both written in Russian *and* in code! The *art* is *ships*, and the numbers, eighteen and thirty-six — are guns!"

"They are planning to steal ships," said Delain, worried.

"And Lupien's book is the shopping list!" added Gorman.

"All o' the ships 'e had documented were thirty-six guns or smaller," said Frey.

"That means their targets will be schooners 'n sloops," added Fairchild, "the size of the *Paladin* and the *Echo*, for example."

"At least the *Paladin* is safe," she said. "The *Echo* as well."

"How do you know that?" asked Gorman.

"I received a letter from Jonathan only a day ago," she said. "He has seen the *Echo*."

Gorman looked at the girl with a questioning frown. He thought of his meeting with Slater, who reported that the *Echo* was missing and that no one had seen her. He let out an audible gasp.

"Delain," said Gorman carefully, "what did Jonathan say about the *Echo*?"

"He said they saw her," said Delain.

"Are you sure? The *Echo*?"

"Why, yes," continued Delain. "It was peculiar, he said, that the new captain, a Captain Andrews, I believe, was unknown to him. The *Echo* was handled poorly. Jonathan said it was no match for the military precision of the *Paladin* and her crew."

Gorman ran to her and held her tightly by the shoulders.

"Delain! When was this letter written?" Gorman asked in a frantic voice.

"The seventh of this month!" she said, now afraid.

"Where was he when he saw the *Echo*? Did he say?"

"I'm not sure, I —"

"Quickly, Delain! Think!" Gorman shook the girl, hoping to aid her concentration.

"Near Gibraltar, but the *Paladin* was headed toward

some other place. It was called…Tesla…Telass—"

"Telašćica?" suggested Fairchild.

"Yes!" Delain said. "Telašćica!"

"Delain, the *Echo* is missing. It never reported to Gibraltar Station. It is now weeks overdue," said Gorman, "and her captain, according to the Admiralty, is Lieutenant Joshua Gray."

"But how can that be?" asked Delain. "How could the *Echo* have a captain other than Gray, and the Admiralty be unaware? And how can she be missing if Jonathan has just seen—oh my lord!" she exclaimed. "She has already been taken!"

"It appears so," said Gorman, now releasing the girl. "It is the only explanation. The crew of the *Paladin* must have seen the *Echo* and believed the story of a new captain being assigned. Obviously, this Andrews from Jonathan's letter must be an imposter. He is posing as an English captain."

"Why? Why steal an English ship and then approach another English ship? Why not just run away?" asked Delain.

"Because, they want to get as close to the *Paladin* as they can, keeping her unaware—"

"So they could steal her as well! Oh! Jonathan! My friends!" said Delain, immediately almost breaking into tears. "What are we to do?"

The men tried to calm the young girl, however, she carried on for some time. She thought of her last few moments with Jonathan, and of all the things she wished to say to him. She regretted not telling him exactly how she felt and what her dreams might be. Would she ever see him again?

After a while, she ceased sobbing and simply asked, "What are we to do?"

"Our plan must be this," said Gorman finally and firmly. "We must confirm our suspicions. At this point it is all circumstantial. Wilder is certainly at the center of this. Gentlemen? Get me Lord Wilder. I don't care how you do it. I don't care if you damage him. I don't care what your methods. Just don't let him know who we are until we reveal ourselves. Bring him here."

"How?" asked Frey.

"Delain, assist them by devising another note, identical to the one you have seen, telling him to be ready for a meeting in the carriage on this Thursday night. Place it on his person somehow. I am sure you can find a way to deliver it and ensure he reads it?"

"I will think of something," she said with conviction.

"I will see Captain Spears first thing in the morning," continued Gorman. "I will get some answers from him, and ascertain who this Andrews character is and what he knows about Wilder and his plans."

They all stood to leave, Frey and Fairchild donning their hoods and stepping into the alley, checking to make sure all was clear. It was only an hour before sunrise, the air still chill, the neighborhood quiet. Delain and Gorman received the all clear and exited the building. Delain turned to Gorman and held his arm firmly.

"We must not fail them," she said—a question more than a statement.

"We will not, Miss Dowdeswell," said Gorman. "And we do have one advantage they did not think of nor plan for."

"What is that?" she asked.

"Jonathan Moore is on the *Paladin*. And he will not go quietly."

Delain smiled, and they disappeared into the night.

20
Flotsam and Jetsam

Captain Harrison had graciously accepted Viscount Ragusa's offer to use his private yacht, the *Kérata Vátrachos*, in an attempt to search for survivors. Along with Marine Sergeant Hudson, Corporal Hicks, and Private Sean Flagon, Harrison left the Villa Ragusa immediately, and met with the rest of their party in town. The others had been sent ahead to look for witnesses and uncover any details of the attacks as seen from shore. Luckily for all, they also located Stewie, sitting on a post of the pier, a small pelican by his side, each fighting for a piece of some dead fish — mostly bones and scales, though for them, a delicacy.

Sean was understandably numb to the entire affair.

Once aboard the *Kérata*, they had no trouble commanding the yacht across the bay. It was a fine little ship, a yacht by some measure, but as large as an English cutter at sixty-eight feet long, twenty or so in the beam, and possibly one hundred tons. The large single mast held three triangular jib sails running fore and aft — and square-rigged courses and topsails as well. A spanker was mounted aft. Though smaller than those of the *Paladin*, the *Kérata* mounted considerable canvass, and they passed swiftly into the open ocean as the sun rose to noon.

At first, they saw nothing. No hulk floating in the water, no mast protruding from the calm waves. As they moved farther north, they could see something large underwater, but it was too deep to discern.

"It could be a ship," said Harrison. "But it is too deep

to see. The water here is murky and deep. We must continue toward shore."

Piloting the yacht himself, Harrison moved the *Kérata* closer to the shallows. There, they began to see flotsam in the water. And bodies.

"There is Miller!" exclaimed Hudson. "One of my marines!"

Certainly, there he was, still in uniform, floating face up in the turquoise water. They recognized others.

"There is Smith!" called Welty. "And Jones!"

All ran to the rail and observed the bodies of their dear friends who had been with them since the *Poseidon*.

"Dear Lord, I can't believe this," said Sean as he collapsed to the deck.

"I see an officer's coat!" cried Bowman. "Off the starboard rail!"

All save Sean ran to starboard. The body they saw was floating facedown in the water.

"It looks like a…a midshipman's coat," said Harrison, choking back his tears. The hair, the size of the body—it could only be Jonathan.

Hicks had grabbed a long spar and reached out to the floating form. He struggled, and as he moved the body closer, it began to roll over. The face of the form now lay upward.

"Southcott?" said Hicks.

"What in the wide world is going on?" asked Harrison.

Sean now joined them at the rail. He stared at the body. Then through his tears, he sensed some odd form of relief. He took in a breath.

"Southcott? When did he get promoted to midshipman?"

"This is no midshipman's coat," said Harrison. "The piping is wrong. Look! The insignia on the lapel has been removed. This is a lieutenant's coat."

They did their best to lash a rope around the body and bring it aboard. They also did the same for the others found in the water, and soon, they had six bodies on deck. It was a macabre scene to say the least, but with each body found, they were more and more relieved. None of the bodies had been Jonathan. Or Jenkins. Or Garvey. Or the brothers Stredney. And though they grieved for their lost friends, they could not help but be encouraged.

Sean began wrapping the corpses in blankets he found below in the small hold as Harrison moved the yacht closer to shore. When he felt the keel scrape the sandy bottom, the commander ordered the anchor dropped. The *Kérata Vátrachos* swung stern first toward shore. Harrison surveyed the beach; it was strewn with barrels, planks of wood, charred lumber, and all nature of debris.

Harrison stared into the water, at first, absentmindedly, and then looking at floating bits of wood, some charred, some not. On one particular piece, large enough to have possibly been a deck plank, he could make out the striations of the holystone that had been used to clean the piece. The edges were slightly singed. It looked like oak, from what he could tell, and the plank itself was wide, as the decking was wide on the *Danielle* and the *Poseidon*. This struck him as being incorrect. He looked closer, then surveyed several other pieces.

"This is not right..." he said, his voice trailing off as a smile came to his face.

He immediately took off his jacket, his shoes, and his sword and then stood on the rail.

"Harrison?" asked Sean.

"What is 'e doing?" asked Hicks.

Sean thought for a moment, then shrugged his shoulders, took off his shoes and coat, and without hesitation, followed his captain, performing a beautiful swan dive into the sea.

"Going for a closer look?" postulated Hudson.

Harrison swam as hard as he could toward the shoreline, now and then stopping to inspect a piece of floating wood or a barrel. Sean did the same.

"They are onto something," said Welty.

"Good swimmers too, they are!" commented Bowman.

Within two minutes, Harrison and Sean were on shore, running to and from the many items that were there on the beach and in the surf.

"The sextant!" cried Harrison.

Sean approached him and said, "On the beach? Could it have been blown here by the blast?"

"Yes," said Harrison, "but look at it closely. It is barely scratched."

They moved hurriedly down the shore. A few yards away, they located Alexander's locker, being a set of drawers, actually. The drawers themselves were nearby, some of their contents spread about the beach, with papers blowing about.

"Alexander's locker," Harrison said excitedly. "Not a burn mark on it!"

"And the kegs I saw in the water as we swam," added Sean. "They were almost completely empty and unscathed. How could this be?"

"The answer is in the flotsam and jetsam. Do you know the difference?"

"Aye!" said Sean. "Flotsam is from wreckage. It's pieces of a ship, usually. We saw that in the water and on the beach. Spars, rigging, planks —"

"And jetsam?"

"Jetsam is what we toss over willingly. Sometimes to lighten the load. Kegs of water, powder, guns."

"Right," said Harrison. "Now, some of the flotsam we found was burned and strewn about. Interesting is what is *not* in the flotsam."

"What?" asked Sean, truly lost.

"Teak," answered Harrison.

Sean thought for a moment. He had not seen any teak planking.

"Yes," said Sean, waiting for explanation. "There was no teak."

"Odd, isn't it?" said Harrison. "An all-teak decked

ship, the *Paladin*, is blown to pieces, yet no pieces of teak?"

"But the sextant and the locker!" said Sean. "Those are undeniably our effects!"

"Yes! *Jetsam*! Tossed overboard! Anything that was not tied down was easily sent over the rail, our lockers, clothes, bodies of the dead, the sextant—which, by the way, would sink, not end up on a beach! And all magically drifted to this spot!"

"But where did all the flotsam—the burned wood and such—where did it come from? Something blew up! We saw the flash from the villa!"

Harrison smiled as he pointed to the place they saw the hulk under the waves. "From that hulk. It was most likely floating, packed with powder. They blew it up!"

"Yes, this is not right." Sean said slowly, now understanding.

"Andrews, or whatever his name is, has stolen the *Paladin*," said Harrison, "though he wishes us to believe it was destroyed!"

Harrison now looked to the south, to the last direction he saw the Turk ship. His heart began to swell with hope. "It all is now making sense."

"So," said Sean, adding all the facts. "Andrews stole the *Echo* and then tried to take the *Paladin* at Telašćica, but they failed! You didn't take the bait!"

"And Jonathan and Jenkins foiled the cutting-out attempt, so Andrews tried a third time, in Zadar, and succeeded!" said Harrison. "The letter from Gogomán was a fake, meant to direct us here. Sean, from the beginning, the change of orders set this all in motion, delivered by Quinn, who is as dirty as they come! I have been a fool!" cried Harrison.

"But Harrison!" protested Sean. "Why fake the *Paladin*'s destruction and allow us to see it?"

"They can't have us and the entire Royal Navy looking for them, can they?" said Harrison. "I can only assume that they wanted us to believe that the *Echo* was taken and that the *Paladin* also was lost. They want us to tell the Admiralty so they can get away with it."

Sean scratched his head. There was one piece that still didn't fit.

"Harrison, I see it all now, mostly. However, why would they dress Southcott in a lieutenant's coat, make it look like a midshipman's garb, and toss him overboard?"

Harrison smiled. "Andrews and his men did not dress Southcott in the lieutenant's coat."

"They didn't?"

"I am sure that the coat that Southcott is now wearing has been altered to *look* like a midshipman's. Who would want his captors to think he was dead? Someone who did not want to be recognized—"

"Oh!" exclaimed Sean. "Because *he* had wounded Aggar on the cheek at Telašćica! Jonathan! He is alive!"

"And probably right where he belongs!" laughed Harrison.

"In the thick of it! I can't wait to hear his side! We must tell the viscount!" said Sean. "He can help us!"

"No, Sean! He is in on this," said Harrison. "He was there to obtain the treaty, but I would not be surprised if it is all poppycock! The viscount's true purpose was to hold us there, off the ship, so it would make taking the *Paladin* easier."

"We are on our own then—stranded!" said Sean, suddenly concerned.

"Not quite," said Harrison with a smile.

21
Southcott's Twin

Harrison was correct. As he had watched from the home of Viscount Ragusa, Jonathan, aboard the *Paladin*, had seen the *Echo* turning easily away to the north after striking her colors. The *Navarkhia,* turning slightly toward shore, was readying to deliver a port broadside. Jonathan and the *Paladin* had been running, but the sight of the third ship appearing ahead had dashed all hopes.

This last ship, however, had a peculiar set of characteristics, and they all registered in his mind in a fraction of a second. First, the ship was a barge, not a warship. Second, there were no sails set. Third, it was at anchor; both the bow and stern were completely immobile, hawsers tight. Fourth, there was no crew. And most intriguing was the fact that there, stacked on the stern, sat keg after keg of gunpowder.

The *Navarkhia* fired her broadside from behind the *Paladin*. Jonathan saw the rounds come from the thirty-six, now ball instead of shot. It missed the *Paladin* completely, sailed past her starboard side, and then struck the kegs on the barge. The hulk exploded spectacularly, sending flame, smoke, and debris high into the air. The blast and heat could be felt by all remaining on deck.

In the middle of all this, Jonathan could only wonder what was happening. He knew one thing: that the *Navarkhia* could have blasted the *Paladin* hard — and damaged or sunk her with another broadside fired at close range. Why had she not? Because the captain of that ship wanted *Paladin* alive.

"They will board us, surely," Jonathan said, now

standing.

"But how do you know?" asked Jenkins.

"They could have easily sunk us right then and there, but they didn't. And look at the *Echo*: colors struck without a fight? I tell you this: Andrews is no Englishman. He was on our deck in Telašćica!"

"Mister Moore, how can you know this?" asked Fawcett.

"Look at him!"

The men stared intently at the *Echo*. It had completed its turn to the north, and now turned again, back to the *Paladin*. Andrews could be seen giving orders, the crew following them to precise execution, now appearing almost capable.

"They have recently developed some technique!" exclaimed Garvey as he came down from the crow's nest.

"Andrews had our English brothers belowdecks the whole time," said Jenkins. "That is why they bumbled and gaffed. Look, now they are in the tops, guns pointed at them to make sure they follow orders."

"He stole the *Echo*!" said Fawcett.

"And we are next!" said Jonathan. "Look at Andrews—closely. Do you see his face?"

It was unmistakable. As the *Echo* drew nearer, they saw a loose patch under Andrew's eye, tied by a white rag across his face.

"A wound, still bleeding!" said Jenkins. "By all the saints, Mister Moore! You did that to him with your blade."

"Yes, as I politely kicked him off the *Paladin*! And where is Quinn?" asked Jonathan. He ran to the nearest gun and checked the touchhole. "Something is jammed in here. Quinn was to check all the guns."

"This one as well!" said Garvey has he inspected the next gun down the line.

"Quinn sabotaged the guns to make sure we could not fire! That explains it!" added Jenkins.

"Harrison was right," offered Jonathan. "Quinn and most likely Crump and Crystal are all part of this. And I will make them pay."

The *Echo* had come about and positioned herself directly along *Paladin*'s port side. The *Navarkhia* was now at her starboard. Both ships drifted with the breeze, closing in on their prey, gun doors open. Men on their decks prepared to board.

"Mister Moore, if I could be so bold as to suggest a course of action?" asked Jenkins.

"I am all ears," the midshipman replied.

"Andrews, or whatever his name is, will be looking for you. And it will not be to dance. He will not recognize you by face, but certainly he will find you once he speaks to Quinn and his lackeys."

Jonathan thought quickly. He realized the course of action he must take.

"Sir," said Jenkins firmly, "we must kill Quinn and his men, Crump and Crystal."

Jonathan looked horrified. He swayed visibly. Had it really come to this? Was this what being in command meant? Is it truly the only way? After some hesitation, he realized that there was only one answer.

"I will do it," said Jonathan flatly. "It is my command."

"And take off lieutenant's coat," suggested Garvey.

"I will report to our guests that Midshipman Jonathan Moore perished in battle," added Jenkins.

"Then I am off to do some business below with my wardrobe and with Lieutenant Quinn, or whatever his real name might be! Keep them busy, Jenkins."

With that, Jonathan ran to the stern ladder and disappeared below.

"My fine English sailors!" called Aggar from the deck of the *Echo*. "Strike your colors — or we will send you to the bottom!"

"We are leaderless!" called Jenkins. "We have no officers to command us!"

Aggar wondered at this. Surely not all the officers could have perished. Though with their captain delivering the useless treaty, and much of his marine guard with him, that would only leave, possibly, a lieutenant and certainly one midshipman.

"Where is your lieutenant?" called Aggar.

"Dead. He perished in Telašćica," answered Jenkins.

"Then your midshipman? I know you have one," countered Aggar.

"He is dead as well. Just killed. His body is below."

Aggar realized his hopes for revenge were now dashed. Though he was angered, he was satisfied that at least the English brat was gone.

From the *Navarkhia*, a voice was heard, a deep bellow calling to the *Paladin*.

"Then who in hell are you?" bellowed Kharitonov.

Jenkins turned about to see the large cruiser. It had been her captain, a mean-looking brute, who addressed him.

"I am Jenkins, able seaman."

"I command you, Jenkins, to strike your colors," said Kharitonov as he hopped from the deck of the cruiser down to the *Paladin*.

"It will be done," Jenkins replied.

"And who are you?" Kharitonov said to Fawcett.

"I am sailing master," Fawcett replied.

Kharitonov produced a pistol and fired into Fawcett, who fell immediately, dead.

"I already have one," said the commodore.

Down below, Jonathan made his way toward the stern and Harrison's hidden locker by the ladder, the one Streen had built. Once there, he quickly took the key from his pants pocket and opened the lock. The tall, thin door swung easily, and inside, Jonathan could see his old, short sword from Lisbon, as well as Sean's. He had placed them there at Harrison's suggestion. A wool, capelike jacket that Harrison wore in his cabin at night to stave off the chill hung in the far corner. Also there were a few boxes containing Harrison's personal effects, his telescope, and a wooden box, which Jonathan opened. There he found the pistol Harrison had asked him to carry. He quickly removed the gun and loaded a charge and ball.

As he returned the box to its position, he noticed the lid did not fit well. Odd, he thought, and he removed the box to see what was underneath. There, in the bottom of the locker, was a burlap bag. Jonathan opened it. Inside: the diplomatic pouch holding the treaty. Harrison had not taken it with him. And now it would fall into the hands of these marauders. Best to destroy it, thought Jonathan. But how? It needed to be tossed overboard, which of course would be almost impossible with these pirates, or whoever they were, running all over the main deck. Hide it? It would be found eventually. Burn it?

A lantern above his head contained oil. A simple dousing and striking of a flint would do the trick, and though smoky and an open flame, if done correctly, with a small amount of oil, it would put itself out once the paper was consumed.

He opened the pouch, broke the seal of the large envelope, and took out the pages. He stared at them. The pages of the Treaty of Akbar were unreadable, for there was not a stroke of script on them. The pages were blank.

Stunned, Jonathan put them back in place, set them inside the locker, took the sword and the gun, and closed the locker door. He would think of this development later, but now, he was more than busy with the issues at hand.

Jonathan made his way amidships on the lower deck. Hammocks had been cleared for action, and barrels and crates were positioned securely, yet some were out of place, jostled recently by someone, or a group. A skirmish? wondered Jonathan. He heard voices ahead, angry ones, and he crept up closer, using a few sacks to hide himself.

As he moved forward, he could see bodies on the floor—Smith, Jones, and Southcott among them. Once amidships, he looked over a stack of barrels to see a small group of crewmen, anger on their faces. Finally, he saw Quinn just ahead with Crump and Crystal, all with their backs to him, each with pistols pointed at the crew, keeping the *Paladins* at bay.

"I said not a move or a sound!" snapped Quinn.

"Quinn! You dirty traitor!" said Colin Stredney.

"You will be next if I hear another word!" said Quinn, motioning to the pile of the dead. "And my name is not Quinn! I am Sublieutenant Tretiak, of the Russian Black Sea Fleet!"

Russian! thought Jonathan. What was this? The war must have started once again, and Russia has joined Napoleon against us!

"All of you, stay in line until I say to move, or we will cut you down, right here and right now!" ordered Quinn. He realized that he and his Russian compatriots were still in danger—the *Paladin* had not yet been taken, and until that happened, he would be on edge. It was his idea to try to turn the tide of the battle in favor of Kharitonov. Knowing that the letter from that fool, Gogomán, was sending them to Zadar, he reasoned that it had to be sent from Aggar and that another attempt would be made to take the English ship once they arrived. His plan to render the guns inept worked almost perfectly. He and Crump and Crystal had made sure of that by jamming shanks of metal and wood into the touchholes of every gun. Moore's last-minute call to sound the three-gun warning almost foiled his plot; however, he thought quickly and volunteered to fire those weapons himself. A quick removal of the obstruction, a firing, and a replacement was all that was necessary.

Jonathan gripped his sword. It had served him well and would take care of one man, if he could sneak up from behind. He needed a special plan to take out the other two. He reached underneath his shirt for Harrison's pistol, then stood ever so slowly, making sure that only the *Paladins* could see him.

Colin glanced for a moment, seeing Jonathan as he lifted a sword and a pistol. The midshipman then motioned with his head toward Crump, as if to say, "You take that one." Colin nodded ever so slightly.

Jonathan had never killed a man like this, with no warning. A thought for later, but for now, his men, his ship, and he himself were in danger. He leveled the pistol at Quinn's head, using his left hand. He was less than four feet away.

He fired.

Quinn's body slumped forward and fell to the deck.

As Crystal turned to see where the blast had come from, Jonathan was already there. His blade was thrust into the man's chest.

Colin and several others rushed Crump, who was immediately overtaken.

"Kill him," ordered Jonathan. And it was done. To his horror, he witnessed death up close, and though not the first time he had seen such actions, this occasion was due to his direct order. These deaths were on his hands, and it shook him deeply. But there was no time to reflect now.

"Men! Quickly!" Jonathan said as he removed his coat and motioned for them to come.

"Listen fast, and no questions. I am in danger. Do not call me Jonathan, Moore, or Midshipman. Do you understand?"

They all nodded in reply.

"Good," said Jonathan. "Their captain—Andrews, or whatever his name is—will recognize me."

"Oh!" said Graham, "And you cut his face! He will be angry!"

"He will kill me because of it. We need to show them I am dead. We must dress up someone, someone who was killed, as a midshipman, and call him Jonathan Moore."

"So they will think he is you? And that you are dead?" asked Nicolas. "Then they will leave you alone?"

"Exactly!" said Jonathan. "Here! Let us use this coat I have—"

"The dead man's coat from Alexander?" asked Colin.

"Yes, yes," said Jonathan, "and put it on—Southcott

there."

"On *his* dead body?" asked Colin.

"Yes, we are about the same size and age," said Jonathan as he removed the coat.

"It's bad luck!" said Colin.

"It's true!" said Nicolas. "It's bad luck to wear a dead man's clothes!"

"What are you saying?" asked Jonathan, now frustrated with the idiocy and the delay in execution of his orders.

"They are dead! Both Southcott and Alexander!" said Graham.

"Then it's probably *double* bad luck!" said Nicolas, almost crying. "Please, sir! Don't make us—"

"By all the saints!" hissed Jonathan, unable to yell at full power to express his wrath. "They are dead! They can't get any unluckier!"

The surrounding crew considered this.

"Oh," said Colin, understanding.

"Then it's proper...I guess," said Nicolas.

At last, the boys went to work, completing the grisly business of dressing Southcott in the lieutenant's jacket.

"And though Southcott is...dead, he is now *Midshipman* Moore. He did everything I have done in this life. Do you understand?"

"Yes, sir," they called softly.

"No! Just say '*aye*'!" Jonathan corrected. "Please! This you must understand!"

"It's a lieutenant's uniform!" said Colin. "You said he was a midshipman!"

Jonathan reached over and roughly ripped the bars off the shoulders of Alexander's uniform.

"He is now demoted," said Jonathan.

"What was that? A gunshot?" cried Aggar as he ran aboard the *Paladin*. He was followed by several of his crewmen, all carrying guns.

"They must still be fighting down below!" said Kharitonov. "Lieutenant Skryrabin! Get down there and bring them all to me! And find Tretiak! We must be moving!"

Skryrabin ran to the ladder. Then cautiously, with sword leading the way, began his decent. Behind him came a dozen armed men from Kharitonov's crew.

Others from the *Navarkhia* assisted in rounding up the remaining English on deck and arranging them in a line along the portside rail. Aggar's men began climbing the lines, ordering the Englishmen to add sail.

Below, as expected, Jonathan and the others watched as the Russians were now descending the ladders to the lower decks.

"Eh? What are ya doing there?" asked Skryrabin as he appeared with his men.

Jonathan and the other *Paladin*s stood quickly and dropped their weapons at the sight of the superior force. No one said a word. Starikov approached and roughly pushed the Englishmen back toward the ladder.

"What's this? Tretiak is dead?" asked Skryrabin. "How did this happen?"

Jonathan realized that this man was referring to Quinn.

"T-they f-fought," said Jonathan, affecting a stutter to disguise his voice. "Our m-midshipman here," he said, motioning to Southcott, "was also k-killed, as were our c-c-crewmates."

Skryrabin looked about. This made sense to him. Obviously, a few pistol shots, a few scuffles with swords, and the scene played out.

"All of you," he directed, "up to the main deck—hands on your heads!"

He led Jonathan and the others up the ladder, and in a single line, moved them to the starboard rail next to Jenkins and the others. Starikov then left them under the watchful eye of his men, all with pistols and muskets ready to fire.

Jonathan saw Jenkins, and nodded slightly, as if to say,

"All has been done." Jenkins, relieved, gave a quick smile.

The sudden burst of anger from Kharitonov shocked everyone on the ship, even the Russians.

"Tretiak is dead?" he boomed. Obviously, his lieutenant had informed him of his discovery. There was a flurry of words exchanged in Russian. Finally, Kharitonov turned to Aggar.

"Tretiak anticipated our attack and spiked the guns! A bright one he was! Nikomed Aggar, you will command the *Paladin* and fix those weapons. Have Cherepanyanko take the *Echo*. Proceed as planned and sail north, away from prying eyes. Cherepanyanko will join me at first to complete the ruse, then meet you before Istanbul."

"Yes, sir!" said Aggar.

Kharitonov departed. Aggar barked a series of orders to his men, who in turn, commanded the English to perform strange duties. They were made to grab almost anything that was not nailed down: barrels, rope, loose lumber, and even the plaque they had pried off the stern of the ship. Jonathan watched with sorrow as the proud name "*Paladin*" was now a simple plank of wood, floating in the sea toward the shore.

Most disturbing was the ordering of a group of *Paladins* to take hand axes, under guard of the guns of their enemies, and begin chopping something off the bow. After a full fifteen minutes, Jonathan and Jenkins heard a large splash. Looking over the side, they saw to their horror a large construction of wood, recognizable as their figurehead, floating in the sea. And as their sister ship prepared all sail and began to pull away, they heard another splash. The lovely girl, Echo, had joined the horse and rider.

Within moments, the *Navarkhia* added sail, and moved southward, crossing the entrance to the bay of Zadar. The *Echo* followed close behind.

Aboard the *Paladin*, other Russians returned from their

searches below decks. Mission orders, books, and even bodies of the dead were either tossed overboard or placed in the jolly boat. They saw the bodies of Smith, Jones, and Southcott being tossed overboard. Harrison's spare uniform went into the jolly, along with his sextant and Alexander's personal chest, and were rowed away toward shore.

Aggar also posted his Russian crewmembers at intervals about the ship, guns pointed, to police the Englishmen. The ones who were not busy assisting the Russians were lined up against the rail. For what seemed like an hour, they waited. The jolly boat that had gone ashore had now returned, and the men came aboard. The boat was secured by a team of Englishmen, who then joined the others in a line.

To Jonathan, the water and shoreline to the north looked as if two ships were destroyed. The lumber of the barge that exploded was now intermixed with the remains of Harrison's command.

"They are Russian," whispered Jonathan to Jenkins. "I heard Quinn, or *Tretiak*, as he is really named, admit it below."

"And what are they doing tossing our effects overboard?" asked Jenkins.

"They are now trying to make it appear as if the *Paladin* was destroyed."

"Aye," he whispered back. "Even bodies and such. Why?"

"They want to make sure Harrison and the British Navy do not come looking for her," Jonathan said softly.

Aggar now turned his attention to the line of men. He took a deep breath and addressed them.

"I am Captain Nikomed Aggar of the Russian Black Sea Fleet! Your vessel has been commandeered to assist us in our war against the Turkish Empire. Serve us well, and you will live. Disobey orders, and you will die!"

He produced a pistol and walked the line of Englishmen, looking each one in the eye. As he reached Jonathan,

Aggar paused. He examined the boy from all angles, then leveled the pistol directly at his head.

"You look familiar to me, young Englishman," Aggar said.

"Y-yes, sir," was all Jonathan said as the gun was pressed hard against his temple.

"Have I seen you before?" continued Aggar.

"I-I don't think so. I-I am Southcott. I tend to the powder, I do."

"Oh?" said Aggar. "You are a powder monkey, is that what you call yourself?"

"A-aye, s-s-sir."

"You look like a midshipman I saw on this ship," said Aggar, looking intently at the young man.

"Oh!" said Colin Stredney who was standing next in line. "That makes perfect sense, it does! We used to call him Moore's twin, we did—right, Garvey?"

"Wha? Oh, oh, yes, we did! Looks just like that Midshipman Moore. Fair of face and dark hair. If it weren't for the uniform, we...well, poor Moore. Dead as a door knocker. The best midshipman in the service, we used to say. And a swordsman! Could best even the captain!"

"Really?" said Aggar. "I will see about that. Where is this Moore?"

"T-they j-just t-tossed him over-b-b-board," said Jonathan.

Aggar lowered the pistol, then ran to the rail to see the body floating away. It did indeed resemble the midshipman he had seen in Telašćica.

"Well, I can say this about your midshipman: he excelled with a blade," said Aggar.

"Thank you," Jonathan muttered under his breath.

Aggar now turned from the rail and addressed all on deck.

"Listen, my fine English sailors! Your Mister Jenkins is now in charge of you. Do what he says, because he does what I command! Jenkins! Have the topsmen man the sails.

And send that powder monkey to his post. I need a complete accounting of all stores. I assume, Southcott, that you can count?"

"Only up to a hunnert," lied Jonathan.

Aggar laughed heartily. "Ha! That will do!"

With that, more men went up into the sails as Aggar's men continued to toss a few additional effects and supplies overboard. Jonathan went down below to the powder room to count barrels of gun powder and supplies, and to contemplate the possibilities of his next move.

The *Paladin*, now nameless, continued to add sail and travel north, in the opposite direction of the *Navarkhi*a and *Echo*. Once she reached the end of the islands to her port side, she would turn west, then south along Dugi Otok. Shielded from the Englishmen now stranded in Zadar, she would set course for the Black Sea.

*   *   *   *   *

Later that same day, a small band of sailors reached a rocky beach surrounded by scruffy pines and white-trunked olive trees on the northern point of Dugi Otok. The men were tired and hungry. To supplement their diet of dried fish, they had been forced to steal some bread from a house in the village of Savar and to take a goat they found wandering near the farms of Dragone. It made for a decent meal, but that had been days ago. All that was available at this moment was dried, unsalted fish.

The leader of the group did not rest nor eat. As the others sat upon the ground, chewing, he looked northward to the open sea.

"Anything, Lieutenant Gray?" asked Hayes.

"Not as of yet," Gray replied. "However, this beach must be passed by many ships heading into Zadar, at least those from San Marino and Venice. I wish it had a cliff or a hill to afford a better view. However, we must make do."

It was now April the twentieth, over six weeks since they had lost the *Echo* to Aggar. Escaping the bay that held them captive for three weeks, they had made their way over rough terrain toward the village of Telašćica. The going was slow. To remain unseen they mostly traveled at night, and with no map, there were many fruitless paths taken. This limited their progress to slightly over two miles a day.

After reaching Telašćica, they had waited, hidden on the hillsides, watching. Though it was horribly cold at night, Lieutenant Gray had instructed them to refrain from building any fires and to remain out of sight in the daytime. Unsure of the status of the war, if there was one, it was impossible to ask for help. Who knew if the local Dalmatians had sided with friends or foes? There was no way to ascertain allegiances. They were only to venture into the small village at night, search for food, and locate a suitable craft to make their journey to British-controlled Malta, over seven hundred miles through the Adriatic and Ionian Seas. If found, the craft would have to be stolen, and though they regretted this course of action, it was unavoidable: they had nothing to trade with nor any money.

They had waited in the hills of Telašćica for three days. In that time, nothing but small boats were seen. By April the eighth, Gray had decided to move north to the more populated areas of the island, specifically Morska. From the beach there, he hoped to see ships on their way east to the large city of Zadar on the Dalmatian coast. If a friendly ship was seen, a signal fire could attract attention, and that might possibly lead to rescue. Also, the towns on the northern edge of the island were larger, and the possibility of finding a suitable craft were certainly greater than at the sleepy settlement of Telašćica.

Along the twenty-five mile journey, the party used the cover of night to search the small villages on Dugi Otok as they passed northward. They had seen a few small fishing boats in seaside towns, mostly one- or two-man affairs, though nothing that could hold all seven of them—let alone survive the long trip to Malta. In the end, it took another twelve days for Gray and his men to reach the remote and desolate northern beach of Morska.

After a short rest, Sherland and Neil ventured into the shallow, rocky water near the beach to look for fresh fish or crabs. Little Ike Williams sat upon Sherland's shoulders, pointing to the water where he could see fish moving in the clear, turquoise shallows. Neil had fashioned a net of sorts from pieces of string and mesh they had "borrowed" from the villages they visited, and he would toss it in the general direction of lunch. During one such attempt, he caught a good-sized whitefish and immediately ran to the beach to alert the others that fresh meat was back on the menu.

As Sherland turned to wade back to shore, Ike believed he saw something in the offing: a sail.

"Lieutenant Gray! Sails!"

Gray ran from the cover of the nearby trees and stood in the gentle surf. He could see Ike pointing to the east. Yes, there were sails.

Hill, Wilson, and Hayes ran from the shade of the brush and rushed into the water, shouting and waving their arms.

"What are you doing?" boomed Gray. "All of you! Take cover!"

"But, sir!" said Wilson. "It could be our savior!"

"And it could also be an enemy! Now get to the shadows!"

The men quickly made their way to the trees and peered eastward. As the ship came closer, Ike, with his keen eyesight, described what he saw.

"Two masts with a spanker…raked sails…still too far to make her colors, sir."

"Two masts and raked sails?" asked Gray.

"It could be the *Echo*!" said Hayes.

Within minutes, the ship changed course and headed southwest now angling close to their position, maybe two hundred yards or less from the beach.

"The masts are raked as the *Echo*'s are, but this one…she's got taller masts, and the sails look larger," said Ike.

"*Paladin*?" offered Gray.

"There's no flag," said Hayes, "but it does look like her."

The men breathlessly waited as the ship approached. Gray wondered why there was no flag, and after considering this, his heart sank. It was either not the *Paladin*, though, by God, it surely resembled her, or it was — and she had been taken.

"Oh dear!" called Ike. "Her figurehead!"

The men looked as close and as hard as they were able. As the ship neared, it became clear: the figurehead of this ship had been brutally hacked away.

"It is *Paladin*," said Gray, the sorrow clearly heard in his voice. "She has been taken."

It was true. As the ship passed, they could see the recognizable purple stripe, the teakwood on the rail, and the missing nameplate on her stern.

"Dear God!" said Hayes.

"What are we to do now, Lieutenant?" asked Hill.

Gray thought for a moment or two. Then, with a determined voice, he said, "We will find a ship. We will remain here for a while, and if unable to signal safe passage, we will scour the coast until we are successful. Then we'll sail to Malta."

They remained unlucky in Morska, and after twelve days, Gray led them away south. The men marched over two nights along the eastern coastline and found their way to the large village of Veli Rat. The moon had lit their way, and it shed enough light to reveal a small pier in the bay. Tied up were three vessels. One was a simple fishing boat, another a flat-keeled skiff of some type. The third was a felucca, a trim ship of about twenty feet in length, lateen-rigged, capable of carrying three small triangular sails on three short masts. It would do nicely.

Gray's men approached the pier once the moon set behind the hills to the west. With a minor protest from two surprised men who were sleeping onboard, the British quickly took the felucca. The men set all sail as Gray took the tiller.

The felucca swiftly sailed northwest out of the bay and then turned to port. With minutes, they were moving past the beach at Morska. A simple course change southeast had them heading into slightly deeper water. They would use the coastline to their port side and follow Dugi Otok and the southern islands into the Ionian Sea — and then to the British port at Malta.

22
Snakes and Guttersnipes

In the late morning of April the nineteenth, Captain Gorman strode hastily up the steps of the Admiralty Building at Whitehall, gave a fast salute to the flag flying atop the dome under a still darkened sky, and disappeared inside.

In a small office in the basement, lit by an old ship's lantern, sat Captain Derrick Spears behind a dark mahogany desk that was in bad need of repair. One leg of the desk was missing entirely; another was cracked. Previously, Spears had an aide stack a dozen or so heavy bound books under the corner with the missing limb, and the cracked leg was bound with some sail cloth taken from Spear's last ship's stores. A lone chair was placed directly across from the desk, facing Spears. It had all four legs intact; however, to make sure that Spears was literally *above* whoever might be seated there, Spears himself had sawed three inches off the bottom of each leg.

Spears was now bent over a written ledger, grumbling to himself about the poor performance of the ships' captains listed there. It was the injustice of the world that allowed *them* to command, he thought, and had placed him in this dreary office, serving men supposedly superior to himself. He was paid modestly, though he wanted more, and his mood was constantly and entirely sour because he had long ago realized that he would be in this dungeon forever. His chances of commanding a ship once again were even less than slim.

There came a strange knock at the door. It was three or four raps, a pause, and then two more.

What is this? he wondered. No one comes at this hour.

Ever. Who could be bothering me at six in the morning?

The strange knock came again.

It seems to be in code, he thought. But no code I know of. Unless it is…

"Wilder?" he called softly. It *could* be Lord Wilder with another secret assignment for some poor unsuspecting captain. This spy business was odd. First was the *Echo* having secret orders to deliver a prisoner, then the *Paladin* to carry a treaty to the Adriatic Sea. And now, the *Echo* was long overdue; surely it was due to the bizarre new assignment.

"Wilder? Is that you?" he said again in a hoarse whisper.

The door opened. Spears saw a shadow, a tall man in uniform. As he stepped into the light, the red of his coat could be seen, and the grim look on his face made him instantly recognizable.

"No, it is not Lord Wilder," said Gorman, "though he is the reason I am here."

Gorman kept his piercing eyes on Spears and reached behind himself to shut the door.

"I have nothing to say to you, Captain Gorman," said Spears with a sneer.

"Oh, you have quite a lot to say to me," said Gorman as he turned to the door and slid the locking mechanism into place. "You will tell me what I want to know, snake."

At nearby Piccadilly, the sun had broken through the clouds as Lord and Lady Wilder began shopping. Lady Wilder had prepared a list, and though servants could usually perform this duty, it had been so long since they'd had any real spending money that both gladly accepted the chore. Lord wilder was thankful that the money from 'the boss,' whoever that may be, had finally come in, and this first installment was a healthy one. He told his wife his investments in his new shipbuilding venture in Scotland were now paying off handsomely, and he was pleased that she accepted his explanation readily, asking no questions.

Lady Wilder had already taken a share of the newly

earned profits to buy a completely new wardrobe and was now resplendent in a dark-maroon wool coat and matching hat. His shoes were direct from Paris, as were her matching gloves — all of the finest quality. She had also chosen a new carriage and two fine horses — absolutely stunning. Now, it was high time that Lord Wilder had a proper suit and over-coat — maybe two — with a pair of French tailored blouses and a series of colorful ascots.

"'Ello! 'Ello gov'na! Missus! A few tuppence for the poor?"

Before him was a child, a common street urchin, dressed in rags, with matted hair, a dirty face, and a stench that could have gagged anyone. Lord Wilder considered the creature with charity and understanding in his eyes, but he could feel his wife's hands on his arm, squeezing tightly. On her face was a look of disgust. She was frowning and thought that maybe it was not too late to simply cross to the other side of the street. However, the lane was crowded.

"Tuppence, tuppence, please! For just a few crusts o' bread!"

"Excuse me, I have no time for any of this —" Lady Wilder said.

"Oh, Missus! And you with such a loverly new coat! Is it new, perhaps?"

"Yes, it is," said Alina, proudly, then catching herself, she frowned. "And none of your business."

"Gov'na!" said the child, turning to Lord Wilder. "I've no parents and no one ta care for me. A few tuppence is all I need! A penny?"

"What are you?" the lady asked. This seemed to take the beggar by surprise.

"W-what do ya mean, Missus?"

"I mean, are you a young girl or a boy? You are so rag-ged I cannot tell!" said Lady Wilder, with a small laugh of superiority.

The beggar stood up a little taller, offended, and stared at the couple with a small amount of pride and defiance.

"Ooo! I'm a lit'le girl! Just barely 'leven! I'd take a bath 'n dress pretty if I 'ad a few pennies to get by! Then ya' might see me for what I really am?"

"And what is that?" asked Lord Wilder, smiling somewhat. As dreadful as the creature was, she had some spirit.

"I'm a fra-gile flower, I am. Use ta be as pretty as a pansy, I was."

A man walked by and slowed down. He reached in his pocket and handed the beggar a few coins.

"'Ere ya go, child. Ya won't get nothin' from the likes o' these 'igh-society types!" he said with a nod toward the Wilders.

"Oh, I don't know 'bout that, sir. The lord seems kind. Now, 'is wife. Well, she seems a bit *off*—and cru-el!"

Lord Wilder laughed inside.

Lady Wilder was not amused in the very least.

"You little wretch!" said Lady Wilder with a scowl.

"Thank ya, mum," said the beggar girl.

"Well," said the man, as he turned and began to walk back in the direction he had come. "Good luck to ya then, li'l lady."

At that moment, the girl began coughing, slightly at first, but soon, she was bleating harder, and arms wide, she gasped for air between convulsions. She fell to her knees as Lady Wilder backed away in horror. A few people began to gather to see what the excitement was about, and soon a small crowd had gathered, jostling for a front-row view of the scene. Even Lord Wilder was pushed slightly. After a moment or two and some additional bumping into each other, the people moved off as the beggar's spasms subsided. Within a few moments, the young girl had recovered.

"Dear, dear, dear!" said Lord Wilder. "Here, my child. Here is a single crown. Please find a place to stay. Get a hot bath and some food."

"James!" exclaimed Lady Wilder. "Don't encourage her! How can you give that much money to a common guttersnipe?"

The beggar checked the coin, and reacted in kind, her face lighting up through the dirt and filth. She smiled widely.

"'Cause the gen'elman is a saint!" she said loudly. "A true saint 'n savior 'e is! God bless ya sir! God bless ya!"

The young girl was now groveling, kissing Lord Wilder's shoes and stroking his shanks as if she were a dog, heeling at her master's side.

Lady Wilder simply shrieked and moved off ahead of her husband.

"Yer a kind soul, sir," said the girl quietly.

"Yes, yes. Please take care...little lady!" said Lord Wilder as he extricated himself from the clasps of her hands. Smiling, he moved away.

The girl watched him go—all the way until he turned in to the tailor's shop a few doors down. The man who had approached her earlier appeared at her side.

"Did you place the note?" asked the beggar excitedly, not taking her eyes off the tailor's shop.

"Indeed I did, Miss Dowdeswell!" said Frey. "As you began coughing like a typhoid-infested guttersnipe, well, it was the perfect diversion! I slid the note right in during all the jostling 'n machinations of the crowd. I could 'ave picked 'is pocket too, but, well, I *am* a member of His Majesty's Secret Service."

"And Fairchild?"

"'E's in place in the shop, posing as an apprentice tailor. 'E'll stay on him, watching. Ask 'im to empty 'is coat pockets ta make sure of a perfect fit. That will surely expose the note."

"Well, then," said Delain, "that is that! I'm sorry it's all over. I enjoyed it so."

Indeed, she was excited and pleased to play the part she had invented; in fact, the entire scheme was her doing. The disguise of the beggar was particularly a favorite, and it was created by borrowing clothes from none other than

Frey, as he was only slightly taller and had an extra set of workman's clothes he used from time to time as his own disguise for his extensive investigating.

"Well done, Miss Dowdeswell," he said. "You know, it wouldn't be inconceivable that you take up *espionage* as a profession, little lady."

"Spying?" she asked. "Hmm. That has some promise!"

In the basement office of Captain Spears, Gorman leaned heavily on the desk, making sure Spears was well aware of two things: one, that Gorman was at least twice his size, causing the desk to creak and shake dangerously as he leaned on it, and, two, that Gorman was deadly serious.

"Captain Spears, I am sure you will cooperate with me and answer my questions."

"I will do nothing of the sort. I am a captain in His Majesty's Navy. I do not answer to you —"

"I am also a captain in the service of His Majesty," interrupted Gorman with a hiss, "and as you must know, I also curry special favor. Do you remember Admiral Barrow and Admiral Worthing?"

Spears did remember. They had been mysteriously assigned to assist the governor of Australia — a truly dreadful assignment, managing a prison colony filled with the most despicable sorts and teeming with disease. Could that have been Gorman's doing? wondered Spears.

"Yes" was all that Spears could say.

"They may need some assistance. I wouldn't want to ask His Majesty to reassign one of his *desk* captains for interfering with my investigation."

Spears audibly gulped as Gorman stood fully erect and crossed his arms. "What can you tell me of the *Echo*?" the marine asked.

Spears paused for a moment. He couldn't seem too eager to help Gorman. He had to appear as if he had some control over his own affairs. Also, depending on where this meeting would lead, he had taken an oath to remain discreet about all matters dealing with Lord Wilder's assignments. How to play this? he wondered. But in the end, Gorman would probably get what he wanted — by cooperation, coercion, or, from what he had heard told, by force.

"The *Echo*?" said Spears, somewhat matter-of-factly. "She is on a packet mission."

"That's all you know?" asked Gorman flatly.

"Specifically?" asked Spears. "She left port March the third for Gibraltar to deliver mail and orders, pick up London-bound correspondence, and then return. Quite typical."

Gorman paused for an instant, then slowly took a seat in the chair facing Spears's desk. He noticed the lower height and looked down at the legs, easily noticing the saw marks. He sighed.

"You have some peculiar issues, Captain Spears. And don't you also find it peculiar that a ship in peacetime, on a packet mission, in the most traveled part of the known world, literally swarming with His Majesty's ships, is missing — missing two weeks and has never even reported to Gibraltar Station?"

"It is not unheard of," said Spears, thinking that the change of orders he delivered might be responsible for the ship's delay, though he could not reveal *that*. "The ocean is deep, Captain Gorman. The *Echo* could have sunk beneath the waves after running aground, swept out to sea in a storm —"

"There were no storms reported of any consequence," said Gorman. "Nor any battles. To run aground, my dear captain, you would require some ground. There would be the remains, a wreck, flotsam."

"I am not a Nostradamus," retorted Spears. "I can't predict nor conjure up answers from the ether."

Gorman smiled. He now had Spears where he wanted him. A well-placed bit of information here would do the trick.

"I have a report that the *Echo* has actually been seen

afloat as recently as April the seventh. And with a new captain."

Spears tried to hide his surprise, but it was difficult. His face was flushing as red as the queen of hearts.

"T-that is good news, honestly, Captain."

"And I also have learned," continued Gorman, now feigning surprise, "that the previous captain of the *Echo*, Joshua Gray, is not aboard. He and his officers are missing. So it begs the question, who is this new captain?"

"I have no idea," said Spears. It was the truth. He knew of the mysterious changes made to the *Echo*'s mission, all in haste, yet Gray was still the captain, as far as he was aware.

·"Spears," said Gorman. "You know something about the *Echo*. And I know you know something. If you don't tell me, I will personally escort you to Australia, and the cruise will not be pleasant for you."

"Is that a threat?" said Spears, trying to be smug.

Unfortunately, Gorman was in no mood to play today. With lightning-fast speed and surprising agility he leapt from his chair, jumped to the desk, and slapped Spears across the face with the back of his hand, sending him tumbling backward with enough force to knock the man out of his chair and onto the hard floor. Continuing over the desk, Gorman was on him in a second, pinning him to the hard floor with his left knee. He raised his hand for a blow to the head.

"All right! All right!" said Spears. "The orders were changed!"

"Yes?"

"At the last minute! Before Gray set sail!"

"How so?" asked Gorman.

"The packet mission was canceled. Instead," gasped Spears, "they took on a prisoner for exchange at Telašćica. In the Adriatic."

"Telašćica? Who was the prisoner?" asked Gorman.

Spears, still slightly breathless as he remained pinned

under the larger man, struggled to breathe. "Aggar. Nikomed Aggar," he said as his breath was running out. "You are hurting me!"

Gorman now had another piece of information: Aggar, the Russian, who had been easily captured by Frey and Fairchild, was aboard the *Echo*.

"Who changed the orders?" demanded Gorman.

"I-I cannot say," said Spears.

"Tell me," said Gorman.

"I am under oath! I swore on my life I would not speak of—" cried Spears.

"Then I will choke you to death right here and now," said Gorman.

"It was Wilder!" said Spears quickly.

Gorman was not surprised at that. He stood up and helped the shaken Spears to his feet. Gorman righted the chair and motioned for Spears to sit.

"It seems that Wilder is interested in small vessels, and the *Echo* is not the only ship he is interested in. Why the *Echo*?"

"I am not sure," offered Spears as he caught his breath and rubbed his chest. Certainly some bones had been broken.

"Captain Spears, I will let you in on something. You are being used. The *Echo* was stolen by Russian operatives, and their new captain, who calls himself Andrews, is most likely your prisoner, Aggar. It was not an exchange; it was a capture."

"No," said Spears. "It can't be…"

"The orders were altered to set the ship in a particular position as to make the theft easy. A remote place. Telašćica."

Spears thought of this. He looked off, dazed, then murmured softly, "Yes, it is clear now. All the secrecy, the waiting until the ships were ready to depart, the *Echo*…and Aggar. And now, now…Treaty of Akbar and th-the *Paladin*."

Gorman froze. His face now turned white, his heart

raced. It was true.

"The *Paladin?*" he asked.

"Yes," said Spears. "The Treaty of Akbar! She is carrying it as we speak. *Paladin's* orders were also changed! Just as we did with the *Echo!* I had no idea they were stealing the ships! I tell you the truth, Gorman! I-I thought they were delivering the signed treaty to the Russians!"

Gorman rose. "I will verify this treaty, though I will bet my life that there is no such thing. I would know. His Majesty would have told me."

"Then it is part of Lord Wilder's deceit!" said Spears.

"Where did you send the *Paladin?*" asked Gorman.

"Again, to Telašćica," whimpered Spears.

Gorman now had all the puzzle pieces. The *Echo,* and now more than likely, the *Paladin,* stolen—crews murdered and ships altered to disguise them. For what purpose? Russians like Lupien were involved. The letter Delain had copied was in Russian, so it only followed that the ships would be used by the Russians and taken to one of the only areas in the world that was still at war: the Black Sea. There, Russia and the Ottoman Turks were fighting as they had been for ages. Jonathan, Sean, and Harrison, along with the crew, were probably there under the command of the Russian Fleet. If not, they were already dead. Gorman glared at Spears.

"You have aided the enemy. They are stealing ships of His Majesty's Navy and murdering crews. And for your part in this, Captain Spears, I will assure you, you will not go to Australia."

"I-I won't?" inquired a surprised Spears.

"No," said Gorman flatly. "Unless you assist me and tell no one of our findings, I will have you hanged as a traitor to the Crown."

23

The Kérata Vátrachos Gunfight

After inspecting the flotsam and jetsam north of Zadar, Harrison's shore party had returned to the pier and slept in the *Kérata Vátrachos* the previous night. They now wondered about food and their next steps. Their moods were sour.

At the arrival of daylight that warmed the city, Harrison had taken the men to a small public house on the edge of town overlooking Zadar Bay. Welty, Bowman, Marshall, and Marron, the other marine who accompanied them, remained outside with a few other crewmen, watching. They did not know exactly what they were watching for; however, they were on edge and looked quite imposing holding their muskets.

Before joining Harrison at a large table in the corner of the house, Sean had brought them each a cup of water and a large plate of anchovies to share. The vile little creatures, as Sean thought of them, seemed to be everywhere on the planet that was within walking distance of a shoreline. The men ate them, as did Stewie.

The house itself was uncrowded; only four or five others were in the room, all keeping to themselves, only now and again glancing at the English sailors. Their table in the corner of the main room was next to an arch that opened to a small patio with a fountain and a view of the bay. Here they observed the few ships in the harbor and the men working on and about them.

"We have a series of decisions to make, gentlemen," said Commander Harrison. All were sitting, intently watching their captain as he paced the room.

"The first decision is this: do we go home and report,

or do we go after Jonathan and the others?"

Without any hesitation whatsoever, they said in unison, "Jonathan!"

That was easy, thought Harrison. And no use arguing with them; it was his desire as well. Normally he would not ask for their permission; he was the ranking officer and the commander. However, he felt this was a particular circumstance, and he needed these men with him, willingly. His failure to heed his own advice had brought them here — his own suspicions that he discounted. In the end, it was his ship that was lost and his fault the men were stranded in Zadar.

As he looked them each in the eye, nodding, he recognized his truly gracious good fortune to serve with these men — and his honor to command them. He also assumed he would never get another assignment. Maybe the criticism that he was unlucky and that he was one who doomed any ship he boarded was true. Facts were facts. Regardless, these men trusted him, and now they were all in it together. Unfortunately, Harrison alone held all the responsibility for the *Paladin* and for her crew. He had to admit, he didn't feel like a captain anymore.

"All right, then," he said. "We will probably hang for not reporting; however, I am in no mind to be chastised by the Admiralty for losing the *Paladin*!"

"And losing an admiral's son," said Hicks without really thinking. "S-sorry, sir," he mumbled.

"We will speak on your behalf," said Sean, giving Hicks a condemning look.

Harrison frowned and looked over the courtyard to the bay beyond. "To speak for me, we must return home someday, and for that, we will need a ship," he said.

"We could ask the viscount if we could take 'is yacht," suggested Hicks. "He seemed like a nice feller."

"He is caught up in this mess," said Sean.

"Indeed," said Harrison with noticeable disdain. "I don't trust him, and I would suggest that we stay away from his viscountship at all costs. The fact that the *Paladin* was not attacked until we came ashore to see *him* about that blasted treaty means he must have signaled someone. No, we cannot ask the viscount for aid."

"Then we wait for a British ship," said Hudson. "These waters are well traveled. One should come along any day now."

Harrison had thought of this already, and he did not like the idea.

"I do not believe we can afford to wait about Zadar until a Royal Navy vessel appears," said Harrison. "If it takes only a day or two, Jonathan and the *Paladin* could be hundreds of miles away. And we would need to persuade the captain of the ship to assist us. More than likely he would agree to return us to Gibraltar if he were heading west."

"Then that only leaves one choice, as far as I know," said Sean. "We steal one of these pretty young ladies in this harbor. And since we are already familiar with the viscount's fine yacht…"

"And since he is a devious devil who deserves death, which I wouldn't mind serving to 'im…" said Hudson.

"Why not take 'is li'l darlin' then?" asked Hicks.

They all joined Harrison at the railing and looked over the harbor, at the *Kérata Vátrachos*.

Two of the men inside the alehouse had noticed the Englishmen as they entered. One had risen from the dark corner where he sat and had moved, unnoticed, closer to Harrison's party. There he listened and observed them looking about the harbor. Believing he understood the Englishmen's intentions, he quietly exited the house and headed up the long hill to the viscount's villa.

"Too bad we didn't just sail away before we came in 'ere," said Hicks. "We could 'ave been on our way."

"We need provisions, though," Harrison said. "At over fifty feet, she'll be sturdy enough to carry us and our supplies all the way to the Black Sea."

"The Black Sea?" asked Sean.

"If the large ship we saw attacking the *Paladin* was a Turk," said Harrison, "their home port will be somewhere in the Black Sea, most assuredly on the southern shore, past the mouth of the Bosphorus Strait. I only hope that if we meet up with that old thirty-six-gun brig, this little girl will have some speed to her."

"Just in case we are on the hunt for an extended period of time, we will need some supplies. Sean, look for water and some limes or lemons. Salt and flour. Hudson, we will need salted pork. Anything else we can eat would be welcome."

"You may skip the anchovies," suggested Sean quietly.

Harrison gave them each a gold coin.

"The Black Sea is three days' sail," he said as they walked away. "We will search for a week, then attempt to get additional stores. Meet at the *Kérata* within the hour!"

As the men left to perform their duties, Harrison exited the house and gathered the rest of the crew. He positioned them about the yacht, casually, as if they were relaxing. He walked about the pier, inspecting the ship — but trying not to be noticed.

Sean and his two marines returned first. The men pushed a cart with two large wooden barrels riding atop. Sean held their guns.

"That was an interesting purchase!" said Sean. "The first three barrels of water I found were horribly spoiled. Another keeper had only a small amount. I finally found a man who said he had collected fresh water from a stream by the foothills. He sold me these barrels and cart, so we filled them ourselves! I also found a small supply of flour and salt."

"A fine job, Private Flagon," said Harrison as he looked about hastily and motioned for the men to board.

"Hurry now! Hide those barrels below and stay there. As soon as Hudson returns, we will all board immediately, drop all sail, and fly. And, Sean, take your feline with you."

"Stewie!" Sean called, and the cat jumped on a barrel now being carried aboard.

Within minutes, Hudson returned with a small cart pulled by the men. He had gotten some fruit, salted fish, and two chickens.

"A man tried to sell me a dog," he said. "But I heard they are tough to eat!"

"I thought 'e meant as a pet!" said Hicks.

"Interesting," said Harrison. "Load this all onboard and—"

"Captain Harrison!"

It was the viscount. He appeared on the pier and approached with a small gang of men—ten in all, and each looked tough and mean. Harrison recognized some from the villa and others from the alehouse.

"May I ask what you intend to do with my yacht?"

"Viscount, so nice of you to come and see us off. I only assumed that your earlier offer to borrow the craft would naturally be extended for a week or two as we report to our nearest port in Malta."

"What will you report?" asked the viscount. "The destruction of the *Paladin*?"

"Probably not," said Harrison.

"I have some news for you," said the viscount, smiling. "My sources say you are planning on going after that Turk. That would be pointless."

"We are not going after the Turk," said Harrison.

"No?" said the viscount.

"No. We are actually going after the *Paladin*, the ship that you and your friends tried to make us think was destroyed. But it was the barge. You forgot to add some teak to your trick, Viscount."

"Teak?"

"Yes," said Harrison moving his right hand to his sword hilt. "The *Paladin* was famous for its teak deck, but there was no teak in the flotsam. You did not fool us, Ragusa."

Two of the viscount's men revealed small pistols. Another drew a sword.

"We will not permit you to leave," said the viscount.

"I did not ask for your permission," said Harrison coldly, "nor do I require it."

Out of the corner of his eye, Harrison could see that Hudson, Hicks, Sean Flagon, and a pair of other marines had muskets trained on the viscount's men. They had been hiding on deck, and now nodded ever so slightly to signal that they were in position.

"Sergeant Hudson?" called Harrison as he drew his sword.

Hudson stood, as did the rest of his team. Welty, Marshall, and Bowman, along with the others, revealed themselves at the side of the pier, holding knives and clubs.

One of the viscount's men fired, missing Harrison, who heard the ball whiz past his right ear.

Hudson fired, and the viscount's men ran for what cover they could find.

Ragusa now produced a pistol and aimed it at Harrison.

Sean Flagon, however, aimed his musket but shook in fear. He had never shot—or even aimed his weapon—at another human being. He tried to will himself to pull the trigger; however, he froze in his distress.

"Your secret will die with you," said the viscount as he aimed at the young commander.

Suddenly, a shot exploded from behind Harrison. The center of the viscount's chest burst in a cloud of smoke. Red blood seeped through his garment as he collapsed.

Harrison turned.

Standing by the smoking musket was Sean Flagon. Still shocked with what he had just done, he could only stare at the body of the crumpled viscount.

Another pistol shot rang out, this time from the viscount's men.

A ball struck Sean in the thigh. He screamed in pain and fell to the deck.

"Sean!" yelled Harrison. He ran to the marine and picked him up in his arms, and the fight continued in earnest. "Dear God!" he cried and quickly moved him behind a few barrels and boxes on the deck, away from gunfire. He hastily inspected the boy's leg. It was bleeding heavily.

"Get aboard!" Harrison called to the others as he applied pressure to the wound. "Hurry! Cut the lines! Drop all sail!"

The marines set up a defensive perimeter about the ship, firing until all had expended their powder and ball. One by one the remaining crew fought their way back to the *Kérata*. A marine fell, and Welty was slightly wounded as a ball scraped his brow. Both were pulled aboard by Marshall and Bowman just as the yacht eased away from the pier.

"Ah! I am hit!" called Welty dramatically.

Bowman and Marshall inspected him. With a simple wipe of a sleeve, Marshall saw that the ball had only slightly grazed the skin above his left eye.

"A bit lower an' you'd be wearing a patch," he said.

"Nothin' serious," said Bowman. "A minor scrape it is."

"Nothin' serious?" asked Welty. "A bandage is all?"

"More than likely," said Marshall. "So to your feet, and help us get this barge to sea. Come on, now."

Harrison continued inspecting Sean's wound and pressed his hand against it to stem the flow.

"I killed him!" said Sean in his delirium. He did not boast—quite the contrary. Tears streamed from his eyes, and he looked to Harrison for an explanation, absolution.

"It is all right now, Sean!" said Harrison as he removed his jacket, folding it as a pillow for Sean's head.

The *Kérata* collected the wind, and though a few more shots rang out, the fighting was over. Hudson took the wheel and piloted the yacht into the harbor. A few smaller skiffs tried to pursue, but the Englishmen, experts at sail and rigging, had the canvas spread in only a few moments. They were now leaving the harbor swiftly, and entering the

Aegean.

"Sean," Harrison said as he held the boy, "stay calm! Hicks! Some cloth! Tear a blouse! Hurry!"

"I am injured," said Sean matter-of-factly.

"You saved my life!" said Harrison.

"But I killed the viscount. In cold blood!" cried Sean.

"No, not in cold blood," said Harrison. "In battle!"

Sean didn't seem to understand the words. He could see Harrison's mouth moving and hear the tearing of cloth, though none of it made sense. He could feel the pressure of hands as cloth was applied. Then he felt himself drifting off into a dream, and he heard himself murmuring something about Ireland and swimming and his mother. Then all went black.

24
Turning a Spy

Lord James Wilder, dressed in cloak and hood, patiently waited on the edge of his estate in Van Patten. Again, fog and a drizzling rain covered the scene. Hiding in his usual spot, he felt it was most *unusual* that he had been contacted so recently by Orvislat. However, after a few moments, he saw the familiar carriage appear. The driver seemed a bit different—smaller—but no matter, he had never met the man, and who was to say that Orvislat had only one driver and one carriage? It was 3:00 a.m. on the night prescribed in the note, and the cart was slowing to a stop, literally right in front of him, as it always did. Checking about himself and his surroundings, he was satisfied that no one was watching. He left the confines of the bushes and entered the carriage.

On his face was a look of utter surprise when he realized that Orvislat was not inside but some other man in a woven mask, with his white beard protruding out from underneath.

"Welcome," he said, and immediately, Wilder felt a club smash into his head. The carriage seemed to spin, and he collapsed to the floor.

Delain had once again stolen away in the night when all in the house were asleep. Successfully making it to the stable, she again selected the black filly, Lilliput, and this time, without the Airedales, whom she had let out earlier in the evening and were assuredly now happily rampaging through the wood. She headed toward the small flour warehouse on Channing Street, where Gorman had planned to conduct his interrogation. No one had invited

Delain per se; however, she had overheard Frey and Fairchild discussing the next step of the plan. She had no pressing engagements for the evening. Why not attend?

Making her way through the dark and mostly vacant streets, she noticed only a few other souls—mostly vagrants and revelers. This area was not the worst section of town, and it was so near to home she felt safe. As she approached the northern edges of the great city, her pace and heart quickened. Ahead, she saw the warehouse and went immediately to the back door, as that seemed to be Gorman's choice. She dismounted, entered with the horse in tow, attached a feed bag to the filly's face, and tied the beast to a nearby railing.

Immediately, she heard a scuffling, then the sound of a wooden chair being dragged across the hard stone floor. The noises came from deep within the building and, she could only assume, from the location of her own interrogation: the furnace room in the lower level. There is where she headed.

"Is he tied well?" growled Gorman, putting on his harshest voice and demeanor.

"'E is, sir!" said Frey, also hissing and growling.

"'E's goin' nowhere, this one is!" added Fairchild.

Lord Wilder was secured tightly. Though bound about the eyes with a rag, he tried to look out from underneath. He could only murmur through the cloth gag tied firmly about his mouth. His hands and feet were fastened expertly to the chair with several knots that seemed impossible to budge.

Gorman walked around Wilder several times, making sure the captive could hear his hard boots hitting the floor. Not being able to see and only hearing the sounds of his captors would frighten Wilder to the point that he would most likely cooperate. At least that was Gorman's expectation.

Wilder had never been mentioned by Gorman's superiors or operatives as anyone who would be suspected of any crime, especially treason. He was an outstanding British subject by all accounts. Though he had been recently appointed to the Admiralty in a position to command assignments, all knew it was a purely ornamental position. He had no real power. It was an honor, no doubt, but one with no teeth.

No matter, thought Gorman. He is deeply involved in this mess — and most probably a traitor. I have been in this business a long while, and I have been surprised more than once with who was a player and who was not. I will let him stew a bit more.

There were three pieces of information the captain desired to extract from Lord Wilder: his admission that he was working with Mister O, exactly who Mister O *was*, and what his role was in this plot.

"Take off the gag," said Gorman, "but leave him blind."

Frey removed the gag. Lord Wilder took a huge breath of air, then another. Apparently recovered, he went on the attack.

"Who are you?" Wilder asked firmly once he had begun to breathe more or less normally. "I demand, in the name of the king — "

"Oh, dear me, Wilder!" said Gorman harshly. "You name His Majesty? We know all about your *treason*. You will surely hang, if there is anything left of you to hang when we are done with you."

"Do I now get the tools?" laughed Frey evilly.

"Yes. Sharpen them up first!" replied Gorman.

"Right, sir," said Frey, knowing his part in this. Keep the victim on edge, keep feeding the fear. He will talk. They all did for Gorman. It just depended upon how and when.

"It is you who will hang!" cried Wilder. "Do you know who I am? I am Lord James Wilder! Let me go now, and I will press no charges!"

Gorman laughed. "I don't think that is a possibility."

"What do you want from me?" Wilder demanded.

"Some answers, to begin with, traitor!" yelled Gorman.

"I am no traitor! I serve the Crown!"

"Oh, really? Then explain why you have been serving a known Russian operative."

"W-what do you mean?" Wilder asked. Since his abduction, he had wondered who these men could be — French spies, surely. Napoleon's minions would certainly benefit from the knowledge he had of the Treaty of Akbar. Lord Wilder would show them what a British spy could withstand!

"We have seen you in his carriage, taking your three a.m. rides about Van Patten. Do you deny it?" said Gorman.

Wilder felt faint. He reasoned that this abduction might have something to do with his secret meetings with Orvislat. Now he knew.

"Who are you? Let me see you!"

"I will remain anonymous. You are *my* prisoner, until the hangman takes you, *spy*!" Gorman said, as if the word were vulgar and despicable.

"I will tell you nothing. It is you who are spies! French spies!"

"You think we are Frenchmen?" laughed Gorman. "Funny coming from a Russian spy!"

"Russian? I am a member of His Majesty's Naval Board —"

"Yes, yes. We know all that," continued Gorman. "What we don't know is *why*. Why did you hand two of His Majesty's ships over to the Russians? Why did you change their orders? Just to make it easier for your friend in the carriage to murder the crews and capture His Majesty's vessels of war?"

"You are mistaken!" cried Wilder. "I handed over nothing! I serve His Majesty's commands."

"Odd," laughed Gorman. "I spoke to His Majesty just this morning. He knows nothing of your doings, Wilder. In fact, I must say, he couldn't even remember who you are or what position you hold."

Wilder caught his breath. Could this be true?

"Who are you?" Wilder asked again.

"Loyalists. Loyal to England. That is all you need to know," said Gorman.

"This is ridiculous," said Wilder. "Let me go before you do irreparable harm to yourselves. All you have correct is that I took a few rides with my friend, the son of the Russian ambassador."

Ah, thought Gorman, I have the answer to one of my three questions! Mister O is Seeja Orvislat, the son of the ambassador. He had been the object of a few simple observations by Slater and other operatives. A suspected spy, a player in more than a few shady dealings.

"Orvislat? He is known a spy," said Gorman, now standing still in front of his captive. "I have been following him for years. We will pick him up soon."

"I will say nothing further. Kill me if you must," said Wilder. These men knew nothing, he thought. Whoever they were, he would not give them a single bit of information.

"You know," said Gorman, pausing for effect, "Orvislat will be shot as a spy. Or maybe you can hang together, along with your tool Spears, of course."

"Spears?" said Wilder. He now saw his entire case falling apart. They had gotten to Spears. He must have told them everything about how the orders had been changed to ensure delivery of the treaty. Yes, that is what they were after! he thought.

Gorman smiled. Looking at the posture of Wilder deflating, he knew he was on the right track. A bit more pushing and Wilder would think he had been found out completely.

"Ah! Your loose end, Captain Spears," said Gorman in a raised and condescending voice, "Yes, I spoke to him this morning. What a tongue wagger he is."

The blood drained from Wilder's face.

"Possibly Spears is innocent; however, he will be a

great witness to prove *you* are *not*. He has already turned
over on you, Lord Wilder. He told us about the orders you
commanded him to change. He told us of the treaty —
again, a fabrication, according to the king."

"Fabrication?" said Wilder softly.

"There is no agreement with the Russians," said Gorman. "No secret correspondence. That is handled via the
British ambassador in Saint Petersburg, not during some
midnight coach rides with your friend Orvislat. There
never was a Treaty of Akbar, Wilder. We know all this. You
intended to use the treaty and prisoner exchange as a ruse
to have the *Echo* and *Paladin* set up for capture. Oh dear,
dear, dear! Conspiring with the enemy — and theft of His
Majesty's ships! That is treason with a capital *T*. And two
of His Majesty's finest ships. The king is not pleased; I can
assure you of that."

"They are just names and numbers of armaments on
paper to me," Wilder whimpered. "I knew n-nothing about
the *Echo* or the *Paladin!*"

A voice came from the darkness behind them all.

"Nothing of the *Paladin?*"

All turned, save Wilder of course, to see Delain Dowdeswell emerge from the shadows and join the interrogation, not as a calculating interrogator but as a crazed
madwoman.

"My friends are on that ship!" Delain said, completely
giving in to her madness and crying out loud. "And now,
they are most likely dead!" She lunged at Wilder and began
striking him. He could only allow it. After a moment, Gorman pulled the girl off.

"We know of your blood money, the letter, and the
notes placed in your library!" she continued.

"In my l-library? W-what are you t-talking about?"

Gorman held Delain in an effort to silence her, but she
would have none of it.

"I saw them there!" screamed Delain, now leaning to
just inches from Lord Wilder's face, "hidden in the books
of your library! I followed Orvislat there as well. He placed

them all there for you!"

"Money? Letter? I have no idea what you are—"

"And I have seen you enter Orvislat's carriage only last week," continued Delain. "You *will* hang—if I don't strangle you myself, right now!"

It was all crumbling, thought Wilder. Whoever these people were, they knew everything. But who were they? Maybe, he could give them a little something, show some cooperation, and in exchange, they might expose their plan.

"Yes, there was a single payment to me from Orvislat," Wilder offered. "He acted as the king's agent. The money was a form of His Majesty's gratitude, I swear to you! It came through Orvislat, yes, and was deposited directly into my account at Blackman's Bank. One thousand pounds!"

"You lie!" said Delain. "I counted five thousand!"

"Five?" asked Wilder, truly stunned. "But…"

This seemed odd to Gorman. He could be lying; however, if it was true that Orvislat paid money directly into Wilder's account, something he could verify easily, then who received the rest of the money Delain had found? Had that person deposited some for Lord Wilder and kept the rest? He looked to the girl, who also seemed a bit perplexed at the statement.

"And the notes with a date and time written in sloppy handwriting?" asked Delain. The anger and worry she felt had completely turned into rage.

"Sloppy handwriting?" asked Wilder, sincerely confused. Then, after a moment, he said, "The meeting notes? You mean the meeting notes? B-but I never found them in my library! They were always in my shoes, or in my dessert!" said Wilder.

"Your dessert?" said Delain. "Preposterous!"

"Once they were in my coat pocket, but I never did figure out how they got there. Their purpose was to alert me to the meetings requested by the king!"

"Then what of the art letter?" Gorman asked.

"I know of no art letters!" pleaded Wilder.

"The letter cleverly disguised as a request for art?" pressed Delain. "It was also in your library, and we know that it was in code! A code directing you to steal more ships!"

"No! No! I tell you the truth!" said Wilder. "I know nothing of letters. I only saw notes with a date and time on them."

Delain reached in her pocket and produced the letter she had taken from Wilder's library and had decoded. Gorman motioned for Frey and Fairchild to remove Wilder's blindfold. They quickly removed it and untied his hands from the chair.

Delain thrust the pages into Lord Wilder's face.

"You are working for the Russians! They pay you! Your wife had suddenly become a fashion plate—a new carriage! Shopping in Piccadilly! All appearing right after I saw the money in your library. And this letter! Addressed to you!"

Wilder briefly regarded the letter, then looked again at Delain.

"You are the guttersnipe from Piccadilly!"

"One of my many *master* disguises!" said Delain proudly.

"I have seen you before that," said Wilder.

"We met at the races," she said, "where you saw the *Paladin*, and you asked questions about her."

"You are Delain Dowdeswell," he said matter-of-factly.

"Dear, dear..." muttered Gorman. "She is one of my...*operatives*."

This made Delain blush. She had only thought of herself as her own operative; however, to be included in the branch of the Secret Service of the king, with prestigious men such as Gorman, Fairchild, and Frey—well, that was compliment enough.

"Slightly young to join the world of intrigue and espionage, don't you think?" said Wilder with a laugh.

"Her code name is *Midget!*" said Frey. Fairchild snorted.

"Hush!" said Gorman. "What of the letter, Wilder? Do you deny it is addressed to you?"

Wilder inspected the letter again, this time in earnest. His curiosity actually helped calm him for a few moments. He recognized it as Russian, as he had a working knowledge of the language. His wife's grandparents had come from the small southern port city of Tsaritsyn, and he had picked up some of the difficult language over the years. It indeed was a discussion of art, some disappointment about the delays in delivery, and an order for additional pieces. He then looked at the translated version. Yes, it was correct as far as he could tell. Completely vexing, however, was that it was written to "L. W."—and surely that was he, Lord Wilder. It was also vexing as the writing was simply signed with the Cyrillic letter *K*.

"Hmm," he murmured. "L. W.? That could be me...But *K*? In the Cyrillic alphabet? Who is *K*? And why haven't I seen this if they were addressed to me? Who could have written me—"

He stopped cold. Like a bolt of lightning it hit him. "It can't be..."

"What?" asked Gorman, now notably calmer, as if trying a different tack.

"No. No..." Wilder said, his eyes welling up in tears.

He knew it was true. He had been deceived by them all. It now explained why Orvislat did not want the captains of the *Echo* and *Paladin* to know too much—and why he was not meeting with the king himself. And the easy acceptance of his sudden change of fortune. He began to sob.

A rush of pity came across Delain. She now considered the man and wondered if indeed he had been innocent. Could there be someone else at the head of this snake? Looking about, she located a small sink and cup. She poured him a bit of water and handed him the cup.

"Orvislat was my contact," Wilder said softly, accepting the cup. "He told me we were sending ships to deliver treaties and exchange prisoners—"

"Aggar," said Gorman.

"Yes. That is what I thought I was doing!" cried Wilder. "The notes simply instructed me to meet Orvislat at specific times. I believed they came from the king himself. I..." his voice trailed off as he stared at the letters before him. Who told him the notes were from His Majesty? It was Orvislat. At their first meeting. Dear God! he thought, How could I have been so foolish?

"Lord Wilder," said Gorman. "Many English lives are at stake. If you are truly loyal to the Crown, you will tell us all you know about Orvislat and his purposes."

"They wanted only the fastest ships," said Wilder, "to support swift communication. But I see now that they wanted small, maneuverable craft to steal. Why, I do not know."

"I suspect for battles in the Black Sea," said Gorman. "Larger ships would be easily outrun by the Turkish galliots. They need powerful warships—but fast and maneuverable. The *Paladin* and *Echo* fit that bill."

"They suggested that for the prisoner exchange involving Aggar, we assign the *Echo*. I agreed. That was to begin the treaty negotiations. "I simply changed the orders to send them to Telašćica. I had Spears do the paperwork."

"That fits with what Spears told me," said Gorman out loud.

"When they asked for a ship to deliver the treaty to the tsar, I suggested the *Paladin*," Wilder said flatly, almost resigned to the fact that he had been totally cheated and used. "Orvislat told me it was an honor. But now I see. It was the second ship he was stealing. I didn't know!"

Wilder held his head in his hands.

Gorman now had his admissions. Wilder had worked with Orvislat. He had sent the ships to Telašćica. But most likely, he was innocent. He could have been used, and it would be hard to convince any court that a lord of the House was a spy. Unless he could get his last piece of information.

"There is someone else involved, Lord Wilder. Someone who knows Orvislat, but who also would have access to your library, your shoes, your dessert, and be able to make account deposits without your involvement."

"The other L. W.," Wilder said. "The one who was to receive this letter."

The room was silent. Another L. W.? The letters were to another person? All anticipated the lord's next words.

"That is why I never saw them. The letters weren't for me. They were for...Lady Wilder," he finally said.

Delain was speechless, almost. Now it made sense to her. Lady Wilder certainly had motive. She needed money. Delain never trusted her, nor did she like her. But to become a traitor?

"My wife is Russian born."

"Russian?" said Delain.

"From the town of Tsaritsyn. I met her years ago, before the war of the first coalition. In Paris. We fell in love. I think we did, at least..." His voice trailed off, and his breathing stopped for an instant. He shook his head in disbelief, then took a deep breath. "K could be a relation of hers. Yes, she had an uncle," said Wilder. "I don't know much about him, nor have I ever met him, but he is Russian."

"The uncle's name?" Delain prodded.

"Kharitonov," said Wilder.

Frey and Fairchild gasped, their faces turning white with shock.

"Ian Kharitonov?" asked Frey.

"*Commodore* Ian Kharitonov?" asked Fairchild.

"Of course," said Gorman, nodding.

"Yes. Yes, that is his name and title," said Wilder. "Yet I believe the title of commodore is perfunctory. He is a man of little importance, I have been told."

"You have been lied to," said Gorman, rising. "And Kharitonov is no pawn. Ian the Cruel, he is called, a ruthless villain. I am certain he has set this all in motion. He is the one requesting the ships. Orvislat is in his employ, as is

Aggar. As are you, unknowingly."

"Orvislat mentioned the boss," said Lord Wilder, "the person at the head of this snake. He must have meant my wife." Wilder paused, then added, "She assisted him! And used me to change the orders."

He now lapsed into silence, only now and again looking up to the others, taking a breath, and then hiding his face again in sobs and self-pity.

"The *Paladin*'s crew is either stranded," said Gorman, "serving under the command of Aggar and Kharitonov or —"

He stopped himself short, knowing that Delain was following his every word. He could not bear to say the words.

"If Jonathan, Harrison, and Sean are smart," he continued, "and they are, they would try at all costs to remain alive. Alive long enough to escape or be rescued. It will take months to find them. I will send word for a ship. There are a few in port that owe me a favor. But we all must keep this silent."

"Why keep silent?" asked Delain, defeated.

"It is our duty now to keep this out of the papers and gossip channels," said Gorman. "If word gets out, our targets will flee. We must capture the culprits of these foul deeds and bring them to justice. Telling anyone outside of this room will jeopardize our efforts to catch them."

"Who are you, if I may now receive an answer?" asked Wilder.

"Lord Wilder, allow me to introduce myself. I am Thomas Gorman, Marine Captain and special intelligence envoy to the king of England. Swear to me your allegiance to the Crown and aid us in proving your innocence!"

Wilder, for the first time that night, saw a ray of hope. He looked up to Gorman and, struggling with the bindings on his legs, stood. He looked Gorman in the eye and said proudly, "I swear!"

"Then we must look for our friends —" said Delain.

"And capture our enemies," added Gorman. "The

whole lot!"

"And I have just the idea!" said Wilder. "I know how to get them all in the same place and the same time!"

The plans were made, parts rehearsed, and the final points agreed upon. Within the hour, Wilder was driven back home in the same carriage that had abducted him and set at the end of his drive. At this point, Delain Dowdeswell was put on her filly that had been in tow and headed through Van Patten, slowly, under the escort of Captain Gorman.

Wilder quickly walked inside his home and told his wife of the horrifying mugging that he had been victim of as he walked home from a late business meeting. After a cool towel and a quick shot of brandy, he retired to his bedroom, and slept with one eye open.

Outside the estate, in the dark shadows of the oaks, the spy Lupien had observed the entire scene: the odd carriage, the mysterious figure on the horse going into the woods with Gorman, and the faces of the two carriage men, Frey and Fairchild. He watched them park the carriage in the wood, then disappear into the shadows of the Wilder estate.

25

The Sea of Marmara

After leaving Zadar, Jonathan and the crew of the *Paladin* spent the next week cruising the eastern edge of the Mediterranean Sea, repairing sail and spar, and becoming familiar to their new masters. Many of the crew were simply happy to be alive and to have their skills of value. After witnessing the murder of Fawcett by Kharitonov, they worked diligently for their new masters out of absolute fear. The ship, in more or less proper condition, headed swiftly southeast.

The *Echo* had also been undergoing minor repairs and, almost immediately upon leaving Zadar, had left the *Navarkhia* for the eastern edge of the Adriatic to meet the *Paladin*. If all went as planned, the sister ships would reach Istanbul, the Turkish city at the western entrance of the Bosphorus Strait, by the evening of April the twenty-fourth.

The single bright spot in this heavy, cold blanket of despair for the Englishmen aboard both ships was the fact that the *Navarkhia*, and therefore Commodore Kharitonov, was on her own somewhere, hunting, leaving Aggar and Cherepanyanko with their small squadron in relative peace. Aggar even seemed to brighten slightly, thought Jonathan, almost becoming human.

Jonathan had successfully executed the ruse of being Southcott, and he even kept the stutter to his voice, except when privately speaking to Jenkins. Being the powder monkey, and being left alone for hours on end, Jonathan mostly remained in the magazine. He used this time to contemplate his position and attempt to develop a plan to return at least one of these ships and some of the crew to

England. It was his responsibility, he reasoned. These were also his friends, his brothers, and he owed them his life. They had agreed to keep his identity secret, and any one of them could alert Aggar to his true identity and thereby gain favor. So far, they had not, and that gave him hope.

As his thoughts turned to Delain Dowdeswell, he fumbled for the silver star-and-moon charm about his neck that she had given him. What would become of her if he could not return? he wondered as he examined the piece. Certainly, Delain needed no one to complete her life; she would excel at anything she desired, probably becoming the first woman ever to captain of one of His Majesty's fighting frigates or somehow casting herself as an adventurer, continuing on her destined path to break the mold of what was expected of a lady in civilized society. And this is what he loved about the blond-haired girl: her independence meant that he too was independent. Delain Dowdeswell would understand his absences at sea, and he would understand her adventures, whatever they would be. Their reunions would be sweet. That would be, to say the very least, an *agreeable* future, though one that at this moment seemed in serious doubt. As he thought of her, his heart broke.

For now, he would remain here, in the magazine, counting stores. At least he could sit quietly and think. On deck, or in the gunroom where he now slept, he was always being watched.

Looking about the room, Jonathan saw that the *Paladin's* store of gunpowder was made up of primarily English kegs from Harrison's command, and a much smaller number of new, slightly larger, Russian kegs, most likely brought aboard from the *Navarkhia*. Like the men on board, he thought: some English and a few Russian.

How many Englishmen had the *Paladin* sailed with from London? One hundred, he recalled. The *Echo* most likely had the same complement. Both ships had lost men from battles, in cutting-out attempts, and to stranded shore parties. After some calculation of these additions and subtractions, Jonathan figured that the *Paladin* and *Echo* must have approximately sixty men left of their original crews.

However…how many Russians had he seen aboard? Twenty? Twenty-five? Yes, that was probably correct. The *Echo* must have a similar number.

Jonathan smiled as he realized that right now, the *Paladin* and the *Echo* both had almost three times as many Englishmen aboard as Russians. Guns and swords were either locked up or in the hands of his captors; however, an advantage in numbers was an advantage.

The next morning broke clear and warmer, the *Echo* and *Paladin* sailing in tight formation into the rising sun. Jonathan strolled the deck, casually looking about as if searching for a sunny place to sit. He made his way forward and to a spot just past the foremast and right behind Jenkins.

"Jenkins," he whispered from behind the man. "A word with you?"

Jenkins simply nodded his head and continued his work, splicing together shorter strands of rope to make larger ones. Jonathan worked on his cloth.

"Southcott," said Jenkins, "you have no duty at this hour."

"I need to speak to you," Jonathan whispered. "I believe I have developed a plan."

Jenkins paused from his work and stood as if stretching his back. He smiled ever so slightly.

"I was wondering when you would have an idea."

Jonathan looked about to see if anyone was near, and seeing that the coast was clear, Jonathan began.

"Do you have any idea where we are?" asked Jonathan.

."We have just entered the Sea of Marmara," said Jenkins. "We are surely headed east to the Black Sea, where the Russian fleet is active.

"Yes," said Jonathan. "That would make sense. Jenkins, I believe that Aggar has taken this ship and the *Echo* for use in battle."

"Or he wants the treaty, at least to make sure it does not get delivered," said Jenkins.

"He will never find the treaty. I assume he will never even consider it," interrupted Jonathan. "I found it on board right after we were boarded in Zadar. I opened it."

"You did? Jonathan—"

"It was blank. It was a fake, and the fact that Aggar hasn't asked for it means that he is not after the treaty, if there ever was one."

Jenkins held a look of puzzlement on his face for an instant, then nervously looked around. He returned to his work.

"Yes," continued Jonathan, "the treaty, delivered by Quinn, the traitor, the change of orders by Wilder and Spears, Gogomán's letter—all were deceptions."

"They wanted the *Paladin*, pure and simple," the old hand said, "and the *Echo*."

"That was why the *Echo* was tailing us," said Jonathan. "She had been taken long before we ever appeared in the Mediterranean."

"And the barge with explosives at Zadar?" said Jenkins.

"Placed there to look as if the *Paladin* was destroyed. They jettisoned our supplies overboard, and our dead, to resemble flotsam," said Jonathan.

"Why?" asked Jenkins.

"To make Harrison and the shore party believe the *Echo* was taken by the Turks and the *Paladin* destroyed," said the young man.

"Sweet mother of God!"

"No one would think to look for a ship that had been destroyed," said Jonathan. "But they will come for us."

"Jonathan," he said, "how would Harrison and the others know it was all a deception?"

"Harrison knows the *Paladin* more than any other man

alive. She is his love. If he inspected the wreckage, he will notice things. And if he sees Southcott in an officer's coat, my coat, he will know we are alive."

Jenkins was visibly relieved and could not help but smile and slightly nod his head in satisfaction.

"We have figured out the past, Jonathan. However, we now need a plan for the future. I assume you have one?"

"I do," said Jonathan. "I was sitting in the magazine and it came to me," said Jonathan. "There are more Englishmen than Russians on the *Paladin*, and I assume the same is true of the *Echo*. Each time a ship is in battle and another ship is taken, the Russians will have no choice but to man the ships they take."

"That means fewer officers and fewer Russian crewmen," said Jenkins.

"On *each* ship," added Jonathan. "So…we need to pick a fight with a Turk."

"That will be difficult, Jonathan," said Jenkins. "The Ottoman Navy—the Turks, that is—are a shadow of what they once were. A few score frigates and a handful of small galliots are all they have to protect their waters. They have been neutral in these wars with France and Napoleon, content to hold on to what little they have. Finding a ship to attack will be difficult."

"There must be merchants, yes?" asked Jonathan.

"Yes, that is our only hope."

"Then let us hope and pray we find one, Jenkins, and then, after we are victorious, we must get you to the *Echo* and coordinate a mutiny on both ships at the same time."

"How could we do that? Even with you here and me there, well, I can't just yell across the waves," said Jenkins. "We need a signal, an unmistakable sign."

"Where do they send us all before a battle?" asked Jonathan, smiling.

"To the guns," answered Jenkins.

"Then our signal," said Jonathan, "will be when they call for us to fire."

"That would work well," said Jenkins, smiling. "During the fog of battle, many things happen fast and are unexpected. If we are successful, we may take both ships back. But it is very risky, Jonathan. If you fail to take the *Paladin*, they will use it to catch the *Echo*."

"I thought of that. I will arrange for some insurance against that possibility," Jonathan said as he stood up and looked Jenkins in the eye. This man had become a close friend of Jonathan's; they had been through much together. He deserved a better end after leading the life he did in service of his country. Leaving him, and all the Englishmen, aboard the *Echo* and the *Paladin*, stranded and practically enslaved, would not stand. "As long as I breathe, Jenkins, I will not allow them to take the *Paladin!*"

Jenkins could not be sure how Jonathan would be able to offer such assurance, but weighing the choices and considering the circumstances, why not attempt this? The best-case scenario would be that they return both ships and what remained of the crews to England. If they failed completely, and there was good chance of that, they would remain in the hands of their enemies.

"Well, then, *Southcott*," Jenkins said, "we need to take part in a skirmish or two."

On the sixth day since leaving Zadar, the *Paladin* and the *Echo* sailed southeast through the Adriatic, then northeast through the Sea of Marmara, and they were now approaching the Turkish capital of Istanbul. These waters would surely contain a prize or two, and if the opportunity presented itself and the situation was right, Aggar could take a ship, and that would please Kharitonov.

As the city was just becoming visible to Garvey in the crow's nest, he saw it: a single sail.

"Captain Aggar! A sail! No, two sails! Three points off the starboard bow! They have not seen us!"

Aggar took up his glass and looked to starboard. Indeed, there was a ship, a galliot, either a rare one from the

Ottoman Navy or a merchant. He surveyed the surrounding water in all directions and then smiled.

"Ah!" he said. "She sails low in the water! Belly full of treasure! And no frigates to defend her! Set a course for her stern! Battle stations! Jenkins, get your men in position!"

The *Paladin* led the charge, the *Echo* close behind with the wind at their backs as they approached their prey. Within minutes, they had closed to only a few hundred yards.

The captain of the merchant had finally noticed them, and seeing he was outmatched and the incredible speed at which the pursuers were approaching, he knew his only hope was to head straight for the Golden Horn, the channel leading northward past the village of Egri. If he could make it before being caught, possibly the shore batteries might assist.

"Position the men, Jenkins!" called Aggar.

"Battle stations!" Jenkins called, and the men who were not already in position ran to their locations at the guns, in the tops, and on the deck.

"Ready the starboard guns," called Aggar. "Jenkins, have a gun fire a warning shot across their side!"

Jenkins ran to the foremost starboard gun and assisted the men. As the *Paladin* began her turn to port, the merchant came into his view. Closer and closer they came, until the ships were aligned just so, and the sea had tilted *Paladin* to a perfect angle.

"Fire!"

The shot sailed true, skidding across the stern of the merchant galliot, just striking the rigging on the aft mast.

"Roll out all guns!" called Aggar. "Show them we would like to dance!"

As the captain of the merchant vessel witnessed the remaining guns rolling into position aboard the pursuing ship, he realized that his luck had failed him. The two sloops were upon him, the gunners had him in their sights, and he had nowhere, nor the amount of sea needed, to run to safety. He ordered his crew to strike colors and reduce sail in surrender.

As the *Paladin* drew alongside the merchant, lines were tossed and the ships temporarily secured. From deck, the men could see the name of the ship: *Umutlu*. Aggar decided to send six of his men aboard — three from the *Echo* and three from the *Paladin*.

"Kowalski! Command the *Umutlu* and get a full accounting of her cargo. Set anyone unneeded adrift in the boats. Make haste!"

Jonathan, who had been watching the entire exchange from the ladder leading from the magazine to the top deck, smiled slightly. The odds were now greater in their favor. Now all that remained was to have Jenkins assigned to the *Echo*.

As if in answer to his prayers, the call came from the tops. "Ships approaching!" called Garvey. "Astern! A frigate! No, two! They fly the flag of the Ottoman Empire!"

"Turks! They are too large for us!" said Aggar. He was immediately aware that if he did not act quickly he would be boxed in, and escape would be difficult.

"Set all sail!" Aggar cried, and the men performed with precision, as they had been trained. "Well done!" he called. "It will be close! To the strait!"

The frigates were approaching fast, and though the *Paladin*, the *Echo*, and their prize had successfully made the turn, both frigates were now within range, and soon, with a slight turn, the guns were rolled out. It would be a close race to the Strait of Bosphorus, and the frigates could very well pursue them in there, but maneuvering for all would be difficult. Aggar was confident that once on the run, the *Paladin* and *Echo* would fly away — if they avoided damage.

Instinctively, Jonathan ran to the bow, calling to the gunners on deck.

"Be ready! Be true! You fight for your lives! We escape and live — or we die! Fight, my English brothers! Fight!"

The men cheered heartily, and the guns were prepared

for firing.

Aggar watched this, and seeing "Southcott," he smiled.

"That is no powder monkey," he said.

The frigates fired. The explosions were heard seconds after the bright flash of the Turkish guns lit the twilight sea. Balls screamed across the waves, and many were wide or shallow; however, two did reach the *Echo*, skidding across the deck, sending splinters and men about in a trail of destruction.

"Captain, come fast to starboard!" called Jonathan from the bow. "We will answer with accuracy."

"To starboard!" yelled Aggar, and it was made so. The *Paladin* came quickly to the south, exposing her guns to the frigate.

"Fire as she bears!" yelled Jonathan, and he and Jenkins ran aft, slapping the men on their backs, cheering them on.

The rippling broadside of nine carronades tore through the twilight air, streaming hot and cruel iron toward the first frigate. Ball after ball violently struck her bow and deck. The foremast was severed and, creaking loudly, fell to her port side, then dipped into the waves, sail and spar dragging in the water, effectively spinning the frigate hard to port and almost turning her completely about. The first frigate was out of the fight.

The second frigate was not deterred. She sailed on to take the lead and approached the *Paladin* and *Echo* with great speed. She turned to starboard to place her guns in position to fire.

"We will not survive her guns should her aim be true!" called Aggar.

"Another ship!" called Garvey from the tops. "It is the *Navarkhia!*"

Indeed, as all looked astern, the *Navarkhia* did approach and was soon in position to fire. Seeing this, the captain of the second frigate broke the engagement and returned to his sister ship to protect her and her crew. The *Navarkhia* sent a broadside toward her, missing completely; however, the effect was desirable: the frigates withdrew, and the *Paladin* and *Echo* took their prize north into the Strait of Bosphorus, with the *Navarkhia* covering their rear.

"Southcott" said Aggar as the ship was set on her course, and all duties returned to relative normalcy. "Come before me!"

Jonathan turned from Jenkins and stared at Aggar.

"M-me? Sir?"

"Come here!" yelled the captain. As the night crept about them, all that lit the stern were a few simple lanterns, glowing amber, and casting an eerie light upon the face of Nikomed Aggar.

All eyes were on Jonathan as he reluctantly made his way from amidships to the stern. He cautiously stopped a few yards from Aggar, who took one large step forward, now standing directly in front of the boy.

"Y-y-yes, sir?" said Jonathan, truly stuttering and afraid.

"You," said Aggar, pausing for effect, "fought well. It is amazing how you inspired the men. Like an officer you were. Continue to perform well," he said loudly, now addressing the entire crew, "all of you, and you will be rewarded!"

Now, turning back to Jonathan, he smiled.

"Southcott, well done."

Jonathan, relieved that he was not to be punished—or worse, killed—for revealing his talent and his identity, relaxed.

"Captain Aggar, if I may?" said Jenkins as he bowed and took off his hat in a sign of respect. "The *Echo* seemed to take damage. If I could take Streen and Garvey, we could assist in repair, and I have some experience as a loblolly boy and could be—"

"A loblolly boy?" asked Aggar.

"A doctor's helper, sir," said Jenkins in an apologetic tone. "An old English term, so old I don't even know where it came from."

"Once we enter the Black Sea, we will anchor. Jenkins, you may go to the *Echo*," Aggar said. "See if you can assist the wounded."

The plan was working, Jonathan thought, as he tried to hide his smile. Our luck has turned! No, not luck, Jonathan said to himself. Jenkins seized the moment. He would soon be aboard the *Echo* and could alert her crew to the plan.

26

The Hunt

Saturday morning at seven, the guests began to arrive at the home of Lord and Lady Wilder. Some parked their carriages on the drive while servants rode their horses to the stables. Those coming from the surrounding estates of Van Patten Wood simply awoke early and rode their mounts through the forest the most efficient way. Soon there were twenty-odd riders on their horses, laughing, drinking tea — or something stronger in a few cases — while they waited for the hunt master's signal. Somewhere off in the distance was the fox.

In the nearby stable near the pendunculate oaks, a nervous Lupien waited behind a bale of hay and a few planks of wood. He knew Orvislat was to take part in a fox hunt, but unable to reach his master at home, he decided to stay by the estate all night and find his way to the stables and wait there. Seeing the crowd conversing and laughing, Lupien had bumped into Orvislat, literally and on purpose, muttered the word *stable*, and then disappeared into the small crowd that had gathered for the hunt.

"Lupien?" came a hushed voice from the stable door, now closed.

"Orvislat," came the reply.

Lupien stood and motioned for Orvislat to join him behind the bales.

"I hope you have a good reason for this meeting," whispered Orvislat somewhat angrily. "Meeting in daylight and in an unsafe location is going to cause trouble if we are found."

"We have enough trouble as it is, Orvislat," said Lupien.

Orvislat noticed his partner's face. In the dim light it was still possible to see that Lupien was as white as a sheet, he was worried, and he was blinking somewhat uncontrollably. Whatever the trouble was, it was serious. Lupien motioned to a pile of straw in the corner of the stable. Then he brushed a few pieces away, revealing two corpses.

"Who are these souls?" asked Orvislat, disturbed, but even more disappointed. Two dead bodies are rarely a cause for celebration, even in the business of espionage.

"May I introduce to you the English spies, Frey, on the left, and Fairchild, on the right."

"Why did you kill them?"

"They saw me here. Luckily, they came at me separately. I killed Frey first, just as Fairchild appeared."

"Indeed this is bad news," said Orvislat. "Dispose of the bodies, then."

"There is more to it. I saw Wilder last night after I placed the note for the next meeting in his library," said Lupien.

"Was he up, roaming the halls of his estate?"

"No. I saw him *outside*. He was exiting a carriage, much like yours. At first I thought it *was* yours."

Orvislat felt a cold chill crawl up his spine.

"Continue," he said.

"He exited the carriage and had some companions. Frey and Fairchild here, one other, and unfortunately, also Gorman."

Orvislat now looked about nervously. If Wilder was talking to Gorman and his agents, this could all get ugly in a hurry. What could he have said? Anything? Or did he keep quiet?

"You said there was another?" asked Orvislat.

"Yes," said Lupien. "A smaller man. I mean *really* small. Like a midget almost. Maybe a dwarf."

"What are you saying?" asked Orvislat in disbelief.

"I couldn't make him out. And he had long, yellow

hair as well. It slipped out of his cloak. He almost looked like a young girl, getting out of the carriage. But at three in the morning? It had to be a midget."

"I wouldn't put it past Gorman to use some wretched, stunted troll to do his dirty work," said Orvislat. "This is bad. Very bad."

"I agree, said Lupien. "But what could Wilder have said? Only that he was reassigning boats to deliver a treaty, right?"

"Unless Gorman knows something more," said Orvislat.

"What could Gorman and his stoolies know?" asked Lupien.

"Gorman may have discovered what happened to the *Echo*," said Orvislat. "There are many ships about the seas—and mostly, they are British. And if Frey and Fairchild somehow retrieved the notes you threw into the Thames…they could know of our interest in ships. It would not be hard for them to put it all together."

"But how did they suspect Wilder in the first place?"

"I don't know," continued Orvislat. "They surely have suspected him for a while. They must have set a master spy to root out his actions, I am sure, watching the Wilders' house and their doings."

"But who?" asked Lupien.

"Someone who could get close to the Wilders, or with access," said Orvislat. "Someone whom no one would suspect, someone your operatives wouldn't know. Someone *new*."

"The midget!" cried Lupien. "Who would consider a midget?"

"Shhhh! Obviously not us!" said Orvislat. "Wilder could have told them everything if they confronted him with the truth! I have heard rumor that Gorman has a line straight to the king. It would be easy for him to disprove our story of the Treaty of Afgar."

"Akbar. The Treaty of Akbar," corrected Lupien.

"Whatever the name!" said Orvislat hoarsely. "The

point is: Wilder may have talked. We need to find out if he did."

"How do we do that without raising suspicion?" asked Lupien.

"I will ask the boss. She will know."

"Better you than me!" said Lupien. "This is quite a mess. The boss will be furious."

"I will make sure to ask her in public. That way, there will be no outbursts. Listen, Lupien, my friend, we have had a good run. We must be ready to disappear. You can dispose of these bodies in the woods after the hunt, then wait in the trees and brush. If you don't hear from me by midnight, go to Paris, at the Rue de Challis, and await me there each midnight. If I do not appear by the end of the month, go to Kharitonov and tell him what has happened."

Lupien nodded. The men shook hands, then departed. Lupien knew that he would eventually disappear, but he had no intention of seeking Kharitonov; that would be suicide. He would take the small fortune he had collected all these years and hide somewhere, far from all this, for the rest of his days. He had heard that there was much need in the new world for men of his talents.

Riding through the woods and now just moments away from the Wilder Estate was Miss Barbara Thompson in a fashionable outfit, riding her sleek chestnut mare. The horse's tail was bobbed and looking quite fancy with red ribbon. Next to her, in a riding ensemble that included boys' white pants, was Delain Dowdeswell on her black filly. Both women were riding aside. Steward sat on a small cart pulled by a single large horse. Not the usual beast, Steward had taken Captain Walker's own personal black stallion.

In the cart he pulled were a few refreshments and gifts for the after-hunt party being held in honor of the newly engaged Admiral Moore and Barbara Thompson. They had bottles of wine and champagne, boxes of chocolate-covered cherries soaked in brandy, and a few assorted cakes and pies baked by Claise.

That was not all the cart carried. After a brief meeting with Captain Gorman early in the morning, Steward was given a pistol—loaded—and instructions to stay as close to Delain Dowdeswell as possible.

Also following the train were the two Airedales, Daffodil and Daisy, who somehow had stayed with them the entire time instead of rushing off to the muck and filth as was their custom. Possibly they smelled the cherries and other treats.

Delain had attempted conversation with Barbara; however, since their earlier argument, there seemed to be a coldness between them: single-word answers, no questions being asked, no commentary on the surroundings nor the guests. Was she distancing herself? wondered Delain. Were they so different? Maybe. Even the sleek mare Barbara rode upon seemed to say that this rider was a proper lady of London, and that meant sophistication. The black filly Delain rode? That stated young exuberance.

"I can trust you, can't I?" asked Delain, not able to stand the silence any longer.

"Is this your long-awaited explanation of your, your tea-party adventure?" asked Barbara coldly.

"Please hear me," said Delain. "Then you may judge me if you will."

"I, of course, can be trusted," said Barbara. "How can you even suggest otherwise?"

"Well, then," said Delain, "now I will tell you. Lord Wilder is involved in intrigue and scheming of the highest order, and Lady Wilder is the worst of the lot. She is not who she appears to be."

Barbara looked at Delain in shock. She slowly thawed.

"You make it sound like one of Captain Gorman's spy stories—"

"It is. Funny you should make that comparison," interrupted Delain. "It *is* a spy story, yet it is no fiction. I have seen spies entering this estate, payments made, secret notes that even Gorman has confirmed."

Barbara stared at the young woman deeply, now a look of horror on her face. Moving slightly away, more out of reflex than defense, Barbara's mind raced. Finally, she recovered once again.

"Is that what made you leave the carriage?"

"Yes, and I have been in league with Captain Gorman for most of this *adventure*, as you call it. We confronted Lord Wilder. He told us everything. They are stealing ships, Lady Wilder and her spy ring—"

"Lady Wilder? A spy? Really, Delain. Your imagination has gotten out of hand."

"Fine," said Delain, and she halted her explanations. They road on in silence. After a few moments, Barbara spoke again.

"All I ask is that you calm yourself. Calm these urges to find adventure where none may exist. Be more of a—"

"Lady?" Delain blurted out. "A priss? A captured bird like you?"

Immediately after saying the words, Delain realized she had gone too far. The look on Barbara's face reflected the shock and hurtfulness of the comment. She turned and looked away, speeding her horse's pace.

"I am sorry," said Delain.

But it was too late. Barbara rode on without her.

When this was all over and Lady Wilder was in the hands of the authorities, thought Delain, Barbara would see the truth, and then, possibly, our relationship could start anew. Until then, I must do my part to bring the mission to a successful conclusion.

The plan was simple. Frey and Fairchild were to wait outside the mansion all night, and upon Lady Wilder's appearance, quickly grab her and bring her to the police station. But as Captain Gorman had said, sometimes, more often than not, "events do go awry and plans to shambles." Delain's role, then, if Frey and Fairchild somehow failed, was to watch Lady Wilder as long as she possibly could, and report her whereabouts to Gorman at the stable at the

Bracknell Estate after the hunt. Lord Wilder had made certain that Orvislat was invited to the event, as Gorman would be waiting in the shadows, preparing to subdue and retain the spy. They all knew that if he or Lady Wilder got wind of the plan, they would be off like foxes. At least these contingency plans would keep the hounds close on their tails.

A clear trumpet announced that the hunt was about to begin. Lord Wilder had his servant manage the newly acquired dogs, all hounds from the best breeder in all of England, ready and willing. Earlier, the hounds had found a covert where foxes had been lying and picked up a scent. Now, with tails wagging, they pulled at their chains, as if to say: "Let us free! We are ready to work!"

The Airedales were also excited, though it was mostly because of the barking, the horses, the trumpet, and the two dozen laughing riders. Daisy and Daffodil ran ahead to the hounds and joined in the baying.

Looking ahead, Delain strained to see who was in the crowd, and more importantly, to witness the arrest of Lady Wilder. As embarrassing as it would be for Alina, Delain had to admit the great sense of satisfaction she would feel witnessing the event. Now nearing the end of the drive, she could make out a few guests from the tea party and others she had seen about London. Few new faces were there.

Delain turned her attention to the front door of the Wilders' home. Shortly, it opened, and out stepped Lady and Lord Wilder. The lord paused and looked about, allowing his wife to walk a few steps ahead. He looked right, then left, then stood in shock.

Where were Frey and Fairchild?

Delain's eyes met with Lord Wilder's. They read each other's concern and bewilderment.

Even more shocking was the appearance from the main road of a horseman on a large black stallion. Lord

Wilder recognized Seeja Orvislat, son of the Russian Am-bassador to England. Delain saw him as the Black Rider.

I must assume, thought Delain, that the entire mission has gone to shambles.

Wilder thought the same.

As the guests continued enjoying their morning re-freshments, Orvislat casually rode to Lady Wilder as she mounted her horse. Seeing him, she followed Orvislat to the rear of the group.

"A word, Lady Wilder?"

"Orvislat," she said, keeping her eyes on the guests in front of her and smiling. "How nice to see you. Is the con-versation business or pleasure?"

"My apologies, Lady Wilder. It is business, unfortu-nately," Orvislat said softly. "Bad business."

Lady Wilder stopped smiling and looked at him with a frown.

"I believe your husband has had a conversation with Captain Gorman."

"The marine? The spy?" asked Lady Wilder. She could feel a cold streak beginning to run along her back.

"Yes. And just a few hours ago, my associate found two of his men hiding in your stable. He disposed of them."

Lady Wilder was now completely shocked. She worked hard to hide her emotions, though soon anger took over.

"How did Gorman and his band of idiots find out that my husband was involved in this?"

"A new player," said Orvislat. "Last night, my assis-tant saw your husband leaving a carriage. There were four others with him. Frey and Fairchild, Gorman, and another. A new operative formerly unknown to us. We fear he has been watching your house."

"And no one saw this new spy?" asked Alina.

"We believe this new spy is a *master*," said Orvislat, "and a midget."

"A-a *what?* A-a midget?" she asked, understandably perturbed.

"Yes, with long hair, and possibly effeminate."

"Indeed," she said, putting two and two together. "Blond, perhaps?"

"Why, yes. My associate said the hair fell out of the cloak he was wearing."

Alina halted. Orvislat stopped beside her.

"The *he* is a *she*, Orvislat! And she is no master spy. It is that boyish brat, Delain Dowdeswell! She is a clever one, there is no doubt! Feigning illness at my tea party and traipsing about my house! The pillows! I should have known why they were left that way in the bedroom!"

"Pillows?" asked Orvislat.

"Never mind," said Lady Wilder. "Delain Dowdeswell was surely in my library, and she must have found the money!"

"So she is the one who tampered with it!" said Orvislat.

"She saw the notes and the last letter from Kharitonov! She probably copied it!"

"We must know if your husband told them anything," stated Orvislat. "Otherwise, we must all flee!"

"What could he have told them?" Her face was now clearly flushed, her heart racing.

"It depends on what Gorman and Dowdeswell knew before they spoke to him. They almost captured my assistant a few weeks ago by the wharf. If they have found his list of ships, or if they got wind of the *Echo*'s capture…"

"What would that prove?" Lady Wilder asked.

"It could lead them to Captain Spears. Then they would learn that the ships' orders were changed. That would lead them to your husband, and he may have told them about me. We must assume that they know everything!" said Orvislat.

I am safe, for now, thought Lady Wilder, unless Orvislat is captured. He could always talk to save his own skin.

"Find Lord Wilder," she said. "He is somewhere about. As his contact, you must ask him about this."

"And if he admits to talking to Gorman and telling our secrets?" asked Orvislat.

"He is a witness that could testify," said Lady Wilder. "See what my husband has done. If necessary, eliminate him. Is that what you say in your business?"

"Your own husband?" asked Orvislat.

"If need be," said Lady Wilder. "I will deal with the brat, Dowdeswell, myself."

"Gorman will be the only one left," suggested Orvislat.

"Actually, Spears is the one who could testify," said Alina. "He can be bought. I will arrange for additional funds."

Within moments, Orvislat left Lady Wilder and headed to the periphery of the group. He waited a few moments, seemingly listening to conversation, then drifted away.

A horn sounded. The hunt was now underway — both of them.

"Barbara Thompson!" called Lady Wilder, who approached on her horse, making her way to her friend. "Or should I say Mrs. Moore? Let me be the first to congratulate you on your engagement!"

Delain stared at Lady Wilder, having a difficult time hiding her scorn. This woman was responsible for the deaths of hundreds of His Majesty's sailors and possibly her best friends as well, including Jonathan. I must stay by her side, she thought, and I will collect her somehow and tie her up! I know a few knots from my days aboard the *Danielle*! Then I will sit tight until Gorman appears.

"I have already congratulated them, Lady Wilder," said Delain. "However, you may be second."

"Miss Dowdeswell," retorted Lady Wilder, flatly. "In pants? It seems wherever there is action, you are in the thick of it."

"Please ride with us," said Barbara, shooting a challenging look to Delain.

"It would be a pleasure!" said Alina. "Just us girls! And I know a secret way! Follow me!"

As they began, Delain looked behind to see if Steward happened to be nearby. He was, sitting at the entrance to the drive of the mansion, but for some odd reason, he was still fiddling with the bit and harness of the horse pulling the cart and now had the entire apparatus off. Not now, Steward! thought Delain.

Fortunately for the fox, many of the guests were too involved with conversation and drink and had forgotten, for the most part, the creature, the hunt, and even where they were. The morning was warm, sunny, and fine, the company of the best quality, and the idea of actually exerting effort grew distasteful as the refreshments continued.

Barbara Thompson, riding sidesaddle, took position behind Lady Wilder, who, to Delain's surprise, rode as a man. This gave Delain the excuse to ride astride as well. The trio moved quickly as the path led them deeper into the woods. The sound of their horses' hooves on the hard turf and the beasts' labored breathing was all that was heard. Over a small stream, around a large oak, and into deep thicket they went. Though the day was bright, there was much shadow, and the canopy of leaves above blocked out a large portion of the sun. Delain turned to look behind, and a chill ran up her spine. There was a rider following them, a long way back, but she could see that he rode a black steed. Almost upon seeing him, Delain saw the horse and man leave the path and dive straight into the thicket.

The ladies kept a brisk pace, and the trail narrowed as it made its way up a small rise. As soon as they had reached the top, Lady Wilder halted her mount, and the other horses instinctively stopped.

"The fox! I see it!" she called

"Indeed?" asked Barbara.

"It has just crested the next rise!"

Delain looked ahead, though she could see no fox. Instead, there were only more trees and brush. She saw that the path split, ascending a slight rise on the left and down through the small ravine on the right. Something, besides the appearance of the Black Rider, was wrong. Surely Lady Wilder was up to something. If I were her, thought Delain, I would try to flee.

"The path divides here," said Lady Wilder. "We must split up."

"I will go with you, Lady Wilder," said Delain quickly. She was not about to let this traitor out of her sight.

"Are you certain?" asked Barbara.

"Splendid idea, Miss Dowdeswell," said Lady Wilder. "Barbara, you know the paths well and can proceed alone. The fox was moving toward the old mill. If you take the rightmost way, we can corner the thing, and the trail is easier — and, darling, riding sidesaddle will be slower."

"She is correct, Barbara," added Delain. "We will move faster like this."

"Really," interjected Barbara. However, it was no use.

"Dear, you are such a prissy one!" laughed Lady Wilder as she sped away. "Meet us at the mill!"

Delain rallied the filly and was off in pursuit, leaving Barbara alone.

Prissy? What is wrong with that? Barbara thought. And how will they get to the mill by that path? I know these paths; most of them anyway, and there is no trail connecting their way with mine.

Feeling somewhat offended, she slowly took her sleek chestnut mare on the path to the right.

27
The Torpedo Kérata

Once the *Kérata* had cleared the bay of Zadar, Harrison assigned the wheel to Hicks. There was a short instruction period of about five minutes, and then Harrison gave the order to hold her steady and sail due east. There was a slight mountain range in the distance, and after being told to head directly at its peak, Hicks concentrated as hard as he could. He steered for a moment and waited for the result to take effect, and then made other corrections as needed. Though he had never piloted a ship before, the *Kérata* was steady and maneuverable, and at just less than five knots, there was little that Hicks could do to worsen the situation. Nevertheless, it took all his effort.

Harrison was now free to attend to Sean. He had instructed Bowman to move the boy into the lower hold and cover him with blankets. Bowman had done well and kept Sean's leg elevated; he looked as comfortable as one could under the circumstances.

The little experience Harrison received in the area of medicine and aide was from his observations while assisting various ships' doctors. During these circumstances he learned some basic techniques of care, including simple remedies for cuts, bruises, splinters — and after battle, more serious procedures that at times included extricating foreign matter from deep tissue. These were bloody, unpleasant affairs. Many men did not fare well. Harrison believed that most of what the doctor did had little or no effect on his patients; however, there were two procedures he took to heart, and they did the most good: keeping the patient warm and elevating the wound.

Sean had lost a good amount of blood. He lay still and

pale, unmoving. Harrison contemplated his friend, one who had been so full of life and humor and goodwill, always one for a laugh, and always one who could be counted upon.

"Find some salt and tools, any kind," said Harrison, and Bowman ran to do his bidding.

Harrison, with a tear appearing in each eye, leaned close to Sean's face. He rested his head upon the boy's chest. He couldn't help but blame himself. He was, after all, responsible for all the crew. And they were good men, especially Sean.

"Yes," Harrison said as he sat up, "you are still breathing, and your heart sounds strong."

Harrison next inspected the wound. The bullet had gone into Sean's leg in the thickest part. Luckily, he found the exit hole. That would mean that the round had gone clean through. The issue, however, would be if any cloth had been brought into the boy's body by the round as it pierced his flesh and made its way out. That could be disastrous. There was only one way to tell: go look for it.

"Thank God you are asleep, Sean," said Harrison.

On deck, the men seemed nervous and anxious, not so much due to their position being on a small yacht and sailing strange waters to execute a rescue of their crewmates on the *Paladin*, but more about the condition of their friend, Sean Flagon. Sean had become more than just a marine private aboard one of His Majesty's vessels; the young Irishman was a part of all their lives. He provided friendship, made them laugh, and was a stout fighter, especially with a blade. Many believed he was a good-luck charm, and a rare one at that, being Irish. It was unusual to see one from that country with any rank beyond that of a seaman. But Sean Flagon, now technically a royally appointed private in the Royal Marines, had single-handedly crippled the French seventy-four *Danielle*, allowing the *Poseidon* to locate a vast treasure for England. He had been part of the small band that turned the tide of the war at the Castle of

Fire and now had saved the life of their captain. He also was the master of another good-luck charm: Stewie the cat.

"'E's our Irish charm, I call 'im," said Hicks as he steered the *Kérata* eastward.

"All of us are lost," said Welty as he adjusted the bandage that had been wrapped around his head to protect his wound. "Without Flagon, well, why go on? We will fail…if 'e doesn't make it."

Harrison now emerged from the lower hold. All eyes turned to him as he approached the wheel and took control of the ship. Men gathered around their captain, some with hands still clasped together in prayer.

"We will go on," said Harrison.

"We'd been prayin' 'e would live," said Welty. "Did we pray 'ard enough?"

"You did," said Harrison. "He is still asleep, but he is breathing steadily, and his heart beats strong."

The men rejoiced.

"Now, I am no doctor, but we did find a piece of cloth in his wound. I was able to take it out, and we dressed his leg with salt and lemon, so keep praying, and let's feed him well. I will need someone to look after him—"

"I will!" came a chorus from the crew. That made Harrison smile.

"And I will also need at least one or two of you to assist in the running of this ship. If you all attend to Flagon, I will have my hands full!"

The men laughed.

"Then we will take turns!" said Hudson, who proposed a system of watching and caring for Sean based on who had known Flagon the longest being first, second, and so forth.

"As I have known Sean the longest," said Hudson, "and have already taken my turn, that would mean that, Hicks, you are the first in line."

"Aye, sir!" said Hicks, proudly. "I'm an original *Poseidon*, I met him on his first day. Was with 'im at Skull Eye

Island. Sat next to 'im while he ate bowl after bowl of Steward's fish stew."

"Well, if he could survive that, he will easily recover from this small scrape!" said Harrison, causing a wave of laughter. "Marshall, find something better for him to eat. But do not wake him."

"Aye, sir," came the reply. "Some fish broth."

"And also," added Harrison as he addressed the others. "I noticed something odd as he slept."

"What was that, Cap'n?" asked Marshall.

"He had a gold earring. I never noticed that before."

"Sir," said Welty. "Must have been fer passin' the equator?"

"Good luck it is," added Marshall.

"Got one myself, sir," added Bowman.

"Yes, yes," said Harrison. "I just never noticed it."

Harrison now assigned duties to the crew, broke them into two watches of twelve hours each, and had them scour the ship to locate maps, arms, string, rope, and any other devices that could aid them in their quest. Finally, alone with his thoughts, the crew busy and relieved, he began to consider his options. He called for Hudson, and they plotted together as they sat on the few crates present at the stern.

"Certainly, we could just sail about, hoping to find the *Paladin*, but then what?" asked Hudson.

"Somehow," said Harrison, "we must recapture her, which is my first choice, or at least rescue the crew. That is my duty."

"Knowing Mister Moore," said Hudson, "he would be hatching his own plan. He's not one to sit back and let things play out."

"You are right," said Harrison. "He will want to be moving the pieces. We will need to be ready to decipher whatever his course of action may be and supplement it."

"So, what are the possibilities and movin' parts? What do we know?" asked Hudson.

"Well, whoever took the ship, be it Turks or Russians,

would be outnumbered by the Englishmen," said Harrison. "They would have to deplete their own crews to keep control on the *Echo*, that cruiser we saw, and the *Paladin* — at least until they arrive in a home port and take on more of their own."

"And there would be other ships, possibly enemies of Britain that would be in those waters," said Hudson. "Do you think the war has started in earnest once again?"

"It very well may have. And either way, it would be best to continue sailing without a flag for that reason. Eventually, though, we must find a way to signal Jonathan. We have no Saint George aboard. He will not know the *Kérata*. He needs to know we are his friends."

Hudson thought for a moment, as did Harrison. What could Jonathan see that would tell him the *Kérata* was not only a friendly but, specifically, was manned by Harrison and the remainder of the *Paladin*'s crew? There must be some way.

"I think I have it!" said Hudson.

Harrison smiled, as he too realized the one and only signal, developed by Jonathan himself, that would be instantly recognizable.

"Does it have to do with Miss Delain Dowdeswell?" asked Harrison.

"It does!" said the marine, laughing.

"You will have to find a way to fashion that flag out of something," Harrison said with a laugh.

"Aye, sir," said Hudson. "If I may ask, what do we do after we signal Jonathan and the *Paladin*?"

"Unfortunately, we would need to attack it, and then Jonathan, Jenkins, Garvey, and the rest could join the battle on our side."

"But what of the *Echo*?" asked Hudson. "What if she was nearby? If they don't recognize us as friendlies, they may attack us."

"Hopefully, whatever ship our friends are on will know we are friendly and will mutiny. If the Englishmen aboard the other ship notice, they will likely do the same.

They will not fire upon us."

"And the cruiser?" asked Sergeant Hudson. "Her thirty-six guns will most likely be manned by enemy crews."

Harrison hadn't thought of that. He pondered the possibility, wondering how he could somehow disarm a ship five times his size—one bristling with guns. He had a few muskets and fewer swords. He would not be able to take any ship, let alone disarm any vessel with those mere resources.

"We must think of something," said Harrison.

"What if Mister Moore's plan is simply to disappear, swimming ashore and making his way home?" asked Hudson.

"That doesn't sound like Jonathan Moore," said Harrison. "He would never leave his crewmen, his brothers. No, Jonathan would plan to take the ship back and sail home."

"Yes, sir," said Hudson.

"Sergeant, we have the beginnings of a plan," said Harrison, standing. "Let us think on it and find a way to turn the odds in our favor. We are but a half day behind them, and my guess is that they will sail Marmara and maybe even the Black Sea. We will check all the ports; we will have eyes in all directions. They took these ships for a reason, and it is not to break them up for firewood. They will use them, they will fight with them, and that will be easy. to see—and hear of. We will ask in every town if we must."

"We will find a way, Captain," added Hudson.

The *Kérata* continued on, sailing all through the night and into the next day. Captain Harrison continued to instruct Hicks on maneuvering. The marine was surely willing to learn, and though almost petrified most of the time, he did exactly what he was told to do, and that suited Harrison's purposes. After two days' sailing, Hicks was almost like a second pair of hands, and Harrison thought that soon

he would teach him some actual tactics, instead of just calling commands to the man every few minutes.

Harrison had men positioned permanently on lookout
all about the ship and up in the tops. There was no proper
crow's nest, but the *Kérata* had adequate rigging, and Everett was placed as high as he could climb, eyes in search of
sails, preferably sails of a two-masted sloop with raked
masts.

The *Kérata* was actually a well-made double-masted
yacht, maybe half the size of the *Paladin*, with smooth lines,
relatively new sailcloth, and even some rope for tightening
stays to achieve a little extra speed. Though they had no
board to throw aside, Harrison was well known for his ability to gauge the speed of a ship by sight alone. After a time,
he announced to the small crew that they had exceeded six
knots. Not enough to overtake the *Paladin* or even the *Echo*
in a race, but enough to outrun that big, lumbering cruiser,
and that offered some comfort to the men.

The crew had found a few useful items in the holds of
the *Kérata Vátrachos* and brought them to Harrison. Most
useful was a map of the Black Sea, including ports, islands,
and even a detailed chart of the Strait of Bosphorus. Along
with Harrison's sextant that he had taken from the jetsam
at Zadar, he could now navigate. A good amount of lumber
was also found. It had obviously been used to begin the
creation of a bed and cabinets for the lower cabin where
Sean now lay. Various tools also were located that were
common on sailing vessels: awls, axes, small saws, and a
tiny bit of extra cloth.

Toward the afternoon of the second day came the surprising and sudden appearance of Bowman on deck, escorting a slightly wobbly Sean Flagon, who held his cat,
stroking the animal's fur lovingly. Sean was led to a small
wooden box, whereupon he sat, with difficulty, put the cat
down on deck, and propped his leg up on the edge of a
crate. He saluted Harrison.

"Marine Private Flagon reporting for duty, sir."

The men erupted in cheers: "Huzzah! Huzzah! Huzzah!"

In turn, each member of the crew gave Sean a slap on the back, offered him some small tidbit to eat, and adjusted the box, brought a blanket, propped up the leg, and generally fawned over the blond-haired favorite.

"If I would have known I'd get this kind of treatment, I'd have jumped in front of a few more rounds on our last voyage!"

The men erupted in laughter.

"It is good to have you back and in spirits, Private Flagon," said a smiling Captain Harrison.

"And now our marine rank returns to full strength!" added Hudson.

"I'm not so sure about full strength," said Sean, "but I do feel a lot better than I did at the pier in Zadar. Captain, where are we now?"

"We are in the Sea of Marmara, and, as far as I can tell, about forty miles south of the city of Istanbul," said Harrison. "It lies at the mouth of the Strait of Bosphorus."

"Has there been any sign of the *Paladin*?" Sean asked.

"Not yet," answered Harrison. "However, I would assume they would not stop sailing or even attempt to do battle until they entered more friendly waters, and that means the Black Sea."

"The Black Sea?" said Sean as he accepted a fresh roll from Marshall and a cup of coffee from Welty. "Is it really black?"

"Yes," said Harrison with a laugh, "Though only at night!"

The men laughed.

"Actually, in ancient Turkey, color was used to describe direction. Black was north, so since it is north of many of the Turkish lands of the Ottoman Empire, it was called the North—or Black—Sea."

"Hmm," said Sean as he bit into his soft tack. "Mildly interesting, Captain Harrison."

Harrison laughed.

"I am pleased I can entertain your senses, Flagon."

"I would be more entertained, sir, if I could become privy to the plan."

Harrison explained what he had discussed with Hudson, and how they needed to not only locate the *Paladin*, signal Jonathan and the others, and incite them to take over their ships, but also to watch out for the cruiser.

Sean seemed angry, his face turning slightly red as he thought more and more about what had happened. He kept scratching his head, listening to the details, and now and again, shaking his head in anger.

"If we only had a ship with some firepower!" Sean said. "We could take out that dirty cruiser, I just know it! But all we have is this silly...pleasure boat! We might as well have a target raft for all the good it will do us against thirty-six guns!"

"We don't even 'ave a gun to shoot at a target raft," said Hicks.

"All we could do is, well, ram into it!" said Sean, laughing. "But it would do no good. Not against that big garbage scow!"

The crew chuckled, agreeing, and offering other colorful and disparaging words to describe the ship they had all seen.

Harrison, however, was staring straight ahead, and in deep contemplation. A plan seemed to be warming in his mind. Sean had just said "ram into it," and that sparked a memory. He thought and thought, and soon a smile appeared on his face.

"It could work," he said aloud.

The crew stopped their joking and turned to look at their captain.

"What would work, sir?" asked Hudson.

"Do any of you know the story of the *Eagle* and the *Turtle*?"

"A nursery rhyme, Captain?" asked Bowman.

"No," said Harrison. "HMS *Eagle* and the American ship—well, not a ship—a device made by our continental cousins called the *Turtle*."

"During the American War?" asked Hudson.

"Yes," said Harrison. "The *Eagle* was Lord Admiral Howe's flagship. It was anchored in New York Harbor one evening in the fall of '76. A rowboat of sorts was seen approaching the *Eagle*, and a marine spotted it. They called out. The boat rowed back the way it came; however, not before it had released a small submersible craft they had brought with them."

"Sub-merciful?" asked Sean.

"Sub-mer-si-ble," corrected Harrison, "meaning under the water."

The men gasped.

"Like a large keg, with tubes and passageways built into the top that allowed a man inside to breathe. There were small oars also, enabling it to move slowly under the water. The *Turtle*, it was called, and it had attached to it a charge of powder that was to be screwed into the hull of the *Eagle*, then somehow set off."

"Did the *Turtle* destroy the *Eagle*?" asked Hicks.

"No!" exclaimed Harrison. "The *Eagle* still sails, however, the *Turtle* released the charge, which detonated when it struck something in the water many yards away. The explosion was quite large. Later, the inventor of the doomed craft was said to have called it a *torpedo*."

"Tor-pee-do," said the men.

"Yes," said Harrison, falling back into his thoughts.

Sean thought of the story, and though it was interesting and very entertaining, he knew there was a reason Harrison told the tale. Then it hit him.

"If, Captain Harrison, you could get me a few barrels of powder," suggested Sean, "I think we could take care of the cruiser if we had to, eh?"

"Yes," said Harrison. "If it interferes with our recapture of the *Paladin* and *Echo*, we will replace the *Turtle* with the *Frog*."

"The *Frog*?" asked Hudson.

"The *Kérata Vátrachos*. It is Greek for *horned frog*."

"*Kérata* ends in an *a*, sir, and all ships that end in *a* are doomed!" added Bowman. "It's the oldest saying in the navy."

"It's a superstition," said Harrison. "However, in this case, we will not tempt fate, if you believe in it or not. Let us from this moment forward refer to our *Turtle* only as the *Frog*."

Within two hours, the *Frog* sailed with a slight breeze at her back through calm waters of the Sea of Marmara, and by sunset they had reached the great city of Istanbul. Now controlled by the Ottoman Empire, the city was divided into three regions by the Strait of Bosphorus and the passage that continued northwest into the European continent's interior, called the Golden Horn. To the east, on the Asian continent, referred to as the Anatolian Shore, was Skutari. To the west was Istanbul proper, the large Turkish metropolis that in previous centuries had been called Constantinople by the British. It was the northern area that Harrison desired to see, specifically Port Kirej. He had heard Captain Walker speak of it in earlier days, referring to it as the Lime Gate, and how there, for a price, almost anything could be bought.

The *Frog* continued on carefully toward Kirej, all lanterns extinguished, under only her mizzen sail, and silently maneuvered into position amid a group of small caïques and fishing skiffs. There, she was anchored.

Gathering the small crew, Harrison addressed them, having changed from his uniform into some simple clothing: a pair of black breeches and a dark cloak found below in the small storage hold.

"Men," he said softly, "I am not sure what the political or military situation is in Istanbul, though I aim to find out."

"Sir," said Hudson. "Who will you ask? It's not as if the Ottoman people here respect the king of England, or speak his tongue, if you catch my meaning."

"I do catch it," said Harrison. "And I also know that inland, just a mile or so, is the Church of Saint Benoit, now managed by Christian French Lazarists, I believe."

"Lazarists?" asked Sean with a tremble in his voice. "Dear me!"

"They are not as terrifying as the name sounds," said Harrison with a smile. "Priests, we would call them, allowed by the ambassador from France, of all people, to persist here as a diplomatic favor."

"What will you *do* with them?" asked Sean.

"I will ask the brothers for information on any sightings of that Turk cruiser," replied Harrison. "If she is Turkish, someone will have seen her about. I will also try to purchase, or borrow, a keg or two of gunpowder for our plans. Stay quiet and out of sight. If anything unfortunate should delay my return, either temporarily or permanently, and I don't return by sun up, sail to the deeps and come back tomorrow after the moon has set. I will take the small dinghy, by myself, and see what can be done."

The men protested respectfully, suggesting that Harrison take at least a marine with him, but he refused.

"If I do not appear, you are to return to London—"

"But what of Jonathan?" protested Sean.

"My duty is to all of you," Harrison said somberly. "Please, follow my orders."

The boat was made ready, and shortly, Commander Harrison was lowered into the bay, and he rowed himself to the darkening shore of Kirej.

28
The Black Sea

As Harrison made his way to the shore of Kirej, Jonathan stood on the stern deck of the *Paladin*, now entering the Black Sea, watching the hands aboard the captured merchant *Umutlu*. Aggar had set some of the original crew adrift on planks; they were not far from shore, and the men would be on dry land soon. Others had been moved to the *Echo*. Jonathan could see Lieutenant Starikov and three Russian sailors managing the handful of Turkish hands that remained aboard the *Umutlu*. They were to follow the *Navarkhia* and leave the *Paladin* and *Echo* to hunt on their own.

Aggar did keep a small prize from the battle: one of the merchant ship's small boats, a twenty-six-foot lateen skiff. Towed behind the *Paladin*, it had a single mast and a long, angled yard forming a triangular rig to hold a large triangular sail rigged fore and aft. For now, the sail was furled. The name on the stern read *Alexandria*.

The sun was setting, his eyes were heavy, his heart heavier. So many friends had died, and his most dear were miles away. They probably think I am dead, he thought. Even if our plan works, can I ever get home again? There are many perils between here and London.

He could not stop thinking that maybe all the cursed happenings—the ringing bell, Sean's earring, the last-minute changes to orders—all these things spelled trouble. And now, as the *Echo* and *Paladin* sailed with no figureheads at all, what else could befall them?

What was worse was the fact that since the lone galliot the *Paladin* and *Echo* captured earlier, there hadn't been a single sail seen by either crow's nest. Jonathan grew edgy and nervous. He realized that if they reached some port city or if Kharitonov returned, the Englishmen might be split up or moved into a labor camp inland or some worse fate, before they even saw a chance to execute the plan.

He had been lucky up to this point in his life, to say the least, and had seen more of the world than many men three times his age. It was a long way from the streets of London to where he stood tonight. Some of his travels had been enjoyable, many not so, but all with his friends. If it weren't for Jenkins, Garvey, and the others, he would simply dive into the water and accept the fate that the sea offered. He thought that there could still be a remote chance he would see Delain again, and fingering the silver compass star about his neck, he decided to continue on, and he fought back a wave of sadness.

"Southcott," came a voice. It was Aggar. "Anything of interest in this twilight?"

"N-no, sir," said Jonathan, affecting his stutter.

The *Paladin* slipped through the placid sea effortlessly, barely a sound of the water splashing alongside could be heard above the strengthening wind. Aggar joined Jonathan at the stern rail.

"Now that we have snuck past the Turks watching the Bosphorus Strait, we will enjoy smooth sailing for a few days. Here in the wide-open Black Sea, we are safe."

"With the fastest ship in the world, yes," added Jonathan.

"Ha! It is good and true!" Aggar said with a laugh. He noticed the boy looking astern, staring blankly at the darkness in the waves and the night sky; the horizon where they met was almost indistinguishable, lost. His countenance was not one of fear or anger but of complete acceptance of his fate, and only sadness could be discerned. At once, Aggar saw his own son, his son who would have been, had situations turned out only a little differently.

"Southcott, may I ask you a question?"

"Y-you are the c-captain," answered Jonathan flatly.

"Your age?"

Jonathan was taken aback. He expected some other question, possibly about the ship's performance or the stores in the hold. Not knowing where this line of questioning might go, he realized that telling the truth might help him. How could his situation grow any worse? he thought.

"I am just now fourteen."

Aggar stood tall, away from the rail slightly. He nodded. Fourteen. The age his son would have been today.

"A fine lad, tall and strong. They must feed you well in England."

"N-not always, but r-recently, y-yes," offered Jonathan.

"How is that?" asked Aggar.

Jonathan looked ahead, remembering a past long ago and a faraway place of comfort.

"Until recently, I was a citizen of the streets. 'Homeless,' some call it. I was reunited with my f-father only l-last year."

Aggar thought of this. As hard as Jonathan's story must be, he too had a hard life, and all one could do was make the best of it.

"Maybe you will see him again, someday," said Aggar. "Sailors and soldiers we are, and our lot in life is not dictated by our own desire. Servants of others. All of us serve another, eh?"

"Y-you are the c-captain. I believe your p-position will have more to do with our f-fates than any other," said Jonathan in a slightly angry tone. A moment passed before either man spoke.

"Across these waters, dead ahead, lies the Sea of Azof," said Aggar softly, "and then the Russian port cities just south of Dimitria. Eventually, we will sail upriver and take in supplies there."

"Is that your home?" asked Jonathan. "It must be n-nice to go home."

"No, *Southcott*, that is not my home. I grew up due north of here, in a small fishing village named Kylia, right by the river Danube."

Jonathan remembered his history and study of maps. The mouths of the Danube, the river that flowed almost two thousand miles from the mountains in Germany to the Black Sea, were located not in Russia but Romania.

"Yes, I am Romanian," said Aggar, as if reading Jonathan's mind. "I lived in a small house by the sea, and since I was a young boy, I built ships with my father. I learned the trade. We made small craft for the local fishermen, effected repairs, and had a simple, enjoyable life. I married a young girl I had known since I was three, Daria Makarenko. We had three children. But, my friend, things do not always work out as we plan them."

"How did you become a Russian Navy captain, then?" asked Jonathan, forgetting his stutter completely.

"Ha!" laughed Aggar. "You call me captain, but I am not *officially* in the Russian Navy. We are a ship with a letter of marque. I am indebted to a Russian commodore…Kharitonov! It is he whom I serve."

Jonathan noticed that when Aggar said the name Kharitonov, his face contorted into a grimace, and he looked as if he were about to spit.

"How is that?" asked Jonathan.

Aggar's face turned red. He held his breath as he regained his composure.

"My father was conscripted into the service of the Russian Navy. Against his will, I will add. I was away, visiting a mill to obtain lumber for our business. When I returned and found my father gone, I was outraged! So, young and foolish man that I was at the age of twenty-eight, I went to save him. I was…unsuccessful. In my attempt, I was brought before Kharitonov. To make sure that I would submit to his will, he killed my father. And my son. My son, Dimitri, would have been fourteen this very day. Kharitonov! He threatened to kill my wife and two daughters unless I sailed with him. That was…seven years ago."

Jonathan was speechless. As horrible as his circumstance was, it paled in comparison to the tale he had just heard. The look on Aggar's face was complete sadness. He had to be telling the truth.

"Why don't you just sail away? Take the *Paladin* back to Kylia, and see your wife and children?"

"They are not there, Southcott. I have checked. Kharitonov has hidden them from me. So, I do his bidding, as horrible as it is. It is all I can do, my little friend. My midshipman."

Jonathan was suddenly shocked and numb.

"Yes, I know you are no powder monkey. I saw you assume command during the battle," said Aggar. "And I saw Jenkins taking orders from you."

Jonathan realized that he now had let down his guard, and would soon feel the wrath of Aggar, a man with a reason to live, even if it meant killing another.

"If it matters at all," said Jonathan, "I am truly sorry about that scar—"

Aggar laughed aloud, heartily, and clapped the young man on the back. "I took your ship and changed your future; you gave me a charming scar. Never mind that. Just tell me one thing, and we will be even! I would like to know your real name."

Jonathan stood erect, faced Aggar, and saluted.

"I am Midshipman Jonathan Moore of HMS *Paladin*, at your service, sir!"

Aggar returned the salute.

"Ah, well and good, Mister Moore! It seems we have both lost our families, and wish to return to them someday. I will make a deal with you, eh? If we make it to the Sea of Azof, and Kharitonov—"

A shout from the tops interrupted the deal.

"Sails ahead, Captain! Four of them."

Aggar and Jonathan ran to the bow. Immediately, Aggar raised his telescope. He adjusted the lens as he searched straight ahead. After a moment, he found them. He offered the glass to Jonathan.

"Yes," he said to Jonathan, "four small galliots, possibly of the Ottoman Navy, and that means they may have

guns—however, only a few. They will not be as easy to subdue as the *Umutlu*. Rusescu! Get the men to their guns!
Gregoran! Send men to the tops! Be ready to reduce sail!
Mister Moore, attend to the powder! These little chickens
will put us in favor of Kharitonov and buy us some peace
and quiet!"

The light continued to fade as the unbelievable speed
of the *Paladin* and the *Echo* were unleashed. Leaving the
Umutlu behind, they rushed upon the wind toward their
quarry like beautiful yet deadly raptors. The decks on both
ships were alive with activity, though soon, when all were
in position, the noise and bustle calmed. The once-small
ship forms ahead grew larger in their sight. Yes, they were
fleeing, but they were also arming their guns. Jonathan
could tell that these galliots were of at least six guns apiece,
and this battle would be more evenly matched than the last.

"Gun doors open!" cried Aggar.

Jonathan ran to the stern and down the hatchway past
what used to be Harrison's cabin. He descended one more
deck and then began his insurance plan. One by one, he labored to move several smaller kegs of powder from the
magazine to the deck just outside of the captain's cabin. He
covered them with a tarp and lashed them down. Four
more kegs he laboriously moved to the main deck, along
the starboard rail, and then surrounded them with several
now-empty water barrels. Effectively, he had created a fuse
of sorts, a line of kegs on the main and second decks, directly above and alongside the magazine that held almost
seventy kegs of gun powder.

Hoping against all hope, he returned to his duties as
powder monkey, and listened for the order to fire.

The first part of Commander Harrison's mission was
successful. As Captain Walker had said, the port of Kirej
was a bustling marketplace, and Harrison had arranged to
purchase four kegs of gunpowder to be placed in the dinghy, and for a few gold pieces, he was able to have them
protected by a dock hand, watched until his return.

It was a short walk due north on nameless, twisting streets to the area known as Galata, where Harrison located the French Church of Benoit. After a brief wait, he secured an audience with the head of the order, Brother Janis. They sat in the priest's office, a small room with a fireplace and only such furniture as was needed: a pair of chairs and a small, low desk. In the corner of the room was a set of candles, and it was here that Janis stood, preparing coffee beans. A pot of water began to gently hiss as it boiled on the fire.

After a discussion of the status of the French monastery, and the fact that Harrison was obviously English, both parties agreed that their homelands were not at war. They could safely assist each other if it suited them.

Harrison explained what he believed had happened in Zadar, and asked if the priest had noticed the appearance of a thirty-six-gun Turkish cruiser accompanied by two smaller sloops.

"My intention, Brother Janis," said Harrison, "is only to assist my dear friends. I care not of the ships but only the lives of my crew."

Brother Janis nodded and handed Harrison a cup of steaming, dark coffee. Harrison thanked him and took a large sip. It was very strong coffee.

"I believe many have seen the ships you describe," said Brother Janis as he began to prepare a cup of coffee for himself, "though I can tell you that it was not a Turkish vessel."

"How would you reach that conclusion?" asked Harrison.

"There was no flag being flown," said Brother Janis.

"Many do not fly flags in battle, unfortunately," said Harrison, eyeing the coffee with suspicion. Some cream was needed, perhaps?

"Ah. But this was no Turk," said the Brother. "I was a witness myself. The cruiser I saw was in action just off the coast, at the mouth of the Golden Horn. A large ship it was—thirty-six guns, most likely—and ahead were two smaller craft."

"Twins you might say?" asked Harrison, hopefully.

"Yes!" said Janis. "Sleek they appeared to me, and both with…with…"

He motioned with his hands to show a ship with a sail, then tilted his top hand backward a bit.

"Raked sails?" asked Harrison.

"Yes," said Janis, "and one of these smaller craft had sails that appeared larger than its twin."

Harrison smiled. He now knew that the cruiser, the *Echo*, and the *Paladin* had been together.

"They were attacking a small Turkish galiot. A merchant," said Janis.

This took Harrison by surprise.

"Then the cruiser could not be a Turkish ship," said Harrison, "though we saw it flying a red flag with the crescent moon and a white star when it appeared at Zadar."

"Commander," said Janis with a smile, "indeed, the flag sounds like the Turkish banner; however, is it not common to see a ship display the flag of another state to hide its identity? Yes?"

"Indeed," said Harrison. "I have done so myself from time to time. So my next question: who would attack Turkish ships so close to shore? Is the Empire at war with anyone? Or is the Treaty of Amiens still valuable in these waters?"

"I cannot speak for the government of the Ottoman Empire; however, I do know from my history lessons, and actually by living in this city for the past decade, that the Turks have been neutral in the recent wars. They and the Russians have *never* trusted each other. They have, throughout the years, been more than enthusiastic in their hostilities."

"Russians, then?" asked Harrison. "But wouldn't that be a breach of the conditions of the treaty? Surely the Ottoman Navy would request aid against the Russian Fleet."

Brother Janis sat next to Harrison and sipped his coffee, nodding that he understood the question. He smiled.

"I never said that the ship was part of the Russian Black Sea Fleet. However, they were Russians."

"A privateer?" said Harrison.

"I believe that is what you call them," said Janis. "Legal pirates, carrying a letter of marque, possibly from the tsar himself. They have been operating in these waters quite heavily, preying on small craft. The new ships — the sloops — they are nimble. We watched them maneuver with the greatest of ease. They quickly captured their prey. The large ship appeared as Ottoman frigates approached the sloops. The cruiser — she sat back, as if watching."

"Protecting the sloops in case of the appearance of the Turkish Navy," added Harrison. "How long ago, Brother Janis?"

"Three days past. The whole town witnessed the battle from the pier at Egri. They ran north, through the strait, into the Black Sea. None could catch them."

Three days, thought Harrison. The *Paladin* and *Echo* must have made great time. He silently cursed the doggedness of the *Kérata*.

"Thank you, Father," he said as he rose from his chair. "The coffee was splendid. Strong, I must say. I do not think I will sleep for over a week; however, I am grateful for it, as I have much to do."

"Be careful, my son," warned the priest as he walked Harrison through the office and into the courtyard outside. It was now late and the wind chill. Harrison wrapped himself in his cloak.

"These Russian privateers are cruel, acting with impunity and abandon," continued Janis. "If it were not for the treaty, I am sure the war would break out again."

"I can assure you, it will, eventually," said Harrison. "I will be careful, Brother Janis."

"The commodore of this little band of ships is none other than," Janis paused for effect, "Commodore Ian Kharitonov. Ian the Cruel."

"I see," said Harrison. "Well, I am, supposedly called

by some 'Harrison the Unlucky.' We will see if I can transfer some of that title to Commodore Kharitonov."

With the priest's blessing, Harrison walked south to his ship.

29
The Hunted

There were many paths in the Van Patten Wood one could take when hunting foxes. Many of the Wilders' guests took the center choice: wide and well maintained, the one suited more for revelry than hunting, and also the one the refreshment cart had taken. Others, thinking they could actually catch the fox, followed after the dogs, who split into several columns, each team taking a different path.

Lord Wilder, now in the saddle, stayed behind. He was nervous now. What could possibly have gone wrong? Where were Frey and Fairchild? Had Orvislat and Lady Wilder somehow found out? All morning he had been careful, through breakfast and in dressing for the day, making sure that he appeared as normal as possible, being certain his wife could not read the terrible anger he held inside. Obviously, the plan had gone bad. What to do? He decided to simply take a short trip into the woods, so if anyone was looking, it might seem as if he were in the hunt. Then he would immediately return to his home and hide.

He trotted through the woods for a few minutes, and looking around the trees and brush, he saw he was alone. He turned the horse about and then headed to the stables. He dismounted the animal and led it into the barn.

Once inside, he heard a sound, a definite creaking of a door. His pulse quickened. He dropped the reins and crouched down low, hiding behind the stall wall. It had to be Orvislat or one of his agents. Had he been seen last night? Was Orvislat watching his home? After a moment of breathlessness, he realized he must leave, must escape. Wilder slowly willed his legs to move toward the rear door just beyond the feed bin. However, all hope was dashed when he heard another sound. Looking up, he saw the rear door being closed, and a dark shape enter. He was surrounded.

Lord Wilder now crawled to the rear of the stall and tried to hide under the straw. It was a futile attempt to conceal himself, but he could think of nothing else. As he moved the straw about, he felt a sharp pain in his hand. A pitch fork. At least now he had another option. If Orvislat, or whoever was in the barn, found him, he might be able to get one of them out of the way with the pitch fork and then escape the second one. At least, he thought, the odds would be slightly more balanced.

Another sound: the opening of a stall door. Then the squeak of it closing and the next door being opened. Someone was looking, and it was only a matter of time before they reached him. Wilder readied himself.

The door opened. A dark shape entered. It was Orvislat.

"My friend," he said. "What are you doing hiding in here?"

"What are you doing following me?" asked Wilder.

Orvislat smiled. "I simply saw you come in and wondered why you would be leaving the hunt."

"Then why not call my name?" asked Wilder. "Are you trying not to be seen?"

"Are you?" asked Orvislat. "I think we both know each other's game now, or you would not be holding that pitch fork under the straw. And your hand? Is it bleeding?"

Orvislat took a step forward, but Wilder raised the tool from the ground, and struggled to his feet.

"How bold," said Orvislat as he reached into his jacket and withdrew a long knife. "But, my *lord*, I do not think you have as much experience using murder weapons as I. Shall we find out?"

Orvislat lunged at Wilder, easily parrying the fork with his bare hand.

Immediately, Orvislat had Wilder by the throat. They

had a brief tussle; however, Orvislat was larger and obviously trained in the brutish art of physical subjugation. Wilder had all he could do to stay alive for a few more moments—a knife at his throat and no means of escape. He struggled, but his adversary was not shaken.

I accept, he said to himself, that this death is my own fault. I was too dull to realize the ruse, too proud to check out the veracity of the claims. I could have gone to the king. I will now die for my stupidity.

"Anything you want to say before you die, Lord Wilder?"

"Yes, Orvislat. Simply this: I hope you go straight to hell, along with my wife!"

Orvislat laughed. "So you know the boss, eh? Good! We will see you there, then!"

Wilder now saw the other man, who must have been the one entering from the back door, approaching slowly.

"And your friend here can go along as well!" said Wilder.

"Friend?" said Orvislat, with a questioning look coming over his face.

"I wouldn't exactly call us *friends*," said the man behind Orvislat. There was a quick movement, and a muffled cry from Orvislat, who immediately released his grip on Wilder and fell to the floor. The man from behind stepped into the light.

"Gorman!" said Wilder.

The marine knocked the long knife from Orvislat's hand and quickly removed his own that he had placed deep into the back of the Russian's knee. Grimacing in agony, Orvislat spun around and looked up from the ground into the face of his enemy. He made a fist and swung at Gorman's lower torso, but the marine easily moved away from harm by spinning to his right side. By continuing this momentum, his booted left foot came all the way around and slammed into the rear of Orvislat's head. Gorman followed with a series of kicks and punches. Orvislat, completely beaten and almost unconscious, could only collapse on the ground.

"I must decide," said Gorman after a few well-earned breaths, "if I kill him now, kill him later slowly, or just turn him over to the gallows. Your opinion, Lord Wilder?"

"Well," said Wilder, "they all sound just and fitting to me!"

Barbara Thompson rode along the path at a brisk pace, the sun still shining somewhere above the treetops, and birds could be heard chattering above. However, the feeling of impending doom had surrounded her, and she couldn't put a finger on exactly why she felt anxious. Was it the comment on her prissiness? No. That was not it, though it *was* offensive.

As she rode on, her eyes searched for the elusive fox, and she soon realized that something was missing. There were no sounds of the dogs. Certainly, if the fox was near, as Alina had claimed, wouldn't the hounds be close, as they must have picked up the scent by now? Yet, after what must have been an hour of riding, there was no barking, nor the sight of other riders. How could Alina have seen the fox, but the hounds were still clueless? She listened for a moment, and could only just barely hear the faint baying of the dogs, a far way off.

Barbara also had a feeling that Lady Wilder desired to get away from her and be alone with Delain. Why would that be? What if, she thought, Delain and her impossibly ridiculous tale of the Wilders being some manner of criminals were true? Was it pure fantasy to think that maybe Delain was correct, and the situation had turned ugly? Nonsense, Barbara thought.

There came a rustling in the nearby brush ahead. Something low to the ground was moving toward her. The small bushes and trees were swaying from side to side. Could it be the fox? No. It was too large for that. Barbara had been in these woods and knew that there was nothing in them that posed a threat. An otter maybe? Or maybe a man, crouching low? Possibly, but a very agile one, and one that growled and panted like a beast. It was almost upon her. She was about to spin the horse about and run, when she caught a glimpse: a pink tongue. Then: button eyes. The *thing* sprang from the bush.

"Daisy! Daffy!" she said, relieved.

The Airedales were certainly glad to see her, hopping and jumping like acrobats, tails wagging furiously. After a few moments, the dogs simply sat still and waited, as if to say "Now what do we do?"

"Odd," said Barbara. "Do you girls smell the fox? The fox? Where is it?"

No response. Just panting and tails wagging. The chestnut mare huffed.

Barbara considered this.

In another part of the wood, Delain rode swiftly ahead of Lady Wilder. The woods were thicker now, and the branches on either side of the path seemed to reach out, scratching the horse and tearing at Delain's clothes. It seemed that Lady Wilder was either intent on catching a fox in the deep forest...or losing Delain.

She spun about in her saddle to check behind. There was Alina, and behind was the black horseman, again approaching and closing the distance quickly. A chill ran down her spine. Turning forward, Delain saw that the path narrowed, and ahead several yards was a clearing with an old brick building to the side. It had to be the mill.

"Miss Dowdeswell!" called Lady Wilder, "The fox! It ran behind the mill! I will go left! You go to the right!"

They picked up the pace, almost as if racing to the mill.

I know what her game is, thought Delain. I will not let her give me the slip by placing the mill between us!

Once they reached the clearing, Lady Wilder reached out to Delain, who was now alongside, and grabbed the girl's collar.

Delain looked at her and in an instant knew that Lady Wilder, now smiling smugly, had not meant to lose Delain in order to escape; she meant to get her alone.

Delain attempted to swat her hand away, but Lady Wilder retained a firm grip. The girl tried to slow the filly, hoping that after some yanking and straining, she could free herself. Instead, the change in speed pulled Delain from her saddle, and she fell to the ground. Rolling with the force of the fall, Delain bumped along the path, and stunned, came to rest on the edge of the trail against a row of thorn bushes.

Lady Wilder halted and dismounted, took a quick look about, and then made her way to the girl.

"Oh goodness!" she said with exaggerated concern. "Did you fall and bump your head? Poor dear!"

Delain was dizzy. She could barely focus on her surroundings. There was a loud ringing in her ears and a mad spinning of her vision, as if the world were on a merry-go-round. It was impossible to focus. She strained to stay conscious.

Her view was of the path and of a figure walking toward her. She had to do something. At first, in her delirium, only air escaped her lips, then some slurring and puffing. After a moment or two, she was able to put a few words together.

"Won't...get...away," said Delain. "Our...network is...onto you."

"Oh? Really? You mean Frey and Fairchild?" she laughed aloud. "They are dead. My friends found them out early this morning."

The pain in Delain's body now grew to a sharp pounding. She could feel her ribs aching and her legs burning. At least, she thought, her vision was clearing and the merry-go-round began to slow.

"No matter," said Delain. "Your husband...told us everything."

"My husband? I am a *widow* as of a few moments ago, I can assure you. You are not the only one with a network, Miss Dowdeswell."

"How many bodies...do you now have...lying about? Three? And I am...the fourth?" Delain managed a laugh of sorts. "You will be…caught!"

"No. No I won't. I will dig two graves in these woods, only for your two spy friends. My husband? I will simply say he left on a business trip. And do you know what? He never returned! Why? A scandal! Yes, that is it! He was a traitor to the Crown! Stealing all those ships! And selling them for profit to the highest bidder! Russians! Tsk, tsk!"

Lady Wilder now glanced from the fallen girl, who was obviously going nowhere, and began looking about the area.

"And for you, little Miss Nosey," said Wilder, "I will let them find your remains right here in this clearing, a victim of a terrible fall that crushed your dainty little head!"

"I'm not dead," said Delain deliriously.

"Not yet," said Lady Wilder as she began to search the ground, looking for something in particular. "Would you wish to be buried in London or back in the jungle where you came from in the Bahamas? I am sure your parents will be so upset! But, knowing your recklessness…"

"Gorman…has seen the letter," said Delain, trying to gain some advantage. "He knows everything, and he will come…for you. The courts will hang you…"

"Using your letter as evidence? But it is a *copy* of a letter, Miss Dowdeswell—obviously written in your hand! A made-up story from a spoiled little adventurer who is bored with London after all her previous excitements. And is dead, so no testimony could be given, as weak as that would be."

"I know even more!" said Delain, now almost fully conscious, but still barely able to move. "I was onto you at the yacht race, in your…ragged clothes and rented dog cart. And your sloppy ruse! Pretending…to not know a thing about ships, but…at your tea, you slipped up enough to have me notice. You knew particulars of the *Danielle*. Odd for someone who knows nothing of ships."

"How clever you are!" said Lady Wilder. She picked up a stone about the size of her hand, considered it, then dropped it to the ground and continued her searching.

"And I am clever as well. I knew someone was in my library and had carefully put the money and notes back in their proper place, but not *exactly*. The money, my dear, was to be on the bottom, not the top of the bag. Then I found the pillows and wondered, Who sleeps like that? Who puts the pillows in such a strange fashion? It pointed to you. Because…you *are* strange."

Delain needed to buy time. Lady Wilder was no prissy; she seemed larger than before — and certainly more ruthless. Under normal circumstances I could teach her a lesson, I am sure, thought Delain. However, I am in no condition to join in fisticuffs. I need to delay until my senses return or help arrives. And where is Steward? Probably the Black Rider, Orvislat, has gotten him. Both of us trapped like foxes.

"So now," said Delain, "you have your money from your ill deeds, your payments for selling those ships?"

"Yes, in a way. I have recovered from my momentary lack of funds," said Lady Wilder as she continued to search the ground. "I was able to purchase a few necessities and a few niceties, such as this *lady's* riding outfit — "

Delain tried to stand but was unable. She fell to the ground.

"And this handsome pistol. Do you like it?" asked Lady Wilder as she showed Delain a pearl-handled pistol pulled from her jacket. She replaced it immediately and continued to search the ground nearby.

"Is that pearl on the handle?" asked Delain. "How gauche."

"Coming from someone like you?" said Lady Wilder, amused. "One who wears pants?"

"At least I am no traitor!" said Delain with as much venom as she could produce.

Lady Wilder turned to Delain and looked astonished.

"Traitor? Traitor? You don't understand at all, do you?" Wilder said.

"I understand that you are stealing ships from His Majesty's Navy. That makes you a traitor!"

"It makes me a hero!" hissed Lady Wilder in anger. "I am not even British! I do not serve your bumbling king, the one who lost the greatest treasure discovered in the last thousand years! An entire continent! I serve the *tsar of Russia*, and *his* interests! Dear, dear, dear! Did you think this was about money, and—and—about *shopping*?" Wilder laughed aloud and then stooped to the ground.

She had found what she was looking for: a large stone, slightly larger than two fists.

Delain realized the stone was meant for her, to make her fall appear significantly more lethal. A simple crack to her skull and a quick washing of the stone in the nearby creek, and no one would doubt Lady Wilder's tale.

Panicking, Delian began to crawl away. Each movement, each inch, sent searing pain through her chest, legs, and head. Her left arm now also throbbed, certainly broken.

"My friends were on those ships!" cried Delain.

"Your friends could *still* be on those ships, if that is any comfort to you in your last moments, Miss Dowdeswell," Lady Wilder said as she went after the girl. "They are now most likely in the service of a special Russian naval force, in the Black Sea. Doesn't *that* sound like an adventure? And under the command of Commodore Ian Kharitonov!"

"Kharitonov. I have heard of him," said Delain. "So you work for him?"

"I work *with* him!" Lady Wilder said, angrily. "He is my *brother*!"

Delain had made it to the edge of the clearing, and now, with all the remaining vigor left in her body, rushed into the brush.

"Oh no, no, no, no, no!" said Lady Wilder. She dropped the stone in the clearing and quickly darted to the girl. Grabbing Delain's ankle, she began pulling her out of the undergrowth.

"For the first time in your life, you will behave!" Wilder said as she pulled hard, dragging Delain through the sticks, thorns, and thistles.

Delain grasped the trunk of a small sapling, hoping to stop the crazed woman from her attack. Lady Wilder simply pulled harder. The sapling tore from the ground.

Delain spun around to her back, still being pulled by the ankle. She swung the sapling at her attacker with her one good arm, striking her ineffectively on the face. Wilder simply laughed. With a massive show of strength, she yanked Delain harshly by her leg, sending her skidding across the ground into the clearing. In an instant, Lady Wilder had retrieved her stone and was upon Delain's chest, pinning her down.

Delain cried out in pain and then began yelling for help, screaming like a wild animal.

Lady Wilder promptly placed a hand over the girl's mouth, stopping her from calling for aid.

"Now," said Lady Wilder, "let us finish our little adventure!"

Delain realized that all her adventuring, all her life, all her expectations and dreams, now had no future at all. She opened her eyes and saw her wrist and the dainty dolphin bracelet that Jonathan had given to her. She thought of the day they had saved turtles on Conception Island; their meeting at the Governor's Ball in the Bahamas, Jonathan looking so handsome and shy in his new uniform; the discharging of the great cannons at the Castle of Fire, and the sea battle she witnessed. She would never see Jonathan again, and they would never marry. Yes, that is what she had dreamed of, though she'd never told anyone of that desire. He was just like her, and he accepted her for exactly who she was. No one had ever treated her as an equal, except for Jonathan. He had given her the affectionate title of "Miss Delain Dowdeswell, Adventurer." She would never hear his voice utter those words again. She could now only hear a horse's hooves approaching. Orvislat. He had returned to assist his master.

With her free hand, Lady Wilder raised the stone over her head, though she paused to look at the rider.

"Aye! What in the 'ell do we 'ave 'ere?" asked Steward.

Steward! thought Delain. It was not Orvislat, the Black Rider, who was following them. It was Steward!

Delain turned her head slightly to see the old sea hand leap from the horse and produce a pistol, aiming it directly at Lady Wilder.

"Oy! What are ya? Daft? Get off that girl and put the stone down slowly, ya ugly salt-withered harpy!"

Lady Wilder set the stone down, keeping her eye on Steward the entire time. But as she released the weight, she reached into the folds of her jacket with her other hand and, with amazing efficiency, produced her pistol and fired.

Delain saw Steward react in shock, clutch his belly, and fall to his knees. Their eyes met, and all Delain could read from the man's face was his failure.

"S-s-s-sorry, Miss Delain..." he said, and he fell to his side.

Horrified, Delain could only look away.

"Where were we?" said Lady Wilder. "Ah, yes! I was about to smash in your beautiful little head." She took up the stone, now with both hands. "Shall we?"

Delain was helpless. There would be no one riding to her rescue. She could hear the fabric of Lady Wilder's jacket rubbing against her blouse as she raised her arms, once again, over her head.

From behind and to the side of Wilder, there was an odd sound—again a horse's hooves, but moving at an incredible pace. Had the hunt come this way?

Delain turned her head toward the sound, as did Alina Wilder.

Seeing what was approaching, Delain summoned all her strength. She quickly coiled herself into a ball and rolled hard to her left, away from her attacker.

Lady Wilder remained sitting fully upright, shocked, with no time to react.

The sleek chestnut mare struck Lady Alina Wilder

with amazing force and at such an angle that the noble-woman was immediately slammed into the ground. The stone flew into the brush as Wilder was dragged away from Delain. The horse's rear hooves slammed into Wilder's back and head with thunderous cracking, and she rolled under the beast for several yards, being pummeled severely. Finally, the brutal attack ceased. Wilder lay in a heap, barely breathing.

Delain looked up at the rider.

Barbara Thompson, siting astride in the western style upon the sleek mare, stared down at the trampled Wilder, a harsh look of victory on her face.

"I never liked her," said Barbara. "Too...*prissy* for me."

"Miss Thompson!" was all Delain could manage as she drifted out of consciousness.

"Well, that was a fine piece o' riding, Miss Barbara," came the muffled voice of Steward. "I-I never liked 'er neither. And remind me never to get on *yer* bad side."

30
Mutiny and Pity

On the other side of the world, Jonathan sat in the magazine, listening. The *Paladin* and *Echo* were now near enough to engage the Ottoman ships, and at any minute, he expected to hear the call to fire. That, of course, and according to his plan, would touch off the mutiny.

He was shocked to hear a call from the crow's nest come once again.

"The *Navarkhia*! She is approaching from the south!"

Jonathan ran up the stern ladder to the main deck and looked off the port side. Indeed, even in the failing light, he could make out Kharitonov's ship slightly ahead of the Turks and choosing a tight angle to intercept.

As the guns were only minutes from firing, he needed to consider what part in all this the *Navarkhia* would play and exactly where she would be in the upcoming battle. Close enough to see what was happening aboard the *Paladin* and the *Echo*? Would she engage to stop the mutinies or chase the Turks? Certainly the answer was not good news. In Jonathan's mind he could see the mutinies taking place simultaneously, and Kharitonov deciding to assist at least one of the captains, either Aggar or Cherepanyanko. His heart was now beset with absolute despair. He had not planned for Kharitonov's appearance.

Jonathan realized there were only two options. One was to call off the mutiny and wait for another time and place when the situation would be more favorable. But what if it never *was* more favorable? What if Jenkins was put back on the *Paladin*? What if the two ships were separated? And how would he signal Jenkins to stand down and abort the mission? It would be best, he reasoned, to go ahead with the plan. He held on to the hope that if both mutinies were successful, he and Jenkins could set all sail and outrun the *Navarkhia*.

Jonathan quickly ran to the hidden locker, opened it, and there found his sword. The same blade had been with him now for years, and though "short," it actually was longer than the usual dirk blade of a midshipman. It was only two inches in length less than a full sword; however, it fit him well, and together, they were a deadly pair. He slipped on the light cape-jacket hanging in the corner, hid his sword beneath, then closed and locked the small door.

Returning to the deck, he moved aft. There by the wheel was Aggar.

"They are breaking up!" came a call from the crow's nest.

It was obvious that the Turks also saw the newly arrived Russian ship and had decided to take their chances separately. They split into pairs, one heading straight ahead, hoping to outrun the *Navarkhia*. The last pair turned to starboard and ran almost due southeast. Within a few seconds, the pairs split again. The farthest pair now ran north together, into the wind, to hopefully escape the *Navarkhia*. She would have a hard time coming about.

"Ha! Those two little chickens will evade capture!" said Aggar, laughing. "A sound maneuver. Let Kharitonov chase them if he will! Leave the real battle to us!"

At that moment, the closest pair also split. One continued onward to the east; the other, larger Turk came slightly to starboard and headed almost due south.

"Ah! They have decided for us!" said Aggar. "We will choose the one to starboard. She thinks the wind will aid her escape, but it will also give us speed! I assume Cherepanyanko can take the smaller one!"

"Our Turk will turn sharply for a moment, Captain," said Jonathan. "He will try to damage you as he catches the wind from the north."

Aggar turned and, noticing Jonathan, smiled.

"That is correct, Mister Moore," said Aggar, "and I

will allow him. With our superior speed, we will be upon him in a minute. I am watching his wheel and rudder. As soon as he turns, I will also turn, and we will trade broadsides, his three against my nine. I think I will win this one easily."

"A sound tactic, sir," said Jonathan. He inched forward and held on to the aft mast with his left hand. In his right, he gripped the hilt of his sword. A quick glance about the deck and he saw almost all of the Englishmen stealing glances at their captors; some slightly nodded to him as if to say, "We are ready." Graham stood to the other side of Aggar, eyes upon the Russian. He too nodded to Jonathan.

It was now or never.

Aboard the *Echo*, Jenkins and Garvey were manning the stern deck gun on the starboard side. They had originally been assigned the second gun on the port side, along with Cardew and Adams, two of the original *Echo* crew, though after their quick and secret conversations about the plan with their English brothers, all agreed that Jenkins and Garvey should be as close to Cherepanyanko as possible. It would be their role to gain control of the wheel. The *Echoes*, thirsty for revenge, would lead the attack against any Russian holding a weapon and then hurry to the sails.

All were tense. All were ready.

Cherepanyanko had held his original course eastward, gaining on the fleeing Turk, an oddly shaped two-deck affair of less than a dozen guns. She looked more like an ancient Spanish galleon than a modern warship—and most likely, she was just that. Her crew could now be seen on deck, manning the guns, but there looked to be some confusion on their part.

"Ha!" cried Cherepanyanko. "They are scared! Aim at the decks! Do not damage the rigging or sails! Do you understand?"

"Aye!" yelled the gun crews in unison as they readied their weapons. There were a few glances about from the

Englishmen as they noted where the Russians were positioned. As expected, half of the Russians who were guarding them had moved to other areas, directing men in the tops, or readying themselves to board the Turk should its men surrender quickly or need to be subdued through hand-to-hand fighting.

"There are only a handful watching us now," said Jenkins into Garvey's ear.

"Aye," replied Garvey cautiously. "You go for Cherepanyanko. I will take the guard to his right."

The *Echo* was almost upon the Turk, less than fifty yards astern.

"Ready guns!" said Cherepanyanko. "Steady!"

The Turk turned slightly to her starboard side, and Cherepanyanko matched the move to position the *Echo*'s portside guns to fire. The Turk fired first, aiming to slow her pursuer. Though only three guns could be used, the shots were accurate and aimed high at the *Echo*'s sails. Balls of hot lead ripped into main course and topsails, leaving large holes.

"Steady!" called Cherepanyanko.

Garvey slowly stood and moved backward, positioning himself near the guard.

"Port side!" yelled Cherepanyanko.

Jenkins reached for a cannonball, one he hid under his shirt, the one he was supposed to load into the gun. He turned to see Cherepanyanko, intent on the Turk, his face red with the fever of a warrior. Jenkins hefted the ball, a six-pounder. Heavy, but not extremely so. He was only four feet or so from the Russian commander.

"Fire!" yelled Cherepanyanko.

Jenkins stood quickly and using the ball as a weapon, attacked Cherepanyanko, knocking him to the deck.

At the same time, the other gun crews erupted in revolt. Only two guns were fired at the Turk, and loaded with grapeshot, they streamed red-hot balls into the deck of the galliot. Some went higher than expected, and small flames burst into being as the shot struck canvas. Soon, smoke filled the decks of both ships. The Turk, now preparing to run, fired rounds at the *Echo*, doing little if any damage, just sending more smoke and ash into the air.

Aboard the *Paladin*, Aggar had read his Turk correctly. When the smaller ship turned, the *Paladin* was in perfect position to fire. In fact, she had been moving so fast that Aggar was forced to immediately call for a reduction in sail. The Turks fired first, exploding in succession. The first ball struck hull of the *Paladin*, causing no harm. The second and third blasted the mizzen gaff at the mast, sending it downward to tear the spanker. The sail was torn in half. The gaff dropped over the stern. The *Paladin* was damaged, however, her speed would only be slightly affected.

"Fire!" yelled Aggar.

The signal was heard, and the English gun crews rose and charged their captors.

The fighting was ferocious. There were pistols being discharged, hand-to-hand struggles, men using ball, wooden clubs fashioned from spare lumber, gaffs, poles, and bare fists. The guards were certainly caught by surprise, though they quickly rebounded.

Aggar watched this eruption and turned to Jonathan with a questioning look on his face. Realizing what had happened, the Russian immediately exposed his pistol.

"You," said Aggar. "This is your doing!"

Jonathan and his blade were in the *en garde* position. He smiled. "Yes, Aggar. I suggest you surrender before your men suffer serious injury."

Aggar laughed.

"Ha! I do love your boldness, my little powder monkey!" he said, raising the gun. "But you have brought a blade to a gun fight!"

"No, he brought a friend!" said Graham as he swung a six-foot gaffing pole at Aggar's right arm, knocking his pistol from his grip and sending it skidding across the deck. Jonathan added a slight kick to the gun, forcing it out a scupper and into the sea.

"He is all yours, Mister Moore! And don't go easy on him this time!" With that, Graham ran to assist his mates, leaving Jonathan to deal with Nikomed Aggar.

"I will have to kill you," said Aggar as he produced his sword. "And I will regret it."

"Then surrender," said Jonathan. "Both of us may live."

"I cannot do that, Mister Moore. I answer to Commodore Kharitonov."

Aggar lunged at Jonathan with a surprising power and speed, driving the boy backward. Jonathan's nimble feet and excellent reflexes allowed him to remain upright and in fighting position. With a few retreats, he soon was able to parry Aggar's strong but brutish lunges and to counter with quick and accurate thrusts. The opponents continued their dance about the stern, into the lower ratlines, and across the main deck.

Aboard the Turks, the captains observed the action on the decks of the Russian ships, and though puzzled, rejoiced and fled into the night. With the smoke clouding the vision of their enemies, their escape seemed imminent.

On the *Echo*, as Cherepanyanko fell, Jenkins immediately grabbed the wheel of the ship. The *Echoes* were infused with a deadly potion: power and anger, born out of revenge for their murdered brothers and for their lost captain. They fought with such vigor that they screamed like wild animals and stunned their enemy. Within moments, they were well on their way to controlling the ship, tossing Russians overboard and unfortunately killing a number of them.

Jenkins, now at the wheel, and secure that victory was only minutes away, maneuvered the *Echo* toward the *Paladin*.

"Jenkins!" said Cardew as he approached the helm. "Why do you turn? We are to flee! That is the plan!"

But Jenkins shook his head in disagreement. He remembered his promise to Admiral Moore that morning in London, which seemed so long ago. I promised to keep an eye on Jonathan, I did, he said to himself, and aid him if I can! I will not run to safety. I will run into battle and be by his side!

Aboard the *Navarkhia*, Kharitonov was bearing down on the two Turks who had headed north. He would have to come about quickly or lose them in the darkness.

"Run if you can!" Kharitonov said, laughing. "One of you will be my dinner this evening! The other I will save for another day!"

"Sir!" came a call from the crow's nest. "Aggar and Cherepanyanko! They are not engaging! Their Turks are fleeing!"

"What?" yelled Kharitonov. "Not engaging? The cowards! The imbeciles!"

He took up his telescope and glanced back at the *Echo* and then the *Paladin*. Silhouetted by the fading glow from the setting sun, he saw them fighting—but not the Turks. They looked, at first, as if they were fighting each other. The longer Kharitonov watched, the clearer it became. Men were being tossed overboard, and on the *Echo*, the fighting had almost stopped altogether, yet men were still being pushed into the sea.

"Mutiny?" he said aloud. "Mutiny!"

"Technically, sir," said Morozov at the wheel, "they are recapturing their own ship. It can't be mutiny."

"Shut up, idiot!" yelled the commodore.

As he continued to watch, Kharitonov saw a flag being hoisted to the mainmast of the *Echo*. It was the Union Jack and cross of the British Royal Navy. Kharitonov yelled in despair. He turned his gaze to the *Paladin*. There, fighting was still in earnest.

"Morozov!" Kharitonov bellowed, "Take us to the *Paladin*! Directly! She is closest, and not yet taken!"

Still in battle, and with no one at the wheel, the *Paladin* drifted south. The Englishmen fought for their lives, and it seemed to some that they would soon be triumphant. For Jonathan, however, Aggar was not quite ready to surrender, and their swords continued to clash as they fought on deck.

At times, it seemed Jonathan had the upper hand, his agility and precise technique having a distinct advantage over his larger opponent. He set his point to Aggar more than once, and blood flowed from the man's body in several places, yet none were lethal—at least not yet.

Aggar also had an advantage: he could press Jonathan in close quarters with his weight and strength, but up close, his arms were too long to do any damage; in fact, he was at the mercy of the boy's quick ripostes and counterattacks. He then moved to keep Jonathan at a sword's length away and stretched with his longer reach to attack the boy from a safe distance. During one such attack, he was able to slash at Jonathan's right leg. The boy cried in pain, his limb hot with blood from the sting.

"Ah!" said Aggar with a laugh. "This is not all fun and games, my boy! This is real life—and real death!"

"And this," said Jonathan, not missing a beat as he executed his most lethal maneuver, a double-advance lunge that kept him airborne, covering the distance between them in a flash of a second, "is a *real* lunge!"

His point pierced Aggar's shoulder, deeply. Shocked, Aggar staggered backward. Jonathan, still in agony from the slash to his leg, retreated.

Unexpectedly, the *Paladin* lurched violently, as if she had run aground. The sound of deep scraping and cracking boards could be heard. The *Echo* had come alongside.

Aggar had been thrown to the deck by the force of the collision, dropping his blade. Jonathan was also thrown, and he landed against the starboard rail. He quickly regained his sword as it slid across the deck, and he stood quickly. He rushed toward Aggar, flicked the man's blade over the side, and placed his tip against his enemy's neck.

Aggar looked up to Jonathan, and the familiar emotion of defeat washed across the man's face.

Again, I am close to victory, he thought. But now, as always, my sad life has no hope. I will never see my family again. And I am tired. Tired of it all.

"Kill me, Mister Moore," he said, exhausted. "I will be in the wrath of Kharitonov if you don't. Knowing him, it would be better to die at your hand."

Jonathan now regarded Aggar and remembered a similar situation he'd faced a year ago, on the island of Ribeira Grande. Then, it had been Midshipman Wayne Spears begging for death. Jonathan could only feel for that boy, a victim of misguided advice, regret, and blame. He could have killed Spears, though he chose not to. Aggar, however, was a different story. He was responsible for the deaths of many Englishmen aboard the *Echo* and the *Paladin*. He certainly deserved death. He would have killed Jonathan if he'd discovered his identity any earlier than he had.

However, wasn't Aggar also a victim of cruelty being forced into his position by a devil incarnate? Kharitonov had murdered his father and his son and, for all practical purposes, destroyed Aggar's family and enslaved the man. Wouldn't Jonathan do anything to return to his family? In a way, he had.

"Stand up!" yelled Jonathan. "Stand up now, Captain Aggar!"

Aggar did so, trying to avoid the blade Jonathan had pressed to his throat. The man's arm was still bleeding. Soon, he would become light-headed.

"Move to the rail!" Jonathan said sternly.

Aggar complied. Once he reached the rail, he believed that Jonathan meant to kill him and toss his body overboard. He closed his eyes.

"Finish it, Mister Moore. Go home to your family before Kharitonov arrives."

Jonathan looked to the sea astern, and there he saw his bane: the *Navarkhia* was approaching, the wind at her back.

"The commodore," said Jonathan, motioning with a

nod of his head. "We will not make our escape."

Aggar looked to see the *Navarkhia* moving steadily on a course to intercept the *Paladin*. He did not smile—quite the contrary. He looked even more defeated and spent.

"Then run to the *Echo*," said Aggar. "Jenkins has taken her back. Sail away. Be free, powder monkey, and with your blade, release me from this hell we call earth."

"No," said Jonathan. "I know some would say that you must answer for the men you killed aboard the *Echo* and the ones who died when you attacked the *Paladin*. But you were being used by Kharitonov. If he did not command you, if he did not hold your family prisoner, none of this would have happened…to either of us. I will send you back to your family."

Jonathan stepped back and quickly slashed at the rope that had been towing the small skiff, *Alexandria*, behind them.

"Jump, Aggar. There are a few of your men who have been tossed overboard. They have made their way to the skiff. They will help you. Go and find your wife and daughters."

"Kharitonov will find me," said Aggar as he glanced aft and saw the *Alexandria* slowly drifting away.

"He may," said Jonathan. "But first, he will have to deal with me."

Aggar smiled, nodding. He looked back at the small skiff. The men aboard struggled with the sail. He turned back toward Jonathan.

"Mister Moore," he said, solemnly. "As I was proud of my son, surely your father is likewise proud. I am indebted to you. May we meet again someday. Good-bye, powder monkey!"

With a quick salute, Aggar turned and leapt into the sea.

31
Paladin's Fate

Though Jonathan could see that his friends were fighting bravely, there were still enough Russians resisting to make the outcome of the mutiny uncertain. He hadn't the time to wait. The *Navarkhia* was almost upon them. His only hope of returning home and saving the crew was to board the *Echo*. She was ready to sail, after suffering only minor battle damage.

"Mister Moore!" came the call from the *Echo*. It was Jenkins. "The *Navarkhia* is almost upon us! Your orders!"

The *Navarkhia*, though slow and cumbersome, had something the *Paladin* and the *Echo* had in short supply: men. Jonathan knew that a ship of that size, almost the size of HMS *Poseidon*, his original assignment, carried two hundred men or more. He could not fight them off. They would take the *Paladin* within minutes.

"Your orders, Mister Moore!" called Jenkins.

One in the hand is worth two in the bush, he thought. "*Paladins!* Abandon ship!" he called, fighting back a cry of despair. "A-Abandon ship! To the *Echo!*"

Men immediately repeated the order, spreading the word. Some looked about in wonder, as they knew the ship was almost won. Then others saw the *Navarkhia* and realized they now had only precious moments to withdraw to the safety of their sister ship.

Immediately, the English sailors began to literally jump ship. The few Russians who were left seemed confused and, not understanding what was happening, surrendered. The brothers Stredney escorted them to the *Echo*.

Jonathan watched them all and then realized his mistake. Immediately, he ran to the bow and opened the box by the *Stowaway.*

"Mister Moore!" yelled Jenkins. "Now would be a good time to leave!"

"On my way," Jonathan said, as he grabbed an incendiary shell from the box.

Kharitonov was now gaining on the two English ships, the *Navarkhia* still moving with greater speed; however, that advantage would disappear in a wink of an eye when the sails of the *Echo* were let down. Though she was fast, at this moment, the English ships were effectively standing still.

The *Echo* seemed to be ahead in its preparation, the commodore observed, the *Paladin* not so. In fact, Kharitonov could see men abandoning the ship. The easier prey would be the *Paladin*. This he accepted, and he somewhat relished the fact that he could personally address Aggar, who had disappointed him yet again. Possibly he had outlived his usefulness. It was time to be rid of the Romanian.

"We will board the *Paladin!*" he called as he maneuvered his ship into position. "Do not fire! I want that ship in condition to sail! Prepare a boat! The large skiff! We will come alongside her! Be ready to board!"

The *Navarkhia* closed to within fifty yards.

"Skryrabin!" called the commodore to his lieutenant. "Take a party in the skiff and regain the *Paladin*. Make her ready to sail! I will continue after the *Echo!*"

Jonathan was the last to leave the *Paladin*. Reluctant to depart, he searched his mind one last time. Was there anything else he could do? Was there any way to save both ships?

"Mister Moore!" called Jenkins. "Hurry! We are adding sail!"

The *Echo* almost lurched as the wind caught the mainsail and the topgallants. Jonathan turned to the *Navarkhia*. She was less than twenty yards away. He could see the boarding party ready to attack. Some fired rounds, hitting the deck and the spars above him.

"Hurry, Mister Moore!" called Jenkins.

"Jump, Jonathan! Jump!" yelled Garvey.

Jonathan ran to the port rail and leapt across the waves. Jenkins and Garvey caught him as the foremast sails let out. They wrestled him over the rail and onto the deck as the *Echo* pulled away.

Jenkins and Garvey helped Jonathan up to his feet as they looked astern. The *Navarkhia* had come alongside the *Paladin*, and not stopping, the skiff with Skryrabin's party inside were dropped into the sea. As Kharitonov continued onward, heading toward the *Echo*, only fifty yards to her stern and gaining, Skryrabin rowed to the *Paladin*.

"We might outrun the *Navarkhia*," added Jenkins, "though the *Paladin* will certainly catch us. We must make haste!"

"But with *Paladin*'s foremast damaged we should have an advantage?" suggested Jonathan.

"*Echo* has taken some damage to the hull, and a few sails are burned beyond repair," said Jenkins. "Some are afire in the tops. We will not have the speed we require to outrun *Paladin*."

They could now see the Russians cheering as they began to swarm over the deck of their sister ship and climbed the lines to let down sails on the main and spanker.

"Garvey! Get the men to those fires! Cut the sails and rigging if need be," commanded Jonathan. "Let out all available sail!"

"Yes, sir!" replied Garvey.

"She will still catch us, Mister Moore," said Jenkins.

"I will not let them take the pride of the British Navy!" said Jonathan. "Nor will I let them take us again!"

"Jonathan!" said Jenkins. "We cannot take her back!"

"Graham! Stredney!" Jonathan called. "Find an *Echo* who knows the stern chaser and have him join me there! Jenkins! Get us out of here. Head due south, as the wind will be at our backs."

"What are you doing, if I may ask, sir?" said Jenkins.

"Cashing in my insurance!" said Jonathan as he ran aft past Jenkins and the wheel.

Cardew joined Jonathan at the stern chaser and assisted him in preparing the gun to fire. Jonathan calculated that the *Paladin* was several minutes away from pursuit, but the *Navarkhia* was moving into position between them—almost directly behind.

Cardew now rammed a wad down the barrel.

Jonathan took the shell from his pocket and loaded it into the breech.

"She will block my shot!" he said aloud and bent down to take aim. "I hope this fires true!"

"She is as true as a first love, sir!" said Cardew.

"Is all sail out?" called Jonathan.

"As much as we have left, sir!" called Garvey from the tops.

On the *Navarkhia*, Kharitonov watched as the men on the stern of the *Echo* readied the chaser. He laughed heartily.

"Ridiculous!" he said aloud. "That little piper couldn't damage us! Like a fly it is! Send a volley to their deck! Muskets! To the bow!"

A group of men with long guns appeared and took firing positions about the bow of the Russian cruiser.

"They are only a few yards ahead!" said the commodore. "Aim for their officers! It is our only chance before they are gone!"

"The smoke from the *Paladin*!" said Jonathan. "It is in my view! I cannot aim!"

"At what are you firing?" asked Jenkins.

"Come to port, two points! I need a clear shot at her stern!" called Jonathan.

Jenkins complied with the order. He then turned the wheel over to Graham and ran to the stern rail to watch the positions of the ships.

Through the smoke and haze, in the failing light, Jonathan could see the *Navarkhia* entering his view. It would be blocking the *Paladin* completely in a matter of seconds. He reached to his neck, and from there grasped the silver star-and-moon compass.

"A little luck, Miss Dowdeswell," he said and kissed the charm.

"All sail is out!" called Garvey as the *Echo* caught the wind and leapt forward.

In an instant the breeze came across the stern, giving Jonathan a clear view of the powder kegs he had positioned on the main deck of the *Paladin*.

"Forgive me, Mister Harrison!" yelled Jonathan.

He pulled the chain of the chaser.

The gun exploded, sending the hot shell, the explosive round, racing toward Harrison's love.

Kharitonov glanced to his side and witnessed Skryrabin and his crew boarding the *Paladin*. Smiling, he called to his men, "Fire!"

The muskets erupted.

Jonathan's shell sailed speedily from the gun, with no arc, straight past the bowsprit of the *Navarkhia*. It cut a portion of the rigging of the foremast, then the mainmast's ratline. It flew alongside the Russian ship and then across the few yards of ocean. It struck the *Paladin* within inches of the stacked kegs Jonathan had prepared.

He could see the powder kegs ignite with a blast of fire and a loud *bang!* Then the second set of barrels underneath the deck exploded, sending a larger flame and a thunderous *BOOM!* into the night. Finally, the entire magazine of the *Paladin* exploded in an astonishing wall of white flame, sending heat and a shockwave in all directions.

Aggar, now aboard the *Alexandria*, saw the explosion. He gasped and shuddered at the thought that Jonathan might be aboard. It was clear that the *Paladin* and whoever was aboard were lost.

Men on the *Echo* and the *Navarkhia* were thrown several feet across deck; some Russians were sent overboard.

From Jonathan's angle, it was as if the sun itself were burning on the sea where the *Paladin* once sat. The light placed the *Navarkhia* and the stern of the *Echo* in silhouette against the explosion, highlighting the form of Jenkins.

Jonathan saw musket rounds from Kharitonov's gunmen strike the man, knocking him from the rail and onto the deck.

"Jenkins!" called Jonathan as he ran from the chaser, rushing to his friend.

Jenkins tried to stand, though he could only sit up partially. He looked down to his chest and became stunned as the fires in the sails glowed about him, showing his blood seeping through his white shirt.

"Mister Moore?" he asked, and in shock, he fell back to the deck.

"Jenkins?" Jonathan cried. "Jenkins!"

The men on the *Echo* surveyed the scene, and though happy to be alive, still could not enjoy the moment of triumph. They too had seen Jenkins fall.

Reaching his friend, Jonathan could see the wounds to his chest and legs. He winced with horror and despair and then collapsed at his side.

"No, no...Jenkins! Not this! Not now!"

Jenkins looked up to Jonathan. "Mister Moore. I am sorry. Did we get away?"

"Yes, yes we did. Y-you will be all right, don't you worry!" Jonathan said.

The *Navarkhia* was firing as Kharitonov desperately tried to stop the fleeing *Echo* from escaping. He had turned to port and loosed an eighteen-gun broadside. The noise was deafening, and Jonathan was sure none could hear his calls for help.

The shot from the Russian ship had hit the *Echo* hard.

The stern mast was damaged, and men ran to attend to the now-tangled mess of rigging and sail.

In the middle of this maelstrom of battle, fire, and smoke, Jonathan held Jenkins, the man's head cradled in his arms. He could see blood running beneath this broken body onto the deck.

"Don't be afraid, Mister Moore. You must…return to England, for all of us."

"But how? I-I—"

"You will think of a way," Jenkins said between gasps for air. "You always do."

Jonathan could only weep, though he tried to be strong for this man, his friend.

Jenkins's face was going pale, and his eyes seemed to gloss over slightly.

"Jenkins!" Jonathan called. "Stay with me!"

Jenkins focused on the boy as best he could.

"I need you here, Jenkins! That's an order!"

The older man frowned.

"You don't need anyone, Mister Moore."

"I need you, Jenkins! I can't do this alone."

Jenkins stared at Jonathan, using all his energy to focus.

"No, you d-don't. R-remember, Mister Moore, *you* are the same man that defeated Champagne. You saved the mission aboard the *Poseidon*. You turned the tides…of the battle at the Castle of Fire…" Jenkins paused, swallowing hard from the pain racking his body. "And now you have freed us from the Russians. All that remains…is to find a way to get the men home. You can do that. You…are a hero of the Crown…remember?"

"No, no. I am no hero…" Jonathan said softly.

"You are…*my* hero, Mister Moore," said Jenkins.

Jenkins breathing stopped, but his eyes remained fixed on Jonathan. The man reached his hand upward and stroked the boy's face tenderly.

Jonathan could not hold back his tears. "Call me Jonathan."

And Jenkins smiled. Then he closed his eyes.

"Goodbye, Jonathan."

With a sigh, Jenkins was gone, and Jonathan Moore wept for this good man.

It was Garvey who came to him, helping his new captain to his feet. Adams and Cardew, along with a few others who could be spared, carefully took Jenkins below.

"We are not out of this yet, sir," Garvey said.

Jonathan looked about, the rushing wind drying his tears, and took account of his position and heading. He could barely see the shadow of the Russian frigate in the distance.

Jonathan took the wheel from Graham and placed the wind directly at his back. "We head south," he said, exhausted and numb. "We need distance from the *Navarkhia*. We can outrun her, but only just barely."

The *Echo*, wounded but still under sail, moved off into the darkness of the southern Black Sea.

* * * * *

After traveling many miles due south toward the mainland of Turkey in her escape from the *Navarkhia*, Jonathan knew that eventually he would have to run west, and he made that course change as the sun rose behind him. Though he had no map or sextant, he did know that the simple fact of keeping the rising sun at his stern and the setting sun on his bow meant he was heading west and toward home. If he could reach the Mediterranean and locate any British port, or even a passing friendly ship, he would be saved. The farther west he could sail, the more chance he would have at success. Working with Graham, they took turns piloting the ship, learning as they went. The few lessons from Harrison were now invaluable, yet he feared that at any moment he would do something horribly wrong, and the ship would run aground or fall helplessly into a windless doldrum, where he would drift uncontrollably into the hands of Kharitonov. Adding to his woes was the fact that the Russian commodore was certainly looking for him, and that sent chills up his spine. Even the *Echo's* speed was of little use, as damaged as she was. The *Navarkhia* had many more guns and a seasoned captain who knew exactly where Jonathan was headed: the Bosphorus Strait.

"I can't even outwit him," said Jonathan to Graham. "He knows where I am going, and unless he was stupid enough to chase me south, he is waiting by the strait for me right now. How could I have been so foolish? Why did I head south?"

Nervous and second-guessing himself, he continued west throughout the day, alternatively looking ahead to the strait, and to port, starboard, and astern for the *Navarkhia*.

He wondered about Harrison and what he would ever say to him if they met again. He had deliberately sunk the *Paladin*. Not only would that surely ruin their friendship, but it would possibly get Jonathan hung. Even his father, an admiral, couldn't save him. Jonathan, in his depression, actually smiled. I have a wild card, he thought. The king said I had a favor. I guess I will use it for a pardon, if he is willing. But then what of me? I will be disgraced. My friends, if they are even still alive, will want nothing to do with me. Captain Walker, Miss Thompson, and Gorman — they will be shunned if they are seen with me, the pariah. And Delain? Though she has a golden heart, I would understand that her whole life ahead should not be wasted on one such as me. She deserves better. It would be better if I just departed now.

He looked around the ship, wondering, even just for the folly of it all, if he could simply jump overboard and sink beneath the waves. Every story has to end, he thought, and this may as well be my own ending.

As he looked about him, he heard a laugh. It was Garvey and Adams, repairing what they could of the damaged sails and rigging, laughing at some simpleton's joke or strange superstition. They seemed happy — at least as happy as one could expect after all this strife. The men had all continued to work hard, repairing many sections of the damaged yards and sail. Though not back to her original condition, the *Echo* was moving much more swiftly than Jonathan had thought possible. The crew had all worked beyond their watch, all dedicated to the hope of seeing home. They would not be held accountable for the losses he had caused. They would return to a normal life, just as the others would: Graham, Garvey, Berkeley, Boston, Colin, Nicolas, and the rest of the remaining crew. All had a future of promise, if Jonathan could get them home.

"For their futures," he murmured, "I will go on."

Sailing west for hours, the *Echo* saw nothing, not even smaller craft. At the toss of a log, Garvey had happily reported they had attained seven knots.

"Amazing," Jonathan said.

"The strait, Captain Moore! Dead ahead!"

Indeed, as the sun began to set, he could see land to port and starboard ahead, marking the opening to the strait. Jonathan recognized a few landmarks from their earlier crossing, and with a full moon visible behind him, its light guided the way and set an eerie glow about the ship.

"Tighten the stays!" he called, and the crews ran to perform the duty. "Light no lanterns."

With some speed and a good amount of luck, which certainly in Jonathan's opinion was long overdue, the *Echo* could try to slip past the *Navarkhia*. Possibly, Kharitonov mistakenly followed them south and then assumed they would abandon ship and head out on foot. Perhaps the commodore thought the *Echo* was damaged and had tried to make repairs in some port. It could be that Jonathan's luck had finally changed.

The crew not otherwise engaged ran to the bow and beheld the approaching strait. They cheered and hollered.

"Huzzah! Huzzah! Huzzah! Three cheers for Captain Moore!"

Even Jonathan smiled. Yes, he had finally found some luck.

Then, a call from the tops.

"Sails! Three masts full to the north! Two points off the starboard bow!"

All looked, straining to see the ship that had been spotted.

Jonathan held his breath. He prayed and prayed that it would not be—

"The *Navarkhia*!" said Nicolas from the crow's nest. "She means to cut off our escape!"

"There they are, those little gads!" said Kharitonov as he lowered his glass. "Predictable! Get the men to their guns! I will hold the course steady, blocking the strait!"

Pleased that he had plotted correctly, Kharitonov smiled. The young British captain, whoever he was, had made a fatal mistake.

"Orders, sir?" said Garvey.

"Garvey," said Jonathan. "We have had one hell of a ride, haven't we?"

"Yes, sir," said Garvey, smiling. "We have. But it ain't over yet, as the 'mericans say."

Jonathan smiled. "It was a wild ride indeed. From the streets of London, to the Caribbean, to the coasts of Africa, the Canary Islands, and even the entire expanse of the Mediterranean."

"Yes, sir," said Garvey. "And the Black Sea! Who would have thought? We have seen more than many could 'ave dreamed. And we are sailing the fastest ship in the known world!"

Jonathan laughed.

"Yes, it is painful to say, but the *Echo* is now the world's swiftest," laughed Jonathan. "So...let us not go down without a fight! Get the men to the guns. Open doors and await my command. Have them aim low! I may have one more trick up my sleeve!"

The ships continued onward toward the mouth of the

strait. The *Navarkhia* was now four hundred yards ahead and to starboard, but she had the wind at her back and was moving faster than the *Echo*. With only part of the wind and damaged sails, she had lost her best weapon: her speed. It was clear to Jonathan that the Russian cruiser would beat him to the strait.

"Garvey! Get the men to their guns," Jonathan called as he turned the great wheel. "Coming two points to starboard!"

"That is directly at her!" said Garvey as he ran to position the crew.

"Exactly into the wind!" Jonathan said.

The *Navarkhia* was closing fast on the strait. Kharitonov knew his ship would beat the *Echo* to the mouth. He could then turn, placing his guns directly at the *Echo*.

"Open gun ports!" he yelled.

As his crew executed his command, Kharitonov noticed the change in his enemy's direction.

"What is this? He is coming…straight at us? Morozov! Hold course!" he called to the helmsman. "We will fire the port side and blast her from the sea!"

Aboard the *Echo*, Jonathan could see the gun doors slowly opening on the *Navarkhia*'s port side. He held his course, just ahead of the cruiser. It is now or never, he thought.

"Coming hard to starboard! Let's luff these sails!"

The *Echo*, now only one hundred yards from the *Navarkhia*, came hard into the wind, heading almost due north. Losing all of the draft in her sails, she slowed rapidly, almost coming to a standstill.

Kharitonov, now at the rail, observed Jonathan's maneuver with a sense of awe and confusion. The swift sloop had turned incredibly fast and, with sails fluttering from the loss of the crosswind from the north, seemed to stop in the water. It was a truly amazing sight; however, why do this? he wondered. Did the Englishman not want to run to the strait and attempt escape? Will he attempt to fire his port side as he passes? The imbecile! I have twice the guns.

Then it hit him: though his guns were prepared to fire, the *Navarkhia* was now moving as swiftly as she had ever sailed. And the *Echo*? She was facing into the wind. Barely moving.

"Fire! Fire as she bares!" he called.

But it was too late. His crews were unprepared, expecting to fire when both ships reached the strait. The speed of the *Navarkhia* now caused her to run past her target.

Jonathan watched as a full broadside from the cruiser was released—all missing the mark. The rounds fell harmlessly into the sea to his stern.

"Kharitonov!" Jonathan called across the waves.

Now less than fifty yards away from the *Navarkhia*, Jonathan took the wheel hard to port. *Echo* responded slowly at first; however, once her sails caught the strong wind from the north, they filled, and the ship increased in speed rapidly. She was now in position to cross the stern of *Navarkhia*, all nine carronades on the port side ready to fire; and as the *Echo* was sitting lower in the water, all her guns had a clear view of the target, just twenty yards away.

"Kharitonov! A little bit of street justice for you, my dear Commodore!" Jonathan shouted. Turning to his gun crews, he called the command. "Blast her rudder! Fire!"

BOOM! BOOM! BOOM! BOOM! BOOM! BOOM! BOOM! BOOM! BOOM!

The *Echo*'s guns roared. Ball after ball sailed toward the target. The first two rounds were fired early and missed the rudder but rammed into the cruiser's port side, doing little damage as they struck the heavy timber at an angle. The third and fourth rounds slammed into the hindquarter, sending splinters from the rail and light lumber in all directions about the stern deck. No real damage. The remaining five rounds, however, struck squarely into the

Navarkhia's stern.

At first, it looked as if there were no major damage. Then, after a moment, as Kharitonov called for his ship to come to starboard and ready to fire, the topmost portion of the *Navarkhia's* rudder literally cracked in half from the strain. Several large planks and the metal pintle fittings that secured them fell into the water.

"*Fekalii!*" swore Kharitonov. "You, you, English *parshivy ublyudok!* Starboard guns! Fire as she bares!"

"But Commodore!" yelled Morozov. "You may destroy the Echo!

"Fire as she bares!" repeated Kharitonov. "Sink her!"

The *Navarkhia*, grunting and groaning as the damaged rudder fought to adjust her course, angled slightly westward, allowing a few of the starboard guns to train on her prey.

The guns roared. Balls sailed toward the *Echo*. As she pulled away, Jonathan could see the first of several rounds sailing high into the sails, some screaming directly through the cloth, some hitting rigging, severing stays and rope. The rest of the rounds missed completely—all but one. That round hit the mainmast just below the topgallant sail, and as if a saw had been applied, the lumber and rigging were severed, and a portion came crashing down to the deck within two feet of him as he still manned the wheel.

"Nicolas!" called Jonathan, fearing the young crewman he had stationed in the top would come crashing down with the remains of the mast.

"Aye, sir!" he called.

Looking upward, Jonathan could see the youngster extricating himself from the ratlines and climbing as high as he could on what was left of the mainmast.

Still ahead of the Russian, Jonathan steered directly for the mouth of the strait.

"Reload! She may come again!" he called.

He looked over his shoulder. The sun had set completely, and a full moon was now shining brightly, lighting his way and silhouetting the massive form of the *Navarkhia*.

She had struggled to follow and was now astern and slightly to port, about two hundred yards behind.

"We may make it!" called Nicolas from the tops.

Jonathan realized that without her topgallant staysail, *Echo* was slower than before, and the torn rigging was causing the lower mainsails to twist in the wind. She was losing speed, and the Russian, though corkscrewing on her course, was still gaining.

Kharitonov had taken the wheel from Morozov and soon, after some experimentation, was able to get the cruiser to handle, and he held her more or less on course.

"We are gaining!" he called. "Get on the bow chaser! Ready the guns!"

Aboard the *Echo*, a call came from Garvey at the bow: "Sails dead ahead!"

Jonathan could not leave the wheel. He could only wait for more information. Dear God, he thought, if this is another Russian ship or a Turk who is out for revenge, we will be finished!

"A small craft!" said Garvey. "Coming out of the channel!"

"Any markings?" called Jonathan.

"It is too dark!" called Nicolas from the top of what remained of the mainmast.

The *Navarkhia* was gaining quickly now. Jonathan watched as she fired a round from her bow, the glowing shot visible as it sailed through the night air. It fell into the sea less than ten yards from the *Echo*'s rudder, sending up a harmless splash of water.

"Again!" cried Kharitonov. "We will be in range in another few moments!"

His men laughed as they reloaded the chaser.

"We will catch them regardless," said the Russian commodore. "But now, we will toy with them!"

"Garvey!" called Jonathan. "What do you see?"

"She is hoisting a flag!" Garvey replied. "Hard to see at night!"

"Whose flag is it?" called Jonathan.

"It's...it's..." stammered Garvey. The flag, now at the top of the small mainmast, began to flutter in the wind. As it gained strength, the banner rose and shone in the moonlight. "Well, it's not a flag, sir!"

Jonathan was perplexed. Probably some Turk, trying to confuse other ships. The devil has gotten his due, thought Jonathan. His luck had run out.

Jonathan heard a laugh. At this strange time, in the last moments of his desperate plan, he heard the joyous laugh of the men at the bow. They are mad, he thought. Insane with grief.

"It is not a flag, sir," cried Garvey. "They are bloomers! Bloomers, Captain Moore! Bloomers!"

Aboard the *Frog*, Welty tied off the rope that held the bloomers, actually canvas cut into the unmistakable shape of a woman's undergarment, to the top piece of the mainmast.

"The *Echo*! Does she see it, sir?" asked Sean.

"I am not sure," said Welty. "But I can see that blasted thirty-six chasing her down. *Echo* just fired a round. Whoever is on her is English, and he's no friend of the Russians."

"Jonathan?" asked Sean.

"We will know in a moment," said Harrison. "Hudson! Is the raft ready?"

"Already overboard and tethered, sir!"

"Sean, how is your latest bomb?" asked Harrison.

"Two full kegs tied to the bowsprit, with the wonderful fuse I made. 'Bout twenty feet long it is! I laced it with powder, so it will burn fast! One foot per second, I'd reckon."

"I will do the math in my head," said Harrison

"A flag is being raised on the *Echo*, sir!" called Welty.

"Bloomers?" asked Harrison.

"Well, something that looks like 'em," Welty responded.

Harrison could barely make out the shape as he headed swiftly at the coming ship. Yes, it looked like a hastily cut-out cloth in the more-or-less pantslike shape of a woman's undergarments.

"Close enough for me! All crew abandon ship! Sean, hand me the torch," he said. "I will light it at the last moment. You, bomb maker, get aboard that raft."

"No, sir!" said Sean. "I'm lighting it!"

"Hicks!" called Harrison as he quickly snatched the torch from Sean.

"Yes, sir," the marine answered, approaching the wheel as the rest of the crew ran to the stern.

"Take Private Flagon to the stern, toss him over, and then assist him onto the raft!"

"Oy!" said Sean. "Not fair!"

"This is the British Navy, Flagon," said Harrison, smiling. "It's never fair!"

"But it is plain ol' excitin'!" added Hicks as he swept up his friend and ran aft. "Over the side we go!"

"But where is Stewie?" asked Sean.

"'E's in me jacket!" said Hicks. Stewie peaked out just above the marine's collar. Though he scratched and complained, Hicks withstood the torture. With a fast prayer, all three went over the side. Hudson and the rest of the crew followed. Within moments they were on the hastily built raft and had severed the rope tethering them to the *Kérata*. They drifted away as the yacht sped ahead.

Harrison remained aboard, now almost even with the *Echo*. He waved as he passed, the larger ship sailing by on his starboard side.

"Jonathan!" he called. "Jonathan Moore!"

"Commander Harrison!" Jonathan called with joy. "Thomas!"

"Pick up the raft—and the little rats that left me alone! I will sink that garbage scow and the grobian that sails her!"

"How?" called Jonathan. However, he had gone past the small yacht and could hear no more. His heart soared as he called for his men to reduce all sail and look ahead for a raft and survivors.

"Who in the name of the Devil is this?" asked Kharitonov as he gazed through his telescope. "And what in the hell is that atop the mainmast?"

"He's heading straight at us!" yelled Morozov.

"Ha!" laughed Kharitonov. "The little fly wants to play? Well, we will cut him in half!"

Harrison knew that someday his ability to gauge the speed of a sailing ship with almost magical accuracy would come in handy—for more than just winning a few wagers with his shipmates. He could apply that ability to the question of when to light the fuse. He could tell that the *Frog* was moving at four knots, and he assumed that the heavier cruiser, with more sail than he had, was moving about the same speed. Burning at one foot per second, it would take just twenty-two seconds to ignite the powder. And that would take one hundred fifty feet of sailing at four knots. The combined speed of both ships, eight knots, meant that he would light the fuse when they were three hundred feet apart.

Harrison watched as the ships continued toward each other in a straight path. Four hundred feet. Three hundred fifty feet. Three hundred.

He lit the fuse.

"Enjoy the ride, you—" Harrison released a long string of interesting and heartfelt profanities, obscenities, vulgar invectives, and uncomfortable expletives as he leapt over the rail.

Kharitonov could barely see the form of a man leaping over the side of the approaching ship. In a moment, he lost view of the oncoming vessel, as his bow, sitting much higher than the smaller craft, blocked it from view. He did see, however, the white-hot flash and felt the subsequent thunderous explosion burst from what appeared to be right below his bow rail. A wall of flame shot upward in an instant, and as Kharitonov blinked, the force of the blast reached the foresail, engulfing it in flame. Within seconds, the mainsail also caught fire. Within another moment, the aftsails had ignited, and all above the commodore burned with an intensity of the noon sun. The air, the sails, the entire world was on fire.

Harrison, treading water, watched the explosion from his position in the Black Sea. He had a front-row seat, certainly the only one, to the entire performance. The *Navarkhia* was literally a shining lantern as the sails continued to burn. Men tried to address the flames, but it was all a loss. Soon the masts were consumed, and the *Navarkhia* sailed past him, thirty yards away, glowing like a specter, aflame.

"Ha!" laughed Harrison. "Ha ha! A fast fuse indeed!"

Aboard the *Echo*, Jonathan sent men to attend the damaged mainmast and reduce its sail. The *Echo* needed little speed now; the *Navarkhia* was aflame, and a stupendous sight it was. The glowing light helped the crew easily find the raft, and then, after securing the men aboard, all cheered and danced in joy.

The ending to the battle was accentuated by the detonation of the magazine on the *Navarkhia* as it caught fire and exploded in a deafening roar. The *Echoes* felt as if all the lightning in a great storm were released at once and concentrated in the small space that at one time had been occupied by the great cruiser.

A certain marine met Jonathan on the deck, hobbling toward him, and then smiling, cheering, and laughing as they embraced.

"Sean! Sean Flagon! You came for us!" said Jonathan.

"Of course! What would ya expect? And we need to get Captain Harrison! He jumped off the *Frog* right before she rammed that cruiser!"

"The *Frog*?" asked Jonathan.

"Yes, yes," said Sean. "We will all tell tales, as usual, once we retrieve the captain!"

With that, the last remaining boat of the *Echo*, a small dinghy piloted by Jonathan Moore, went in search of Commander Harrison.

The remaining fragments of the *Navarkhia* crackled with flame, and through their faint light, Jonathan could make out his friend, laughing as he floated on his back in the water. He turned to look at the approaching rescuers.

"Did you see that?" the commander cried from the water. "Did you see it?"

"I did, Harrison, I did!" said Jonathan.

"Flagon may be the king's bomb maker," called Harrison, "however, he knows no restraint! There was enough powder to sink a line of first rates! Though I am not complaining!"

Jonathan ordered the men to toss several lines to Harrison, who gladly accepted them and was somewhat unceremoniously hauled aboard the dinghy and delivered to the *Echo*.

"Well, *Captain* Moore," Harrison said with a laugh, accepting the blankets offered and a cup of hot coffee, "I assume now we retrieve the *Paladin!*"

Jonathan swallowed hard. Amid this joyous occasion, this reunion of friends, the terrible news had to be delivered.

32
Justice and Reward

Just past midnight on the twenty-ninth of April, the crew of the *Echo*, now enhanced by the members of the *Kérata,* sailed southwest in silence through the Strait of Bosphorus under the English flag, the Cross of Saint George.

Jonathan and Sean remained below as the ship was rightly turned over to Commander Harrison. They had agreed to find a safe harbor, for then all tales and fates would be told. By the avoidance of any information being offered about the whereabouts of the *Paladin*, Harrison knew something was amiss, and he stood at the wheel, alone in his thoughts. He feared the worst.

In the Sea of Marmara, just a few miles southwest of the opening to the strait, lay the island of Kinaliada. Harrison had decided it would be an adequate spot to anchor, being such a remote isle, quiet and unassuming, allowing them all to take a long-needed breath.

The moon set as Kinaliada came into view. Jonathan and Sean appeared on deck and stood next to Harrison. Upon seeing his friend, his commander and mentor, standing proud and strong, Jonathan felt pity and shame, and he suddenly become overwhelmed with grief. How could he tell Harrison of the loss of the *Paladin*, and, most horrifically, the loss due to his own plan? Completely overcome, Jonathan wrapped his arms about his friend and shook with regret.

"Jonathan?" asked Harrison, still holding the wheel. "Whatever is the matter?"

"Let's drop anchor," suggested Sean, who had been told some of the tale. "Maybe take a boat to the beach. I could use to get some hard ground under my feet for a change. It would do us all some good."

The *Echo* sailed to the leeward side of the island where the sea had calmed to glassy perfection reflecting the stars above. Harrison ordered the makeshift anchor the crew had˙fashioned from twisted iron bands and shot to be tossed overboard. All sail was furled, and the *Echo* came to a silent rest.

Jonathan, Sean, and Harrison had boarded the dinghy along with Hudson and Hicks, who were rowing. The beach at Kinaliada was reached easily.

Dark, yet under a starlit sky, they built a small fire near the shingle of the beach. The mound protected the flames from the slight wind, and the fire gave some sense of place across the vastness of the long, sandy coast. At the moment, the only sound was the gentle hiss of the waves against the sandy shore and the occasional cry of some lonesome bird.

Only Jonathan sat by the fire, silent, deep in his thoughts. The others busied themselves looking for additional dry wood to use as fuel, searching for anything that could make their stay more comfortable; but mostly, they kept a casual eye on Jonathan. The events of the past days since Zadar weighed upon him, and his friends knew by looking at his form that he was greatly troubled and concerned about all that had transpired. Could it be the death of Jenkins that Garvey had told them of? Was that the final blow to him? Did he feel responsible?

Jonathan sat staring into the fire, the flames giving him no comfort. He felt lost, confused; yet he knew that it was all his own doing. Could someone complete noble and honorable actions, yet still be wrong? he asked himself. He had been a pawn in the schemes of Spears and Wilder and then a slave to Aggar and Kharitonov. He had witnessed the passing of Patrick Jenkins, the value of that friendship now defined in the most holy manner — forged in the heat of battle, and ending in the cold loss of death. Only his memory remained — and his kindness.

Right or wrong to some, destroying the *Paladin* was

the only course of action that would ensure his crew's survival and freedom. If he was to be hanged for it, then that would be his fate. He hoped that those who loved him and mattered to him most would understand his decision.

He stood after a moment and smiled to no one but the sea. "You give me hope," he said to the waves, "and you take from me as well."

As the sun began to rise, so did his spirit, and he was at peace with his past and his future. He turned away from the water and saw his friends standing respectfully in the distance, looking at him with kind eyes.

"Well? What are ya? Daft?" he called. "Come to the fire! It is time for you to hear the tale. And, my friends, it is an amazing one at that!"

The *Echo* set sail the next morning for the village of Gallipoli, on the northern shore of the Dardanelles Strait between the Sea of Marmara and the Aegean. The crew hoped to reach the port on the thirtieth, an easy goal. There, they would acquire needed fresh water and other supplies and then continue to the British naval base at Malta some eight hundred miles away, or three days' sail.

Jonathan had been correct in his assumptions pertaining to the loss of the *Paladin*. As he recounted the trials under Aggar and Kharitonov—and the desperate plan to save his men—he was relieved. As shocked as Harrison was at the death of Jenkins, the loss of the *Paladin*, and that the ship's end came from the guns of the *Echo* and Jonathan's hand, he understood.

"I would have done the same, Jonathan. I would have done the same," he said, and he shook the hand of his friend.

And though Harrison took his own time to stand alone on the beach at Kinaliada, he soon turned back to his friends and congratulated Jonathan, assuring him that he was a hero, just as Jenkins had said, and that the Admiralty would never hang a hero.

On the sixth of May, the *Echo* sailed from Malta, in the

center of the Mediterranean, with fresh supplies, and after some repair to her sails, masts, and rigging, she picked up a few packets for delivery to Gibraltar and London.

A brief stop in Gibraltar and a report to Admiral Crampton eased the minds of many. Here was the *Echo*, missing now for some time, with a new commander and an amazing tale. The loss of the *Paladin* was also reported, and the hearts of those who heard the tale sank deeply.

One Englishman, going by the name of Marine Lieutenant Slater, had been granted a private interview with Harrison and Jonathan after their report to Crampton. Once revealed as a member of Marine Captain Gorman's network, he was told as many of the details as they could remember, without Harrison's usual embellishments. Knowing that Gray was still missing, they feared the worst. Slater decide to request a ship to return to Telašćica, and whished Harrison and crew safe passage home.

Harrison and Jonathan, along with Sergeant Hudson, had also taken the time to document their doings in the ships' logs. With the assistance of Sean, Garvey, Graham, and the others, the retellings and embellishments of each became almost comical. Eventually, it was Harrison and Jonathan, alone on deck one night, who completed the ships' logs of the *Echo*, the *Kérata*, and the *Paladin*.

"One thing about these superstitions," said Jonathan, seemingly choosing the subject out of the blue.

"Yes?" asked Harrison as he closed the logs.

"I witnessed the beheading of the *Paladin*'s rider and the *Echo*'s beauty. I saw them discarded into the sea unceremoniously. And I thought of all the ridiculous things Jenkins said about superstitions…"

"And?" asked Harrison. "Do not tell me you believe that rot?"

"Fawcett said that if ever the *Paladin*'s rider was to be changed or damaged, that would be the end of her. He was right."

Harrison nodded his head in agreement—but only

slightly.

"Well, this beautiful lady here, Little Miss *Echo*, I will call her, has no head either, and she just saved scores of men and a cat and will return to fight another day, so I guess that superstition proves nothing."

Jonathan smiled.

"I'll rely on good old-fashioned drive and determination over a bunch of cocky," said Harrison. "Yet, they also say that ships that end in the letter *A* are unlucky. So the *Kérata*, even though we called her the *Frog*, is now at the bottom of the sea. Or in a million pieces, floating on top! And what was the name of that Russian cruiser?"

Jonathan began to laugh.

"*Navarkhia!*"

"It must all be true then! I am now convinced!" Harrison said, laughing.

* * * * *

Just one week after the sailing of HMS *Echo* from the Royal Navy port of Malta, a lone felucca carrying six men and a boy docked at one of the smaller piers of the same port. As a flag, the three-sailed craft flew a Royal Navy commander's jacket above the mainmast. This was enough to allow them permission to dock.

The men were recognized as British sailors, and though dehydrated and famished, they were able to tell their story to a nearby lieutenant. The seriousness of their tale, as fantastic as it sounded, certainly explained a few rumors the officer had heard about missing ships in the area, and he immediately brought the men before Admiral Troubridge.

After the men devoured a brief meal and obtained new clothes, Commander Gray and his lieutenant were quickly shown into the office of the admiral to give their accounting of the happenings over the past months—and of the loss of HMS *Echo*.

Troubridge smiled as they finished their account, nodding in acceptance. "I have the greatest of news, Commander Gray. It seems you are mistaken. You have not lost the *Echo*."

"I beg your pardon, sir," said Gray.

"The *Echo* left Malta on May the sixth," the admiral said as he checked his master log, "just eight days ago."

Gray was shocked into silence. He looked to Hayes, as if his lieutenant could explain, but of course, he was equally surprised.

"Sir? How can that be?" asked Gray.

"Commander Harrison and his midshipman, Jonathan Moore, recaptured her."

"Commander Harrison and Midshipman Moore? I know them, sir. We met in the Battle of Fire…" Gray's voice trailed off as he regained the memory of the two men formerly of HMS *Danielle*.

"Yes," said the Admiral. "It seems they found your vessel and took it back. At the loss of their own ship, if you must know."

"The *Paladin*?" Gray asked. "We saw her on the twentieth of April. She was headed southeast off Morska Point on Dugi Otok."

"Taken by Russians of all people!" said Troubridge with a laugh. "The *Echo* and *Paladin* were both captured and taken to the Black Sea."

Gray was now even more stunned. How could this transpire?

"Midshipman Moore started a mutiny aboard both ships—well, actually it couldn't be classified a mutiny as he was taking back his own ship!" Troubridge laughed heartily once again. "He fled south in the *Echo* after losing the *Paladin*. Being chased by a Russian cruiser, they met at the Strait of Bosphorus. Harrison arrived as well. He commanded a stolen yacht that he rigged with explosives. A torpedo? Yes, that is what he called it."

"Amazing," said Gray softly.

"As was the destruction of the Russian cruiser, I must

say," said the admiral. "Burned to the waterline. *Echo* was in need of minor repair, mostly sail work. She and her crew should be in Gibraltar by now — or already on their way to London."

Gray could not fathom the events that had happened, though the accounting certainly explained what they had seen. After clearing up a few details, Gray and Hayes were satisfied, grateful, and still astonished at the news.

"One request, Admiral," said Gray. "Would there be a ship bound for London? One on which we could obtain passage?"

"There is one. In fact, it is looking for you," the admiral said, now pointing out the window of his office that overlooked the bay. "HMS *Dasher* arrived this morning. An operative of the Royal Marines, Lieutenant Slater I believe his name is, is readying to sail to Telašćica. I assume your arrival will change his course."

Elated, Gray and Hayes excused themselves, gathered their remaining crew, and rushed to the *Dasher*, requesting permission to come aboard.

On the bright summer afternoon of May the twentieth, HMS *Echo* reappeared at the docks at South Sussex to no fanfare, no special greeting — just the familiar sights and sound of a working shipyard.

Word was sent immediately to Nathaniel Moore and Captain Walker, who came from the Admiralty together in a large four-horse coach to retrieve the boys.

The words *unbelievable* and *dear God* were exclaimed many times during the discussion on the ride to Walker's home in Golden Square — and again during the retelling of it all to Barbara Thompson, Mrs. Walker, Gorman, and the slightly recovered Steward, once they sat in Captain Walker's den.

It was then that Barbara Thompson and Captain Gorman told of their tale, and of the treachery of Lady Wilder and the spy Orvislat, and how Delain had found them out and joined forces with Gorman and his network.

"So Lady Wilder, not Lord Wilder, was behind this!" said Jonathan.

"I will teach them a little about street justice myself!" exclaimed Sean. "My friends! Many are dead! Because of their treachery!"

"They are awaiting trial," said Gorman. "They will hang; I am sure of it. And if not, well, they will have an accident. Fatal, I am afraid."

"And where is Miss Delain Dowdeswell?" asked Jonathan, thinking she would be along any moment. "I so much need to see her and hear the details of her adventures."

A hush came over the room, and all looked to Miss Thompson to explain.

"Jonathan, she is well, though, she was injured, I am afraid. And so sorry. But she will be all right."

The story about her attempted murder by Lady Wilder sent Jonathan into a rage; he became uncontrollable. Tears streamed down his face. Even Gorman could not contain him. Sean, equally upset, began to gather his coat and hat. Immediately they ran from the room, heading to the front door.

"Jonathan! Wait!" called Barbara. "She is not home! She is still under the doctor's care!"

Eventually they had calmed him down enough to explain that she was still at hospital at Saint Paul's, and since the time was now approaching eight in the evening, it would be better if they would take him to see Delain in the morning.

"I will run there on foot, right now, if you will not take me!" he said.

"Me as well!" added Sean.

"I will take them," said Harrison. "I have business with Rebecca Dowdeswell. It is on my way. Well, not really."

"Fine," said Jonathan, "we will leave at once!"

"Yes, sir," said Harrison, smiling.

On the second floor, in a private room away from the bustle of the hospital routine, Delain Dowdeswell sat awake in her bed, propped up with pillows, having her hair brushed. Penelope attended her and would stay in the hospital this night. They had been greeted earlier by Claise, who had rushed from Captain Walker's kitchen once he greeted the boys and ran to tell Delain that they were all home, all well, and each in one piece.

As Penelope placed the brush down on the table by the bed, a soft knock came at the door. The girls looked up. Two faces peeked around the opening, concerned.

"Delain?" asked Jonathan.

"Jonathan!" she cried. "Oh, Jonathan Moore! You have returned!"

He ran to her and gently held her in his arms. She smiled through her tears and laughed when she could finally breathe. Jonathan smiled as best he could, though his heart, finally relieved, ached for what might have befallen them both. He could see bruises on her arms and face; yet to him, she remained as beautiful as ever.

"Delain, I-I am so sorry!"

"No, this is not your fault!"

He looked into her green eyes. *Now is the time for strength,* he thought, and without hesitation, he kissed her.

"I will be in the hallway," said Penelope softly.

"I will join you," said Sean with a smile.

Once alone, Jonathan and Delain lay holding hands, sharing the pillow, and smiling.

"You certainly don't look as if you are injured, *Miss* Dowdeswell," said Jonathan, feigning formality.

Delain smiled.

"I will tell you, *Mister* Moore," she said, affecting a slight air of superiority, "that I have two broken ribs, a bruised left femur, a scar along the back of my neck that will probably never heal—so says Lady Bracknell—and both my ankles were broken. Not to mention contusions to my skull—which is still under observation!"

"Dear me!" said Jonathan. "All that from boring tea

parties and dull school lessons!"

"You *are* a cad!" she said with a giggle.

"I am only jesting, Delain," he said. "Seriously now, are you all right? You have certainly looked better. Tell me your adventure."

She recounted it all for him, from the yacht race where she suspected something odd about the Wilders, to the tea party, the Black Rider, the money in the library, and her subsequent copying of the notes. She then explained her plan to follow Lord Wilder and her capture by none other than Captain Gorman, and their joining forces and turning lord against lady.

"The final trick was to get her and her spy, Orvislat, in the same place—a fox hunt as it turned out—so we could capture them for arrest!"

Delain now seemed to lose some of her excitement and actually pulled away from Jonathan a bit as she remembered what happened next.

"She tried to kill me, Jonathan. As I raced alongside her during the hunt, she pulled me off my filly, and then, with a stone, tried to strike me. I-I couldn't defend myself."

She began to cry, and Jonathan held her tight. After a moment or two, she continued.

"Just as she was about to crush me with the stone, Steward appeared, but she shot him!"

"Dear God!" said Jonathan, truly horrified.

"He is fine now. Captain Gorman said the extra padding in Steward's belly saved him, and the shot was not powerful enough to kill him. I thought I was dead already, and then—oh, Jonathan—then the most amazing thing happened! A horse appeared, in full run, and cut her down! I was saved! Saved by the rider: Barbara Thompson!"

"Miss Thompson?" said Jonathan in disbelief. "Delain, that is truly amazing! Amazing!"

"And she was riding *astride*!"

"Now I know you are lying!" he said with a smile.

They both laughed long and hard, Jonathan asking for more detail, and Delain saying that her story did not even need "Harrisonesque" embellishments to be entertaining.

Soon they were joined by Sean and Penelope, and all sat together on the bed — old friends, older friends now — and all thankful for a well-earned respite from the sea and the subterfuge of London's dark side.

"Now your turn, Jonathan," said Delain. "We were so worried about you once we knew Orvislat and Wilder were stealing ships! We feared you were dead!"

"I thought he was, for a few hours at least!" laughed Sean.

"Well?" asked Penelope. "What happened on your side of the world?"

Jonathan and Sean looked at each other and smiled.

"I was shot," said Sean.

"I was a slave," said Jonathan.

Delain frowned. "Now *you* are embellishing!"

The boys laughed and began their tale.

The trial of Lady Alina and Lord Wilder was expected by many Londoners to drag on for months and months. In actuality, it did not. Beginning on May the twenty-eighth, an unlucky Friday, according to Sean, many appeared to witness the trial, including Delain, now out of hospital. With the help of Midshipman Moore as an escort, she was able to observe and eventually give testimony. Sitting next to them for most of the trial was the newly engaged Nathaniel Moore, in his splendid admiral's uniform of navy blue, and the proud and just-a-bit-full-of-herself-in-a-very-ladylike-way Miss Barbara Thompson. Harrison, and yes, his fiancée, Miss Rebecca Dowdeswell, also attended.

Lord Wilder was certainly disgraced but was found innocent of any traitorous deeds. Spears also was cleared of any wrongdoing.

Lady Wilder believed she might escape punishment, her lawyer arguing that there was no real evidence connecting her to the ships, and in the end, the copied letter supposedly found in her library was presented as a forgery, a prank, perpetrated by a bored and frustrated little girl, Miss Delain Dowdeswell.

Of course, there was more than the charge of treason leveled against her. There was the attempted murder of Delain and Steward, with expert testimony by the two victims and the eye-witness account of Barbara Thompson, now celebrated in the papers as "the young horsewoman of justice." She not -too-secretly enjoyed the notoriety.

Additionally, there were the two bodies—those of Fairchild and Frey, found in the Wilder's stable, under the hay—discovered by the police after Gorman and Lord Wilder had tipped them off. It seemed that Orvislat then tried the defensive tactic of "rolling over" on his boss and testified that Lady Wilder killed the men. She then shouted, over calls for decorum by the judge, that it was Orvislat who had orchestrated the entire thing and forced her to attack the young girl. After much yelling and gnashing of teeth, the courtroom finally settled down.

The magistrate was not impressed.

The final nails in the coffins of Lady Alina Wilder and Seeja Orvislat came from the sudden and dramatic appearance of Captain Gorman as he escorted into the court Lieutenant Joshua Gray, formerly the commander of HMS *Echo*. Just recently arrived in his homeland, the lieutenant explained the change of his orders and how the Russians had taken the ship and murdered over half of his crew. Gorman then explained the relationship between Kharitonov, a commodore of the Russian fleet, most likely sailing under a letter of marque, and Lady Wilder. This was confirmed by the final testimony of Lord James Wilder himself, explaining that his wife was a Russian spy, and he had the payments to prove it: the thousands of pounds his wife had received from her brother, Kharitonov, part of the money still hidden in his library. With no explanation of where the money came from, Lady Wilder was judged guilty of high treason and attempted murder. Orvislat was also found guilty of espionage and murder in the first degree. They were both jailed immediately.

No letter or request for pardon came from the Russian

embassy. In fact, the ambassador, the elder Orvislat, had mysteriously disappeared a few days after the arrest of his son.

On the eleventh of June Alina Kharitonov and Seeja Orvislat were hanged—a Friday, an unlucky day, as pointed out once again by Sean.

"Most unlucky for her," he said solemnly as he read the news.

In contrast to the grim scene of that day, on June the twentieth, all celebrated the happy occurrence of a long-anticipated wedding. Initially set for Saint George's at Hanover Square, Jonathan had overheard the true wishes of the bride-to-be. Delain had been privy to a private conversation where Barbara Thompson had revealed her true wishes: her dream, even as a small girl, was to be married in St. Paul's Cathedral. This was a rare occurrence, and though she and Nathaniel had tried, it was just not allowed for anyone, unless, of course, they were related to the royal court. From this information, Jonathan requested and received an audience with his friend George, and after the telling of his recent adventure, used a promised favor from the previous year to move the wedding to Saint Paul's.

In attendance, in their impressive uniforms, were Marine Captain Gorman, Captain Langley, Commanders Harrison and Gray, Steward (who turned out as well as could be expected), Claise, and of course, Mrs. Walker, Lady Bracknell, and Penelope and Rebecca Dowdeswell.

As maid of honor, standing at the majestically stunning and ancient alter in an all-white gown tapered to her youthful frame and exquisitely trailing behind her, was none other than Delain Dowdeswell. Looking more like an angel than an adventurer, she held in her hands a small bouquet of while lilies and red roses wrapped in white crinoline. About her wrist was the dolphin charm; about her neck was the turtle necklace.

Across the altar from Delain were two young gentlemen, standing at attention. One was dressed in a sparkling red-and-silver dress uniform of the Royal Marines, ceremonial sword at his side, on loan from Captain Langley, the very one he received for his participation in the taking of the *Danielle*. Sean Flagon smiled at Delain, and just couldn't help beaming at the assembled guests, including the one who had given him his nickname, bomb maker.

Next to Sean stood a young midshipman in a dashing new deep-blue navy uniform, with silver piping and waistcoat, also sporting a ceremonial sword, also on loan from his coconspirator and dearest friend, Marine Captain Gorman. Though present in the cathedral were all his friends and the king and queen of England, he could not keep his eyes off the most beautiful flower of all, his dear friend and, yes, his love, Delain Dowdeswell. Jonathan smiled to her alone—and she, to him.

The appearance of the groom, Admiral Nathaniel Moore, caused the assembly to sigh, as he too was dressed in full naval uniform, handsome and alive with the light of joy. He walked with gallantry and purpose to the altar and stood proudly next to his two sons.

As the organ now sang the familiar tune of "Ode to Joy," all rose and turned their eyes to the aisle. At the arch of the west doorway stood the bride, Miss Barbara Thompson. Her wedding gown was made of white silk and lace and was fitted from her delicate neckline to her waist, where it was gathered. Like a sleek waterfall of snow, the gown tapered out ever so slightly and draped to the floor, shimmering in glittering silver gems. Her veil, dainty and seemingly of almost invisible lace, met with the train, silken and flowing behind her. The sunlight passing through the stained glass windows of the church set her aglow, and the guests, to a person, let out a delighted gasp as she slowly glided past, escorted by a uniformed Captain Sir William Walker.

On the other side of the world, another man and woman were also joined, though *reunited* would be a more accurate term.

As the sun set on a sandy beach in the southern Romanian town of Menkalia, a lateen-sail skiff named *Alexandria* slid effortlessly to shore. It had been crewed by a handful of men, all sailors, all being at sea together for the last several weeks. They had visited almost every village along the northwestern shore of the Black Sea, from Nikoniia down to the southernmost towns on the Gulf of Baba. A man with a scar on his cheek led them, and he had originally hoped his search would begin and end in Kylia, his hometown. However, no success was found in that place; just a feeling from the residents that the people he sought had moved to the south years ago. Menkalia would be the final town he would search before all hope was lost.

He jumped from the bow of the skiff to the sand. Immediately, he gazed up and down the beach and then toward the small homes and buildings of the seaside village.

Surprisingly, he was seen by another man, an older gentleman, who recognized him immediately. Excited, they ran to each other and, laughing, embraced heartily. After a moment, the scarred man returned to the boat and pushed it off the sand, back into the sea. He saluted his friends, then waved a happy good-bye as they now departed for their own homes.

The older man led the way across the beach, and they hurried into town, around the village square, and eventually, down a narrow, quiet street in a poor neighborhood. There, the scarred man stood before a small, white house.

"Daria! Daria Makarenko Aggar!" called the man. "Daria!"

After a moment, a dark-haired woman wearing a simple cotton dress came to the door and stepped barefoot into the twilight. Glancing at the two men, she recognized the older one; he had come with her and the others who had fled their former village in years past. Her eyes were then drawn to the man with the scar. Considering him for a moment, she had an odd feeling. Had she seen him before? He looked familiar. Then, in an instant, she recognized him. A flood of memories came to her, memories from an earlier life that seemed to have disappeared seven years ago, when she had suffered so greatly and all hope was lost. Though it seemed impossible to her that he was here, now, her heart was able to guide her, and she flew to him, weeping tears of joy.

From the door, two young girls appeared. Seeing their mother embracing the stranger, it only took them a moment to realize who had finally come home.

"Tata!" they called, and they ran into the arms of their father.

"Your face!" Daria said, touching the wound tenderly. "What happened?"

He smiled at her.

"A reminder. From one who was generous and chose pity over hatred and revenge," he said as he held his girls tightly.

"I don't understand," said Daria.

"Nor do I," the man said. "Though he freed me, and I will tell you of him. A boy, Daria—a wonderful boy, just like our dear Dimitri. He freed me from Kharitonov forever, and now I am here to stay."

The family held each other for what seemed to be ages. Then, after all had cried their tears, Nikomed Aggar was led inside to tell his tale.

After the wedding ceremony of Nathaniel Moore and Miss Barbara Thompson, many attended the splendid reception in the decorated and familiar home of the Walkers. There was dancing, some mild drinking, and of course, delightful food was served, with Steward cackling at Harrison's poor humor and Claise trying to ensure all had plenty to eat. Yes, tales were told.

Jonathan noticed that his father and his new mother now seemed truly happy. He wondered if he would ever be that way, though he thought, Why fret? Today is today, and tomorrow is not. I will think of my future plans...in the future!

Ask if on cue, Sean motioned for Jonathan to step outside. Exiting, he saw that there, on the front steps of the Walkers' mansion, lit by the gaslights of the lane, stood Delain. Now in a simple white dress, she tightened a woolen shawl about her shoulders. The evening was warm for early summer: perfect walking weather.

"It's getting too stuffy in there, Jonny Boy!" said Sean, holding a small, oddly shaped bag in his hands. He pushed Jonathan outside and closed the door gently. "Let us three take a walk."

With the boys each taking an arm, they escorted Miss Delain Dowdeswell slowly down the drive from Captain Walker's door to the street and strolled lazily through the lanes to Hay Market, then east to find Charing Cross, then again due south on King's to Westminster Bridge. Sean stopped them only once, turning down an alley, one familiar to him, and gave his bag, obviously full of food, to a poor boy living in the shadows.

Arriving at the bridge, they stood at the railing. Before them, now at the edge of their town, was the Thames, the river that led to the adventurous sea.

"That ends yet another successful undertaking, my handsome friends!" said Delain with a sigh.

"What's next, Jonny Boy?" asked Sean expectantly.

Jonathan looked to the water, then to the many gaslights glowing about the city. He noticed their radiance reflecting off the waves in swirling shapes that moved in unison, as if some strange and wonderful creatures were performing a harmonized ballet for his pleasure. The worlds of land and sea met at this place, he thought, calm and welcoming to anyone who was about to sail away to adventure or return home to family and a quiet life.

"For now, we are all together," he said, placing his arms about them both.

They stared into the waves, each lost in his or her thoughts.

"But when tomorrow comes?" asked Delain, breaking the silence.

Jonathan thought for a while, and then, after a deep breath, spoke with purpose:
"I have no idea."

The End
of
Book Three

Acknowledgments

I am a true believer in the idea that no one gets through this life alone, and to complete something grand, like the writing of a novel, takes a great amount of encouragement and charity from others. That assistance comes not just during the task, but from a past shaped by many people and their kindness. Most of these are teachers—formal educators or otherwise. In my life, I have had the great fortune to receive advice and direction from many: my parents, my teachers, and yes, even my bosses. Here, I would like to thank the most influential individually.

Jane Beem was my high school English and creative writing teacher at Warren Township High in Gurnee, Illinois. Let's not mention the year, but suffice to say that at that time, computers were items only available to NASA. We wrote everything with number 2 pencils (I preferred a 3H myself) on lined paper in those days.

I specifically remember one assignment. We were told to write a short story, in class, that had action as the main theme. I wrote a piece about the feeling of flying through a snow-covered downhill racing course on skis, something I did regularly in the rock-quarry-turned-ski-hill nearby. I finished the story in less than an hour and turned it in. I liked it so much, I actually copied it during the passing period so I could have a duplicate to ponder over that evening. The next day, Ms. Beem returned the paper to me. There was a bold "A" across the top—no marks of any other kind, except a single word across the entire script: *Wonderful.*

And that did it for me. I have been writing stories ever since, dozens of short and full-length screenplays (one optioned) and so many technical manuals and marketing pieces that I thought my head should explode. The Jonathan Moore Series is the newest endeavour, and no matter what the commercial success, the few words of thanks I have gotten from readers have been payment enough for the years I put into the writing. I am a storyteller, and I remember seeing the word *wonderful* and knowing that someone, somewhere, might enjoy my tales. Thank you, Jane Beem, for starting me on this journey.

Jo Ann Fox was my college acting and creative dramatics teacher at Northern Illinois University. I remember her as a fiery force of talent and energy who believed that anyone could do anything. Jo Ann exploded into the classroom every day, smiling and flamboyant; she didn't just walk in and sit behind her desk. In fact, I don't think Jo Ann ever just *sat*. Conversely, I was shy and reserved—a bad set of traits for an actor—and at twenty years old, I had just switched from a biology major (where I was failing miserably) to theatre education. I thought a class titled "Creative Dramatics" would be about writing plays and such, and I was surprised because Jo Ann had all of us acting as teapots, octopuses, gnomes, cats, Labrador retrievers, and even stones. I don't think we ever wrote or read a single line the entire semester.

Something happened in Jo Ann's class for me: I shed my shell. I took it off, threw it on the ground, and busted the living hell out of it. Confidence followed quickly in every aspect of my life.

One day, I was walking down the hallway to the Actors' Theatre and saw a piano in there. No one was around. I had sat through a few piano lessons when I was younger, and I still fiddled at the keyboard a bit. Being away from my home and my mother's fire-damaged Howard baby grand, I was always delighted to find a piano that was in tune and available. I sat down to play.

I didn't know that after my first few notes, the readers' theatre group that was rehearsing a version of Shel Silverstein's *The Giving Tree* had come in, and not wanting to interrupt, let me play for a few more minutes. The director heard something he liked, stopped me, and after a few minutes of discussion and playing some chords, he cast me as the music to their production.

A week and a half later, I performed a background score I had composed for the play. Jo Ann was in attendance. At the after-performance critique, she asked, "Who is sitting behind that piano? He was as much a force of this delightful production as anyone else."

Seeing me, she stood, hugged me, smiled, and said, "I knew it!" and told the group something to the effect of "Peter Greene looks like he can do anything. I would not hesitate to cast him in any play in any role. He has no shell; he just *is*."

I changed again that day. Those words have helped me attempt and succeed in so many parts of my life, I can't even begin to count them or to acknowledge Jo Ann's effect.

Though a bit out of order in the chronology of this list, I met a man named Dorn Kennison, who hired me as assistant manager of a Chess King men's clothing store. Dorn was rock-star good-looking, an excellent guitar player, and a very young husband and father. He was serious, mostly, but with some goading, I could get him to teach me a few kung fu moves (he was a black belt and would slap me around lightly and laugh, but I always came back for more), and he would draw the most ridiculous cartoons that had me rolling with laughter.

I had been working in retail since I was fifteen, and I had experience, but becoming a manager was a challenge for me. Still in my late teens, I struggled until Dorn decided I was worth working on. He taught me that you had to be honest. A devout Pentecostal, he modelled his management style after his belief in family structure, hard work, simple reward, and honesty. He drilled those necessities into me for a year. He taught me the right way things should be done, the perfect way, and the work ethic that made me realize that whatever it was that I was doing, it was worth doing the *best*. He even taught me how to print numbers neatly and with consistency for the hand-written stock ledger, cash ledgers, and general ledgers we kept for the business — all done with 3H pencils!

Of the many valuable lessons Dorn taught me, he made me see that being neat and organized — and striving to be perfect and do everything to the best of my ability — now had *value* to me. It was my job — my paycheck — and not doing it right meant losing my livelihood. I "grokked" this and succeeded. The result was more confidence and an awareness that I had a value to others and to myself.

I worked for that company on and off for eight years, even after I moved to Los Angeles. I was given a great job as a manager, I trained others, and I made a living. It was because of Dorn, someone else who believed in me. I use what he taught me every day.

Once I was in California, Chess King hired me again and sent me to Bakersfield, north of Los Angeles about one hundred miles. Now managing a mall store, the busiest in California, I was mentored by an amazing man who became like an older brother to me: Mike Aguilar.

Mike was like a college professor. He did everything right, he delegated, he was ahead of the game, and he taught me not to sit idle — in my career and in my life. He forced me to grow up. I was doing extra things that made me stand out, and under his direction, I blossomed into more than a manager. I had learned to be industrious. He was also hard on me, and that helped prepare me for failure and gave me the drive to move on, learn, and persevere. I wanted to impress him. He liked my writing as well and encouraged me to continue.

Thanks, Mike. You fine-tuned me as a person, not just a businessman. I remember the day we discussed my competition for the store in Santa Maria, and you said, "Those guys? They can't hold a candle to you!"

That's because you helped me.

Two years later, back in Los Angeles, I moved to a different company, Wherehouse Entertainment. At the beginning of that job, I met Steve Brown. He was brash, confident, young, chain-smoking, aggressive, tall, ex-military, a fashion plate, a tornado, and right most of the time. He knew this. Some didn't like him. I did. One knew what one was getting with Steve. He was my district manager, and for some reason, he thought I had some potential. To be honest, my sales and P and L numbers proved it. Unlike my other mentors, Steve wasn't interested in honing my skills. That wasn't his bag.

Steve was a pusher. He taught me the political ropes, the idea of honest self-promotion, being competitive, speaking out, getting off the fence on issues, and kicking ass. He was exhilarating to be around. He put me out in the ocean, figuratively, and said, "Swim back, and then we can talk about your worth."

The biggest thing Steve taught me was to look for opportunities and attack them. He gave me all the rope I wanted and ate me alive when I hung myself, but mostly he beamed like a proud father when I was recognized for success. I had become, under his tutelage, a mover and a shaker. I was well respected and was given the opportunity to take any job, within reason, at the company.

Steve Brown made me do something *big* with my talent. I can never thank him enough.

There were two other people who actually tried to tell me all the things I learned from Jane Beem, Jo Ann Fox, Dorn Kennison, Mike Aguilar, and Steve Brown: my parents, George and Virginia Greene, who are now in their nineties.

I remember all of what they told me—all these same things. Quotes like "Try it—you are young! What have you got to lose?" and "You did that wrong. Fix it," and "You can do anything. Just don't give up."

But of all the qualities and skills that both my parents possessed, the one that rubbed off on me was legendary in our family and with our friends: the ability to tell stories.

My mother was a poor girl who lived in the Bronx with her off-the-boat immigrant father and mother, he a barber and her mother, a beautician. She had an older brother and younger sister. The stories she would tell thrilled us as kids. She played piano at Carnegie Hall in a recital at the age of four. After completing her pieces, she bumped her head after her bow and let out a few choice expletives in Italian. Everyone heard. She told us of jumping across alleyways from rooftop to rooftop of the neighbouring apartment buildings, of her rise as a dress designer, her days working at CBS when the new sensation of television was in its infancy, and of her crazy aunt who came after her own family with a kitchen knife—and some darker tales of what we nowadays would call child abuse, but then it was just "not sparing the rod" to raise children. She was always conversational yet at times very emotional in her telling. We always listened. We urged her to tell more.

My father was a master of comedy. Now in his later years, he repeats his repertoire ad nauseam, and he embellishes so much that we wonder what kids he's talking about when he speaks of our younger years. But when we were young, we couldn't get enough. His stories of Ivy League college days, pranks of stealing mascots and cannons, goofy cars that had exploding eagle-sculpted radiator caps, navy stories—not of war, but of corpsman duties stateside, playing trombone in the captain's band in Miami, and silly get-togethers at which he was always the life of the party. Our favorite was his courting of our mother, who understandably wanted to dump him after he left her alone at party after party where he seemed compelled to entertain all the guests. After she told him she would never date him again, he begged her for another chance and promised not to leave her side. At the next party, he actually waited outside the ladies' room each time she used it and figuratively stuck to her.

We loved these tales. Each was rich and detailed, especially the characters. Most of all, my father was funny. He didn't just tell a story; he acted them out, changed his voices, did accents, made faces.

How could I have been anything else but a storyteller? Thanks, Mom and Dad. It was a great gift to receive.

So why write sea stories? Because I love them, and I want to help others enjoy them as well. Knowing that sometimes the terminology and jargon can be a bit rough on beginners, I hoped to create a series that would capture the excitement and thrill of being on one of His Majesty's wind-powered warships during the Nelson era, while taking it easy on the technical aspects of a life at sea.

I am not an expert in sailing matters and have relied heavily on reference material from Dean King's *A Sea of Words*, Lavery's *Nelson's Navy*, O'Neill's *Patrick O'Brien's Navy*, my personal correspondence with Captain Richard Bailey of the now fully refurbished and seafaring SSV *Oliver Hazzard Perry*, and the novels and biographies of Forester, O'Brian, Stephenson, and others.

It is my fondest hope that my readers will explore these works and continue their own adventures in this remarkable period of history.

—Peter Greene, March 2017